RAVE REVIEWS FOR
WHITE WOLF!

"Ms. Edwards' words flow like vivid watercolors across the pages."

—*Rendezvous*

"Susan Edwards [is] an author who readily joins the pantheon of chroniclers of the Westward expansion."

—*Calico Trails*

"*White Wolf* is a captivating tale of passion and romance along the Oregon Trail."

—Candace McCarthy, author of
White Bear's Woman

"Hop on your plush horse (your couch) and enjoy this romantic Western!"

—*Affaire de Coeur*

SECRET LONGING

Jessica's stomach fluttered at the very thought of Wolf. "Stop thinking of him," she commanded herself, willing her racing pulse to calm. This was ridiculous nonsense, pure and simple.

When she heard the sound of someone whistling, she lifted her head, grateful for any diversion that would take her mind off of Wolf. Edging closer to the ledge, she glanced down, then gasped and dropped her head back to the ground, praying that the tall grass concealed her presence from the very man who haunted her thoughts. She slowly inched back from the edge. The last thing she wanted right now was for Wolf to see her here, away from camp, where they were alone. Her lashes fluttered closed and in her mind's eye, she saw him: his golden-brown hair dark from the water, his eyes bluer than the sky above and his lips as soft as his chest was hard.

Her breathing quickened and her eyes shot open, filled with dismay and longing. Her heart raced and she wondered just what it was about the wagon master that drew her like that bee to the sweetly scented bloom. Each day, he intruded into her thoughts, her dreams and, now, even her fantasies.

The silence broke through her thoughts. The cheerful whistling had stopped. Was he gone? Jessie scooted forward, peering through a small bush. "Oh my God." She gasped, her eyes growing wide as she gulped air into her burning lungs. Wolf stood below her—*gloriously naked!*

Other *Leisure* books by Susan Edwards:
WHITE WIND

WHITE WOLF

SUSAN EDWARDS

LEISURE BOOKS NEW YORK CITY

A LEISURE BOOK®

January 1999

Published by

Dorchester Publishing Co., Inc.
276 Fifth Avenue
New York, NY 10001

ISBN 0-8439-4471-4

The name "Leisure Books" and the stylized "L" with design are trademarks of Dorchester Publishing Co., Inc.

Printed in the United States of America.

This book is dedicated to women.

To the frontier women of our past who left family and friends behind to go west. As we women of today continue to forge new frontiers, let us never forget those brave and courageous women in our past.

And to the special women in my life. Thanks, Mom, for giving me the gift of life and a love of reading. Sally, my thanks for all you've done and the incredible courage you've shown. LaVona, you are the best mother-in-law a girl could ask for. And last but not least, Betty. What would I do without your red pen? Love you all.

WHITE WOLF

Chapter One

Missouri—April 1856

Westport teemed with activity. Storekeepers swept weathered boardwalks while customers indulged in spots of gossip. From inside Baker's Mercantile, Jessica Jones stared out the window. "I'll sure miss this town when we leave for Oregon, Mr. Baker."

The store owner wrapped a pair of gloves in some brown paper. "We'll miss you and your brothers, Jessie. Town will be downright dull without you to liven things up. Here's your gloves. Any idea when you're leaving?"

Jessie took the packet. "First of May. Only two weeks to go." Her voice rose with excitement as she thought of their plans to emigrate to Oregon. Suddenly, two weeks seemed so far away. She was eager for the adventurous trip, yet there was so much that still needed to be done. "Guess I'd best get back before James wonders where I've gone."

"I reckon he'll be worrying over what sort of mischief you're getting into."

Jessie grinned as she met Orvil Baker's twinkling gaze. "That too, Mr. Baker." With a farewell wave she stepped outside, greeting Shilo, her black mare. "Ready to go, girl?" The horse nickered softly as Jessie unhitched her. A loud shout in the street drew her attention.

One man, unable to control his oxen, rammed his team into another wagon, which resulted in braying mules and shouted obscenities. She shook her head. Westport had become another jumping-off place. Each winter and early spring, those seeking to join a wagon train bound for Oregon or California arrived in droves.

Stowing her package in the saddlebags, she leaned down to pat Sadie, her black-and-tan dog. She put one foot in the stirrup and grasped the saddle horn with both hands. But before she could swing up, a high-pitched voice hailed her.

"Yoo-hoo, Jessica, don't rush off."

Jessie swore beneath her breath and gritted her teeth. There was only one person in all of Westport who dared to call her by her given name, and that person had the ability to raise her hackles faster than a cornered rattler. Glancing over her shoulder, she saw three young ladies dressed in their Sunday best sauntering toward her.

"Oh, Jessica, I'm *sooo* glad I caught you before you left."

Dropping her forehead into her hands, Jessie swayed, her left foot in the stirrups, the right dangling loose. "Damn, just once I'd like to come into town without running into Coralie and her snotty friends!" Maybe she'd just ignore Coralie Renee Baker's royal summons and ride for home. A drop of moisture splashed onto her nose. Holding her hat in place with one hand, Jessie eyed the sky and groaned.

"Oh, dear; girls, it looks like Jessica will be riding home in the rain. Too bad she doesn't live here in town." Laughter accompanied the false concern.

Given a choice, she'd gladly endure all manner of bad weather if it meant not having to deal with Coralie. "Might as well get this over with," she muttered. Years of dealing with the rich girl had taught her that Coralie's attention always boded ill for her. Jessie stepped down into the muddy

street and turned to confront Coralie. She stumbled when her
boot sank up to the ankle in the mud and had to grab her
saddlebags to keep from falling into the slippery goo.

She tugged at her foot. The rude sucking noise followed
by the release of her boot from the grip of the thick mud
brought forth a fresh wave of snickers from the three young
ladies standing high and dry on the boardwalk in front of
Baker's Mercantile. Jessie clamped her jaw tight. Though she
was used to being shunned because she lived on a small farm
on the outskirts of town with her brothers, their disdain still
hurt. She folded her arms across her chest. "What do you
want, Coralie?"

Coralie twirled her closed parasol in front of her and took
a small step forward. Shilo thrust his raven black nose forward in greeting. The blond-haired girl squealed and jumped
back, fanning herself with her hand. "Keep that beast away
from me, Jessica. He'll ruin my new dress."

Against her will, Jessie admired the other girl's crisp-
looking daffodil yellow dress with matching bonnet and parasol. Just once she'd like to look like a beautiful young lady
instead of a rowdy tomboy. She stared down at her own
threadbare homespun shirt and worn canvas pants dotted
with dried mud. Suppressing a sigh of envy, she patted her
mare. "Shilo won't hurt you, Coralie. Now what do you
want?"

Coralie smoothed her skirt, fingered a silky blond ringlet
hanging over one shoulder and opened her baby blues wide.

Jessie wasn't fooled by the innocent look.

"Oh, dear; do forgive me, Jessica." She smirked. "I forgot, you have cows to milk and chickens to feed." A chorus
of soft sniggers followed her taunt.

Setting her jaw, Jessie turned away, struggling to control
her anger. The last time Coralie'd riled her, she'd shoved the
hateful girl into a pile of manure. The sight of pale pink fluff
gracing the brown pile, like icing on a cake, had been worth
being confined to her room for a week.

But she wouldn't give in to her temper today. She'd promised her eldest brother she'd avoid Coralie—but it was

hard when the snotty rich girl deliberately provoked her! Jessie swung up into the saddle, determined to make her escape before she said or did something that would get her into trouble. "I don't have time for your little games, Coralie."

Coralie pouted. "I'm sorry, Jessica," she said, not sounding the least bit repentant. "There's a dance tomorrow night. Are you coming?"

Jessie frowned, not trusting the innocent question. "Why do you want to know?"

Coralie made a pretense of shaking out nonexistent wrinkles in her skirt. "Well, Elliot asked if you were coming."

Jessie's head shot up, her interest piqued in spite of herself. She glanced in the store window behind Coralie and spotted Elliot Baker standing at the wooden counter beside his father. Why did he care whether she came to the dance or not? Though she harbored tender feelings for him, at twenty-one the man was four years her senior, and Elliot always treated her as a pesky young sister.

"Why does he want to know?" She held her breath in anticipation. Her attention centered on the movements of the fair-haired young man in the store, Jessie missed the look of amusement that passed between Coralie and her friends.

Coralie's lips curved into a malicious grin. "So he can keep away from you!" she declared, turning to join her friends in gleeful laughter. "After last month's dance, who can blame him? What a disaster!"

One of the other girls, a dark brunette named Becky, sashayed forward and slipped her arm through Coralie's. She looked Jessie up and down and sneered. "The dance was ruined before it started, and it was all your fault. Elliot left to change his clothes and never returned; then *your* brothers left to follow you home. I didn't get to dance with Jeremy, all because of your clumsiness!"

Coralie patted Becky's arm in mock sympathy, her voice soft and cajoling, but her blue eyes were hard and filled with hatred. "Dear Jessica, on behalf of Becky and Sarah, I do think it would be most considerate if you stayed home tomorrow night, don't you? We don't want this dance ruined."

Sarah stepped forward, her nose in the air. "Who'd want to dance with her anyway? She looks, dresses and acts like a boy."

"Now, Sarah," Coralie began, "you know that's not true. That fat mama's boy Robbie doesn't care what Jessica looks like. I heard he's courting her."

Becky shuddered delicately. "Oh, do come on, you two. Mama's waiting tea on us." Arms hooked at the elbows, the three young ladies turned away.

"Well, ta-ta, Jessica. Nice talking to you. Tell Jordie I'll see him tomorrow night," Coralie trilled over her shoulder.

Through the narrowed slits of her eyes, Jessie glared at Coralie's retreating figure. She clenched and unclenched her fingers. How dared she throw that horrible night in her face? She groaned with mortification. She'd never forget the humiliation. Wanting to look her fashionable best for Elliot, she'd piled her waist-length hair on top of her head, leaving tight ringlets to dangle past her ears.

Then she'd gone through the trunk of her ma's clothes and pulled out a gray woolen broadcloth trimmed in white lace with leg-of-mutton sleeves. It had been one of her ma's best Sunday go-to-meeting dresses. But to her dismay, when she'd put it on, she'd discovered that it was much too big. The sleeves slipped past her wrist, falling even with her fingertips, and the skirt was several inches too long.

Having nothing else suitable, she'd worn it in the hope of attracting Elliot's attention. She grimaced. She'd certainly done *that*. Lacking the skill to do her own hair and without enough pins to hold the weight securely on top of her head, she'd arrived at the dance with her hair already on the verge of falling.

The older women had been polite and sympathetic in their glances, but not so their daughters. They'd pointed at her lopsided head and snickered behind gloved hands. The boys had laughed outright, but Jessie had ignored them, determined to have a good time in spite of their cruel laughter. Then, in her haste to get away from their taunts, she'd tripped on the hem of her skirt and fallen headlong into Elliot, sending them crashing into the refreshment table.

No, she'd never forget that horrible night, nor would Coralie. Well, she'd teach that spoiled, mean-spirited girl a lesson. After all, she'd started it. Jessie gave Shilo a sharp kick to the flank. They galloped down the street in the opposite direction of the three girls. Sadie followed. When Jessie reached Garvey's Feed and Grain, she guided Shilo behind the store and raced back up the alley.

At the end of the wooden buildings, she reined in Shilo and waited behind one of the town's many saloons that seemed to have popped up overnight. Motioning for Sadie to sit, Jessie cocked her head and listened. It wasn't long before she heard the trill of feminine voices. Backing the mare out of sight, she gripped her hat in her hands.

In a darkened corner room above the saloon, White Wolf stared at the ceiling. The late-afternoon shadows danced their way through the curtained window. His gaze followed the trail of dust motes shimmering in and out of the single beam of light that sliced the room in half. Resting his head in the cradle of his linked fingers, he berated himself for agreeing to go west again. He'd sworn never to lead another party of emigrants west, not after his last trip, not after losing Martha. . . .

Severing the painful train of thought, he brooded over the events that had once again put him in the unwanted position of wagon master. He'd arrived in Westport just yesterday. Each spring he made the journey down the Missouri River to sell the furs he and old Ben spent the winter trapping. Even though the fur trade was dwindling, he'd gotten a fair sum for his goods. In addition to the furs, he'd auctioned off five wild horses he'd spent the long, lonely winter months breaking and training.

While examining the other horses up for sale, he'd found a spirited black stallion that no one had been able to mount. After proving his skill by riding the black beast, he'd heard that Able Bennett, an old friend and trapping partner, hadn't been so lucky. He was laid up with a busted leg after being thrown. After purchasing the black devil, Wolf had gone to visit Able.

The older man hadn't wasted any time in calling in a favor. With a broken leg, he couldn't take his cattle west to sell them, or lead the small party of emigrants who'd already paid him to act as wagon master. Wolf sat up in bed, careful not to awaken the woman in bed beside him. He wished he'd refused Able's request, but both men knew he couldn't; he was bound by honor, for Able had come to Wolf's aid many times. Angry with the circumstances he found himself stuck with, Wolf ran a hand through his mane of golden brown hair and cursed his luck.

Untangling the sheet from around his waist, he eased out of bed. The floorboards chilled his feet as he padded across the room to a chipped ceramic pitcher sitting on a small water-stained washstand. Pouring a small amount of cold water into the basin, he splashed his face, neck and chest. After drying himself with a coarse homespun towel, he paced, unmindful of his nudity. He drew in a deep breath, then wished he hadn't. The small room reeked of stale drink, smoke and the odor of unwashed bodies.

To alleviate the feeling of suffocation, he pulled back the grimy curtains and opened the room's sole window, allowing the weak afternoon rays of sun to streak into the room. He braced his hands on the narrow sill and leaned out, the dark gold of his unbound hair brushing against his shoulders. Desperate for a breath of untainted air, he inhaled deeply, then coughed. His nose twitched at the rank odor that rose from the street below, where waste, both human and animal, rotted. He sighed, missing the crisp air of his home and his clean, well-ordered cabin.

To his left, sounds of fighting drew his attention. Several rowdies from the saloon beneath him barreled through the swinging doors, heedless of the wagons and livestock as they rolled through the mud, their fists slamming into each other. Their angry shouts added to the noise and confusion in the street. Mules harnessed to wagons brayed in annoyance as their owners cracked whips over their heads and cussed to keep the animals moving.

Amid the angry shouts, the trill of female laughter drifted upward. Tearing his gaze from the fight, he spotted three young ladies standing on the edge of the boardwalk, opening their parasols to guard themselves against the light misting rain before tentatively stepping into the street. His lips twitched with amusement as he watched them attempt to cross the mud-slick road without dirtying the hems of their finery. His left brow rose when one of them boldly lifted her skirt high enough for him to see one neatly turned ankle.

Suddenly, from his right, he heard the pounding of hooves. A black horse bore down on the women. He shouted a warning. Two of the women jumped back onto the wooden planks, but the blond-haired woman screamed, frozen in the middle of the street. He held his breath, willing the horse to veer away. To his relief, when the horse was several feet from the young woman, the rider yanked hard on the reins. The horse turned sharply and came to a stop.

Wolf heaved a sigh of relief, then winced when a spray of muddy water flew through the air and pelted the vision of sunlight standing below. High-pitched wails filled the air, along with the dark-haired rider's husky laughter. Furious with the irresponsible rider, Wolf felt his sense of fairness rail at the spiteful act, Wolf leaned forward. "Hey, you, boy," he called down to the rowdy young man. The figure on horseback glanced upward.

Wolf had a brief glimpse of a youthful face framed by a riot of black curls and capped with a weathered hat before horse and rider galloped away like greased lightning, a black-and-tan dog following. "Someone ought to teach that cub a lesson," he said in a growl.

The woman with whom he'd spent the night, Lolita, left the rumpled bed and joined him at the window. "What are you all huffy about, Wolf? What's going on down there?" Peering over his shoulder, she grimaced and shook her head. "Good Lord, there goes another one of Coralie's dresses.

Never mind her and Jessie, Wolf. They're always going at it."

Her voice grew petulant as her hands snaked around his bare waist. "What about me? Aren't you coming back to bed? I have a couple of hours before I have to go downstairs." Her voice turned low and seductive as she crushed her full breasts against his back and slid the long painted nails of one hand down his side.

Wolf released the curtain and turned. He reached out and filled his palms to overflowing with her twin globes of pale, quivering flesh. Kneading the soft mounds, he watched her head loll back on her slender neck. His manhood stirred in response to her pelvis, which ground against him. "Please, Wolf." She gasped, running her tongue over her ruby-tinted lips. "It's been so long since you've come to town. I've missed you."

"How much?" he asked cynically. Lolita was never short of male company.

Her skilled hands traveled from one mat of soft curls to a second forest of springy fur. He sucked in his breath when she dropped to her knees and showed him.

Chapter Two

The crimson sun dipped slowly beneath the skyline, painting the horizon with ribbons of muted pink, purplish blue and golden yellow. Soon, darkness would fall completely, but the sunset went unnoticed by three men. As the glowing sphere disappeared on the horizon, each of the Jones brothers felt the hard knot of dread deep in the pit of his stomach.

James, sitting in the swaying porch swing, was the head of the Jones household. A sick feeling of betrayal—his own—ate at him while he watched his youngest brother, nineteen-year-old Jeremy, pace back and forth across the well-worn wooden planks along the front of the old farmhouse.

"It's times like this I'm glad I'm not the eldest."

James made a rude noise and slumped further down on the wooden seat. He stretched out his long legs, crossed his ankles, and then folded his arms across his broad chest to ward off the inevitable unpleasantness ahead. The creaking of the swing merged with the nighttime rustling of house sparrows in the tall oak trees, the hum and chirp of insects under the porch, and the screech of an owl searching for rodents in the cleared fields.

Cocking his head to one side, he listened to the howl of a lone wolf in the distance and wished he were anywhere but here. Jordan, younger by two years, perched on the porch railing, his boot heel scraping the wooden flooring. Like Jeremy, Jordan looked miserable. He grimaced. How was it that three strong men lived in fear of one slip of a girl?

Tilting his head back to stare out into the well-kept yard, James felt the weight of responsibility taking away all enjoyment of the night. This was his favorite time of day, but today's sunset brought no peace. He had a problem, a big problem who went by the name of Jessica Jones.

Jeremy stopped pacing. "Well, what are we gonna do, James? We're all in for a load of trouble if we can't figure a way out of this mess."

"Thank you for telling me something I didn't know." He scowled. Reluctantly, he stood. There was no sense in putting off the inevitable. After spending a sleepless night tossing and turning, he knew what had to be done. He might as well get it over with.

Shoving his dusty hat to the back of his head, he peered through the open doorway into the darkened house. All was blessedly quiet inside, which meant Jessie was still out in the barn. Stepping lightly, James walked along the porch to the side of the house. Jordan and Jeremy followed. Leaning out from the railing, they all looked out to the barn. Suddenly, the sounds of banging and cursing swept toward them on the evening breeze.

All three men groaned. Jessie had returned from town in a snit. They returned to their previous positions, except for Jeremy. After a couple of minutes, he slapped his hat against his thigh, then hooted with laughter, his pale green eyes lit with glee. "Boy, don't she sound mad. Wanna bet she got into it with Coralie again?" He grinned and eyed Jordan. "And we all know who won, don't we?" He smirked, pleased.

Jordan scowled. "She'd better not have done anything to Coralie," he threatened, pulling on his thick black mustache. "I warned her the last time to watch her temper."

"Yeah, but you know that don't mean a thing with her."

"Forget Coralie for now," Jordan ordered. "Let's get back to the real issue here. We can't let White Wolf do this to us. Not after all the plans we've made."

"Yeah, just who does that half-breed bastard think he is, anyway? He ain't got no right to up and change things," Jeremy added scornfully.

James stared at his brothers, taking in their agitated pacing and tightly clenched fists. He rubbed the bridge of his nose. God, there were times when he cursed their Irish blood. He alone had inherited his mother's calm English temperament; his three siblings had their Irish father's hot temper. "If you boys want to live to see Oregon, I wouldn't let Wolf hear you call him a half-breed *or* a bastard. Seems his father is an Indian chief," he growled, his voice cold and forbidding as he glared at first one then the other face staring belligerently at him.

Jeremy and Jordan stomped past him, their heels pounding on the wooden planks. "Sit down, you two! Them boots of yours are making too much racket. Do you want to bring *her* out here? You know Jess smells trouble a mile away!"

Despite the grim situation, James grinned when Jordan and

21

Jeremy sank onto the nearest bench, nearly tipping it in their haste. He shook his head. If their predicament wasn't so serious, he'd have ribbed them a bit for being so cowardly. He ignored the fact that he too breathed a sigh of relief that Jessie was still in the barn.

He adjusted his hat. "Okay, boys, listen up. As I see it, we've got no choice but to go to Oregon as planned." He held up his hand, stilling the rumbles of protest. His stomach burned. Curse the "no single women allowed" rule that had put him in this situation. "Too much has gone into this move to put it off. I talked to Matt Smith this morning. His daughter, Mary Jane, can't go for the same reason that Jessie can't. He's waiting for another guide and agreed to bring Jessie out with him and his family." He folded his arms across his chest and waited.

"But that means . . ."

"We'll have to split up."

The air hung heavy as each remembered the vow they'd made the day they'd buried their parents: they would never split up. At sixteen, James had become a man, responsible for his younger siblings. He'd stood firm when the wife of the local pastor had tried to take his little sister into her God-fearing home to raise. Though many in Westport agreed that it wasn't proper for three young boys to raise a girl of eight, the Jones brothers had fought the townfolk to keep Jessie with them. And though Jessie somehow managed to get into more scrapes than the other two combined, he'd never regretted keeping them together.

He set his jaw as he faced his brothers. "There's no other way," he said calmly. "We've sold the land, the house, the livestock, everything," he reminded them, taking off his hat to run his fingers through a thick mass of wavy black hair. Silence, as dark as the approaching night, fell between them.

"Yeah, and coming out with the Smiths ain't gonna be the worst of it, either," Jordan muttered, rubbing the back of his neck.

James heard him and frowned at his brother. "Dammit, Jordan, but you've got lousy timing. Of all times to get married! But to choose *her*? Jessie's gonna be in a horn-tossin' mood when she finds out you want to marry Coralie."

Jordan threw back his shoulders and stood. "I got the right to marry anyone I want," he said, daring his brother to tell him he couldn't.

James sighed and turned away. "We'll deal with that problem if Coralie accepts. Right now we've got to break the bad news to Jessie."

Out in the barn, Jessie struggled to calm her temper. Already she regretted her childish act of revenge. She knew better than to let the town girls rile her. Besides, she didn't want her brothers, especially Jordan, to know she'd ruined another of Coralie's dresses.

She shoved her fingers through her unruly black curls. Addressing Sadie, Jessie paced the length of the barn. "I'm in a fix now, girl. Jordan's going to hit the roof when he finds out what I've done. What he sees in her, I don't know! I'll sure be glad to leave her and the rest of those snooty girls behind. Just think, in a few more weeks, there'll be no more Coralie to give us grief."

Jessie closed her eyes and concentrated on taking slow, even breaths to keep the anger at bay, but it did no good. She kicked an empty pail sitting in the middle of the path with the pointed tip of one boot. It flew across the barn and bounced off the opposite wall. The noise sent several barn cats scurrying for cover. The horses, safe in their stalls, kept wary eyes trained on her, and at the back of the barn, the one remaining cow mooed in annoyance.

She planted her hands on her hips and glared at the animal audience. "That Coralie Baker makes me so mad I could just spit! Just because her pa owns the mercantile, she thinks she's better than the rest of us!"

A soft *woof* from the barn door drew her attention. Fearing that one of her brothers had come to see why it was taking her so long to do her chores, she whirled around, then breathed a sigh. It was only Sadie barking at an overturned tub, her rump high and her tail wagging. Suddenly a tiny black-and-white paw shot out and swiped the dog's snout with tiny, sharp claws. Sadie backed off with a whine.

"Best leave them kittens alone, Sadie," Jessie advised. Gathering an armful of sweet-smelling straw, she carried it into Shilo's stall and spread it over the freshly raked dirt floor. Her mare nickered softly and butted her huge black head against Jessie's shoulder, letting her know she understood. Jessie leaned against the animal.

Coralie's barbs had hit home. She glared at her dirty, work-roughened hands and broken fingernails, then frowned at her equally filthy clothing, comparing her attire with the stylish dresses worn by Coralie, Becky and Sarah.

Suddenly the fight left her. Raw pain rose to the surface to devour her anger. Tears pooled in her eyes, blurring her vision, but Jessie set her jaw. She wouldn't give Coralie the satisfaction of making her cry. She lowered herself to the bed of fresh straw and ran her hands through her short, disheveled curls.

How she longed to own a pretty, fashionable dress. "Pale blue," she mused, "or perhaps lavender, with lots of frills, lace and ribbons." Her one and only dress was a plain brown calico, and ugly to boot. She glared at a piece of shredded straw and tossed it away in disgust.

As much as she hated that dress, she couldn't ask James for fancy clothes. Not one of her brothers would understand, and she'd rather die than admit she was jealous of Coralie and the other girls. Sadie whined and nosed her way onto Jessie's lap. "Oh, Sadie." She moaned, burying her face in the dog's silky fur. "I do so want to go to the social tomorrow night. It'll be the last time I see Elliot, but I don't dare," she whispered, "not after last time." Her face flushed with remembered humiliation.

She'd fled the dance to return home, where there was no one to witness her tears. After tossing her mother's ruined dress into the corner of her room, she'd taken the shears to her hair, hating the unmanageable thick strands that had contributed to her downfall. By the time her brothers had returned from town, her bruised and tender heart had been hidden from the world once more.

They'd been very upset that she'd cut her hair. It had previously been her only concession to being a young woman, but she'd ignored them, keeping to herself how betrayed she'd felt—by her own yearnings. There wasn't anyone who'd understand that the emerging butterfly of her femininity longed to spread its tender, budding wings.

Raised by three brothers, she knew every aspect of farming, rode better than many men, could shoot and hunt, and was deadly accurate with her bullwhip. The one thing she'd lacked in her upbringing was advice and tutoring in how to be a lady. After that night, by cutting her hair short, she'd removed the temptation to be something she wasn't.

It was some time before Jessie got to her feet and left the barn. Her steps dragged. "Might as well confess what I've done," she muttered. "They'll discover it soon enough." Just as she rounded the corner, she heard Jeremy say, "Boy, James, I don't envy you telling Jessie."

"Telling me what?" she demanded, springing over the rail. She scrutinized her older brothers. They shared her curly black hair, and all of them had varying shades of green eyes. Right now, not one of them would meet her questioning gaze. Something was going on. She tossed her hat through the open front door. Sadie barked and ran inside after it. Rubbing her work-roughened hands down the front of her faded pants, she addressed the silent group.

"Well? I'm waiting." She speared Jeremy with a glare. "Jeremy Ezra, you didn't get into another brawl at the Wild Stallion Saloon, did you? It took us a month to pay off the damages from your last fight. Really, fighting over some floozy." She grinned with satisfaction when Jeremy dropped his head into his hands.

"Aw, come on, Jessie. Quit throwing that at me, will ya? That was ages ago." Jeremy lifted his head. "Besides, that's nothing compared to all the money James has paid Orvil Baker for Coralie's ruined dresses!"

Before Jessie could protest, James held up one large, callused hand. "Calm down, Jess. Jeremy didn't do anything wrong—this time," he interceded.

"Thanks a lot, James." Jeremy shot his brother a killing look, folded his arms across his chest, then sat back to watch the action.

Jessie turned on her eldest brother and stared into eyes as deep green as her own. "James Noah, tell me what's going on."

"Oh, lordy." Jordan groaned. "She's gonna start in on the *names* now."

Momentarily sidetracked, Jessie leaned back on her heels. "Now, Jordan Phineas. Is it my fault Mama gave you boys such god-awful second names?" Inside, she gloated. Using their second names never failed to get their hackles up.

"Well, yours ain't much better, Jessica Nao—"

A hand clamped over Jordan's mouth. "Don't say it," Jeremy hissed, "unless you want to cook for the next month."

Jessie glared at him. She hated her second name more than anything!

"Jessie, enough!" James shouted.

Startled, Jessie turned away. James seldom raised his voice or lost his temper. She watched him plow his fingers through his hair and wondered what was wrong.

"Look, Jess," James began, "we have a problem. I went to town yesterday to see Able Bennett. He'd called a meeting. There's been a change. . . ."

Eager for news of their departure, Jessie clapped her hands. "The first of May is still two weeks away. Does this mean we're leaving sooner than planned?" She grinned, her mind racing with all that still needed to be done. "If you're worried we won't be ready to leave on short notice, forget it. We can be ready to leave anytime." She squealed, excitement filling her voice. "Oh, I can't believe it's really happening."

James took a deep breath and gripped her slender shoulders, forcing her to look at him. "The trip is off for you, Jess," he announced bluntly.

Jessie's jaw dropped. The trip off? Staring the glum expressions surrounding her, she noted the misery and guilt etched in each of their faces. "What do you mean—" Just then his exact words sank in, and she whirled around to glare at James. "What do you mean, the trip is off *for me?*" she demanded, planting her hands on her hips.

James refused to meet her accusing glare. She turned to Jordan, who brushed mud off his boots, and Jeremy suddenly seemed fascinated by a small brown spider dangling from the roof. "You're going without me?" she cried incredulously. Her temper erupted as she stormed across the wooden floor. "What's wrong, James? Afraid I won't make it? You know I'm tough. I'm not one of them soft, lily-livered town girls. I work hard, as hard as any of you, and you know it!"

A hand at her elbow stopped her tirade. She stared into Jeremy's worried gaze. "Shut up and listen for a minute, Jess," he beseeched, holding his hands out, palms up. "It's not our fault. We have no choice!"

Jordan joined them. "Do you remember why we agreed to help Able Bennett drive his cattle west?"

Jessie yanked away from Jeremy, her eyes stormy as she glared at all of them. "Of course I remember. With the money the three of you earn and what we save because your food is provided, we'll have us a nice bit of cash to start new in Oregon. Stop treating me as if I were a dim-witted clod. We're only waiting for the prairie grass to reach four inches and the mud to harden before we leave."

She paced as she ticked off all the preparations she'd done over the long winter. "I've spent my days gentling and training the oxen, painting the wagon, sewing the double-thickness canvas cover and both tents as well as waterproofing all that canvas. All that's left to do is pack the wagon and buy my share of the provisions." Out of breath, she stopped, her hands digging into her hips.

"Well, what you don't know, little sister, is Wolf . . ." Jeremy stopped and turned away. "Hell," he muttered under his breath. "I can't tell her."

"Tell me what? Who's Wolf?" she asked. The first feelings of fear snaked up her spine when James gave her his laying-down-the-law look mingled with a mixture of regret and sorrow.

"Able broke his leg and can't go," he announced grimly.

Jessie gasped. "How terrible," she said. "But what does that have to do with me?"

"Able found another wagon master, a half-breed by the name of White Wolf." James brushed his hat against one thigh.

"So?"

James stared out into the darkness, his shoulders hunched as if the weight of the world sat on them. "Wolf set his own rules. He's agreed to take Able's cattle and a handful of wagons to Oregon. The bad news is he won't allow any unmarried women in his party, says he doesn't want trouble with unattached females on the trail."

"But we're family! Surely the rule doesn't apply to families?"

"Jess, Wolf made himself very clear. No marriageable girls, period, and as much as I hate to admit it, you're a young woman of marriageable age."

Jessie hugged her arms to her chest, desperately trying to absorb the news.

"Please try to understand, Jess. On such short notice, he's the only experienced guide Able trusts to deliver his cattle, and he's got to get the herd on the trail or risk them not reaching Oregon before winter sets in."

Jessie walked to the far end of the porch, stunned that her brothers planned to go without her. James followed and tried to put his arm around her, but she shrugged him off and moved away. "Fine, let this White Wolf find someone else to drive the cattle. We'll go later." Desperation laced her voice. "We can't split up. There'll be other parties forming."

James shook his head, his eyes clouding with regret and sadness. "We can't, Jess, and you know it. The house is sold, and the Ballous' only agreed to let us stay on until Able is ready to roll."

Jessie closed her eyes and thought hard. "Then we'll stay in town. It won't be for long."

Again, James shook his head. "We have jobs to pay our way west. We can't pass up this opportunity. We have no choice but to accept Wolf's conditions."

Jessie stared at Jeremy and Jordan. "Tell James he can't split us up," she demanded of her siblings. To her dismay, they all refused to meet her incredulous gaze. A deep and searing hurt made breathing difficult. "How can you break your promise to keep us together?" She turned away so they wouldn't see how perilously near tears she was.

How could they do this to her? How could they even think of leaving her behind? Didn't family mean anything to them? If they separated, there was a good chance they'd never see each other again. What if something happened to them and she never found out? She'd heard stories of that happening. She blinked back her tears and didn't see Jordan sneak into the house or James back away as he imparted the last of his news.

"It won't be for long, Jess. There are several other families who can't go for the same reason. Able sent for his brother, who's agreed to come and take the rest of the party west. It won't be long before he arrives from St. Louis. You're going to come out with another family. You might even catch up with us."

Jessie glanced over her shoulder at James and caught the look he and Jeremy exchanged. Her eyes narrowed. She had a bad feeling about this. "Who?" she asked, watching James twist his hat in his hands. He took two steps back.

"I've, uh, made arrangements for you to join the Smiths."

"The Smiths?" she screeched, all hurt and fear of the future gone in a blinding flash of fury. "You can't be serious, James. Not the Smiths, with that stuck-up Mary Jane or her disgusting brother Robbie?" Jeremy ducked into the house, leaving Jessie to stare at James, her face a mask of disbelief and horror.

When he didn't deny it, tears of betrayal slid down her cheeks. "You can't do this to me," she shouted, stomping her foot and throwing her arms out to her sides. "I won't travel with them. Robbie is filthy and disgusting.'' She closed her eyes and shuddered at the thought of enduring close quarters with the slovenly boy whose clumsy attempts at courtship were annoying at the least and ridiculous at best.

When she opened her eyes, James was gone, leaving her alone with her rage. Jessie swore a blue streak, her emotions warring between anger, feelings of abandonment and the worst hurt she'd ever endured. Stunned, she leaned her elbows on the wooden rail and stared out into the heavy darkness. Her world had collapsed around her feet like a poorly constructed shanty.

She wiped at the moisture running down her cheeks and narrowed her eyes. James might think the matter settled, but it was far from decided, she told herself, her mind racing. She'd always been able to change their minds. Why should this time be any different? One by one, she'd sway her brothers to her side and then, as a team, they'd convince James to wait.

A soft whine followed by a wet nose nudging her hand interrupted her thoughts. Jessie looked down to see Sadie standing with her two front paws on the lower rail, her devoted gaze up on her mistress. Near her feet, Jessie noticed her misshapen hat. Sadie loved to fetch her hat whenever she tossed it aside. That small, normal gesture of love calmed her. She bent down to hug her beloved pet, then plopped her hat crookedly onto her head. Staring out into the darkness, Jessie let stubborn determination chase away her fear of the future. ''Sadie, we're going with them,'' she vowed. ''We'll find a way.''

Chapter Three

Sitting on the bank of the Missouri River the next afternoon, Jessie hunched her shoulders against the chilly breeze that swept through the trees. Above her, shiny green leaves rustled, and small greenish flowers drooping from catkins showered down upon her. She scooped a handful from the ground and threw them into the wind.

"There's got to be a way," she repeated as she leaned against the dull gray bark of the tree. Her thoughts returned to the previous evening. No amount of coaxing or threatening, tears or outbursts of temper had changed her brother's minds. For the first time in her young life, she had not been able to sway even one of them to her side. Even her close bond with Jeremy had failed to earn his support.

This morning had been no different. She'd failed. She felt sick and miserable. How could they turn their backs on her? They were family. Families were loyal to one another. Families stuck together through thick and thin. At least that was what she'd always believed—until now, until money and convenience had superceded blood ties.

Jessie felt as though her whole world had been turned upside down with one little sentence. *The trip is off for you.* Over and over, the words hovered over her like a winter's storm, leaving her cold and desolate inside.

Low growls erupted from Sadie's throat. Jessie jumped to her feet and snatched the coiled bullwhip from her belt. Wiping the tears from her eyes, she glanced around and spotted an old man sitting upon an equally venerable-looking horse. The nag nervously eyed the growling dog. Jessie narrowed her gaze.

"Stop right there, old man. Who are you and what do you want?" she demanded, moving away from the tree trunk at her back. She remained wary, her fingers curled around the handle of her whip as she stared into faded blue eyes and a weather-beaten face framed by a shock of white hair.

The old man nudged his mount forward but stopped when she uncoiled the whip. For good measure, Jessie gave Sadie a hand signal. The dog responded by stepping forward, teeth bared. With the daily influx of strangers to Westport, it paid to be careful.

"Mean ya no harm, lad. Name's Rook." He leaned forward, peering down at her. After an intense moment, he lifted a brow, then sat back.

"Keep your distance," she warned, taking two steps back when she saw the recognition dawn that she was no lad. She whistled through her teeth. Shilo trotted back from where she'd been grazing near the river's edge. Jessie felt more secure with her horse beside her. If the stranger's horse was as old as it looked, there'd be no way he'd catch her on Shilo.

The stranger continued to stare at her and scratch his head, leaving tufts of hair standing on end. "Beggin' yer pardon, but you's a lass, if'n I'm not mistaken."

Jessie swallowed. There was nothing in his eyes to make her fear him, yet she had the feeling he was seeing far more than she wanted anyone to see. She felt vulnerable, naked. Vaulting into the saddle, she backed her mare away.

"Wait, lass, can't help noticin' you was cryin'. Sometimes helps ta talk, ya know."

When Jessie remained wary and watchful, Rook held his arms out to his sides. Fringe dangled from his arms. "Look at me, lass. I'm jest an ol' man, don't even carry a weapon on my person." He patted the old horse's scrawny neck. "Me and Bag-o'-Bones here is jest out for a quiet afternoon ride." He drew out a pipe from his shirt pocket. "Whatever you's been cryin' bout can't be all that bad.''

"What would you know about it, old man?" Anger and desperation caused the words to come out harsher than she'd intended. When a cloud of pain dulled the sparkle in his blue gaze, she felt like a heel. She had no business taking her problems out on others. She opened her mouth to apologize, but the old man smiled sadly at her.

"Forgive a nosy old man, but ya remind me of someone very special. My dear, sweet Anabella had jewel green eyes that flashed jest like yours whenever she got her dander up,'' he whispered.

Instinct told her she had nothing to fear from the sad-looking man before her. She relaxed her hold on her whip. She regretted her previous words. "I had no cause to snap at you. Forgive me.''

He fingered his white beard while the two of them took stock of each other. Then he filled his pipe and lit it. "Mebbe I can help if ya tells me what's got ya feeling so down. Some young lad, I'll wager.'' His eyes twinkled as he puffed on his pipe.

Jessie rolled her eyes. "You're close, old man, 'cept it's three rotten men, to be exact.''

His jaw dropped and his bushy brows lifted. She sighed and nudged Shilo forward. "Fine. You want to know? I'll tell you. I'm heading into Westport. You can ride with me if you like, but mind you keep your distance,'' she warned, keeping her whip loosely coiled in her hand.

Nudging his horse forward and maintaining a respectful distance between them, the stranger drew deeply on his pipe, then released the woodsy scent of tobacco. "Call me Rook, lass. What's yer name?''

"Jessica,'' she answered, signaling Sadie to walk between them, "but most folk just call me Jessie.''

"Well, now, who are these men who've left ya lookin' like ya lost yer best friend?''

"My brothers, James, Jordan and Jeremy.''

"And what'd they do ta make their pretty li'l sister cry?''

Surprised, Jessie stopped and fixed her narrowed gaze on Rook to see if he was making fun of her. After all, she knew she wasn't pretty. Staring into his face, she was startled to find he was serious. She grunted and clucked at Shilo. Obviously his eyesight wasn't very good, she thought with a disappointed sigh.

"Me and my brothers were all set to go to Oregon, but our wagon master, Able Bennett, broke his leg. He found someone else, but it seems the new wagon master won't allow single women to go—which leaves me out." Her voice hitched and a thread of bitterness crept into her voice. "My dear brothers are going without me."

Rook drew on his pipe and lowered his brows. "They's leavin' you behind?"

Staring straight ahead, she was tempted to let Rook think her brothers were abandoning her, but she couldn't. Deep down, she knew it wasn't their fault that the rules had changed. Nor could she blame them for making the best business decision they could, but accepting it didn't ease the hurt she felt.

"I'm supposed to follow later, after a new guide is hired." Her lips twisted with renewed disgust. No way was she coming out with the Smiths. She'd go alone if necessary! "James says he can't pass up the opportunity to work their way west. The money he and the others earn will help us get a new start."

"Makes sense, lass. Doesn't sound like they's jest leavin' you."

Jessie closed her eyes. Rook was right, but the fear remained. "You don't understand. We're family. After our parents died, my brothers promised no one would ever separate us, yet they're allowing this White Wolf to do just that. What if something happens to them while we're separated? There's so many dangers, unknowns."

She whispered her greatest fear: "I can't bear the thought of arriving in Oregon and not finding them. Anything could happen. I've heard lots of stories of relatives who've never learned the fate of their loved ones after they left. We have to stick together. No one can separate us. I won't let them.

I'm going. You'll see,'' she finished, defiantly lifting her chin.

Rook stared at her for a long time. "Do ya believe in fate, lass?''

Jessie frowned.

"Sometimes fate is unkind, but ofttimes when things look their bleakest and you've lost all hope, somethin' good comes along. Ya jest have to be patient and watch for it. And when it comes, you grab it with both hands. Understand?''

"If fate is Able breaking his leg and causing this mess, then I have to say it's cruel. Besides, can you honestly tell me fate has always been kind to you?''

Rook stopped, his piercing gaze holding hers, inviting her to glimpse another brief flash of sadness that he didn't bother to hide. "No, lass, Lady Fate hasn't always been kind to me, but there's no use wallowin' in self-pity. It don't change a damn thing. Secret is ta take the hand fate deals you and play it the best ya can.''

Jessie bowed her head under his gentle rebuke. Still, what he said might make sense, but she just couldn't sit by and watch her brothers leave. Too much was at stake. "I can't just give up.''

"No one said anythin' 'bout givin' up, lass.''

"What do you suggest I do? I've spent all night and day trying to think of a way either to go or to change their minds.''

Rook grinned, the sparkle back in his eyes. "Mebbe you're tryin' too hard, lass. Sometimes help comes from unexpected quarters. I suggest you relax and see what happens. Watch and listen. If you's meant to go, a way'll open up. You jest make sure you're ready to take it.''

They traveled the rest of the way to town in companionable silence. Jessie contemplated Rook's advice. Perhaps he was right. If she went to the social tonight, maybe she'd discover something that would help in her quest to go west.

It was dark by the time Jessie and Rook parted company on the outskirts of town. She turned and waved good-bye to her new friend, then headed for the Belshaws' barn. When she arrived, fiddle music already filled the air, along with the jaunty sound of several mouth organs. She smiled. Her brothers were inside.

Still dressed in her worn blue jeans with holes in the knees, a flannel shirt and scuffed boots, she tethered Shilo to a nearby tree, then ordered Sadie to stay. Squaring her shoulders, she headed toward the barn, where light and laughter spilled out into the dark night. Keeping to the shadows, she made her way to the wide-open door and peered in, scanning the crowd for her brothers. James and Jeremy stood on a makeshift stage along with several other men with fiddles. She glanced around but didn't see Jordan. Slipping inside, she kept to herself.

As the minutes passed, her hopes sank. And after an hour of listening to conversations concerning health, poor winters and bleak futures, she'd had enough. There was nothing to be learned here. Time was running out. Her lips trembled. Exhaustion swept over her as she watched her brothers play, stamping their feet and yelling as if they had no worries.

Saddened, she pressed her lips together and hurried toward the exit. Once outside, she stopped and glanced over her shoulder. What a wasted trip, she thought glumly. Not only had she not learned anything useful, she hadn't even seen Elliot. Maybe he hadn't come in case she showed up. That thought was even more painful.

A loud whistle pierced the din inside. Silence, like a soothing balm, fell. Raising up on her tiptoes to see what was going on, she saw Orvil Baker make his way up onto the stage. There was still no sign of Elliot, so she turned to leave and ran smack into a male figure coming up the path. Startled, Jessie found herself staring at a chest covered by pristine white cotton. Her cheeks flamed as she lifted her gaze to Elliot's handsome features.

"What are you doing out here, Jessie? Pa's about to make the announcement."

"Don't know what announcement you're talking about, Elliot," she said, hiding her feelings for him behind a scowl. He was so handsome, it took her breath away. In the light from the moon above and the lanterns inside and outside the barn, Jessie gazed upon his boyishly handsome features. In his go-to-church clothes with his blond hair slicked down, Elliot Baker was unquestionably the best-looking male around.

His eyes widened, then crinkled with devilment. "I'll be damned"—he laughed—"they didn't tell you, did they?"

Jessie crossed her arms across her chest and glared at him. "If you have something to say, Elliot, say it."

He held up his hands. "Hey, I didn't mean anything. I leave the feuding to you and Coralie. But—I uh, suggest you pay attention to what's going on inside."

Jessie gave him a puzzled look when he nodded toward his father. She returned to the doorway, very aware of Elliot's warm male body standing close behind. Staring into the large room, her gaze fell on the two people standing beside Orvil on the makeshift stage. She frowned, puzzled. What were Jordan and Coralie doing up there? Then she heard Orvil Baker announce, "The wedding will be held Tuesday, as the newlyweds are heading west with the rest of the Jones clan."

The color drained from her cheeks. Jordan and Coralie? There had to be a mistake. Jordan couldn't marry Coralie. She'd known he was sweet on her, but marriage? Suddenly, all the times he'd gotten angry with her for one-upping Coralie made sense. She should have seen this coming. Then the impact of what Jordan and Coralie's marriage meant hit her and squeezed the air from her lungs.

Coralie, as a married woman, would be expected to travel with her husband and his family to the new land, yet she, their own flesh and blood, had to remain behind. Anger, shock and despair assaulted her. Her heart sank, and she couldn't draw a breath. The loud cheers and rounds of clapping sounded like thunder roaring in her head, and the blood pounded painfully in her ears. She gasped, drawing air into her starving lungs as cold fury took hold. No way in hell was Coralie going and not her!

Orvil's voice drew her back to what was going on. "Sadly,

I'm losing my only son, Elliot, who has also decided to go west to start his own business." Pride rang in his voice. Jessie gaped in shocked silence. Elliot too? Orvil's announcement slammed into her. Everyone was going but her. Not only was Jordan marrying the woman she most hated, but Elliot, the man she loved, was going, while she'd be stuck traveling with that rotten Robbie.

Well, they had another thing coming. She wasn't accepting this injustice quietly. A flush of rage warmed her cheeks, and her gaze narrowed to furious slits as she took a step into the barn.

"Now, Jessie," Elliot warned, taking hold of her arm to prevent her from barging into the music-filled room. "Calm down and take it easy."

Jessie shoved Elliot's arm away, her eyes blazing as she turned on him. A shaft of pain pierced her heart. It wasn't fair! She sent Elliot a reproachful glare. A hard lump formed in the back of her throat. "You're going too. Everyone's going but me!" she cried, her voice low and husky with suppressed emotion. She moved back toward the open doorway. Never had she thought she could feel such hurt. Suddenly it seemed as if everyone was against her.

Elliot moved quickly, blocking her way. His glance shifted sideways, as if he were seeking help. "Come on, Jess," he coaxed. "Let's go for a walk and talk about this. There's nothing you can do to change the marriage plans. Accept it. You'll only end up embarrassing yourself if you don't."

"It's not just them marrying and you know it," Jessie spat. "Now let go of me."

"No. I won't let you do something foolish. It's not James's fault Able broke his leg. If you're going to blame anyone, blame the new wagon master."

Jessie froze. Her eyes narrowed and her mind raced. Elliot was right. This was all Wolf's fault. He was destroying her family. Well, she'd stop him—someone had to put him in his place. She grinned in anticipation, her eyes narrowed with intent. "You're right, Elliot," she said angrily. "I'm going to give that half-breed bastard a piece of my mind. He can't do this to us!''

With that, she sprinted off in the direction of the livery, where her brothers had met earlier with the new wagon master. If this White Wolf wasn't there, she'd hunt him down, even if it took all night.

"Jessie, wait. Come back—you can't—Jess!''

Wolf patted the flank of his new black stallion and smiled in satisfaction. Speaking Lakota, the language of the Teton Sioux, he addressed the tall, broad-shouldered Indian standing beside him. "He'll father many strong colts and fillies, my brother. It's been a long time since I've found horseflesh of this quality.''

Striking Thunder reached out to touch the horse, but the wild-eyed stallion snorted and pulled away. Wolf held the reins firmly. "Shh, easy, boy,'' he crooned, his voice low and soothing. When the animal calmed, Wolf led him into an empty stall.

"You always did have the touch with the animals who roam across the *Maka*,'' Striking Thunder said. A thread of wistfulness floated through his voice. "Many times I have wished for your gift.'' He swept one large hand toward a corner of the barn. "Wahoska responds only to you.''

Wolf glanced at the silvery white wolf sitting in one corner of the barn, its pale blue eyes watching them intently. His brother's confession surprised Wolf. He lifted one brow. "You envy the second son of our father? You, the bravest warrior of our tribe, the one chosen to lead our people? You, who will follow in our father's and grandfather's, steps? Why would you envy a brother who is said to have received more white blood in his veins from our mother than the Sioux blood of our father?''

Striking Thunder shrugged and leaned against a stall door. "Have you never considered the demands, the responsibilities that I must shoulder in order to protect our tribe, while you are free to spend your days walking the earth or tending your horses?''

Susan Edwards

Wolf turned away, closed the stall door and repacked his saddlebags. The old, familiar resentment crept unbidden into his system. Striking Thunder had been chosen by the council to replace their father, Chief Golden Eagle, when the time came. Though he was happy for his brother, none of his family ever understood that all Wolf had ever wanted was to be part of the family, part of his tribe, not an outsider. "Be thankful you were not sent away from our people, my brother. It was never my choice to live the white man's life," he finished, his voice hard, cold and bitter.

White Wind, their half-English, half-Sioux mother, had taught her children the ways of the white man, teaching them about their mixed heritage. But unlike his siblings, Wolf had been sent away for an extensive education. Memories of the years spent in the white man's boarding school still gave him nightmares.

Wolf hung the lantern on a nail near the door, then tossed the leather bags to the ground by the open door and stared out into the night. He and Striking Thunder were alone. Everyone else was either in one of the saloons or at the social held at the other end of town. In the maze of corrals outside, horses snorted and cattle lowed at the moon. Behind him, bedded down in their stalls, several mares, including his other horse, Lady Sarah, nickered softly. His new stallion answered back.

"At least you have a purpose to your life. You are needed by our people. But look at me, my brother." Wolf waved his hand. "I have no such purpose. I am told by our *Wicasa*, our shaman, that I must live as a white man in order to serve my people with my gift of knowledge. But how? For many years I have searched for the answers, but they do not come." He stared into the heavens above as if what he sought was written in the stars. "I travel across the land, seek visions on the highest mountains and pray to my *Wakan* for answers, but the spirits do not hear."

He turned away, hiding the bleakness in his eyes. "Perhaps I am destined to walk the path of life alone, not needed by my people, neither white nor Sioux. You, my brother, carry our white blood in your veins but not in your spirit—as does my twin sister, Star Dreamer. Her gift of sight, given to her by our grandmother, is revered by our people. Even our youngest sister is much sought after for her knowledge of herbs and healing. But what of me? How am I to use my gift? What good does my knowledge bring to the People?'' His voice dropped. ''There is no place of importance in our tribe for this son.''

Striking Thunder frowned and crossed his arms across his vest-covered chest. ''How can my brother hear the spirits speak? Your heart and mind are filled with bitterness and anger. You must clear your mind, find peace *within* before you can hear the voices of *Wakan Tanka*.''

Wolf glanced over his shoulder and frowned, but before he could dispute his brother's words, Striking Thunder moved to stand before him.

''Clear your mind and heart of all bitterness. Look to your future. This may be the reason that you have been chosen to make another journey across the *Maka*.''

Wolf was long past believing. ''We shall see,'' he said, and changed the subject to a less painful one. ''Why are you here? Your presence will rile the townfolk, especially those coming into town to buy supplies for their trip overland. They already fear Indians on the trail.'' Unlike Wolf, Striking Thunder was all Sioux in looks, thoughts and actions, and showed no outward sign of his white heritage.

Striking Thunder shrugged. ''It's night. The strangers are not about, and the whites who live in town know me as brother to Wolf. I am safe. The spirits watch over me.'' He took a leather thong from around his neck and held it up to reveal a small leather pouch.

''I bring you this. Wear it. The spirits will go with you as you travel far from home. They will keep you safe and return you to our mother and father. My brother is not to worry, I will deliver the needed supplies to our people and inform our parents of the reason for your absence from their tipi.''

Wolf took the leather thong and slipped it over his head, relieved that his brother would be able to deliver the supplies

41

and horses he'd purchased for his family back in the Nebraska Territory. "You and the others are leaving for home tomorrow?"

Striking Thunder nodded. "We leave before *Wi* rises to show her face. Woodcarver-Who-Lives-in-the-Woods will be eager for my return. Do not fear his being alone. Our people will help him with your horses while you are gone."

Wolf grinned, his dark thoughts lifting. Striking Thunder never called Ben, an old friend of their mother's, by his given name, preferring to use the name his people had bestowed upon the old man when his mother, White Wind, had married their father, Golden Eagle. "Go safely, my brother." The two clasped each other on the shoulders. It would be many months before they met again.

Striking Thunder left to join the rest of his warriors camped outside of town. At the end of the street, he heard running feet and stopped—but not in time to sidestep a dark figure who hurtled into him. He reached out to steady the boy, but his feet slid out from beneath him. The two of them fell onto the wet and muddy road, with Striking Thunder taking the brunt of the fall. Flat on his back, he quickly realized that the softness crushed against his chest didn't belong to a boy.

Light from an upstairs window nearby splashed onto them. Looking up, he found himself staring into eyes the color of spring grass. He felt her rapid breathing and watched her eyes widen as she looked at him. She stared first at his jet black braids; then her gaze flickered to the bronzed skin of his high cheekbones. When those bright green eyes narrowed on his hawkish nose, he realized something else. She was very angry.

"Let go of me," she demanded, pushing against him. In her haste to get off him, she fell into a puddle of muddy water.

Getting to his feet, Striking Thunder kept a wary watch on the young girl, unsure of the cause of her anger. He knew from experience that most white people either despised or feared Indians. He wanted no trouble with the townspeople.

Suddenly she jumped to her feet and jabbed his buckskin-covered chest with a mud-coated finger. "White Wolf, I've got words to say to you, you . . ."

Startled, Striking Thunder held up a hand for silence. In an expression of surprise similar to his brother's, he lifted a brow. "I am not White Wolf," he corrected. "I am Striking Thunder, his brother."

The girl seemed momentarily taken aback. She took a step back and glared up at him. "Are you sure?" she demanded.

His lips twitched with amusement. "Of this I am sure." He watched as she brushed her tangled curls from her eyes and attempted to wipe the drops of water from her face. But it only made matters worse. Streaks of mud now covered her cheeks and forehead, giving her the appearance of a young brave painted for war.

"Fine. Where is that no-account brother of yours?"

Striking Thunder shrugged and pointed the way he'd come. "White Wolf is tending to his animals." To his surprise and amusement, she stalked off without another word. Intrigued, he stared after the mud-soaked figure. He didn't possess the gift of sight as his sister did, but somehow he knew with absolute certainty he would see again this strange white girl who dressed as a boy. He headed toward the outskirts of town, but curiosity got the better of him. On silent feet, he kept to the shadows and retraced his steps back to the barn.

Wolf stared out into the night, tired, ready to return to the boardinghouse where he had taken a room. He frowned and hoped Lolita wasn't waiting for him. He'd endured two days of her clinging possessiveness—and that was more than enough. She was shallow-minded, concerned only with money and bedding any male who caught her eye or offered enough coin.

Six months ago, that wouldn't have bothered him. Now he wanted more from life. A strange restlessness had seized him. He felt like a fish tossed on the bank. He was floundering his way through life. To counter the useless feeling, he'd thrown himself into the necessary preparations for the overland trip. He was grateful that the coming year would be hard, leaving little room for discontent. He took one last look at his new horse. The stallion had settled. If he spooked during the night, Rook, asleep in the loft, would be there to calm him.

His gaze shifted to a mound of hay in one corner of the barn. "You stay away from the farmer's chickens, my friend," he told the animal. The white wolf, curled in a tight ball, lifted his muzzle and stared at him with unblinking blue eyes. With a low whine, the animal lowered his head to his paws.

Wolf grinned at his companion's woebegone expression. "Yeah, I know, old boy, but you got shot last time you messed with a chicken house."

Suddenly, an angry voice yelled out, "White Wolf, you no-account scalawag. I want a word with you."

In one smooth movement, Wolf dropped to a crouch, palmed the knife hidden inside his boot and spun around to face the intruder. His brows lowered when his gaze encountered a filthy youngster with furious green eyes standing in the pool of light just inside the barn. He straightened, his weight on the balls of his moccasin-clad feet. "Dammit, boy," he ground out furiously, "you could've gotten yourself killed. Don't you know better than to sneak up on a man like that?"

The boy, barely over five feet tall, stomped toward him. "It's all your fault that my brothers are leaving me behind so they can take Able's cattle to Oregon. You can't separate us. We're a family. I won't let you!"

Before Wolf had time to make sense of the angry words, a fist flew at him, catching him square in the chest. Tossing his knife into the nearest bale of hay, Wolf swore beneath his breath and jumped back to avoid another well-aimed blow.

He wrapped his fingers around two thin wrists, then yelped when the sharp toe of a booted foot caught him squarely on the shin. He grimaced at the pain from the kicks and stepped on the boy's toes to prevent further bruising of his smarting shins. "Settle down, you hellion," he said with a growl. One hand wiggled free of his grip and lashed out, catching him on the chin. Wolf yanked the offending arm behind the kid's back. "One more kick or punch out of you and I'm gonna put you over my knees and paddle the tar out of you, understand?"

His assailant stopped struggling and stood there, breathing hard. Wolf relaxed his hold, grateful the threat had worked—not that he'd have carried it out. He knew firsthand, from his years as a reluctant boarder in the white man's school how demeaning corporal punishment was. Staring down at his unwanted captive, he wondered what to do with him. Who was in charge of this cub?

"Touch me, and my brother James will tear your hide into strips."

Wolf narrowed his eyes. There was something familiar about the kid glaring at him. "What's your name?"

"Jessie," came the low reply.

Something tugged at the back of his mind. He'd heard that name before. Then it dawned on him. Yesterday, at Lolita's window, the dark-haired rider who'd nearly run over the young ladies. Yes, he was sure this was the mischief-maker, yet seeing him up close, there was something else that was familiar. He narrowed his eyes, concentrating on the dirty face and the glaring green eyes.

Recognition dawned. It was the eyes and hair that gave away the boy's identity. The spunky and foolish kid bore a definite likeness to James Jones, the man hired to be in charge of the cattle. He grimaced when he recalled hearing that all the Jones boys—except James—had quick tempers.

Wolf noted the lateness of the evening and wondered why the boy was wandering the streets of Westport. From what he'd seen, Jessie ran unsupervised a great deal of the time. Well, he'd let Jessie's parents know about this latest stunt. They could have been burying their son come the new day. "Where's your pa?"

"Dead."

"Your ma?"

"Same."

Frustrated, but not willing to turn him loose, Wolf frowned. "Who's in charge of you? Grandparents?"

"What do you care? You're taking my brothers away from me. If I never see them again, it'll be your fault."

"What the hell are you talking about?"

"You hired my brothers to go to Oregon. If they go, I go. You don't have the right to separate us. We're family. Families stick together."

Wolf noted the glittering sheen of moisture in the boy's green eyes and wished he knew exactly what was going on. He could have sworn Able had said there were only three brothers, the same ones he'd hired to drive Able's cattle west, but there was no doubting this boy's identity. A slow-burning anger simmered deep inside him. He remembered how it felt to be separated from family, and from what Jessie said, it was obvious James wasn't planning on taking him to Oregon.

He couldn't blame the boy for being angry. Setting his jaw, Wolf pulled Jessie toward the inky darkness outside the barn. "You and I are going to find James and get some answers." Jessie struggled and protested but Wolf tightened his grip. But before he reached the door, James Jones burst into the barn. "Dammit, Jessie," he shouted, "what the hell do you think you're doing?"

Chapter Four

At the sound of her brother's furious voice, Jessie froze. Her startled gaze shifted past Wolf's broad shoulders to James, who stood in the dark opening of the barn, feet widespread and fists shoved onto his hips. He glared at her, his brows pulled into a tight vee.

Oh, Lord, she was in for it now. She'd pushed her even-tempered brother too far this time. Of all her brothers, James seldom lost control, but when he did, she'd swear Hell heard him hollering. She moved slightly behind Wolf; moments before he had been the enemy, but now he seemed a safer haven.

Wolf released one of her wrists, keeping the other firmly encircled with his long brown fingers. "About time you came looking to see what trouble young Jess is getting into. Saves me from hunting you down."

Wolf's annoyance hung heavy in the dark silence. Jessie glanced from one man to the other, noting twin aggressive stances of fisted hands and set jaws. She groaned softly. How had things gone so wrong? All she'd wanted was to convince Wolf to let her go to Oregon with her family, but she'd let her temper get the best of her. She opened her mouth to explain, but James stopped her with an accusing finger.

"What the hell are you trying to do, Jess? Of all the wild, reckless—"

"Reckless is right," Wolf interrupted. "Attacking strangers seems a good way to end up dead."

James's lower jaw dropped. "Jess attacked you?" He stepped farther into the barn, shock and disbelief written on his face. "You've gone too far this time."

Jessie lowered her gaze to the tip of her muddy toes. Yep, she was truly in trouble now. She didn't need to look at James to know his face was red as the lips of the women working in the saloon. She narrowed her gaze, her brief feelings of trepidation giving way to indignation. What had she really done wrong—aside from losing her temper? Nothing! She had rights. She was a Jones. No Jones worth his or her salt would sit complacently and let some outsider split them up. Refusing to cower, Jessie tilted her chin, her green gaze mirroring the anger in her brother's.

She had every right to protest what her brothers were doing. And though White Wolf was responsible, James was allowing him to split them up. He deserved to shoulder some of the blame. "If I've gone too far, James, it's your fault."

"Dammit, Jess! We've talked about this."

Jessie shook her head vehemently. "No!" Her voice trembled as tears threatened to break forth. "*You* made the decision to go to Oregon without me."

"And you know why! We can't afford to pass up this chance, and if you've ruined it . . ." His arms fell to his sides and he sighed heavily. "I'm real disappointed in you, Jess."

Recognizing the familiar tactic meant to make her feel guilty, Jessie yanked herself free from Wolf and stomped over to James until she stood toe-to-toe with him. Over the years, she'd pulled some stupid stunts that he'd had every right to chastise her for—but not this. Oh, no, not this time. She was a grown woman. It was time he realized it. Digging her fingers into her hips, Jessie leaned forward.

"If that isn't low enough for a belly-crawling snake! How do you think I feel? What happened to sticking together?" she accused, her voice low and husky with the effort to hide any weakness. Her voice hardened as she drew a deep breath and continued: "Talk about disappointing! Finding out that money is more important to you is bad enough, but then to learn that Jordan's going to marry Coralie, that she'll go to Oregon but not me, your own—''

''I've heard enough,'' Wolf said in a growl, his fingers closing around her upper arm to pull her aside. ''I want to know why you didn't tell me you had a younger brother, James.''

Jessie stared at Wolf in confusion. He thought she was James's brother? Glancing down at her shirt and homespun pants, she grimaced. One side of her face felt tight. Lifting one hand, she felt the streak of mud on her right cheek. Heavens, she was a mess from head to toe.

She tried in vain to rub it off; unfortunately, her hands were just as dirty. She wrinkled her nose in disgust. In all fairness, she couldn't blame Wolf for mistaking her for a boy. Still, it rankled, illustrating just how lacking in womanly curves she was. Her fragile feminine ego took another bruising.

She opened her mouth to correct him. ''You've made a mis—''

Wolf silenced her with a raised hand. The anger left his cold blue eyes, and the hard line of his mouth softened with compassion. ''Quiet, boy. This is between me and your brother. As the eldest, James is responsible for your welfare. I will deal with this. You will not be abandoned by your family.''

The combination of his change toward her and the sudden realization that she might have caused her brothers to lose their jobs stopped the flow of words gathered on the tip of her tongue. The color fled from her face. What had she done? Did Wolf mean to fire her brothers?

She'd never meant for them to lose their jobs. She'd only wanted to shame Wolf into letting her go with them. Jessie bit her lower lip. As usual, her temper had landed her in a heap of trouble.

She tried once more to correct Wolf. ''You don't under—'' From behind her, bony fingers squeezed her shoulder, silencing her. Startled, she turned her head. Her jaw dropped as she stared into a pair of familiar twinkling blue eyes. Surprised to see the old man she'd met earlier, she whispered, "What are you doing here?"

Rook indicated the two arguing men with a slight nod of his white head. "Come away, lass." His raspy voice was low, for her ears only. His gnarled fingers grasped her arm as he pulled her back into the deep shadows.

Jessie glanced over at Wolf and James. They seemed oblivious to her disappearance. She turned to her new friend. "But Rook, he thinks—"

"Quiet, lass," Rook rasped. "Listen ta me. God gave ya two ears 'n' one mouth so's ya could listen more than ya talk."

Jessie pondered that bit of advice and decided she didn't have anything to lose at this point. Raised voices brought her attention back to her brother and Wolf.

"Now wait one gall-durn minute, Wolf," James sputtered. "No one is abandoning anyone. I arranged for Jessie to come to Oregon later with another family because Jessie's a—"

Wolf's hand rose upward, then slashed downward. His voice roared and echoed in the rafters. "A scamp. An unmannered cub, that's what he is. But where I come from, we don't abandon our children no matter how badly they behave. You should've told me you had a younger brother. We could have worked something out. I hire honest, hardworking men. You came highly recommended, but I don't cotton to any man running out on his responsibilities."

"I don't believe this." Jessie groaned softly as she watched her brother gesture angrily. "Someone needs to kick some sense into both of them."

Rook grinned and pulled a pipe from his shirt pocket. "Kickin' never gets you nowhere, 'less'n you's a mule. Jest relax. I gots me a feelin' things is gonna work out jest fine."

Jessie released her pent-up breath in one long disgusted sigh. Let them fight it out. No matter the outcome, she was going to Oregon and that was that.

As the seconds ticked by, Jessie's gaze kept returning to

the imposing figure of the wagon master. Up until now, she'd been too distracted to pay much mind to what he looked like, but now the raw masculinity vibrating from him slammed into her, taking her breath away as she experienced her first taste of instant attraction.

He wore an unfastened buckskin vest, buckskin breeches fringed down each side, and moccasins. Except for his coloring, he looked Indian. She continued to study him. The faint glow from a lantern hanging on a nail revealed tantalizing glimpses of glittering golden curls coating the bronzed expanse of his chest beneath his vest. A strange fluttering in the region of her stomach caught her by surprise. Surrounded by grown men who oftentimes went shirtless, walked around in their long johns and spoke frankly within her hearing, Jessie had figured she was immune to all those symptoms of desire that the other girls giggled over. Yet staring at Wolf, she discovered she was very much affected.

His features were a study of shadows and smooth planes. Finely etched cheekbones placed high and prominent contrasted with sharp, angular jaws and a straight but gently sloping nose. Her eyes latched onto his mouth. Moments ago it had been soft and full when he'd looked down at her. To her surprise, she wondered what it would be like to be kissed by him, to have those blue eyes look at her with love and tenderness.

Jessie made a face. Why was she thinking of such things with a man she'd never met before when she had her sights set on Elliot? Some inner voice pointed out that Elliot's handsome features had never taken her breath away or set her heart racing as the man arguing with her brother had managed to do in one brief meeting.

She was grateful when Wolf joined both her and Rook, putting an end to her disturbing thoughts. Staring into his set features, she noted that the brief flash of compassion she'd glimpsed earlier was gone. Though he stared hard at her, he addressed James.

"It's settled. Jessie goes—with you—where he belongs. But from what I've seen, he's not responsible enough to work with the cattle,'' Wolf announced grimly, drawing himself up to his full six-foot-plus height.

Resenting the slur on her abilities, she stepped forward, hands on her hips. ''I'm as good with cattle as my brothers are, aren't I, James?''

James choked and refused to meet her pleading gaze. His fingers massaged the back of his neck as he paced behind Wolf. ''If you'd just listen to me, Wolf. You don't understand. Jessie is short for—''

Rook stepped out of the shadows behind her, cutting James off. ''I could use some help with the cookin'.'' His bushy white brows winged upward as he winked down at her. ''Can ya cook and wash dishes, *boy?*''

Holding her breath, Jessie stared into Rook's amused blue eyes. His use of the word *boy* let her know he'd had the same thought as she. She recalled his parting advice to her earlier: *If you's meant ta go, a way'll open up. You jest make sure you're ready to take it.* It looked as though one had. The question was, did she dare take it?

''Well? We're waiting,'' Wolf reminded her.

''Jessie . . .'' James warned.

Jessie averted her gaze from her brother. Could she really do it? Pass herself off as a boy for the entire two-thousand-mile trip? Yes! If it meant going to Oregon with her brothers, she *would* do it. She hid her grin of elation under a scowl. ''I can cook as well as any girl,'' she bragged.

Strands of golden brown hair scraped the tops of each leather-shrouded shoulder as Wolf pulled Jessie to his side, then addressed James, who was swearing beneath his breath. ''My decision is final. The boy goes or none of you go.''

Stark silence met his ultimatum. Jessie held her breath and waited anxiously as James strode to the open doorway, one hand leaning on the rough planks of wood as he stared out into the night, his shoulders stiff with tension. Please, James, she begged silently. It was the perfect solution. As the silence stretched, she stared at the straw-strewn ground, unable to watch him wrestle with his conscience. She felt bad knowing she was the cause of his inner turmoil. She tried to go to him but strong fingers dug into her shoulder.

Warmth seeped through her shirt beneath Wolf's firm touch. Jessie puzzled over her reaction to the man at her side whose close presence sent heated blood thrumming through her veins. She sneaked a quick glance sideways and frowned. Admitting to any feelings of attraction to a hard, cold, insensitive man like Wolf was unthinkable. If Wolf knew the truth, he'd refuse to let her go. Surely it was the anxiety and tension flowing around the four people in the barn that was affecting her so oddly.

James turned, defeat written across his face. "This ain't what it seems, Wolf, but you're the boss. I just hope you remember that I tried to tell you."

Jessie released her pent-up breath, her heart filled with joy. She was going to Oregon after all. The look James threw her way warned her that things were far from settled between them, but she'd worry about that later. For now, she was so relieved, she grinned happily.

Wolf glanced down at her. Jessie wiped the grin from her lips and ducked her head, unable to face those bright cobalt eyes that seemed to pin her to the spot. She shivered, struck with the sudden knowledge that she'd rue this day should Wolf discover the truth.

"It's settled then. As of now, Jessie Jones, I'm the boss, and when I'm not around, Rook's word goes. You work with him and do as he tells you or you'll answer to me, understand?"

Jessie glanced over at Rook. It was his sly wink that gave her the courage to answer with a snappy, "Yes, sir." With that, she bolted out the door.

Tuesday morning arrived, bringing with it clear blue skies, warm temperatures and lilting song as sparrows frolicked in the oak trees and swooped down to investigate the half-packed wagon. Standing on the porch of the small white-washed farmhouse, Jessie watched Jeremy roll a barrel of rice into position. The wagon shifted and creaked under his movements. He straightened and smacked into one of the hickory slats arching from one side to the other. Rolling her eyes, she called out, "Duck, Jeremy. I swear, that's the tenth time you've done that!"

He scowled at her. "Don't see why we can't just take these off and put them back on when we're ready to put the cover on."

Jessie shook her head and tromped down the porch steps. She handed her brother a small trunk containing her mother's flo-blue china. He tucked it beneath a rocking chair and arranged a quilt-wrapped clock beside it. Satisfied that her mother's dishes and clock were securely packed, she returned to the house for another load. Each trip through the lived-in rooms brought a lump to her throat. Her emotions seesawed. So many memories—of home, childhood and her parents— were being left behind for new beginnings in a land that promised richer tomorrows.

Clutching the family Bible to her breast, she left the house. Staring into the back of the nearly filled wagon, Jesse let hopes and dreams fill her heart and mind. Eager anticipation of the adventurous journey gripped her and left her breathless. She leaned against the side of the wagon while visions of the green grass lining the fertile Willamette Valley permeated her mind. Her lips curved upward as she imagined a rough log-cabin house with her ma's old rocking chair in front of a warm fireplace.

Jessie's smile grew wistful. It had taken her and her brothers nearly the whole winter to pare down what each family member considered essential to take to Oregon, but there'd been no question of whether the chair went or not. They all held dear to their heart the sweet memories of Mary Jones rocking the evenings away in front of the fire with her sewing in her lap.

Glancing down at the porch, she spied her meager pile of personal possessions: a small trunk that held a few of her favorite books, an old rag doll and her spare changes of clothing. Lying on top of the trunk, her new journal beckoned—a gift from Mrs. Bettencourt, the old schoolmarm she'd occasionally helped out. Jessie kneeled and opened the leather-bound book. Staring at the pristine white pages, her fingers itched to fill each page with her thoughts and images of her overland experience.

Heavy footsteps and an impatient voice shook her from her musings. "Jess, start gathering whatever we need from the kitchen. Remember, only the bare essentials," James ordered.

Jessie's stomach knotted into a hard, painful mass under James's icy green glare. He strode toward the barn without another word. Her earlier excitement fled. James was still all horns and rattles. She grimaced, remembering the ugly scene between them when he'd arrived home on Saturday. He'd ordered her to change into a dress and return to town with him right then to confess the truth to Wolf.

She'd refused. Rook was right: Wolf's having mistaken her for a boy was meant to be. A way had opened up for her to go to Oregon. Besides, the thought of appearing before Wolf in the one ugly dress she owned was unthinkable.

Leaving the porch, she dug the toe of one boot into the hard-packed earth, loosening a large rock. Kicking it, she heard it bounce off the porch siding.

An arm slipped around her shoulders. "For what it's worth, Jess, I'm glad you're going with us. So is Jordan."

Jessie looked up at Jeremy and drew a measure of comfort from the understanding in his pale green eyes. She leaned into him. It helped knowing Jeremy and Jordan were behind her—sort of, anyway.

"Thanks. Want to tell James that?"

Jeremy straightened in mock horror. "Hey, you crazy? He gets plenty mad at me as it is."

She tried to force a grin. "Only when you pull some stupid stunt." Her lips trembled and her eyes stung with unshed tears. She couldn't stand being at odds with any of her brothers, especially James, yet there was no way she could back down. "He's never been this mad at me before," she whispered, staring off after James into the dark interior of the barn.

Jeremy ruffled her curls and led the way into the house. "What'd ya expect, Jess? You defied him and involved him—us—in a lie."

At her moan of anguish, Jeremy took pity on her. "Aw, come on, sis. He'll get over it. He's just worried, you know. Wolf ain't gonna like it when he finds out he's been duped."

At the mention of the wagon master's name, Jessica stopped short of the kitchen. This bad air between her and James was all *his* fault. "If it hadn't been for his stupid rule against women, none of this would have happened," she snapped.

"That's beside the point," Jeremy said. "Don't worry. James'll come around soon enough. Now, come on, we've got lots to do before sunset."

Jessie shook her head. "I'm going to talk to James first." She stalked out of the house, determined to clear the air between them. When she reached the open doorway of the barn, she paused to inhale the familiar odors of oiled leather, sweet hay and horseflesh. James sat on the ground, sorting through farming implements. He'd set aside several hammers, a chopping ax, broadax, froe, auger and plane in one neat pile on the hay-strewn ground. Those items would go with them to Oregon.

She watched him untangle an old length of rope. After what seemed like hours, he turned and acknowledged her presence. Deep grooves of displeasure were etched across his forehead. Jessie swallowed past the lump in her throat. She'd never meant to hurt him or put him in an awkward position. Honor was important to James, and she'd compromised it. She sighed. He took everything so seriously. Being left in charge of three siblings while still a boy himself had matured him early. But that didn't mean he was always right. Moisture gathered in the inner corners of her eyes. "Please don't be angry, James," she begged. She wanted her loving brother back, the one who'd nursed her through her childhood illnesses and comforted her through the nightmares brought on by the fear of being taken from her brothers.

It had fallen to James to wash and bandage her skinned

knees and apply the paddle when she'd deserved it, though he'd never hurt her. In fact, she recalled fondly, those lessons in discipline had bothered him more than her. But when James turned his back on her and added the neatly coiled rope and a length of chain to the growing pile, another stab of pain went through her. Never could she recall him staying mad overnight at her—not until now. Defeated, she brushed the tears from her cheeks and turned away. Her feet dragged with each step as she went to the wooden pen where she'd slung her saddlebags.

Retrieving the brown paper–wrapped packet she'd purchased in town nearly a week ago, Jessie returned to James. "Happy birthday, James," she whispered, handing him his gift. She walked away, tears streaming down her cheeks. His voice stopped her.

"Shouldn't have done what you did, Jess."

Jessie stopped in the open barn door. A sob of relief escaped. She turned and retraced her steps slowly. "You should've told me that Jordan was going to ask Coralie to marry him. Do you have any idea how I felt knowing that she was going but not me?"

James stood and stared up into the wooden beams crisscrossing above him. After several long seconds, he turned and gripped her shoulders with his large, callused hands. "You're right, Jess; I'm sorry. We should've told you—but we knew how you'd react." His lips tilted up into a wry grin. "Though I could never have foreseen this."

He grew serious. "Now, will you please reconsider this mad scheme—for me? We can go to Wolf together and tell him the truth. There's still time to convince him that you should go with us. If he refuses, you can come out with the Smiths like I arranged. We won't be separated long. A few months at the most."

Jessie shook her head sadly. "Oh, James, how can you promise that? Can you swear on our parents' graves that nothing will happen to you or the others?"

James sighed and rubbed the back of his neck. "Listen,

Jess, even if you go with us, there's no guarantee that nothing will happen to one of us.''

"But I'd know," Jessie replied simply. "Don't you see? It's the not knowing I couldn't live with. Remember Fritz and Else Fabricus?''

James sighed, his shoulders slumped in defeat. Fritz, their nearest neighbor, had left three years ago with his two eldest sons. He'd planned to return for Else and their three daughters after he'd built their dream house. That was three years ago. No one knew what had happened to him. They stared at one another for long moments. Jessie ran her hands down the front of her torn and dirty jeans. "You can't promise that, James. No one can. Rook was right when he said I'd know if I was meant to go. This is meant to be." An impish grin tugged at the corner of her lips. "Besides, we *did* try to tell him the truth.''

James ducked his head, but not before Jessie saw his lips twitch, and in that moment she knew he'd forgiven her. "It'll work, James. I know it will.''

"I sure wish you'd never met that old man," James grumbled.

Then he lifted his worried gaze to her. "I hate to think what will happen when Wolf finds out. And Jess, he will find out that you're my sister and that we've lied to him.'' He sighed and pulled Jessie into his arms. "But I guess we'll face the consequences together.''

Jessie wrapped her arms around his neck and clutched him tightly.

He stepped back and cuffed her gently. "You're forgiven, brat," he said gruffly.

Poking her hands into the back pockets of her pants, Jessie smiled, happy that he wasn't mad anymore. "Thanks, James. I promise I'll work real hard.''

The sound of ripping paper filled the air as James unwrapped his gift. The brown paper fell away to reveal a brand-new pair of leather work gloves. "Do you like them, James? I bought them with the money I earned selling Mr. Baker eggs and extra jars of preserves.''

"They're great, Jessie. Sure needed a new pair. These will come in right handy during the trip." He reached out to ruffle her hair. "Off with you," he ordered, his voice low and gruff. "We've got to be at the Bakers' by suppertime."

Orvil Baker glanced at the young couple heading up the stairs to the living quarters above the store. Jordan and Coralie had just returned from a stroll around town. He knew his daughter was showing off her new husband. It was hard for him to believe his little girl was a married woman of two days. How he wished her mother had been alive to see this day.

"Father, are you going to join us for tea?"

Glancing from Coralie's beaming features to Jordan's handsome sternness, he prayed that the two kids would be happy. He knew he spoiled his only daughter, but if anyone could handle her, it was Jordan. In answer to Coralie's question, Orvil shook his graying head. "No, dear, I need to gather the supplies you and Elliot will need." He winked. "Good thing I own the store! Now, be sure to come down after tea so I can fit your feet to a pair of boots. Just got in a nice shipment. Your fine kid-leather slippers and spool-heeled ladies' shoes aren't suited for the trail."

Coralie's lower lip jutted out. "Father, I wouldn't be caught dead in any of *those*." She waved her hand toward the shelf of ready-made boots. "And besides, I'm not going to walk. *I'm* riding in the wagon. You know I have to protect my skin from the sun," she said, lifting her skirts to flounce up the stairs.

Jordan shook his head and rolled his eyes. "Pick out two pairs of boots for her. I'll make sure she takes them." He then followed his wife up the stairs.

Orvil grinned. Yep, his little girl would be in good hands. Then he thought of something else. He lowered his voice. "Jordan?"

"Yes, Mr. Baker?"

"She's not going to be happy about Jessie."

Jordan leaned over the wooden banister. "Coralie's a married woman now, Mr. Baker. She and Jessie will have to make their peace.''

Orvil listened to Jordan tromp upstairs. It wouldn't be that simple, and he admitted to being a coward. He didn't want to be anywhere near his daughter when she found out Jessie was going to Oregon.

''You heard right, Coralie. Jessie is going to Oregon as our young brother,'' Jordan announced, leaning one hip against the windowsill, his hat in his hands.

''But how? I mean . . .'' Coralie was momentarily stunned. This couldn't be!

Elliot, lounging in an upholstered Sleepy Hollow armchair, smirked at his sister. ''You'd best start calling her Jessie or Jess from now on, Cora.''

Coralie sniffed and turned to sit sideways in her chair, presenting her brother with her back. She hated to be called Cora and her brother knew it, but with Jordan looking on, she kept her features perfectly schooled as she continued her role as hostess and finished pouring the tea. She delivered a fragile cup and saucer to each man, then resumed her seat. Picking up her own cup, she took a careful sip of the hot liquid. ''Surely you jest, Jordan,'' she said, looking at him through her lashes.

''No, Jessie is going with us, and though I have some reservations about pulling this off, I'm glad. It never felt right leaving her behind.''

''But she can't go to Oregon disguised as a boy! It's—it's preposterous.'' Coralie ducked her head, letting her blond curls fall to curtain her face. Her nostrils flared with displeasure. She didn't want to travel all the way to Oregon with Jessie. She'd planned on using the time alone with her husband's family to establish herself as the lady of the household—a position she refused to share. Though a slow tide of anger rolled through her, she didn't dare let Jordan see how his news affected her.

She composed her features before lifting her head. Her eyes were innocently wide when she looked at her husband.

"But Jordan, how gauche, pretending that Jessica's your brother. Surely you can't expect me to lie?" she asked, her voice high and breathless as her fingers fluttered at her throat.

Ignoring Elliot's muffled laughter, Coralie fanned her flushed cheeks with one white-gloved hand. "Why, the mere thought of practicing such deceit, especially after we had the good fortune to enjoy the reverend's sermon on trust and honesty just last Sunday, does make me feel all-overish."

Jordan coughed and Elliot stood, clapping his hands. "Cora, that was one of your best performances to date. But I do feel I must remind you that truth and honesty or lack thereof have never seemed to bother you before. I propose that you go about your normal business and ignore those virtues in this instance."

Coralie laughed nervously. "Really, Elliot." She turned her head to gauge her husband's reaction and saw his lips twitch.

Elliot sat down with a chuckle. "Jessie has courage and spunk."

Jordan grimaced and moved from the window to stand beside his wife. "Let's just hope she keeps away from Wolf. Catching a weasel asleep will be easier than fooling that one. I wouldn't want that man for an enemy."

Coralie opened her mouth to argue her opinion of Jessica's deceitful plan, but Jordan knelt before her, and her gloved fingers were swallowed in his large, callused hands. She tried to look away but his green eyes, darkened with love, held hers.

"I want your word that you will not say or do anything to reveal the truth to anyone."

Coralie's heart thumped when his thumb caressed the underside of her wrist. Staring down into his loving gaze, she was powerless to deny him. She tipped her nose upward and sniffed. "Well, she does look like a boy most of the time, so I suppose it shouldn't be too difficult to pretend she is one. I'll even try to call her Jessie—but I'm not very good at lying," she warned with a pout.

"Thank you, sweetheart," Jordan said softly.

Coralie grabbed his shirt when he stood and moved away from her. She leaned into his hard length, and in the blink of an eye, huge tears welled in her eyes. "But Jordan, you must make her be nice to me. She nearly ran me down with that huge horse of hers for no reason last week, ruining another gown." She blinked the tears from her eyes, then dabbed her long blond lashes delicately with the corner of a pristine white lacy hankie.

Elliot broke in. "Cut it out, Coralie. Pa and I heard you taunting Jessie. In my opinion, you deserved it."

Twin flags of rage brightened Coralie's cheeks. Her lower lip trembled as she shook out her skirts. "You're so mean, Elliot. You don't know anything." She peeped at her husband through wet lashes. "Are you going to believe him or me?"

Jordan ran a hand over his jaw. His expression, more than words, let her know he wasn't fooled by her female wiles. He tilted her chin, forcing her to meet his stern gaze. "It doesn't matter who started what. What's past is past."

He set his half-full teacup down and gripped her hands. "As my wife, you will go along with this. You and Jess are sisters by marriage now. I won't have any more fighting from either of you. Understood?"

Coralie lowered her gaze and nodded, hiding her resentment. "Yes, Jordie," she replied, forcing meekness into her voice. What she wouldn't give to one-up that tomboy Jessica.

Jordan reached out to finger one long golden curl. "Good. Now, my family will be here by nightfall, thanks to your father's kind generosity in allowing us to stay here until morning. You have the rest of this day to get used to the idea of thinking of Jessie as my little brother. In the meantime, Elliot and I have much to do, as do you. Pack your personal belongings while Elliot and I help your father. Remember, one small trunk."

Coralie flounced out of the room without a backward glance. Jordan cringed when her bedroom door slammed shut, shaking the whole house. The two men looked at each other and shook their heads.

"As I said, this will not be a dull trip with our sisters along," Elliot said. "I just hope we can keep them from killing each other."

Chapter Five

Dusty rose fingers of color raced across the pale blue sky, tinting the fluffy white clouds with the delicate blush of a newborn babe's skin. Down below, dew clung to spring green grass, pooled on bright shiny leaves and freshened tiny wildflowers dotting the landscape. Sniffing the crisp morning air, a shaggy, white-furred wolf sat on his haunches beside a weathered gray barn. His ears perked forward, and his bright blue eyes tracked the movements of oxen pulling wagons past.

From inside the barn, the animal's master silently observed the frenzy of activity out in the streets as his wagon train prepared for its journey west. Wolf knew that by month's end the Oregon Trail would be one endless stretch of white-topped wagons. While most emigrants set out around the first of May, he was leaving nearly two weeks earlier in the hope of getting ahead of the rush and avoiding clogged trails, long lines at the crossings, fouled water and trampled prairies.

Stepping out into the weak warmth of the sun, Wolf saw the approach of the Jones family. He nodded to James and Jeremy, each leading an extra horse as they rode past. Elliot and Jordan followed with two wagons. He glanced down the muddy street, looking for the youngest Jones boy. The fact that Jessie Jones wasn't with his brothers wasn't a good sign. Now what mischief was he up to? Feelings of misgiving assailed him. On one hand, the boy was not his concern, but by hiring Jessie as Rook's assistant, he'd personally assumed responsibility for him.

He knew better than most that the trail was unforgiving of the rashness of youth. This trip would either make a man of the boy or claim his young life. When the ground vibrated beneath him, Wolf instinctively stepped out of the road and back into the shadows to avoid being hit. His gaze narrowed when he noticed that the reckless rider galloping past was none other than the youngest Jones boy. A black-and-tan dog streaked past, then stopped abruptly to eye the wolf.

Hackles raised and head lowered, Wahoska growled low in his throat, but before Wolf could call the animal off, a shrill whistle rent the air. The dog turned away, surging forward in a burst of power to rejoin her master.

Wolf joined his pet in a warm pool of sunlight. "There goes trouble, my friend," he said to his companion, feeling unaccountably uneasy. Tension radiated beneath his fingertips. He glanced down to see Wahoska tracking the dog's movements with his keen eyes. Low rumbling continued to erupt from his throat. Wolf pulled at his freshly shaved chin, his gaze pensive as he stared after the youngest Jones brother, now riding ahead of his siblings. Somehow it seemed fitting that Jessie's dog had agitated the wolf. Heaven only knew the boy managed to get under his skin. Damn. It was going to be a long trip.

The sound of mules braying down the street reminded him that there was work to be done. "Time to get moving, my friend." Resolution filled him. He had a job to do, and he'd do whatever it took to see that every man, woman, child and beast made it safely to Oregon. Mounting his nervous black stallion, he rode out into the sunlight. Giving a low whistle, he commanded Lady Sarah, the Indian-trained mare he'd named after his mother, to follow. Wahoska padded alongside.

He rode to the meeting spot outside of Westport, joining Rook, who stood near four wagons loaded with food and provisions for the hired men. Aside from food, there was also feed and shoeing equipment for the forty-plus horses that were needed to see the cattle to their destination in the Willamette Valley.

Wolf ran an experienced eye over each team of oxen, checked each wagon, then conferred with Rook over the food and feed stores. When he was satisfied that everything was in order, he turned to the older man. "Have the rest of the wagons line up for inspection," he ordered.

"Yes, boss." Rook hurried off. His bowed legs carried his burly figure from wagon to wagon; his deep booming voice rang loud as he shouted out instructions. In short order, the emigrants pulled their wagons into three long lines.

Wolf leaned against the rough wood of a supply wagon, his arms folded over his chest. Tipping his chin to the sun, he breathed deeply and felt his blood race in anticipation of the challenging trip ahead of him. He thrived on pitting his skills and knowledge against the outdoor world he knew so well. What he didn't enjoy was leading unseasoned travelers across the rough and dangerous terrain. Too many of them had heads filled with unrealistic dreams rather than good sense. Often their lack of preparation resulted in death.

He grimaced. To avoid most of the common mistakes green emigrants made, Wolf insisted on inspecting each and every wagon, draft animal and load before setting off. Nothing brought morale down faster than having to abandon a family along the way. When Rook rejoined him, he pushed away from the wagon and squared his shoulders. All resentment at being saddled with the trip faded. From that moment on, he had a job to do, one that required skill and a clear mind. Hands on his hips, he drew in a deep breath and scanned the lined-up wagons.

"All set, boss. They's jest awaitin' on you now." Rook

waved his pipe in the air. "Only the Macauleys' wagon is missin'."

"How do they look, Rook?" He knew the answer in advance.

Years of close association showed in Rook's toothy grin. "Green, boss. All green, but reckon they'll learn fast enough," the tough trapper answered, tugging at his bushy white beard.

"They'd better, my friend. I'm setting a hard pace. We've got cattle to deliver by fall."

Wolf started with the two wagons belonging to the Jones party. With Jordan and Elliot at his side, he checked the rigging, the condition of the oxen, and the wagon from wheel to wheel. Glancing in the back, he ran his experienced eye over the load, mentally calculating the load weight and the food supply.

Hopping over the wagon tongue, he peered into the front end of the second wagon. One brow rose when he saw Jordan's bride. Coralie Jones sat perched on a wooden box wearing a fine linen dress of pale lilac. Her skirts fluffed out around her, and a matching frilly bonnet sat upon her head. Glancing down, he noted the thin-soled and spooled heels of her shoes. He bit back a groan. They were totally unsuited for walking. He pulled Jordan aside. "Don't mean to interfere, Jordan, but your wife is dressed for Sunday church." A thread of impatience crept into his voice.

Jordan let out a long, pained sigh. "Yeah, I know, but she refuses to wear anything else." He sent Wolf a wry shrug. "I packed practical clothing for her for when she's ready to be reasonable. I figure it'll only take a day, two at the most, before she realizes I'm right."

Wolf nodded his understanding, well acquainted with the stubbornness of the female of the species. Watching Coralie lean out of the wagon to talk to her friends who'd come out to see her off, he felt a small measure of relief that Jordan wasn't blinded by his wife's doll-like beauty. "Perhaps you should stay with the wagon for a few days. I can do without you for a bit," he offered, even though the first three days on the trail with cattle were the most difficult.

Jordan knew it too. "No need, Wolf. Elliot and Jessie will be here to help Coralie during the day, and I'll be with her most evenings."

Wolf nodded and glanced around in search of the youngest Jones brother. He spotted Jessie patting one of the oxen on the rump. He winced at the idea of Jessie and Coralie being together all day long. The incident he had witnessed from the saloon window was still fresh in his mind; he could well imagine the boy's idea of "help."

No, expecting Jessie to help his sister-in-law was just asking for trouble. Another concern came to mind as he stared at the two teams of oxen. "Elliot's in charge of one wagon, but who's in charge of the other one? I can't see your wife being up to that task quite yet, Jordan."

Jordan nodded toward Jessie. "Jess."

Wolf frowned and narrowed his eyes at the boy's slender frame. "The boy doesn't look strong enough to handle a team of four yoke. It takes a lot of muscle to handle eight oxen." He kept to himself the thought that Jessie certainly couldn't be trusted to do the job.

Shoving his hands on his hips, Wolf glanced around. "I'll ask Lars Svensson if his youngest boy is free to help Elliot with the other team, unless you'd rather stay with your family instead of riding herd?"

Jordan shook his head and adjusted his hat. "No need, boss. Jessie's stronger than s—" Jordan coughed. "Stronger than he looks. He trained and gentled one team of oxen. Elliot will handle them while Jessie breaks in the new ones on the trail. They'll be fine on their own."

Wolf eyed Jessie doubtfully. The older brothers seemed to expect a lot from their young sibling. The feeling that he needed to keep Jessie well supervised made him shake his head. "No. I'm not willing to trust the oxen or wagons to young Jess until he proves himself. Perhaps later, after I've had time to observe him working the oxen, I'll change my mind. For now he travels with Rook." Wolf turned on his heel, unaware of the look of concern that passed between Jordan and Elliot.

Wolf stopped a few feet from Jessie and watched silently. The boy ignored him and proceeded to the next yoke, talking in low, gentle murmurs to calm the restless beasts. Wolf studied the rigging, which Jessie had expertly adjusted. He found no fault and had to concede that the boy seemed to know what he was doing and handled the oxen well. But some perverse part of him forced him to keep to his resolve.

When Jessie glanced up to acknowledge his presence, Wolf hooked his thumb over his shoulder. "You're riding with Rook. He'll need your help gathering fuel for the fires and fresh greens when they're available while we travel. And remember, you do whatever he says."

Jessie's brows drew together. "The oxen—"

Wolf held up a hand to forestall the protest. With the sun rising at his back, he got his first good look at Jessie. Staring down at the face tipped up toward him, he frowned. Without the dark shadows of the barn or the streaks of mud, Jessie looked different than he'd expected—younger, softer somehow. Not what he'd expect to find in an adolescent boy who should be showing signs of maturing.

He questioned whether the boy was really fourteen, as Rook had said. All the more reason to veto the idea of his taking charge of the oxen. A plaintive sound of mooing came from behind the wagon. Wolf narrowed his eyes as the Joneses' cow tried to break free in order to reach the tender shoots of grass. Glancing around at the other wagons, he noticed the Svenssons also had a cow tethered to the back of their wagon, and he knew that the Macauleys, who had small children, would most likely also have a cow. And if he counted the one Rook purchased, he suddenly found himself in need of someone to herd them during the day.

He snapped his fingers. "In addition to helping Rook, you're also in charge of the milk cows. You will collect the cows from their owners each morning, drive them on the trail, then deliver them back to the wagons each night," he finished, pleased with himself. He'd found a way to keep

Jessie too busy to cause any mischief while they were on the trail.

"But—"

"Don't argue. I'm the boss." He paused and carefully enunciated his next words. "You will not drive a wagon until I'm sure you can handle the oxen. I won't risk any delays or injuries due to your inexperience." Wolf stared into blazing green eyes. "And a word of warning. Keep that temper of yours under control. I won't tolerate tantrums or mischief. Got it?"

Jessie thrust her chin out, glaring at him until the sound of Jordan clearing his throat sent her stalking off, rocks flying out from under her scuffed boots.

Wolf forced back the guilty feeling brought on by those prairie green eyes and that stubborn chin. Boys above the age of ten regarded the care of cows to be girl's work, but Jessie Jones had become a thorn in his side from the first day he'd encountered him. He reached up to scratch his jaw. If the boy learned nothing else during this trip, it would be how to control his temper.

Leaving Jordan and Elliot to finish getting ready, Wolf went on to the next family, shoving worries over the youngest Jones from his mind. Lars and Anne Svensson had two wagons with three yoke of oxen each, and six children: two girls ages ten and eleven and four boys ranging from fourteen to nineteen. Alberik, the eldest son, a tall, sturdy blond, and his father were in charge of the wagons, while Nikolaus and Bjorn, ages seventeen and fifteen, had been hired by Wolf to help Rook with two of the supply wagons. "I have need of another driver, Lars. Can you spare Rickard during the day to help Elliot Baker with the Joneses' wagon? He'll be paid the same rate as the other two for each day's work."

Rickard, standing next to his parents, stood taller. A wide grin spread across his features. Lars nodded to his son, who replied, "Thank you, Mr. Wolf."

Wolf nodded. "Drop the mister. Wolf will do," he said, dismissing the boy to report to Elliot. He then commenced inspection of the wagons. Finding no fault, he moved on to the Nortons' wagon. Mr. and Mrs. Hugh Norton were a quiet newlywed couple in their mid-twenties. To his surprise, the new bride batted her long, dark eyelashes at him.

He ignored her flirting as he checked the outside of the wagon. When he'd finished, he turned his attention to the inside. He lifted a brow. There was only one trunk packed among the stores of food and trail gear. Even the food supply consisted mostly of dried meat, hard bread, and crackers with a small amount of bacon, pork and beans. They were also the only family traveling with horses. Rosalyn informed him in a breathy voice that she and Hugh planned to ride most of the way to Oregon, that they'd hired a driver to deal with the oxen and the wagon, as well as the cooking chores. Wolf took note of the long troughs on the outside of the wagon and made sure they had sufficient grain for the horses, as the animals wouldn't survive the long trip on grazing alone.

The last wagon rolled up into position, driven by a small woman with golden red hair. Eirica Macauley had trouble getting the oxen to stop and fall into line. Wolf took over, explaining what to do, then waited for her to lift her three children, all under the age of five, out of the back of the wagon before checking it over. He found no fault with the wagon or the animals. Jumping onto the wagon tongue, he examined the load inside and found the supplies and provisions to be on the meager side. Lifting a quilt, he peered beneath it.

His brows rose when he found two wooden kegs of whiskey, then discovered two more kegs hidden behind a trunk, and a fifth one buried beneath a gutta-percha sack of sugar. His lips tightened. Food might be in short supply but not the spirits. "Mrs. Macauley—"

Eirica turned to grab her youngest, a redheaded boy who had toddled too close to the restless oxen. Seeing her in profile, Wolf noticed that she was with child. He did some fast calculations and figured she'd give birth in late summer. He exhaled. Birthing added complications and slowed progress. Glancing around, he realized he hadn't seen Birk. "Mrs. Macauley, where's your husband?"

Eirica lowered her gaze to the toddler she jiggled in her arms and whispered nervously, "He's still in town."

"Which saloon?" he bit out, his voice tight with anger.

Eirica stepped back, her arms tight around the little boy. "I don't know."

Recognizing her fear of him, Wolf stalked away. Of all the families making the overland trip, this family worried him the most. Untying his horse, he mounted and rode toward the herd of horses grazing to one side of the cattle. Each hired hand brought with him anywhere from one to three mounts, plus Wolf had purchased an extra ten horses for spares, as each animal would be ridden long and hard during the day. He spotted a tough-looking horse wrangler.

Cupping his hands, he shouted, "Duarte!" The dark-skinned man rode up to him, and Wolf jerked his thumb over his shoulder toward the Macauley wagon. "Mr. Macauley has several kegs of whiskey tucked into the back of his wagon. My rules state that each family is allowed only one small cask of liquor. Take the kegs into town and trade them for food rations. While you're there, fetch Macauley. I believe you'll find him at one of the saloons. Take Bart and Claude with you. If Macauley objects, tell him he doesn't go. We leave within the hour, with or without him."

Duarte rode off, signaling for the two men to join him. Within minutes, the kegs were unloaded and on their way to town with the three men.

Jessie leaned forward in her saddle, excitement building within her as she waited for the wagon master's signal to roll. Watching the young Macauley children run in wild circles across the wide-open land, she smiled. Kerstin and Hanna Svensson ran after them, their laughter mingling with Sadie's sharp barks. She laughed softly at the sight of her dog trying to run herd around the children. After a few minutes, Sadie gave up trying to corral the high-spirited youngsters and returned to her mistress. She lay panting in the grass, her tongue lolling to one side of her mouth, blissfully unaware that within minutes, they would begin a two-thousand-mile trek across the country.

Nudging Shilo, Jessie circled the black-, brown- and white-spotted cows as they grazed lazily. From the corner of her eye, she spotted one lumbering beast breaking away from the small herd. A squeeze of her booted heels against Shilo's side was all the horse needed to move toward the cow. The cow lifted her black nose disdainfully into the air and released a long disgruntled moo when Shilo nudged her back toward the others.

She scowled. "Sorry, girl. I've got orders to keep you away from the wagons." The cow swished her tail and lowered her head to the tender grass of the meadow. A few minutes later, the same stubborn cow made another dash for a tempting dark green patch of grass near one of the wagons. Jessie whistled and motioned for Sadie to take care of her. "Cows," she scoffed, shaking her head, her pride still smarting. But deep down, she knew it wasn't the task assigned to her that left her feeling angry. It was Wolf's assumption that she couldn't handle the oxen that rankled and made her feel as though she had to prove herself.

Shilo pawed the ground, shifting restlessly. Jessie forced the muscles in her thighs to relax and absently patted the mare. Her gaze narrowed with determination. She'd show White Wolf that she was perfectly capable of handling the oxen or any other task this trip required. She frowned at the thought.

What did it matter what he thought? Taking care of cows was an easy job, one that required little or no skill. She should be content, but she wasn't. Wolf's poor opinion of her hurt. Ever since Saturday night, images of the wagon master stalked her like a determined cat fixed on its prey. While she admitted that he was a virile specimen of man, she found him arrogant and vexing. "You don't have to like the man," she muttered to herself. "All you need to do is keep your distance and get to Oregon."

The sun continued its ascent into the sky and the minutes ticked by slowly. Jessie fidgeted in her saddle. What were they waiting for? When would the signal come? She bit her lower lip, anxious to get under way. Her gaze went back to the wagons and settled on Elliot's fine figure. He stood beside his team of oxen, reins in one hand, bullwhip in the other. When the blond-haired man looked up and saw her, he waved. She answered with a wide grin and waved back.

Coralie stuck her head out from under the canvas cover, opened her lacy white parasol and held it over her head to protect her milky white skin from the rays of the sun. Jessie's good humor vanished and she turned her back on her unwanted sister-in-law. "I hope you get lots and lots of freckles, Coralie," she muttered.

Shifting in her saddle, she couldn't resist glancing over her shoulder at Elliot. She hoped to gain his interest on this trip. But glancing down at her baggy shirt that hid her bound breasts, she sighed in defeat. How could she possibly hope he'd notice her when she had to dress as a boy, especially seeing as he could probably have his pick of any woman? Jessie ran one gloved finger along the freckled bridge of her nose. Another sigh of envy escaped her lips.

Ladies were supposed to have milky white complexions, not honey-colored skin the result of spending days outside. She wrinkled her nose, thinking about the smattering of small brown spots flagging each cheek and dotting the bridge of her nose. Removing one glove, Jessie stared at the back of her hand. It too was golden brown. Before she could sink into a pit of self-pity, she heard the sound of approaching hooves. Reeling Shilo around, she saw Wolf riding toward them on his magnificent black stallion. He stopped at Rook's wagon, turned, raised his hand and threw it forward.

Her heart pounded, and feelings of anger and resentment fled as the command to roll was given. A cheer rose from one end of the wagon train to the other. Jessie held her breath when Rook gave a loud shout, raised his hand and sent his whip cracking through the air. His yells turned the air blue as he cursed and swore at the oxen until the stout beasts trudged forward.

Rook was followed by the two Svensson boys in charge

of the supply wagons. The boys' parents were next with their two wagons, which were the only ones in the group to boast seats for their drivers. The rest were just rectangular wooden wagon beds mounted on wheels. The Macauleys came next. Birk Macauley cracked his whip over the team of oxen with more force than necessary, his face red with rage from the angry words he'd exchanged with Wolf. Jessie felt sorry for his wife, who walked behind the wagon, carrying her son. Her two little girls skipped beside her.

The newly married Nortons rode past, then Elliot. Jessie laughed when she heard Coralie squealing and complaining from inside the wagon. As they passed, Jessie glanced into the back and saw her sister-in-law holding on for dear life as the springless wagon bounced over the rutted ground. Jessie twisted in her saddle to watch the departing wagons. Her breath caught in her throat at the sight of the caravan. The wagons stretched out and rolled across the green carpet of grass toward the clear blue horizon of the West. White canvas billowed in the breeze, and the sound of bellowing oxen and whips cracking the air left her feeling giddy.

It was Rickard's turn with her oxen. Resting her forearms across the saddle horn, she watched him try to get the animals moving, but the oxen refused to budge. Rickard yelled at the lazy beasts, pulled on the reins and swatted them with a short stick on their thick rumps, but they wouldn't move. There hadn't been enough time for her fully to train or gentle them, as Jordan had purchased them just three days ago to pull the Bakers wagon.

Jessie grinned with satisfaction. "And he thinks I can't handle them," she muttered, gloating. "This'll show White Wolf." Her gloating came to an end when Rickard turned away, his shoulders hunched in defeat, the stick dragging in the grass. She caught sight of his crestfallen face and felt his feelings of failure. And when no one came to his aid, she decided to take pity on him. She rode toward Rickard and dismounted, her custom-made bullwhip coiled in her hand. After all, it wasn't his fault Wolf was an arrogant bastard.

*   *   * ◀

Wolf and James sat halfway between the cattle and the wagons, ready to follow with the cattle, horses and the fourth supply wagon, which contained feed and shoeing equipment. "Look at them go, boss. Purdiest sight I think I've ever seen," James said, leaning forward in his saddle.

Wolf nodded in agreement. On each trip he made, the sight of wagons rolling westward to challenge the wild country never failed to quicken his blood and arouse the wandering soul that was a part of his heritage.

James suddenly straightened. "Uh-oh, looks like there's a problem," he announced, pointing toward the unmoving wagon holding up the line.

Wolf frowned when it became apparent that Rickard was having trouble. He started forward. "I'd best go lend a hand."

James stopped him. "No need. Jessie's there."

Wolf saw Jessie dismount and take up the reins. He grimaced but didn't voice aloud his doubt that Jessie had little chance of succeeding where the taller and stronger Rickard had failed. But he decided to give the boy a chance, if only to prove to James that he expected too much from his young brother.

James leaned forward, pride ringing in his voice. "Watch this, boss. Ain't nobody in Westport better with a whip. An old cowhand who worked for me taught Jess how to use it. Even custom-made that one just for—ah, him."

Wolf waited impatiently. Three wagons were lined up behind Jessie and Rickard. Suddenly the sound of snapping and popping jerked his attention back to Rickard and Jessie. The air above the oxen was filled with what sounded like musket fire in a raging battle as Jessie snapped the reins and cracked the whip overhead with a precision that came from years of practice. From where he stood, Wolf had no trouble hearing the shouted, "Gee-haw, gee-haw." In seconds, the four-yoke of oxen reluctantly trudged forward. Taken aback by the boy's skill, Wolf raised his left brow with admiration at the graceful movements of rawhide singing through the air.

"What'd I tell ya, boss. Ain't that something?" James bragged.

Wolf remained silent for a long moment. He had the uncomfortable feeling he'd underestimated Jessie Jones, and that didn't sit too well with him. Angry with himself and the Jones boy for showing him up, he turned away, ignoring the knowing look James sent his way. "Get the men in position," he ordered, pulling on the stallion's reins. He rode toward the wagons.

When he reached the two boys, Jessie was already mounted, the bullwhip neatly coiled in hands that looked much too small and dainty to wield such power. With a defiantly raised chin, Jessie made it clear who had won that round. Angry but unsure why, Wolf watched the boy rejoin the herd of wandering cows. His features settled in a grim line. He'd let Jessie Jones bask in this one bit of triumph. The hard rigors of travel would leave little energy for mischief.

Wolf spent the next half hour riding up and down the line of wagons, giving advice where needed. After a while, he pulled off to one side. "Well, there they go," he murmured, his sharp gaze following the long line of wagons. Just then, one of the wagons veered off course.

"Damn," he swore. "Come on, Black Shadow, we're not through yet." He rode up alongside Lars and helped the man halt the oxen who were pulling to the right. With his help, they unyoked the lead pair and put the dominant oxen on the left. Lars, who walked on that side, could control the animal better.

Wolf waited until the emigrants were at least half a mile ahead of the waiting cattle, then rode back and gave the cattlemen the signal to start out. First came Duarte and Shorty with the remuda or remounts. Saul followed with the supply wagon. Then James and Jordan rode forward, driving a few head of cattle between them. The two brothers were pointers. Their job was to point the long line of cattle by guiding the leaders of the herd. The cattle behind them would gradually swell to four or six across and stretch out half a mile in length.

Jeremy came next, riding flank, with Claude and Sunny riding swing near the end of the line. Bart and Gunner came last. They were the least experienced, the tenderfeet. They rode drag, the least-desired position; it was their job to keep the herd together.

When everyone was moving, Wolf hunched low over his horse's neck and urged the mount forward. The stallion's long strides quickly ate the distance as they galloped past the bellowing cattle. Wolf lifted his face to the wind, his mane of golden brown hair flowing behind him. From the corner of his eye, he saw a streak of white racing him. He grinned and wondered if Wahoska would accompany him to Oregon this time or turn around and head for home after a few days on the move. The wolf had yet to make the overland trip.

As soon as he passed the line of wagons, he gave Black Shadow his head. The blue sky and green grass whizzed by as horse and rider became a blur of black and brown. Wolf gave himself up to the wild ride. Adrenaline surged through his veins as he contemplated the challenges that lay ahead. Not wanting to tire the horse, he slowed the animal to a canter and scanned the countryside. His nostrils flared with deep appreciation for the beauty of the *Maka*.

It didn't matter that he'd been schooled in the white man's world. He had an inbred affinity with the *Wakanpi*, the spirits of his world that Indian children were taught to respect, revere and even fear. When he looked upon the green grass, he saw life-sustaining feed for the cattle and horses. He tipped his face up to stare into the clear blue sky and felt the warmth of *Wi*. And when he looked upon the trees in the distance or listened to the birds singing their special songs, he knew these things were *Wakan*: sacred, mysterious.

Finally, his mind and body were free from the driving pace of the last week. He came to a halt and stared back toward the wagons. They were but mere white specks in the distance. But instead of feeling totally relaxed, Wolf found himself gripped by a curious tension, a nagging feeling that something wasn't right. What it was, he couldn't say. He scratched the back of his neck. His brows drew together when he recalled his brother's words spoken two days ago.

Striking Thunder had returned in the morning for a last good-bye and a parting bit of wisdom. "I do not have the gift of sight that our sister possesses, but I know you travel this path for a reason. You will find the answers you have long sought, and, perhaps your match in a woman as well."

A snort of disgust escaped Wolf as his brother's cryptic words played in his mind. What good was all the knowledge he carried in his head when he had no idea how to put it to good use? He sighed and dismissed Striking Thunder's words with a shake of his head. Wheeling his horse around, he rode into the wind, and after a few miles, his brother's words were forgotten.

Back among the slow-rolling wagons, Daisy "Rosalyn" Portier adjusted her bonnet as she rode away from Westport. Nervously, she glanced over her shoulder toward the town. Desperation darkened her eyes and left her stomach tied in knots. Would they make it? Could they outrun Vern? Her lips tightened. They had to.

She chuckled, a low, throaty, pleased sound. Her scheme was brilliant. Who would suspect that the newlyweds, Rosalyn and Hugh Norton, were actually Daisy Portier and Dan Tupper, brother and sister? Once they were on the trail, she and Dan along with their "driver," Sammy, would blend in with the hundreds of other emigrants. Her grin grew smug. Vern Portier would never catch them.

Chapter Six

Far from the traveling caravan, an Indian woman paused in her meal preparations to stare up into the *Paha Sapa*, the towering black hills her people would enter to make their summer camp. Many tribes refused to live in the hills, but her *tiyospaye*, or clan of the Miniconjou Sioux Indians, preferred the secluded sanctuary.

White Wind lifted her head to the cool breeze. She loved the spring and summers, looked forward to the move. Fingering one long white-blond braid that trailed down the front of her soft, unadorned deerskin dress, she smiled softly as happy memories filled her with joy. It was there, in those hills so very long ago, that she'd discovered love. Humming, she lifted the lid of her prized Dutch oven and stirred the simmering meat and fresh herbs. Then she took another pot and heated water for tea, the one luxury she indulged in every afternoon.

She was fortunate to have a husband and sons who provided her with little luxuries, and though she greatly appreciated conveniences like thread, fabric, bowls, utensils and a coffeepot, she was content with her life, had never regretted leaving her old life as Sarah Cartier behind. She had four wonderful grown children and a husband who loved her. What more did a woman need to make her life complete?

The loud report of a firearm intruded upon the bustle of the late afternoon. She frowned. There were some changes to their peaceful lifestyle that worried her, like the need for guns, but worse than those were the cravings for what her husband called the white man's fool water. Alcohol turned warriors into drunkards, and she was grateful her husband had forbidden its presence in their village.

With her evening meal cooking, White Wind entered her tipi and picked up her sewing. She didn't get far on the small pair of moccasins she was beading before she was interrupted.

"Uncheedah!"

At the sound of the soft young voice calling out *Grandmother*, White Wind glanced up and smiled at her granddaughter, who stood in the open doorway of the tipi. She held out her arms.

But a small brown blur pushed past Morning Moon, and hurled himself into his grandmother's waiting arms. White Wind shook her head and laughed softly as she hugged her grandson to her bosom. Over the boy's shiny black head, she glanced at Morning Moon, who still hesitated outside the door. "Come here, child," she invited the shy young girl. Soon, after telling their grandmother about their day, the two children left, leaving White Wind alone with her daughter, Star Dreamer. She indicated that her daughter should sit. "How are you this day, daughter?"

"I am well," Star Dreamer answered, her voice unsteady, distracted.

White Wind studied her. She recognized the faraway look in Star's fawn brown eyes and the lines of worry etched across her forehead. It was the same look her mother-in-law had worn when troubled by visions. "Visions?"

Star Dreamer's eyes clouded. "Yes. Striking Thunder is on his way home."

White Wind stood and wrapped her arms around herself. Her two sons, Striking Thunder and White Wolf, had left to go to Westport together, but her daughter saw only one returning. Her heart pounded with dread. "What of Wolf?"

"He travels across the land with many wagons."

Gripping one side of the hide covering, White Wind went

to the opening of the tipi and glanced outside. Her voice dropped. "Wolf has gone west again?"

Star Dreamer put her arm around her mother's shoulders. "I see many wagons, people and cattle."

Sorrow filled White Wind. She turned away, chewing her lower lip as she paced. A cold, hollow feeling invaded her soul where moments before there had been warmth and contentment. She hugged herself, knowing she should be used to Wolf's long absences from home as he searched for his purpose in life.

Closing her eyes, she prayed he'd find it this time. Each time he left home, he returned restless and edgy. Fulfillment and happiness always seemed out of reach for her second son. She wished he could be satisfied with the cabin that had once belonged to her. He was fulfilling his—and her—dream of raising fine horseflesh. And there were many maidens in surrounding tribes only too willing to become his wife. Why couldn't he settle down and raise a family? But it wasn't enough. He was driven to fulfill his grandmother's visions.

A pang of regret hit her. Wolf had been troubled for so long. Had they been wrong to send him east as a child to be educated? She sighed, knowing it did no good to harbor such thoughts. The deed was done, and she could only hope he'd find whatever it was that was missing from his life. She squared her slender shoulders. "We must offer prayers for his safe return." She couldn't bring herself to ask if Wolf *would* return.

"I know, my mother. I see many things, but none of them make sense," Star Dreamer whispered, her gaze wide and confused.

White Wind understood and drew her daughter into her arms. Wolf wasn't the only troubled child she had. So long ago, her mother-in-law had forecast two children—twins— each born with a special gift to help their people. Wolf had yet to discover how to use his gift of knowledge, and his twin sister, Star, had never fully accepted the gift of sight passed down from her grandmother.

She could only hope these two special children of her heart

would find peace. Cupping her daughter's face between her hands, she pressed a kiss to her forehead. "The visions will clear, my daughter. Do not fight them. Time will reveal what will be. Let us hope your brother finds what he is searching for this time and will return safe, free of his haunting thoughts."

A deep, booming voice spoke from the door. "Our son will find his way. The spirits lead him, my wife. We must be patient."

White Wind glanced up when Golden Eagle entered. Her heart fluttered with pleasure, as it did each and every evening when he returned to her. Her loving gaze slid over his gray-streaked hair and a face browned and wrinkled by years in the sun. His body was still lean and firm, and after twenty-eight years of marriage, her love and desire for her golden warrior continued to grow each day.

"You must be hungry, my husband. Our meal is nearly ready." Golden Eagle smiled at her, his eyes hooded to conceal the desire she knew burned there.

"I'm hungry, but not for food," he said, his voice low and thick.

Star Dreamer left with a smile. Golden Eagle closed the flap behind her. But even as Golden Eagle led her to their sleeping mats, White Wind knew she would worry over Wolf until he returned home next summer.

By late afternoon on the third day of travel, the emigrants reached Blue Mound. Wolf shifted in his saddle and turned his gaze toward the western horizon. The distant blaze of orange and yellow fell toward the earth, flowing into the endless fringe of green stretching out before him. Beneath him, Black Shadow snorted and pawed the ground restlessly, shaking his huge head as the herd of cattle approached. Wolf caught a glimpse of the animals' white eyes, and tightened his knees, ready when the stallion stood on his powerful hind legs to paw the air with his front hooves. His scream of rage blotted out the nervous bawling of the herd.

Wolf leaned forward and battled for control of the high-strung mount. He forced the horse back down on all fours. The black beast continued to prance as Wolf murmured soft reassurances into the animal's ear. "Easy, boy, easy," he crooned, patting the stallion's sleek neck until Black Shadow calmed.

Twisting in his seat, he surveyed their surroundings, then glanced at the sun's position behind a light layer of clouds. Though there were several hours of good travel light left, he decided to stop for the night. Over the last couple of days, he'd relentlessly pushed both men and beasts hard, concerned that the cattle might break away and run for familiar land. But now that there was enough distance between them and Westport, he no longer worried over the herd bolting. He also knew many of the emigrants wanted to explore Blue Mound.

Pursing his lips, he let out a loud, ear-piercing whistle. It was the signal to stop. He murmured soft words in Lakota to the nervous horse.

James joined him. "We're stopping already, boss?"

"Yep. I've pushed the animals hard. They need to rest." He pointed to an area between Blue Mound and the Kansas River. "Graze the cattle there and I'll circle the wagons here, close to the river."

"Will do, boss."

Wolf left James and rode toward the waiting wagons, which were spread out three abreast across the prairie. He'd encouraged them to fan out until single file became necessary. Single file, there wasn't going to be any way to avoid the choking dust that later would become a part of their daily diet.

"Circle to your left, Elliot." Wolf continued to call instructions until each wagon tongue lined up with the rear wagon wheels in front of them, the teams of oxen standing inside the semicircle of white-topped canvas wagons. He left one opening, which would be closed off after all the animals were inside for the night.

Dismounting, Wolf tied his stallion to the back of the supply wagon, then watched Jessie unhitch the oxen, check them over and wash their backs. He watched, looking for fault, but found none. Once again he was forced to admit that Jessie had a way with the lumbering beasts.

Jessie crossed the space in front of him. "Rook, I'm taking the teams out to graze."

Wolf narrowed his eyes. "Don't be long. There's work to be done," he reminded him, making sure that the boy didn't shirk his duties.

Jessie's head snapped up. Resentment-filled green eyes flashed with temper. "I have never shirked my duties and don't intend to start now." Without another word, Jessie drove the weary oxen outside the corralled wagons.

Wolf ignored the frown of displeasure Rook sent his way. His old friend didn't know the boy's penchant for getting into trouble and would be too easy on him. Wolf planned to keep the boy so busy, he'd be too tired to get into mischief.

After the oxen joined the others to graze, Jessie trudged back to the wagons, her boots sinking into the rain-softened earth. She was tired; every muscle and bone ached from the long hours of travel. Aside from keeping an eye on the herd of cows, she'd spent her time on the trail gathering wood.

She smiled to herself when she remembered her shock the first time Rook had ordered her to "keep the bitch filled," and her discovery that "the bitch" was a hide stretched under the wagon, creating a hammock for storing firewood. Jessie knew the importance of keeping it filled. The time would come when trees gave way to dried grass, small twigs and, finally, the hot-burning buffalo chips. Rook had pointed out several nails hammered into the sides of the wagons, which would be used to hang canvas sacks filled with the dried buffalo dung.

By the time Jessie rejoined Rook, he'd already dug a slit-trench in the ground, laid out the wood and unloaded a large box that held several days' worth of food so they didn't have to open the sacks of flour and beans each day. She grabbed a couple of fry pans and slabs of pork to fry but Rook's voice stopped her.

"Leave it, lass," he said, glancing over his shoulder to make sure they were alone. "Take some time off," he ordered gruffly. "We'll start supper a bit later. I'm jest gettin' things ready, so go on an' enjoy the afternoon. When I'm done here, I'll have me a nice, relaxin' smoke 'n' a nap, and if you's here, you'll jest yak my ears off."

Jessie laughed. "Hey, you shouldn't be such a wise old man." During their long days of traveling, she'd eagerly encouraged Rook's trail stories.

Rook grunted. "Off with you. Go climb the mound. Maybe it'll git rid of some of yer cheekiness."

Jessie needed no further urging. Since leaving Westport, Wolf had kept them on the trail until the gray cloak of dusk fell. By the time chores were taken care of, the meal was prepared and eaten, and clean-up was done, it was too late to do anything but go to bed. She glanced around, looking for the bossy wagon master, and spotted him brushing his black stallion.

Awareness rippled through her skin as his hands moved down the horse in gentle strokes. From where she stood, she heard his voice: low, soothing and tender. Tender? Wolf? Ha! Not him. Frustrating and formidable. That was how she thought of him. She wrenched her gaze away and headed for her wagon, unsure what it was about him that drew her but determined to ignore it.

She climbed into the back of her wagon and located her journal. Warm afternoon sunlight streamed in through the canvas opening as she took full advantage of daylight to complete her daily entry. Today she added the names of two California-bound families who had passed them, then logged emerging daily patterns within their own party as everyone adjusted to life on the trail. Her stubby pencil flew across the page as she put into words her impressions of the day and added another one of Rook's outrageous stories for flavor.

Smothering a yawn, she stretched her arms over her head. "Lord, but I could use a nap," she muttered. She and Rook, along with the other women, rose at four each morning to begin preparations for the first meal of the day. When the aroma of fresh-roasted coffee and fried bacon filled the crisp morning air, the men stirred, and by the time the meal was ready, the oxen had been rounded up and hitched and the wagons readied. By seven, they were ready to hit the trail.

Jessie leaned on the tailgate and rested her chin on her cupped fingers as she stared out into the wide-open space. Spotting gray clouds scudding across the horizon, she grimaced. They'd suffered their first rainstorm on the open prairie earlier that afternoon. She was thankful it hadn't been a hard, driving rain, but it had slowed them nonetheless.

Hooking one leg over the back of the wagon, Jessie dropped to the wet ground and winced when the damp bindings flattening her breasts bit into her chafed skin. She'd already exchanged her wet shirt and jeans for dry clothing, but she didn't dare change the bindings around her breasts. That was too risky to attempt in the daylight.

Jessie stuck her thumbs in the waistband of her pants and surveyed the area surrounding their camp. She spotted Anna and Eirica along with their children heading toward Blue Mound in the not-so-far distance. A small, secret grin played at the corners of her lips. The two women had pegged her from the beginning and thought her masquerade a hoot. If she ran, she could catch up with them. Or she could take a walk along the Kansas River and maybe even indulge in a refreshing dip.

Staring at the gentle slope that was but a bump on the wide-spreading prairie, she recalled that her guidebook promised that the view from Blue Mound was well worth the effort. She decided to see for herself. They'd be following the river for many days. Plenty of time later to sneak in a swim. Plopping her hat on her head, she set off.

Across from her, she noticed Jordan unloading supplies from the back of the wagon. "Perhaps he'd like to go too," she said to herself. Since leaving Westport, she hadn't seen much of her brothers, except for a few minutes at mealtimes. She missed them, missed the good-natured arguing and fussing.

The sound of Coralie's screeching stopped her. "*Now* what's wrong with the queen of snobbery?" Jessie didn't understand how her brother put up with it. Quickening her pace, she hurried by.

Elliot glanced up from rummaging through a long narrow box fastened to the outside of the wagon. He looked ill-at-ease, and they exchanged pained looks when Coralie's voice rose an octave. "Jessie, wait," he called out.

Jessie stopped. A deep sigh of appreciation pushed past her parted lips; Elliot was such a handsome man. Her hand lifted to smooth her tangled mass of curls, but she remembered her role, and her arm fell back to her side.

Elliot joined her. "Where are you off to?"

"Rook gave me the afternoon off. Thought I'd go exploring. Want to come?"

He sent her a pained look. "You're not going to climb the mound, are you?"

Jessie laughed. "You bet I am. Come on, it won't be that bad."

"Easy for you to say. You're used to all this." He paused. "But it sure beats staying here. I love my sister, but she's behaving like a spoiled brat. I sure feel sorry for Jordan!"

Jessie bit her lip to still the bubble of laughter that threatened to erupt. Earlier, she'd gotten a good look at Coralie's ruined dress. What had been a lovely rose-and-cream day dress this morning was now muddy and ripped after a day of walking over the rough and rutted prairies. Even the matching bonnet, more suited to shading the wearer from the sun than a sudden rainstorm, hung as limp as Coralie's long blond hair.

Jessie grinned. "Come on. Let's go. At the rate Coralie's going through her dresses, she won't have any left before the week is out."

Elliot grimaced. "Pa and Jordan tried to tell her they weren't suited for trail travel but she wouldn't listen."

"Such a shame." She snickered. "Coralie just doesn't seem to be able to keep her dresses for very long."

Elliot reached out and cuffed her gently on the arm. "You brat. You really put her in a snit by ruining that last dress."

Jessie scowled. No way would she admit to Elliot why she'd lost her temper.

"Look, Jessie. Pa and I heard what Coralie said to you. Pa was furious with her and even refused to let James pay for the dress. My dear sister goes too far sometimes." He looked uncomfortable for a moment, his face flushing. "I want you to know that I don't hold anything against you. Accidents happen."

Jessie sighed. "That's right nice of you, Elliot, but I made a fool of myself even before I tripped and fell into you. I should never have tried to be what I'm not. Let's not talk about it. Some things are better forgotten!"

Elliot ruffled her hair. "Come on, Jess, don't be so hard on yourself. You didn't look that bad. In fact, you looked rather fetching in that dress."

Snorting, Jessie sent him a disbelieving look. Silence fell as they walked up the incline. She slid an admiring look toward the man walking beside her. He'd be such a perfect husband, so kind and gentle. It wasn't hard to imagine him as her husband, but when she tried to picture their children, they had deep blue eyes, tawny brown hair and rich honey-colored skin.

Startled, Jessie realized she was envisioning Wolf's children. She frowned. Why was she so obsessed with the wagon master? He wasn't gentle, kind or even handsome. And he certainly was much too bossy to make a good husband, she thought sourly, thinking of the extra chores he seemed to find perverse pleasure in dumping on her.

Making an effort to put Wolf from her mind, she concentrated on the view. One of the things she loved best about trail life was the constant change in scenery. She loved the outdoors. It brought peace to her soul. She forced herself to relax, inviting the beauty of the afternoon to flow through her. Glancing around, she stretched her arms overhead, working the kinks out of her neck and shoulder muscles. "I can hardly believe we've come forty-five miles in three days."

Elliot grimaced and held out blister-covered palms. The welts were red and angry. "I don't know about that. My hands and feet feel like we've come at least a hundred! Makes the mind spin when I think how many more miles we've got to go."

"Poor Elliot. Except for those nasty blisters, trail life seems to agree with you," she commented, noting the light tan that was beginning to replace the redness caused by walking in the sun all day.

Elliot drew a deep breath, his blue eyes lighting with boyish eagerness. "It's not as bad as I'd feared. Who would have thought I'd enjoy being outdoors all day?" He slid her a conspiratorial grin. "But I can't say Coralie shares my newfound appreciation of nature."

Jessie giggled, recalling their first day. "Didn't take her long to decide that walking is much easier than riding in the backs of those wagons. I heard her complaining that she had bruises upon bruises that first night." Her lips twitched, and suddenly the two of them were laughing and talking like the best of friends.

During that shared moment of understanding, Jessie realized that even though she'd known Elliot for eight years, she'd never felt as close to him as she did right then. She'd always been the to-be-tolerated sister of the Jones boys and treated as "one of the guys." But on the trail, formality, status and all other veneers of society faded. The struggle to keep up with the grueling pace left little energy for airs—something her sister-in-law still hadn't figured out.

They reached the top of Blue Mound, and Jessie let out a gasp of pleasure. Spread before them were miles of flower-spangled prairie. "It's beautiful," she whispered, her gaze soaking up the wonder before her. Even Elliot seemed awe-struck by the view.

"Rook said we'd be able to see the next week's travel from here. I didn't believe him, but look." She waved her hand, indicating the vastness. "It's so open, so endless." She spread her arms wide, as if she could grasp and hold on to the beauty before her. "Oh, Elliot, it's a grand adventure.

Something you'll be able to tell your children.''

After several minutes of companionable silence, Elliot spoke. ''Jessie?''

She looked into his soft, pale blue eyes. ''Yes?''

''I want to apologize on behalf of Coralie. I know she's caused you more trouble with Wolf.'' Elliot glanced away. A slow flush stained his neck. ''It's not right for you to do her dishes along with all those pots and fry pans you have to wash from cooking for the men. Hell, I'm the one who ends up doing our cooking while she takes credit for it. I should be doing them, but—''

''Don't worry about it.'' Jessie shrugged. It warmed her inside to know Elliot cared about her feelings. But reminders of Wolf and his meanness toward her intruded and kept her from basking in that knowledge. Despite her good intentions to enjoy her free time, a shadow had been cast over her and Elliot. Jessie sighed and trained her gaze out onto the miles of endless prairie.

As if sensing her mood change, Elliot wandered to the other side of the mound, leaving Jessie to stew. That first night on the trail, Coralie had whined and wailed that her dress would be ruined if she knelt at the stream to wash her dishes. She'd tried ordering Jessie to do them, but Jessie had refused. Wolf had joined them, demanding to know what was going on.

Even now, the mere thought of her sister-in-law playing the helpless damsel in distress angered her. Coralie had let loose with big, welling tears, as she was so good at doing, and had the gall to lie, telling Wolf that she, Jessie, had reneged on a promise to do Coralie's dishes in return for an earlier favor.

Jessie made a rude noise. Wolf had bought the lie, and she'd been ordered to do her sister-in-law's dishes—and if that hadn't been enough, later that night she'd overheard Wolf telling Rook that if the boy was kept busy, he couldn't cause trouble. So every night and morning for the last two days, Coralie pranced over to dump a load of dirty pans and tin plates on her with a satisfied smirk. Jessie glanced at her red hands, raw from dishwashing.

Glancing up, the deep indigo sky reminded her of the color of Wolf's eyes. But the blue above her was soft and dreamy, strewn with fluffs of cottony clouds. The wagon master's blue eyes were hard and cold. It was so unfair, she fumed. What had she done to earn his disapproval?

After a while, Elliot wandered back to her side and they retraced their steps. Halfway down they met Wolf and Rosalyn Norton coming up. The married woman had her arm threaded through Wolf's, her hungry gaze fixed on him as she chatted. Jessie pulled the rim of her hat down farther over her eyes and ducked her head, prepared to walk by without a word, but Wolf stopped them.

"Enjoying the view, Elliot?" he asked.

"Yep, it's quite a sight. Makes a man feel small and insignificant when viewing the vastness of nature spread out before him."

Jessie studied the ruggedly handsome wagon master. He radiated vitality. Some invisible force drew her to him like a moth to a flame. Unlike the other men, who wore denim, woolen or homespun pants, Wolf favored the buckskin breeches more common to mountain men and trappers. Her gaze roamed his lean form. She understood why. The garments sheathed his lean legs and outlined the bulging strength of his thighs.

Her eyes absorbed each tiny detail; wide brows, long brown lashes with golden tips, a shadowy cleft on his chin and a tiny mole near his jaw all softened the rugged lines. Though he couldn't compete against Elliot's fine-boned, fair-skinned aristocratic good looks, Wolf wore a savage wildness that held a beauty all its own. To add to his untamed appearance, he rarely wore shirts, favoring a leather vest instead. And as on the night in the barn, the front edges gaped open in the breeze, affording her a tantalizing view of bronzed skin.

Jessie felt a curious longing take hold. But a longing for what? she wondered. She swallowed, suddenly afraid of the answer, but fear didn't stop her fingers from twitching with the most irresistible urge to follow the path of the cooling breeze as it feathered through long strands of hair that gleamed molten gold under the bright rays of the sun. Her cheeks grew warm and her pulse quickened as a spark of desire caught fire. She gave herself a mental shake. What was wrong with her? It had been Elliot who drew her admiring looks and made her heart flutter. Then why did this man affect her so? She didn't even like him!

Feeling someone's eyes on her, Jessie tore her gaze from the overbearing taskmaster and found Rosalyn's hard brown glare boring into her. Jessie quickly lowered her gaze and frowned at the toe of her boot. Rosalyn was the only woman in their party who hadn't discovered her secret, which was fine with her.

For reasons she didn't understand, she didn't trust Rosalyn. While she knew Anna and Eirica wouldn't give her away, something about this woman spelled trouble. And her mistrust wasn't just because Rosalyn was a married woman trying to seduce Wolf. No, what made Jessie keep her distance was Sadie's reaction to the Nortons. Her dog normally liked everyone, but she had taken an immediate dislike to the reclusive trio. That was enough for Jessie.

Rosalyn tipped her head back and fluttered her dark lashes. "Are we going to stand here all afternoon, Wolf?"

Jessie narrowed her gaze. Why did Wolf put up with this woman? Jessie reminded herself that what those two did had nothing to do with her. She nudged Elliot with the tip of her boot.

Wolf allowed Rosalyn to lead him forward. Relieved, Jessie started down the hill, but she didn't get far before Wolf called after her, "Jess!"

She glanced at him over her shoulder. "Yeah?"

"Ride out and help Shorty check the horses. I want every hoof checked. That should keep you busy until Rook needs you to help with the meal."

Jessie whirled around, ready to protest the end to her free afternoon. Elliot's fingers gripped the back of her neck and prevented the rash, angry words from spilling from her lips.

"Not now, Jess," Elliot hissed in her ear. "Turn around, and for God's sake, just keep your mouth shut and do what you're told."

Jessie glared at Elliot, then stalked off, her enjoyment of the afternoon ruined.

"My dresses and shoes are in ruins," Coralie screeched at Jordan. "And I don't have anything else to wear. This is your fault for not letting me bring more," she accused loudly.

Jordan struggled with his temper. He was bone-tired. Last night, with the herd restless from the distant rumbling of thunder, he and the other hired hands had spent the night rotating on a four-hour watch, which had resulted in very little sleep.

He sighed. "I tried to tell you that your fancy town clothes weren't suitable for this journey. You're going to have to wear the dresses Mrs. Newley made for you."

Coralie's hands went to her hips. She opened her mouth, but Jordan held up a hand. "Look, Coralie. She went to a lot of trouble to provide them with so little notice. She even made them the shorter, washday length so the hems wouldn't drag on the ground like your other dresses. And as for shoes, your father provided you with a suitable pair. You'll just have to start wearing them," he snapped.

Coralie stomped her foot and shook a finger at him. "I won't wear farmer clothes," she scoffed contemptuously, folding her arms across her chest.

Jordan removed his hat, ran his fingers through his hair and turned to stare out at Blue Mound, his thoughts in turmoil. He didn't know what to do. Marriage wasn't what he'd envisioned. Hell, so far they were man and wife in name only.

On their wedding night, with her blue eyes swimming in a pool of tears, she'd pleaded with him to wait and consummate their marriage later, when they were alone. With her father and brother in the next room and the Jones siblings across the hall, she wouldn't be able to face them the next day if anyone heard them making love. He'd given in, but now each night when he came to their tent before guard duty, it was the same. Too many people around.

Part of him understood her fear and inhibitions. Sound traveled in the still of the night, but no matter how much he tried to reassure her that he would be quiet, she feared the others would hear them, just as they all heard Birk's loud rutting each night. And his suggestion that they move their tent farther away had been met with horror—that was too obvious; people would know what they were doing,

Jordan's shoulders drooped under the weight of his unhappiness. Now he turned and walked away from the woman he'd loved for so long. As a young girl, she'd been so incredibly beautiful and so different from the other girls, with her ladylike airs, that he knew he'd wait for her to grow up. A soul-deep ache tore through him. It looked as though he hadn't waited long enough.

"Jordan, don't you dare walk away from me. I'm not through talking to you." Coralie ran after him and grabbed his arm. He shrugged her off and swung up into his saddle, staring down at her. The resignation in his eyes gave way to determination: She was his wife. While he wouldn't force the issue of sharing his bed, from now on she'd start doing the other things a wife did for her husband.

"I'll be back for supper. Have it ready. And Coralie, from now on, you will do our cooking, cleaning and washing. I know that Jessie and Elliot have been doing all your work. But no more. Elliot will eat with the hired hands in my stead. You and I will eat our meals together—alone." With that announcement, he rode off.

Coralie stood, stunned and silent.

Chapter Seven

Tired from a full day but feeling restless, Jessie left the wagons. Passing the McCauleys' tent, she heard Birk's loud rutting. She hurried past, disturbed by Eirica's muffled cries. This was the third night she and the others had heard Birk forcing himself on his wife, though normally he waited until much later. Jessie frowned, wishing there was something she could do to help the woman. She sighed. Eirica belonged to her husband, and no man would interfere in Birk's business. But that didn't stop the worry she felt over the other woman's pain and unhappiness.

Anne and her children passed her. The girls had wet hair from a bath. "Evenin', Jessie." Anne nodded.

"Evenin'," Jessie returned. She longed to visit and chat with the friendly woman, but she didn't dare draw attention to herself. She sighed. Once again, she was on her own. This time, though, she didn't even have the company of her siblings, as they were all on duty. She thought of riding out to visit them, but Wolf had forbidden her to go anywhere near the cattle.

She picked up a rock and rubbed the smooth bottom between her fingers. Maybe Elliot would like some company. Tossing the rock into the shallow water, she quickly discarded that idea. Coralie would be there, and no way was she going to spend any amount of time in her company. She wasn't that desperate! "Might as well go to bed. There isn't anything else to do," she murmured, turning away from the soothing vision of the flowing river.

An irritated voice answered, "How nice for you!"

Coralie joined Jessie. Jessie lifted a brow when she saw Coralie's armload of dirty pans and plates. Supper was long over, and everyone else had already finished their nightly chores.

Coralie sent her a sly look. "Dearest Jessie—"

"The answer is no, Coralie."

Coralie stamped her foot and set the dirty dishes down in disgust. "I can't believe Jordan made me cook supper. How can anyone cook over a fire? These pots are burned black. They'll never come clean," she wailed.

"Best start soaking them, then. Try rubbing some dirt on the burned areas. It'll help." Jessie bit the inside of her cheeks to keep from laughing at Coralie's look of outrage.

Coralie put her hands on her hips and tapped her foot. Her eyes narrowed to determined slits. "Look, Jessie, what do you want? Name it."

Jessie shook her head side to side. "Sorry, Coralie. Not a chance."

Coralie glanced up from beneath suddenly damp eyelashes.

Jessie rolled her eyes and shook her head. "Don't bother with the tears. It won't work." She took a step back. If she was smart, she'd walk away before things got nasty. Coralie wouldn't give up until she made a scene.

"I'm turning in." She stepped away but couldn't resist adding, "Have fun."

"Ooh," Coralie raged, "you're so mean to me, Jessie. I really, really hate you." She grabbed a cup and threw it.

Jessie ducked and laughed as the cup sailed harmlessly past. "I don't know why you even bother to throw things at me. In eight years you've yet to hit me. Why don't you start acting like a married woman instead of a spoiled daddy's girl."

The other girl threw her a dark look. "If you don't help

me, I'll make your life miserable once we reach Oregon. I'll be the lady of the house, not you.''

"Good luck, Coralie.''

Coralie stomped her foot and fumed. A sly look over came her features. She glanced at Jessie from beneath her lashes. "You know, Jessie, we aren't that far from Westport.'' She focused her attention on her ragged nails, her implied threat hanging in the air between them.

Jessie clenched her jaw, tempted to shove Coralie into the river. After all, she could only take so much. But before she could form a suitable reply to Coralie's not-so-subtle blackmail, she noticed a large grasshopper near her foot. Peeking up at Coralie's smug expression, Jessie felt a smile spread slowly across her disgusted features. Barely moving her boot, she nudged the insect. The grasshopper sprang into the air and landed on Coralie's bosom.

Coralie screamed and stumbled backward, slipping down the wet bank to topple bottom-first in the shallow water.

Jessie threw back her head and laughed. "Guess you might as well wash the mud from your dress while you're down there.'' With that, she left, shrill cries filling the air behind her. Heading away from camp, she reached a stand of shadowy cottonwood, then stopped when she heard the sound of excited barking.

Whirling around, she threw out her hands to try to avoid being knocked down by Sadie's enthusiastic greeting. The two of them went tumbling over the damp ground. Jessie laughed and giggled as she dodged Sadie's wet tongue.

She wrestled the dog to the ground. "So are they through with you for the night, girl?'' Sadie barked happily. Earlier, Jeremy had fetched the dog to help with the bedding-down of the cattle. Sadie was a working dog as well as a beloved pet.

Suddenly a low, menacing growl filled the air. Jessie's blood turned to ice and her mouth went dry when she glanced up into the cold blue gaze of a large white wolf standing near the clump of cottonwood trees. Gooseflesh rose on her arms and she slowly got to her knees, her fingers tightening on Sadie's nape. But the dog tore out of Jessie's grasp and positioned herself in front of her mistress. With teeth bared, hackles lifted, shoulders hunched and head lowered, the dog growled, warning the intruder away.

Before Jessie could move, the silhouette of a man strode out from the shadowy stand of trees. "Wahoska! Come," a deep, vibrant voice commanded.

Heart racing, Jessie recognized the voice. Her sense of relief changed to one of incredulous surprise when the wild-looking beast moved back to stand at Wolf's side. The animal's fur stood on end, his fangs bared as he continued to eye Sadie with mistrust. It was only then that she noticed a rawhide collar around the animal's neck. Jessie grabbed her dog and got to her feet. Her disbelieving gaze never left Wolf or the animal at his side. "That wild animal yours?"

Wolf inclined his head. "I apologize. You weren't at the meetings when I introduced Wahoska to the others. He tends to keep to himself on the trail, but he won't harm you. He was only being protective."

Jessie put Sadie in a sit-stay and shoved her hands down on her hips. "Protecting me from what?" she demanded, "my own dog?"

Wolf shrugged. He rocked back on his heels, his face concealed by the shadows. "He didn't know she was your dog. From where we were standing, it looked as though Sadie was attacking you. Wahoska won't bother you or the dog again. You have my word, young Jess."

To her amazement, his voice was soft and tender, just like it was when he had soothed his new stallion. Staring at him, Jessie was mesmerized. She'd never have thought that the simple act of smiling could bring about such a difference to one's features. But his whole face softened. Gone was the forbidding wagon master and in his place was a man, a man who tempted her into forgetting her resolve to have nothing to do with him. Unconsciously, she swayed toward him.

Sadie growled low in her throat, bringing her back to her senses. For just one moment, she'd forgotten who he was and that she had to avoid close contact with him at all costs.

Besides, she was still furious with him for ruining her afternoon, and now his pet wolf had scared the wits out of her. She stalked past him.

"I owe you an apology."

Those words stopped her in her tracks. She glanced over her shoulder. Surely she hadn't heard correctly. "For what?" she questioned, her voice betraying her surprise. She eyed him with the same mistrust with which his wolf eyed Sadie.

"Rook informed me you'd earned yourself the afternoon off. He also made it clear that you're a hard worker. I agree and I've found no fault with the care and attention you give to the animals. You handle them as well as any man in this party, better even than some. If you want to reclaim your team of oxen on the morrow, they're yours." He looked uncomfortable for a moment before adding, "And judging by what I just witnessed between you and your sister-in-law, I may have misjudged the situation there as well."

Stunned, Jessie stared at Wolf. Not only had he apologized—on two counts—he'd actually praised her. She closed her mouth as a horrible thought came to mind. Earlier, she'd been so angry with him that she'd embedded some nasty thorns in his bedroll.

Adding to her guilt, Wolf sent her an appreciative look. "You're not too bad with a whip either."

Now she felt wretched. There was no way for her to remove the thorns; he'd fetched his bedroll from the supply wagon immediately after the evening meal. But his next words dashed all feelings of remorse.

"There may be hope for you yet—if you learn to control your temper and wild ways. It's my aim to see you do so by the time we reach Oregon. So no more of those grasshopper stunts," he added, the tenderness in his voice gone, replaced with harsh promise as he strode back into the night.

Jessie snapped her mouth closed and narrowed her gaze, his threat dashing the glow brought on by his praise. "Damn him." Trust him to ruin her evening. She narrowed her gaze, then grinned wickedly. "Sweet dreams, wagon master," she whispered.

*   *   *

Wolf slid into the shadow of a lone cottonwood and watched Jessie stalk toward the circle of wagons. Shaking his head, he glanced down at the wolf. "You leave that dog alone, hear me? She's the best cattle dog I've seen," he told Wahoska. The white animal bunched its muscles and dashed off, eyeing Sadie one last time.

He stared off into the shadowy night, watching until Jessie's slim form faded from sight. A small crease marred his forehead. Something about those expressive eyes bothered him. "This is madness!" Wolf headed off toward camp with his churning thoughts. But Jessie's wide, innocent features returned to his thoughts. His pace quickened until he was running, his heart pounding in rhythm with his moccasin covered feet. He sought to outrun the niggling worry that he'd missed something. Something was out of place. The feeling that had begun the day they'd left Westport had grown.

His nostrils flared but his breathing remained steady as he drew upon his warrior's training. Running always helped put things in perspective. With his blood pulsing loudly in his ears, he attempted to sort out his feelings and discover what was bothering him, but images of Jessie once again intruded. The smooth pace of his gait faltered. He stumbled, then stopped. So much for training! Wolf tipped his head back and rolled his shoulders, worried about his inability to focus. He'd always been able to identify and solve his problems.

Disgusted, he shrugged off the unsettling feeling, returned to confer with Rook one last time, then headed for the separate camp set up near the livestock for the hired hands.

"Wolf?"

He stopped reluctantly when a shadowy figure stepped out from behind a wagon and sauntered toward him. His brows lowered. Damn the woman. Now what was she up to? "What do you want, Rosalyn?"

She sidled up to him, slipped her hands around his neck and pressed her lips to his. Her pelvis rubbed against him, making her invitation clear. "You, Wolf. I want you." She tipped her head back and licked her lips.

Disgusted with the woman's wanton behavior, Wolf clamped his fingers around her arms, freed himself of her grip and stepped back. "Forget it."

But like a bitch in heat, she batted her eyes at him and slid one hand beneath his vest. "Uh-uh, I don't believe you. A big, handsome man like you has needs, and I know just what you'd like." Like a snake striking, her fingers dipped beneath the waistband of his buckskin breeches.

Wolf yanked her hand away and stepped back. "The answer is no, Rosalyn. I suggest you go to bed—with your husband."

Wolf stalked off, heading toward the herd of cattle in the distance. By the time he'd rolled his bedroll out and slipped inside, he was both exhausted and frustrated. This trip was proving to be fraught with problems. He had the troublesome Jones boy, a she-cat determined to hook her claws into him, and the uncomfortable feeling that his problems were only beginning. Sliding down further into the cocoon of warmth, he cradled his head in his hands and stared up into the star-studded sky, wondering what else this trip would bring.

Too tired to contemplate the rest of the emigrants, he closed his eyes and took several deep breaths. On the verge of drifting off, he shifted his shoulders. A sudden, piercing pain between his shoulder blades caused him to bolt upright.

"What the hell?" he said in a hiss. Shoving aside the top quilts, he ran his fingers tentatively over the bottom blanket. A sharp jab to his thumb brought another exclamation of pain. After a careful search, he found a nasty-looking thorn embedded in the wool beneath him.

"Damned thorns." He found two more wickedly pointed thorns. As he stared at them, his eyes darkened with fury. There was only one way for these to get inside a person's bedroll. Someone had deliberately put them there, and he'd wager all his breeding mares that the culprit had rebellious green eyes.

*   *   *

The following days were a blur of travel, chores and sleep for Jessie. They passed the small town of Lawrence on day four, and today, day seven, they were camped on the outskirts of Topeka. After caring for her horse and the oxen, she tackled the biggest chore of all: the preparation of two meals for a dozen-plus men. She groaned at the thought. After a long day on horseback, Wolf's hired hands devoured everything she and Rook fixed for the evening meal, which left no choice but to cook two meals and put one aside for the next day's noon stop.

She was sure glad she hadn't taken back the grueling job of driving the oxen. The Svenssons had little money for their new start in Oregon; most of their cash had gone into outfitting their family for the trip. And while Jessie didn't have the heart to take away Rickard's job, neither did she want to baby-sit cows all day, so she was paying Kersten and Hanna to herd them. The girls were happy to earn money for their family.

That left her free to ride and explore the trail or search out small game for fresh meat for their meal. Making a face at the thought of just beans and rice with salt pork for dinner, Jessie decided she'd go hunting. Rabbit or prairie chicken added to the stew sounded good.

With the ease of two people who'd established a working partnership, Jessie and Rook set about their duties. Rook started the fire and cooked slabs of salt pork while she grabbed the ingredients needed to make bread—two days' worth. Kneeling, she placed the bread board on a wooden box and mixed the ingredients. Turning half of the sticky dough onto the board, she sprinkled it with flour, and soon her hands moved in a rhythmic rolling motion as she kneaded the flour into a soft ball with the heels of her hands. When she was finished, she began the process again. Halfway through, she heard laughter and glanced to her right.

Eirica and Anne were standing among a group of five other women, talking and visiting. Resentment warred with frustration as she watched the women walk over to Anne's wagon. For the first time since leaving Westport, they were camped in close proximity to other travelers, and she wanted to meet new people, people who might end up being her neighbors in Oregon.

Glancing around, she noted that most of the train had set aside their normal routine of chores so they could visit and exchange trail news and gossip during the light of day. Having traveled less than ten miles that day, they had several hours before the sun set. But she and Rook had mutually decided to get their meal preparations done early and have the evening to relax.

The tangy smell of tobacco smoke drifted down to her. Jessie smiled. When Rook lit his pipe, it meant he was in a good mood. He joined her. ''Goin' to be some merrymaking tonight, *laddie*, if'n I'm not mistaken,'' he announced.

His emphasis on the word *laddie* warned her that they weren't alone. When it was just the two of them, he reverted back to ''lass.'' From the corner of her eye, she saw a shadowy figure near the wagons and knew without doubt it was her taskmaster. Turning her back on him, she answered Rook.

''That should be fun.'' She bent over the dull brown blob, kneading with more vigor than needed, very aware of the man who watched her every move with nerve-shattering intensity. Jessie was grateful when Wolf engaged Rook in conversation, leaving her to her bread making. Shaping the dough, she gave herself up to her silent contemplations, troubling though they were. Her whole being seemed to be on edge—waiting, but for what?

The sudden appearance of a pair of jean-clad legs brought her head up with a snap. Her startled glance locked onto the rough blue material pulled taut across muscular thighs. It was the first time she'd seen Wolf up close in anything other than buckskin. She swallowed, not sure which she preferred him in. Shocked by the direction of her thoughts, she ruthlessly thrust all thought of him from her mind, but his nearness unsettled her, and his continued silence made her hands tremble, causing her to spill precious flour.

Why did his presence affect her so? Whenever he came near, a curious anticipation gripped her. It was as though she came alive, both mind and body alert, waiting. But for what, she was afraid to explore. Tipping her head back to glare at him, she couldn't help but appreciate how the faint afternoon light softened his prominent cheekbones and lent a golden glow to his sun-bleached hair. It made him seem so much more human. Locking gazes with him, she found herself wishing she could lose herself in the wild sapphire blue of his eyes.

What was she thinking? Thrusting out her jaw, she mentally ticked off all the mean things he'd done to her, reminded herself that this man made it a point to push her to the point of anger at least once per day. With one last punch, she shaped the last loaf, putting one half into a Dutch oven, and the other into one of the covered frying pans that Rook affectionately called spiders.

Standing, Jessie felt more in control as she passed Wolf and set the pans beside the others. When she turned, he was still there, watching her. Now she wished he'd say something. His silence was unnerving, as was the glint in his eyes as he stared at her. But she continued to ignore him while she cleaned up her mess. She turned her attention to Rook, who was stirring a big pot of beans for the night's supper. "I'll check the coals in the other firepit to see if they're hot enough to bake the corn bread I mixed up earlier—and it looks like we even have enough milk left for sweetened bread and milk for dessert."

Without looking at Wolf, she went about her chores, but his presence unnerved her so that she continued to babble. "We'll be finished in time to join the others. Did you know Lars plays the fiddle? Rickard told me his pa is going to play tonight. Should be a lot of fun." Her voice took on a belligerent tone as she sent Wolf a look that dared him to ruin it for her.

As if that was precisely what he'd waited for, Wolf

grinned, a knowing, pleased-as-hell grin that boded ill. "I'm afraid you won't have much time for socializing tonight, young Jess." Wolf folded his arms across his chest and met her glare with an impassive stare of his own.

Jessie swiped at a strand of hair that fell over her eyes, unaware of the pale streak of flour she left across her forehead. "Of course I will. There's still lots of day left. My chores will be done in plenty of time," she challenged. She threw her shoulders back and stuck her chin out, her emerald greens clashing with the ice blue of his gaze.

She refused to back down, even when Wolf took a step closer. They stood toe-to-toe. Jessie had to tip her head back. "Give me one good reason why not," she ordered. "No matter how many extra chores you assign me, I'll get them done."

Rook groaned and motioned from behind Wolf for her to keep silent. She ignored him.

Wolf lifted an eyebrow, and a sly grin lifted the corners of his lips. "I've no doubt about that, but don't fret. There won't be any extra chores tonight, but it seems I've neglected to inform you that I've added your name to the guard-duty roster."

Jessie's jaw dropped. "Guard duty?"

Wolf nodded toward the oxen grazing nearby. His eyes gleamed with humor. "As you know, someone has to watch over the oxen whenever they aren't corralled. Tonight's the first night we've not formed a corral with the wagons, and with so many other wagons near, I have to assign guard duty. I can't risk having ours wander off or be stolen. Rickard is watching them now. You'll relieve him at dark, and Bjorn will relieve you at midnight."

Jessie stuck her hands on her hips. He couldn't do this to her. Not after all the plans she'd made. But before she could argue with him, he reached into his pocket, drew out a piece of leather and handed it to her.

"I believe these belong to you." Wolf walked away, whistling.

Opening the leather square, Jessie stared at three wicked-looking thorns.

Rook coughed to keep from laughing. It didn't take a genius to figure out what Jessie had done, but when he saw the fury in her green eyes, he stepped forward and grabbed her arm to keep her from running after Wolf. "Now, lass, don't do it. That's what he's awaitin' fer."

Jessie rounded on him, a she-bear all het up and steaming mad. He took a step back, careful to hide his grin.

"Listen to me, Rook." Jessie's furious voice demanded, bringing him back to the present. He winced when her voice grew in pitch.

He took another step back for good measure when she advanced on him. He glanced sideways, keeping an eye out for objects that she might have a mind to start tossing. He'd never seen her so angry, so out of control, and he figured he'd better calm her down right quick. "Now, lass. Ya needs to calm down. Gittin' angry ain't gonna help ya none."

Jessie paced back and forth, kicking the dirt and grass in front of her until she'd worn a small, muddy path before him. "Why, Rook? Why's he doing this? He hasn't left me alone for one minute since we left Westport. I've done nothing to deserve this! I swear, he was born with a burr up his butt."

At that, Rook lifted one bushy white brow, crossed his arms in front of him and stared at the thorns in her hand. "Mebbe yer just a thorn in his side?"

Jessie winced. Then her gaze went wide with feigned innocence. "The prairie is covered with thorns. He can't prove I had anything to do with these."

But Rook wasn't fooled. He'd seen the gleam of satisfaction in her eyes. But before he could tell her so, her anger deflated. She tossed the thorns down and smashed them into the soft ground with her boots. Standing there, rubbing her cotton-covered arms, she looked young and vulnerable.

Her voice dropped to a husky whisper and quavered with emotion. "That still doesn't explain why he hates me." She turned away, but not before he caught a glimpse of watery green eyes. "And he does, Rook," she whispered. Stooping, she grabbed an empty kettle and stalked toward the river.

Rook frowned and reached for his pipe. She was right. Wolf *was* being hard on her. He drew a deep breath and shook his head, utterly confused over his friend's unusual behavior. Under most circumstances, Wolf was a fair and just man. Why was he singling the girl out for what he had to admit was unwarranted harshness over a bit of high-spirited behavior?

Tapping fresh tobacco into the bowl of his pipe, he stared out over the river. Low growls sounded from somewhere behind him, interrupting his musing. Rook whipped around, much faster than his stocky, old-man's body should've allowed. His hand went to the knife sheathed at his belt, and his faded blue eyes scanned the area, looking for the trouble. When he spotted it, he relaxed and lit his pipe, drawing deeply. "Ah, I should've known it'd be the two of ya at it again," he grumbled, spotting Sadie under the wagon. She growled low in her throat as the wolf approached.

He sighed. The two animals were at odds with one another, as were their masters. Sadie refused to have anything to do with the white wolf, and the wolf wasn't taking no for an answer. A sudden thought came to mind as he watched the two animals eye one another. Each time Wahoska moved closer, Sadie growled and snapped. Rook knew it was just a matter of time before Wahoska won her over.

His bushy white brows rose with sudden insight. Was it possible that Wolf sensed there was more to Jessie than he could see? He chuckled and shook his head, a gleam of anticipation replacing the worry in his eyes. He grabbed his walking stick and poked the white wolf. "Git outta here, you mangy ol' mutt," he said in a growl, shooing the animal away.

Sadie came out and licked his proffered hand. Rook scratched the dog behind her ear and took a big pull of his pipe, blowing out a stream of smoke. "Well, Sadie, ol' girl. Things look to be gittin' mighty interestin'."

*　　*　　*

Jessie mounted Shilo and headed out across the prairie in search of some small game. For her sixteenth birthday, when most girls received fancy dresses, gleaming jewels or golden chains, her brothers had presented her with a new scattergun. The shotgun now lay across her lap. Hunched over the mare's neck, Jessie felt the wind cool her face as she put distance between her and the person who had hurt her deeply. Well, she'd show him.

As her eyes scanned the grass and small bushes for prairie chickens or rabbits, her mind searched for a suitable method of extracting revenge. No one treated her like he did and got away with it. Jessie rode until she calmed.

An hour later she returned to camp and tossed four prairie chickens to the ground near Rook. After taking care of her horse, she helped Rook pluck the birds. By the time dinner was ready to be served, Jessie not only had her plan of revenge, but she'd put it into action.

Hunching over a Dutch oven chock-full of fresh meat, beans and rice, she stirred the steaming mixture. Glancing around, she made sure no one was looking before dropping a small sliver of hot chili pepper into the pot, carefully concealing it near the side of the kettle where she could scoop it up quickly. Jessie grinned in anticipation when Rook rang the large gong to announce the evening meal.

The sound traveled to the hired hands camped a good half mile away. It still didn't make sense to her that she and Rook were so far from the cattle. But according to Rook, Wolf wanted the supply wagons away from the cattle in case they stampeded. She grimaced. He just wanted *her* away from the cattle.

When the men came riding in, Rook took his place next to her. He handed out thick chunks of steaming corn bread while Jessie, her face impassive, dipped her ladle into the thick, spicy meat, beans and rice mixture and served it up onto tin plates each weary man held out to her. With each dip into the pot, she was careful not to disturb the hot pepper.

"Thanks, Jess," Jeremy said.

White Wolf

Jessie glanced up, surprised. She'd been so deep in her thoughts, she hadn't noticed her brother in line. Staring up at him, she saw how tired he looked. But before she could ask him how it was going, he'd moved on and held his plate out to Rook. After serving nearly everyone, Jessie felt disappointed when there was no sign of Wolf. Had he remained with the cattle? At sound of a rider, she glanced up and saw him riding in with Shorty. Surreptitiously, she scooped up the hidden hot pepper. Ladle ready, she waited impatiently.

Rook, seated next to her on a wooden box, turned to her. "Go fetch the rest of the corn bread for me. I'm jest too tired to git up."

Jessie's eyes widened with horror, but she didn't make a big fuss over his request. Carefully, she rested the full ladle on top of the mixture in the kettle, making sure the pepper was covered. Standing, she watched Rook move over and pick up the ladle full of beans and rice.

"Git yer arse over here, Wolf. Some of us would like ta eat afore the food's cold."

Jessie sighed with satisfaction and quickly fled the scene of her crime. Her plan of revenge was going better than she'd dared hope. With Rook serving, Wolf wouldn't be able to point the finger of blame at her. For good measure, she took a moment to stir another pot of beans that would be sent out to the hands still on duty. Then she leaned down and picked up two pans of corn bread.

Carrying them back to the line of men, she sat down and handed Wolf a hunk of steaming bread, keeping her eyes downcast.

Wolf sniffed his plate. "Where'd the fresh meat come from, Rook? You go hunting today?"

Rook grinned and shook his head. "Young Jess here scared 'em up."

Jessie mumbled something in response to Wolf's grudging praise. She kept her head down until he left the line. Her lips curved with glee when he sat down with the others and lifted his fork to his lips.

Chapter Eight

Wolf held the tin plate of food to his nose and sniffed appreciatively. The tantalizing aroma caused his mouth to water in anticipation. Picking up his fork, he scooped a large forkful of beans and rice into his mouth. He chewed, savoring the hot, spicy food. Conversation turned lively as the men seated around him joked and laughed as they ate, complimenting Duarte on the added spice to their meal and going back for more. Normally, trail food leaned toward bland and boring. After one bite, Wolf ate in earnest, enjoying the distinctive fruity flavor that Duarte said made this pepper unique.

But halfway through his meal, he quickly revised his opinion when the inside of his mouth exploded with a burning heat unlike anything he'd ever experienced. The liquid flame spread down his throat and up into his nose and brought tears to his eyes. He dropped his fork, lifted his plate to his mouth and spat out the offensive bite of food. Coughing and gasping for breath, he dropped his plate and ran toward Rook. "Water," he said in a croak, beads of sweat popping out along his forehead and across the bridge of his nose.

Rook quickly dipped a tin cup into the water barrel and handed it to Wolf. "Here, boss," he said, a look of concern in his eyes.

Wolf took the cup and drank with the air of a desperate man. After gulping down three more cups of water, he faced Rook. "What the hell did you put in the beans?" he rasped.

He held his mouth wide-open, willing the cool air to take away the heat that continued to linger and burn.

Scratching his head, Rook furrowed his brow in confusion. "It ain't that hot, boss, 'specially since I was real careful not too use too many of them dried peppers, like Duarte warned. Ain't no one else seems to have trouble."

Feeling a small measure of relief as the burning began to abate, Wolf couldn't believe he was the only one to have felt the heat of those damn peppers. Shorty strode past him, shouting, "Hey, kid, dish me up some more of that there grub. Jest make sure there ain't no peppers in mine. I don't like my food that hot, only my women," he joked.

Rook shook a finger at him. "There ain't no peppers in there, lad. Counted them afore I put 'em in and removed them myself afore I served up."

Wolf held his plate out to Rook and pointed to what was left of a tiny sliver of red-orange chili. "Yeah? Guess you forgot one," he said, his throat and lips still burning. "Damn. You trying to do me in?" He straightened as a suspicious thought came to mind. He studied Jessie Jones. Every instinct within him screamed that he'd been one-upped again. He narrowed his eyes and compressed his burning and swollen lips. "Show me the peppers you removed," he ordered Rook, never taking his eyes off Jessie.

"Now, Wolf—"

"Show me!"

Wolf followed Rook to another wagon, where the back hung down, suspended by two chains to keep it level with the wagon bed. From the waist-high work surface, Rook picked up a tin cup and dumped out the large pepper pieces. With the tip of his knife, he spread them.

He turned in puzzlement. "All there, boss. That piece you got must've broken off durin' the stirrin'."

Once again, Wolf's gaze fell on Jessie. "I'm not too sure about that," he said. Damn. He'd never experienced anything so hot in his life. He took a step toward the boy. If Jessie Jones thought he could make a fool of him, he'd better think again! He planned to give him lots of time to rethink the wisdom of his actions and make him sorry for indulging in his spot of mischief.

Rook's gnarled fingers bit into his arm. "Now, Wolf, the boy didn't have anythin' to do with this. I'm the one who served ya up, not him. Was jest an accident. Why don't ya have a piece of this here peach pie we has for dessert."

Wolf glared at Rook but realized his friend was right. He'd look even more the fool if he openly accused the boy. Ignoring Rook's peace offering, he stalked off. He didn't believe in accidents. There was no doubt in his mind—not one little bit—that Jessie Jones had somehow managed to sabotage his meal. His jaw tightened. Young Jess would soon find himself with so much work on his hands that he'd be too tired to cause any more trouble.

The sounds of fiddle, song and laughter floated across the night air. Small glowing fires danced in the darkness along both sides of the Kansas River, sending smoky fingers upward to obscure the brightness of the heavens and settle over the water, cloaking the land, giving it a soft, muted look.

Several westward-bound parties had joined together for an evening of merrymaking. The young folk danced to the merry tunes of fiddles, work-weary women gathered together with their mending to enjoy a good gossip, while the young children ran gleefully across the green grass. Sitting apart, small groups of men gathered around campfires to smoke, pass around a flask of whiskey and compare notes and stories about the Oregon and California trails.

Guarding the oxen a short distance away, Jessie stared out toward the haze-shrouded river, longing to be a part of that joyous gathering of people who had only one common interest: reaching the new lands that promised richer lives. Turning away from the sight, she walked past the herd of oxen until she came to a lone tree. She leaned against the thick trunk and slid down it, her back resting against the rough bark as she kept watch over the livestock. Except for Sadie, who lay asleep a few feet away, she was by herself.

Once again, she was on the outside looking in. Unbidden, tears of self-pity spilled down her cheeks.

Resting her head on her knees, she knew tiredness played a part in her weepiness. On top of the endless list of chores Wolf found for her to do, her clandestine late-night walks were taking their toll. How she longed for a solid night's sleep. Lifting her head, she let the music flow through her. After a while, the sounds of the fiddles faded to the haunting harmony of several mouth organs. Jessie reached into her pocket to withdraw her own musical instrument. She lifted it to her lips and added a fourth part.

When the last notes died away, she began to play a soft, sad solo. Sadie crawled over and nudged her, then lay down with a low whine. Halfway through the tune, she stopped, unable to finish. She brought her thighs up to her chest and propped her arms across her knees. Chin resting on her fist, she stared into the gray-black of the night.

Wolf stood in the shadows, riveted to the spot. He'd come to check on Jessie Jones but had stopped when he heard the mournful notes. The sound made him feel like a low-down snake for assigning the boy guard duty when he'd been looking forward to having some fun with the others. His actions left him feeling small and petty—even though Jessie deserved it after that last prank. In fact, to his disgust, some part of him admired the boy's spirit. There weren't very many men alive brave enough to put thorns in his bedroll or peppers in his food.

When the softly played tune ended, guilt mingling with anger made his voice harsher than he'd intended as he jerked his thumb toward the river. "Go on, get outta here. You're relieved."

Startled, Jessie jumped up with a cry of surprise. A shaft of moonlight filtered down past the haze of smoke. Wolf found himself staring into eyes filled with wary disbelief.

Jessie's jaw shot forward. "You're relieving me of guard duty?"

Wolf folded his arms across his chest and stared down at

the boy. When he noticed the trail of dried tears on each side of his face, he felt another twinge of guilt for being so hard on him. He resolved to go easier on the kid. "Look, do you want to join your brothers for a while or not?" he said with a growl.

The transformation was immediate and startling. The boy's eyes sparkled like glittering jewels, and his lips curved into a wide grin. "Oh, yes, thank you, Wolf," Jessie cried out joyously.

Wolf froze, all his senses alert and screaming. The blood roared in his ears, muting the drifting sounds of music, laughter and the barking of a dog. The youngest Jones boy had looked almost beautiful with the soft glow of moonlight illuminating his wide green eyes, and his wide grin gave his lips a lush fullness in a face that seemed far too delicate for a boy.

A startling thought flashed through his mind. Jessie Jones would have made one hell of a beautiful woman. The hairs on the back of his neck prickled. His gaze tracked Jessie running across the grass with Sadie. Jessie Jones? The truth hit him like a thunderbolt. Jessie Jones wasn't an adolescent boy. Jessica Jones was a girl on the brink of womanhood. He laughed, the sound more of a bark. "You're crazy!" But in his gut, he knew he wasn't.

Suddenly all the little things that had nagged at him made sense: Rook's protective attitude toward Jessie, the graceful way she moved, her ease with cooking, but most of all, it explained why James hadn't told him he'd had another brother. He didn't. He had a younger sister. Thinking back to that night in the barn, Wolf cursed when he recalled how James had tried to tell him that he'd made other arrangements for Jessie to come out to Oregon.

Wolf's gut tightened painfully as anger overwhelmed him. The truth had been there all along, staring him in the face, but he'd been blind to it.

After the evening festivities broke up, Jeremy and James insisted on walking Jessie back to her wagon. She didn't mind.

It gave them more time together. They wound their way around wagons and canvas tents in companionable silence. After an evening of visiting and listening to conversation about what to expect during the upcoming days and months along the trail, Jessie felt pleasantly relaxed.

Nearing the Macauley tent, she yawned, more than ready to crawl into her bedroll and sleep. "What time do you go on duty, James?"

"We're both on as soon as we get back. Wanted to make sure you made it back without getting into mischief. Now, be good, brat." James fixed her with his big-brother stare. "And no more of those pepper pranks."

Jessie stopped. "Me?" She couldn't keep the glee from her voice, and James nailed her with his no-nonsense glare.

"I'm warning you, Jess. No more. It's a wonder Wolf didn't beat you."

She giggled. "That's 'cause he can't prove I had anything to do with it. After all, Rook served him, not me."

"Yeah, you were lucky this time. Now—"

An angry shout followed by the reverberating sound of a sharp slap interrupted his lecture.

Jessie stopped in her tracks and stared at the Macauley tent. Her eyes narrowed and she clenched her fists at her sides. Drunk, Birk was mean as a tom turkey, and she knew he'd spent most of his evening drinking with a bunch of rough-looking men heading for California.

James reached out and grabbed hold of her upper arm. "Come on, Jess."

But when the angry shouting continued, followed by another slap and the whimper of a scared child, Jessie glared at her brother and tried to break free. "Let go," she said.

James tightened his grip. "Stay out of it, Jess." Jeremy moved closer on her other side, and the two men hustled her away.

When James released her beside her wagon, she rounded on him. "James—"

"No!" His voice was a harsh whisper. "It's not any of our concern."

Jessie's jaw fell open in disbelief. "He's drunk, James. He'll hurt her or the children." She stared at her brothers, bewildered by their lack of compassion. "You've taught me to stand up for what's right. What he's doing is wrong. Eirica needs our help," she pleaded, glancing from James to Jeremy when it was apparent she'd get no help from her oldest brother. Jeremy stared at his feet.

From the first night on the trail when she'd heard Birk's loud rutting, Eirica's plight had haunted Jessie. Hearing a private act hadn't bothered her—living in such close quarters on the trail, it was inevitable. No, what upset her was the soft weeping that had followed.

Since that night, she'd lain awake, sometimes for hours, attempting to blot out the sounds of Birk's harsh anger, the sound of flesh meeting flesh, a crying child, and finally Eirica's humiliation. She'd tried taking her bedroll as far from the Macauley tent as possible, but no matter how far she went, she knew he was terrorizing his wife and children. She glared toward the Macauley tent. How she hated the abuse and longed to do something to stop it.

James dug his fingers into her shoulders and shook her to get her attention. "I know that look, Jess. Forget it. I forbid it! We are staying out of it—all of us, and that includes you. Leave it alone, hear me?"

Jessie stared at him in surprise. James was furious, his features cold and forbidding. Gone was her normally easygoing brother.

"Do you hear me, Jess?" James shook her again.

She nodded. "I hear you," she whispered.

James released her arm and stalked off without another word.

Jessie rubbed her arms as she watched him go, confused by his strange behavior. She glanced at Jeremy, but he stuck his hands deep into his pockets and refused to meet her gaze.

"What's going on with him, Jeremy?" she whispered.

Releasing his breath, he glanced down at her, his green eyes shadowed with worry. "You know he don't like seeing women being beat up on."

116

"Then why won't he do something? Why won't he let me help Eirica?"

Jeremy put his arm around her shoulders. Brother and sister stared off into the dark. "I don't know, Jessie, but he's right about one thing. You keep away from Birk Macauley. He's a mean bastard who won't tolerate interference from anyone. I don't want you getting hurt. Remember that." With another quick hug, he left.

Jessie stood alone, tired and utterly drained. Voices from the Svenssons' tent drifted by as the older boys returned to camp. Then silence fell. Shivering in the growing coolness, she finally grabbed her bedroll and unrolled it beneath her wagon. Leaving her boots on, she crawled on top of her blankets and watched the Macauley tent with her chin propped on her fists. Her work this night was not yet done. After what she'd heard earlier, she knew Eirica would need her tonight.

Jessie yawned again. The soothing sounds of crickets and other nighttime insects lulled her. But she didn't give in to the overwhelming desire to close her eyes for even a moment. Instead, she concentrated on the noises around her: the sounds of snoring, Sadie's soft whimpers as she chased a rabbit in her sleep, the pop of burning embers, and the occasional howl of a lone coyote calling his mate.

To keep her mind active, she thought of her new friends. On their second night on the trail, both Eirica and Anne had joined her at the stream to wash dishes. Though she'd tried to remain aloof, Anne had leaned close to confess that they both knew her secret, and so did Rickard. He'd pestered her from day one to teach him how to use a whip. They all promised to keep her secret, but Jessie worried now that it would only be a matter of time—and not very much time at that—before Wolf discovered the truth. She grimaced, knowing that there was no way in a tight-knit group to keep up the pretense forever. She could only hope they made it a lot farther west before Wolf discovered it.

She groaned at the thought. Anne and her family, along with Eirica, thought her ploy amusing, but Jessie knew Wolf would not find any humor in her deceit. Pushing the fore-boding feeling away, Jessie continued to watch the Macauley tent. The minutes ticked by. The sliver of moon rose higher, and Jessie's eyelids grew heavy. Just when she feared she'd fall asleep, Eirica, a waiflike shadow in the silvery moonlit night, left her tent.

Jessie's eyes snapped open and she crawled out from the wagon, staying low, blending in with the deep shadows of the trees and brush as she followed Eirica along the fog-shrouded banks of the river. In return for Eirica's silence and friendship, Jessie had vowed to look out for the other woman. Eirica needed a friend.

She'd discovered Eirica's nighttime wanderings by acci-dent two nights ago when she'd been awakened by the sound of someone moving past her wagon. Peeking out from under her warm cocoon of quilts, she'd been surprised to see Eirica heading toward the river. Silently, she'd followed to make sure the other woman was all right. Jessie knew she'd be forever haunted by the sight of Eirica bathing in the river, desperately scrubbing herself raw.

Coming to a stop beneath the protective cover of the trees, Jessie watched Eirica walk down the sloping bank to dip a cloth into the water and press it to one side of her face. After repeating the action several times, she left the water's edge and fell to her knees in the grass, her hands splayed protectively around her middle. The tears came, slowly, then flooding into deep, gut-wrenching sobs, empty-of-hope, full-of-despair sobs that tore deep into Jessie's sen-sitive soul.

Eirica's unhappiness brought a lump to her throat. It was difficult to witness her misery in hidden silence. Every in-stinct urged her to go to Eirica, but she forced herself to remain a motionless shadow, allowing the other woman to keep her pride intact. She wished she could leave the woman to deal with her demons in private, but it wasn't safe for a woman to wander alone at night. Until Eirica brought up her husband's ill treatment, Jessie would remain a silent but watchful guardian.

Tears stung her own eyes. She brushed them away, her fury against Birk growing. She pressed her lips together, and her hand gripped the rough bark of the tree. How she longed to give that bastard a taste of his own medicine. Eirica's sobs continued much longer than normal. Jessie frowned. Tonight's tears were different. They were the sound of a woman who'd lost all hope. Jessie shifted, feeling like an intruder. This was private, and she had no business witnessing such personal grief. Just as she turned away, a figure emerged from the shadows hugging the bank. Jessie straightened, alert and watchful, fearing that Birk had followed his wife.

"Well, whadda we have here? Who letcha out here all alone, darlin'?" The tall, thin stranger moved with the speed of a rat, grabbing Eirica by the shoulders and hauling her up against him. His hand covered her mouth, muffling her scream. "My, you's a looker," he jeered, running his other hand down her front, "even if you has a bun warmin' in the oven."

Erica struggled to free herself, but her futile attempts only made her captor laugh. Jessie narrowed her eyes and tightened her lips as her fingers released her coiled whip from her belt. She moved forward, the leather lash uncoiling, snaking through the grass behind her.

Just after midnight, Bjorn Svensson relieved Wolf of guard duty. The last few hours had left Wolf tense and restless, filled with a cold anger that threatened to explode. He headed for the river. Not one to act hastily or rashly, he stripped off his clothing and lowered himself into the dark, swirling water. The cold rush slapped against him, calming his raging emotions. He'd had several hours to think, and while he didn't believe he was wrong about Jessie, he hoped he was. Still, he had to be sure before he confronted him—her.

Sinking down, he leaned back to float, seeking the peace nighttime offered. Staring up into the heavens, he was no longer White Wolf, the Indian boy who'd been sent away from his people, nor was he the half-breed who belonged to neither world. He was just Wolf, a man with a battered soul who walked his path alone.

Trailing wisps of clouds floated across the crescent-shaped moon. Wolf turned and pitted his strength against that of the current until he felt himself tire. But even that exertion wasn't enough to keep his smoldering anger at bay. When the cold became too much, he headed for the bank. Crouched, half in the water, half out, he sensed movement beyond the grass-lined bank. Silently, he crawled out of the water, grabbed his knife and parted the tall grass.

Eirica walked by, unaware of him. Why was she so far from camp at this time of night? It wasn't safe for her to be out alone. He grabbed his clothes, then froze when another figure approached in a low crouch, staying much closer to the tall grass and brushing along the riverbank. Eirica was being followed. Sinking back into the deep shadows and swirling water, he hid as the unknown stalker passed by. He peeked out again between the dense foliage, his frown deepening when he recognized the silent figure of Jessie Jones. He dressed, then followed, his moccasin-clad feet making no sound.

When Jessie stopped behind a thick trunk, Wolf crouched in the grass several feet behind her. From his vantage point, he saw Eirica sitting on the ground, sobbing. His jaw tightened. He knew what went on between husband and wife. He'd seen Macauley backhand her more than once when she didn't move fast enough to suit him, but there was nothing he could do. His gaze switched from the crying woman to the other figure hidden in the shadows. What was Jessie up to now?

Suddenly Eirica cried out. He jerked his attention from Jessie to Eirica. His grip tightened on his knife when he saw a stranger holding Eirica against her will. He surged forward, a cry of rage building deep in his throat, but before the sound could escape, a loud pop sounded overhead. He threw himself to the ground.

Glancing around the tree trunk, he looked for the source of the gunfire. His jaw dropped when he spotted the actual source of the popping noise, but before he could call out or even get to his feet, Jessie lifted her hand and sent the rawhide whip singing through the air again. It split the quiet with a sharp snap, followed by a cry of surprise from the drunken man.

"Let her go," Jessie ordered. The hand holding the whip lifted once again.

Wolf moved to another tree, closer to the scene unfolding at the river's edge. Eirica had fallen to the ground and was sobbing softly; the intruder stood in front of her, holding his shoulder where the whip had torn a path through the faded material of his shirt.

"Who the hell are you?" The man peered at Jessie when she stepped out of the shadows. He laughed and spat on the ground. "Go 'way, boy," he said with a sneer, "else I'll have ta hurt ya. This don't concern ya."

"Leave the woman alone," Jessie repeated, drawing the whip back.

The angry man snorted and reached for the knife stuck in the waistband of his soiled breeches. In a flash, Wolf had his knife ready to throw, but Jessie stepped between him and the drunk. Once again, the whip zinged through the air.

Another roar of pain followed. This time the drunk man dropped his knife and put his hand to the side of his face. When he pulled his fingers away, he wore a look of utter disbelief as he stared at the blood on his palm. A long gash split his cheek. Blood poured down his chin. His pain-glazed eyes never left Jessie as he backed off slowly.

Jessie moved in front of Eirica. "Get your worthless hide out of here before I strip more flesh off your no-good bones." Her voice shook, but she held the whip in front of her, making it clear that she wouldn't hesitate to use it again.

The man spat. "Ya ain't heard the last of me, boy. We'll meet again, and I'll give you what-for," he threatened, his voice filled with hatred.

Wolf narrowed his gaze and watched the man stagger away, muttering vile threats. When he looked back at Eirica, Jessie was on the ground, holding her in her arms, rocking her, comforting her, smoothing the hair from her face. If he'd had any doubts about Jessie's true sex, they were gone. What he witnessed could only be one woman comforting another.

He backed away. It was obvious that Eirica knew what Jessie was, and it served to remind him that he'd been deceived. Fury engulfed him. His fist clenched into a tight ball, and he had an irresistible urge to strike out at something, anything. He turned, searching for a target. Then he remembered the drunken man's threat to harm Jessie. He took off in that direction.

When Wolf came upon the staggering drunk, he sneaked up from behind and whirled him around, grabbing him by the shirtfront. A beam of light from above fell across the surprised man's face, revealing eyes wide with fear and illuminating the bleeding wound on his face. Wolf felt a measure of satisfaction. The scum would carry that scar for the rest of his life. To his surprise and resentment, he also felt a twinge of pride that Jessie had handled the situation with the same fearlessness either of his sisters would have shown.

For long moments, Wolf stared at the man through slitted eyelids. He tightened his hold, his nostrils flaring at the stench of unwashed flesh. "I don't take kindly to others messing with the women in my wagon train," he said in a growl. "Nor do I like scum who threaten them." In the dim light, Wolf looked every bit the fierce warrior. He ignored the no-good varmint's pleas and excuses as he continued to level his glare of rage at the blubbering man. For good measure, he decided to make sure the bastard knew that Wolf protected those for whom he was responsible.

With a lightning-quick movement, he slammed his fist into the other man's nose with enough force to bloody his nose. Though he was tempted to do more, he leashed the savage fury that raged within him. "That's for manhandling the woman," he said, eyes gleaming with vengeance. Wolf reached down, picked up the cowering man once more and struck him again, this time in his soft, fleshy belly.

When the man made no move to rise or flee, Wolf drew his own wicked-looking bowie knife and placed the sharp tip at the middle of the man's chest. The drunken man broke out in a sweat and closed his eyes, his lips moving silently. "If I ever see you near any of my wagons or people again, I'll cut more than your other cheek. Got it?"

Eyes wide with fright, the man nodded. Wolf pulled his knife away and stalked off.

Wolf's fury lasted all night and into the next morning. He shouted out orders to roll out an hour earlier than normal. No one said a word, which made him feel even worse. It wasn't their fault he was in a foul mood. As the wagons pulled away, he felt disgusted with himself for allowing anger to rule his actions.

The discovery that the Jones brothers had a young sister gnawed at him like a bear at a sore paw. He couldn't let it go. One part of him understood the close family bond that had been behind the deceit. He and his siblings were also close and would do anything for each other. But despite that understanding, he didn't know if he could forget or forgive the Joneses for lying to him. Honesty and honor were traits he valued, and if a man had no honor, he wasn't a man. Then there was the question of what he was going to do about it. He drew in a deep breath, his nostrils flaring. He needed the Jones boys to drive the cattle, and had to admit they were hardworking and honest—except for passing off their sister as their brother. His lips twisted into a sneer. "Honest, hah!" he muttered.

"What's with ya, Wolf? You's been techy as a teased snake all mornin'."

Wolf frowned at Rook. His wagon was first in line today and had already headed out. "Who's in charge of your wagon?"

"I put the lad in charge for a bit. Now, what's with ya?"

Wolf lifted his face into the wind, his hair flowing out behind him, his chin jutting out as he gave a humorless bark of laughter. "Lad? Don't you mean lass?" He watched Rook remove his empty pipe. His expression never wavered.

"You knew, old man. Dammit, you knew all along, didn't

you?'' Wolf balled his hands into tightly clenched fists.

Rook measured the extent of his anger and then nodded, fingering his bushy white beard. ''Reckon I did.''

Though he hadn't expected his friend to deny it, the admission stung. Wolf smacked his right fist into his left palm and glared at his trusted friend. ''Why?''

Rook stared out into the clear, sparkling water of the river. ''Guess I didn't want to see her parted from her family.'' His gaze grew watery. ''Once I looked into those green eyes—''

Wolf closed his eyes in defeat as his fury drained. He was probably the only man alive who knew what his friend had gone through after they'd returned to Rook's cabin from a week in the mountains. There they'd found the dead bodies of Rook's wife and young daughter. He couldn't hate the man for his deceit. But that didn't excuse what he'd done, what they'd all done. Wolf was furious with the lot of them. He whipped around, his eyes narrowed to glittering slits. ''You had no right to interfere, old man.''

Rook, far from being intimidated, lifted a brow, his eyes sparkling with amusement. ''Seems if I remember rightly, ya assumed Jessie was a lad. As I recall, her brother tried ta tell ya, but ya kept cuttin' him off, so full of righteous anger no one could get a word in edgewise. Seems ta me it's yer own fault.''

Wolf clenched his jaw, forced to admit Rook was right. Late into the night, he'd replayed that night and each passing day, seeing all the signs that he'd forced the situation. He shook his head. Even in his dreams, her elfin face haunted him: the generous smattering of freckles that trailed across her nose and cheekbones, those green eyes and that mischievous grin.

No, in all fairness, it was his own fault—but he didn't like feeling the fool. His stomach burned as if a hot rock had been dropped into it.

''Ya know, Wolf, not all women are as shallow-minded and deceitful as that Martha gal.''

Wolf glared at him. "Wrong, old man. She's just as deceitful as Martha. All she cares about is getting to Oregon." Jessie's deceit reminded him of Martha. Each had lied to him so he would take her and her family to Oregon. Then had come the discovery that Martha was already engaged to a man waiting for her in Oregon. No, Jessie wasn't any different.

But while his mind searched for ways to redeem his shattered pride, his heart brought forth images of bright green eyes that mirrored her emotions: happiness and joy when she didn't know he was watching her, resentment and anger in his presence, and now that he thought it over, could it be that he'd glimpsed admiration and desire in those bewitching eyes of hers as well?

A thoughtful calm overcame him as he placed her true age at around sixteen or seventeen—which fit if Jeremy was nineteen. Seeing her silhouetted in the moonlight last night, he'd seen the curves that she somehow managed to hide during the day. And while she wasn't well rounded, there'd been no mistaking the curve of her breasts.

The corner of his lips tilted upward as the gem of an idea began to form and grow. He scratched the thick stubble lining his jaw thoughtfully, then lifted a brow and grinned—a wolfish grin. He knew her secret, but she didn't know he knew. His grin widened. What if he turned her role as a boy against her, then built up her awareness of him as a man without letting on that he knew the truth? What a perfectly devious ploy, he thought, anticipating how she'd squirm when he changed his tactics and got close to her—very close.

Then when she gave herself away, he'd let her and her brothers know what he thought of their lying ways. Taking a step closer to Rook, who was watching him closely with a worried expression, he jabbed a finger into the cook's chest. "Not a word, old man. Not a word to anyone that I know."

"Now, Wolf. What are ye up to?" Rook demanded.

"Nothing that concerns you," Wolf said, striding away.

Chapter Nine

Jessie rode along the river with Lara cradled in front of her, aware that Wolf watched her as he rode up and down the line of wagons. There was no doubt in her mind that he knew she was responsible for the pepper in his stew, nor did she doubt he'd find a way to pay her back for it. But what puzzled her was his relieving her early from guard duty last night.

She recalled the ribbing he'd received during supper because of the hot pepper. His very anger over her actions should have made him even more inclined to exclude her from the social gathering. Now she was left wondering what he was up to. That he felt guilty for the way he treated her was inconceivable. No, Wolf was up to something, and she'd do well to be on guard. Putting him from her mind, Jessie urged the horse into a canter and easily caught up with Rook.

"Look at us, Rook." Lara giggled, "Shilo goes ever so fast! How come your horse don't go fast?"

Rook wiggled his white brows, to the little girl's delight. " 'Cause we's in no hurry, lassie."

Jessie sent the old man a mischievous grin. "Uh-huh, I could outwalk that old nag of yours, Rook." Laughing at his indignant 'harrumph', she slowed her horse to the pace of Rook's. Breathing deeply, she enjoyed this relaxation, for she knew once they stopped, she'd find no peace until she crawled into bed.

Lara's chatter claimed her attention for the next hour until the three-year-old fell asleep. She and Rook exchanged amused glances. Jessie stared down at the golden red head resting against her breast. How she enjoyed the innocence of children and envied the girl's ability to greet each and every day with an eagerness to learn and to experience life to its fullest. So she spent as much time as she could during the day with Eirica's two girls, teaching them about the sights along the trail, even instructing them in their letters.

But when she held their little brother, Ian, the desire for her own babe took hold. This longing to cuddle her own child to her breast surprised her. She'd never given much thought to having babies, but now she had visions of little boys with golden brown hair and bright blue eyes.

Suddenly a loud wail pierced the lazy afternoon's quiet. Twisting around, grateful for any distraction from the impossible dreams that had taken hold, Jessie spotted Coralie lying facedown on the matted grass. She clucked her tongue. "Now what's her problem?"

Coralie struggled to her feet, a picture of weariness and defeat as she shoved her tangled blond hair from her face and attempted to brush the caked mud from her dress. Jessie eyed the ragged and torn hem of her dress and shook her head. "Why doesn't she wear the boots and dresses Jordan packed for her?"

"Pride," Rook answered, his voice rough with compassion. Suddenly he squinted at her, his sharp blue gaze drilling into hers. Then he shifted his gaze back to Coralie and jerked his head, sending Jessie a silent command. He lifted his hands toward Lara.

Jessie tightened her hold on the sleeping child. "Not a chance, Rook. I'm not helping her, not after the way she's treated me. Nope, not me. You go help her." She dared him to insist.

But the old cook lowered his arms without a word. He didn't need to. He just kept those penetrating blue eyes trained on her until guilt crept in. She scowled at him. Rook constantly amazed her: crusty and gruff on the outside, but inside lay a tender, caring soul. She gestured toward Coralie.

"Look, she isn't going to want my help. Besides, it's her own fault for being so darn stubborn."

"Ah, lassie. I'm disappointed, I am. I thought ya had a kinder heart than that. That I sure did." He exhaled loudly, his eyes full of reproach.

His disappointment in her hurt. Jessie glared at Coralie, waiting for her to get to her feet. But instead, the girl put her hands to her face and cried. The sight of Coralie at her wits' end stirred something deep inside her. She knew only too well the bitter taste of defeat. She'd felt that same way after finding out her brothers had planned to leave her behind. She had been full of despair, had lost all hope.

"Go to her, lassie. Ferget yer pride," Rook urged, his voice gruff but gentle.

Jessie frowned. "Oh, blast," she swore, handing Lara over. She supposed it was long past time to put the past behind them.

She rode back to her sister-in-law and stopped. Coralie glanced up, her tear-filled eyes laced with suspicion. They stared at one another. Jessie noted the dark streaks and smudges across her cheeks, the girl's sunburned skin, missing bonnet and windblown hair. Just two weeks ago, Jessie would have found great pleasure in witnessing the queen of snobbery's fall from her pristine pedestal, but now she realized Rook was right. Coralie had pride, although it looked to have taken a severe beating. Sighing, she held her hand out.

Coralie bit her lower lip. "You want a ride or not?" Jessie felt awkward and didn't like the feeling one bit. As far as she could recall, this was the first time in their association that she'd offered to help. She grinned. For real, this time.

Coralie shoved her matted hair out of her eyes. "I'm not falling for one of your tricks, Jessica Jones. If I try to take your hand, you'll just ride off and laugh at me or you'll let go and watch me fall like you did that time I fell into that pile of cow manure." Coralie's lips trembled.

Jessie closed her eyes, saddened. There was a time when she'd have done just that. Her arm fell back to her side. She was tempted just to ride off, but, glancing down, she saw that exhaustion had overcome Coralie. Jessie frowned and tried once more.

"I'm sorry, Coralie. This isn't a trick. I really want to help." Her voice roughened. "Now, come on. I'm calling a truce—at least until we arrive in Oregon." When Coralie still sat there, Jessie made the first move. She dismounted and took Coralie's arm and pulled her to her feet. She then removed a knife from the leather sheath hanging from the belt around her waist.

"What are you doing?" Coralie squeaked when Jessie grabbed a handful of her skirt.

"Stand still, Coralie. I'm just going to make a couple of slits so you can ride astride. In case you haven't noticed, I don't ride sidesaddle."

"But you'll ruin my dress," she wailed. "This is my last one." Tears flowed down Coralie's cheeks, leaving muddy trails in their wake.

Jessie gave her sister-in-law a hard stare. "Look, Cora," she ordered, deliberately using the nickname Coralie hated, "quit acting so damn snooty. In case you haven't noticed, this isn't town life. Look around you. Do you see anyone wearing their Sunday best?

"Jordan provided you with brand-new dresses, made from the best he could afford. Don't you dare put them down. Anyone would be proud to wear those pretty prints, me included. Now make your choice: ride with me or walk."

Silence fell between them, broken only by Coralie's sniffs as she bent her head to her skirts and wiped her face. Then her head came up, her arms folded across her chest, her blue eyes bright with tears. She pressed her lips together. "Don't call me Cora," she finally said, her voice petulant once again.

Jessie hid a smile at the familiar tone and slid her knife through the material. After making two slits, she stood and remounted. "Put your foot on mine, grab my hand and I'll help you up." When Coralie glanced around for her other shoe, Jessie sighed. "Forget the shoe; it's ruined. Now, come on. We're falling behind."

Coralie took her hand and Jessie pulled her up behind her, then spurred Shilo forward. Coralie gave a cry of surprise and wrapped her hands around Jessie's waist, terrified. Jessie slowed Shilo out of consideration to her onetime nemesis.

"Dang city folk," she muttered then winced when Coralie pinched her side and made a snide comment about country girls.

Jessie coughed to hide her laughter, and by the time they caught up with the others, some of the resentment and animosity that had built over many years and many pranks melted away. Neither spoke, each recognizing that their truce was as fragile as a newborn babe and needed careful nurturing if it were to be forged into something deeper and permanent. It wasn't long before Jessie felt Coralie's head fall against her shoulder, and the grip around her waist loosened. She reached down and grasped her sister-in-law's arms, holding her so she wouldn't fall off the horse as she slept.

Jordan rode away from the herd of cattle, accompanied by loud whistles and hoots of merriment from his brothers and the other hired hands. He ran his hand over his jaw and knew that come tomorrow he'd be at their mercy once again. He laughed. Right now, he didn't care. Wolf had given him the rest of the day off. At long last, he was going to take his wife away and begin his marriage properly.

His mouth broke into a silly grin full of anticipation as he envisioned taking Coralie to a secluded spot along the tree-lined banks of the Kansas River, which they had followed since leaving Westport. He glanced across it. Tomorrow they would tackle swimming the cattle across, but tonight he wouldn't worry over anything but pleasing his wife.

Tonight it was just them, and the thought of being entirely alone with Coralie for the first time since their marriage sent his blood pumping with the eagerness of a randy pup. Some of his excitement dimmed as he thought of her reaction to his plan. He slowed his horse. Would she go with him and become his wife in every sense of the word? A small frown flickered across his features. He was the head of his household, Coralie his wife, his woman; she would go with him.

A groan rose from deep within him. How he wanted her, needed to be her man, her husband—the one who would stand beside her as they began their life together in a new land and the one she'd turn to in times of need. He straightened in his saddle, squaring his shoulders in determination. A silly, love-besotted grin erased the grimness etched around his lips as he recalled the few kisses they'd shared before the wedding. True, they'd been quick, tame little kisses, but he knew she'd enjoyed them.

With a kick, he sent his horse galloping toward the line of white-topped wagons. He'd just have to win her trust and show her she had nothing to fear. When he drew abreast of his brother-in-law, he slowed. Elliot glanced up from his place beside the oxen and greeted him, but Jordan was more interested in fetching his wife. He peered into the back of the wagon, but she wasn't there. "Elliot, where's Coralie?" A thread of panic crept into his voice. If anything had happened to her, he'd never forgive himself.

Elliot grinned and pointed. "Relax, Jordan. She's fine. Look."

Jordan glanced in the direction Elliot indicated. At first he saw only Mrs. Svensson and Mrs. Macauley along with their children. A few feet from them, Rosalyn and Hugh rode, part of the wagon train, yet separate. Then he saw Jessie on horseback, his wife slumped behind her. "Is she all right? She isn't hurt, is she?" he asked, fearing the worst.

"She's sleeping."

Jordan's brows shot up in surprise. "Sleeping!" he parroted in disbelief. "Can't be. Our sisters on one horse without killing one another? I must be dreaming! Are you sure Jess didn't knock her senseless?"

Elliot laughed softly. "I'm sure. I've been watching them for the last hour."

The two men exchanged looks of confusion. "Hey, don't ask me to explain it. I gave up trying to understand the workings of the female mind long ago,'' Elliot offered with a shrug, swatting the oxen to keep them moving.

''Well, I don't care how or why. I just hope the two of them have finally put an end to their feuding ways!'' Jordan dismounted and hopped into the back of the wagon. He gathered a change of clothes for himself and Coralie, rolled them up into a small bundle, then tied them behind the saddle to his bedroll.

As an afterthought, he added one of the canvas tents, and a sack filled with leftover bread and bacon from the morning meal, plus a handful of biscuits, fruit and two large pickles. When everything was tied down, he slapped Elliot on the back. ''A good evening to you, my friend.'' Whistling, Jordan mounted and rode toward his sister and his wife. Before he reached them, he heard Wolf's signal to make camp. Immediately, each family pulled out of line to find a relatively private spot along the river.

Jordan rode up alongside his sister and motioned for her to stop. Reaching over, he gently scooped his wife up into his arms and cradled her to his chest. She barely stirred when he shifted her into a more comfortable position across his thighs. Staring down at the woman he loved, he narrowed his gaze with concern when he noticed that the translucent skin beneath her eyes was tinged purple, lending her a frail, bruised look. His eyes roamed over her face, lingering on the splotches of red and streaks of dried mud over each cheek, and he vowed to be patient with her and try his best to ease her hardship on the journey.

Glancing at Jessie, he nodded. ''Thanks, Jess,'' he whispered.

Jessie glanced away, shrugging as if it wasn't a big deal. Then she pulled the brim of her hat down, tugged on the reins and raced away. But Jordan wasn't fooled. He'd seen the soft glow of compassion in her eyes.

Jessie watched Jordan disappear through a stand of trees near the curve of the river. Silently she wished him luck. She hated to see him so miserable. Shaking her head, she turned

Shilo toward the river and laughed softly at the irony of the situation. Once upon a time, she'd dreamed of seeing her longtime nemesis looking like some ragamuffin, but when it finally happened, sorrow and regret for a past that could never be changed filled her. "Sure hope Coralie doesn't spurn him again, Shilo," she said, reaching down to pat the horse on the neck.

Shilo nickered softly and pulled playfully at the bit. Glancing up, Jessie spotted Rook watering Wolf's horse. Without waiting for direction, Shilo tossed her head and headed toward him. Huffs of air escaped her nostrils.

Jessie let her go. "Thirsty, girl? Or is it Wolf's magnificent stallion that interests you?" Jessie dismounted, eyeing Wolf's horse. What she wouldn't give to ride him just once. She sighed. That day would never happen. After the horses had their fill of water, she unsaddled the two blacks. Wolf's horse was so skittery, only a few people could handle him: her, Duarte and surprisingly, Kerstin. Right on cue, Kerstin appeared at her elbow to finish caring for the horses.

With Shilo in good hands, Jessie unhitched the oxen and washed their backs, checking for any sores caused by the wooden yokes. Then she gave their feet a once-over before watering them, then turning them out to graze. Frowning, she turned away. One of the oxen had loose shoes. She'd let Rook know so they could take the animal into Fort Kearny; it was difficult to shoe an ox on the trail. Oxen weren't able to stand on three legs, so a ditch had to be dug and a harness rigged to cradle the animal over the ditch to allow the men to work on their feet.

"Jessie, the grain is gone," Kerstin announced, dragging an empty feed sack.

Jessie looked into the trough attached to one wagon. "They have plenty for tonight, plus there's lots of grazing," she reassured the young girl. "Why don't you run out to Duarte and tell him we need more for tomorrow?"

"Can I ride Shilo?" The girl's bright, lively blue eyes were wide as she silently pleaded for Jessie to say yes.

Hiding her smile, Jessie knew full well that she couldn't

deny the girl. "Yes, you may ride her." With a whoop of happiness, Kerstin hopped onto Shilo's bare back and rode away, her blond braids flying out behind her. Jessie watched until horse and rider reached the feed wagon, then allowed herself a few minutes to wander to the edge of the river, where the cry of birds hidden from view among tree branches and the chattering of brownish squirrels called out to her. She absorbed the beauty of life, one so different from the one she'd left behind.

She turned her head and stared down the river's wagon-lined banks. The thought of crossing the fast-moving waters left her innards quivering. From her earlier reading, Jessie knew the Kansas River was six hundred feet wide and forty feet deep. Once again, her gaze roamed down the long string of wagons camped along the south side of the river. In the morning, each of those oxen- or mule-drawn wagons would line up and await its turn to be floated across by ferry. She drew comfort in looking at the wagons on the opposite banks. Some of her worry abated. If they had made it over safely, so would Wolf's group.

Jordan cradled his wife close to his chest. When he came to a stand of trees past a twisting bend in the river, he stopped and glanced around. There was no one in sight. Clucking, he urged his horse deeper into the trees. Perfect, he thought, staring at a secluded place near the river. The trees and tall grass shielded them from view, providing them absolute privacy.

He glanced down at her. She looked so frail and vulnerable. His green eyes softened with love. "Cora? Sweetheart, wake up," he murmured tenderly, careful not to startle her. Coralie stirred and mumbled something. With gentle fingers, he swept wispy strands of blond hair away from her face and leaned down to plant a light kiss on her warm, supple lips. This time she stretched, her lips parting. Jordan bent down for another sweet kiss, but Coralie was wide-awake and struggling to sit up.

"Jordan, what—Where am I?" she stammered in confusion, glancing around.

"I've found us the perfect place to make camp. Just think, Cora, just you and me, really alone for the first time since our wedding." He nuzzled the creamy flesh below her ear.

"Don't call me Cora, Jordan. You know I don't like it." She pouted. Suddenly she grew still as comprehension dawned. She pushed at him, trying to put distance between them, but she was wedged between him and the saddle horn. Glancing up at him, her baby blue eyes grew wide, first with dismay, and then the familiar look of fear marred her doll-like features.

Jordan cupped her lower jaw gently and lowered his lips to hers. Slowly and thoughtfully, he nibbled his way from corner to corner, teasing, nipping and tasting, while murmuring reassurances. How he longed to thrust his tongue inside and taste her honeyed moistness, but he forced himself to go slowly, contenting himself with drawing her lower lip into his mouth to suckle. To his infinite pleasure, she slumped in his arms, her hands clutching his shirt. He drew her tightly to him, his heart beating against hers. "Oh, God, Coralie, I've waited so long." His tongue traced the soft fullness of her parted lips.

Coralie sucked in her breath when his tongue touched hers. She was paralyzed with fear and some other emotion she couldn't identify as Jordan's tongue touched and stroked the inside of her mouth. A strange, lethargic feeling washed over her. Her limbs felt heavy. She couldn't have moved had her life depended on it. Her mind screamed that she should put an end to this shocking behavior, but her heart pounded with the pleasure of it. She slid her fingers up his chest and wrapped her arms around his neck, drawing the two of them even closer, wanting this feeling to go on forever.

Of its own accord, her tongue responded to Jordan's demands. Tasting him, she discovered she liked the feel of him in her mouth. When the backs of his fingers caressed her cheek and trailed across her jaw, then down her throat, shivers of delight followed. He continued to murmur soft, loving words as his lips pulled away from hers to trail along the soft curve of her jaw. Then his tongue darted out to lave the inside of one small, perfectly shaped ear. She jerked with surprised pleasure.

Then his lips were everywhere. Across each eyelid, as fleeting as a butterfly searching out the sweetest nectar, they landed briefly, then were gone, only to touch the tip of her turned-up nose before flitting off to tease the corner of her parted lips. Each breath became a gasp of air, a shallow pant. And when his lips kissed the pulsing hollow of her throat, her head fell back as she gave herself up to his wonderful kisses. Just when she thought she'd go mad with his teasing, he lifted his head. Coralie clutched her husband. "Jordan," she cried out, afraid of the pulsing need building deep within her.

"It's okay, love," he murmured. "Open your mouth, Corie, kiss me back." She did, her first attempts clumsy and tentative, but with each passing second she grew bolder, tracing his full, moist lips with the tip of her tongue.

While she explored and learned the taste and feel of him, Jordan's other hand ran up her thigh, over the valley of her waist and moved upward, past her ribs. But when he cupped one full breast with his large hand and kneaded the throbbing flesh, reality returned, and with it a rush of old fears. She panicked. "No, Jordan." She pushed at him in earnest.

Jordan lifted his head, his eyes glazed with love and passion. He stared into her eyes. "What's wrong, sweetheart?" His fingers traced her brows.

Coralie's cheeks burned with shame and humiliation. "It's . . . daylight. We can't do this. Someone might see us," she whispered, desire and fear warring within her.

Jordan took several deep breaths and glanced away from her. He finally dismounted. Reaching up, he lifted her down, holding her against the length of him, pressing that part of him she feared to her belly. "I want you, Coralie; feel how much I need you. Look around you," he urged, his voice gentle. "We're alone."

Coralie stepped out of his arms, away from his hard heat,

shaking her head. "We can't. Someone might come." Coralie's wary gaze roamed over the isolation of the scene. Panic set in. They were alone, just as he said. She gnawed at her lower lip and looked out toward the river, then up and down the banks, searching for the familiar wagons of their party, but only trees, bushes and water met her seeking gaze. "Where is everyone?" Her voice rose with alarm.

Jordan gripped her shoulders gently as he turned her to face him. "The others are camped down thataway." He indicated the direction. "But tonight it's just you and me, Coralie. No more tears, no more games, no more excuses. Tonight we celebrate our wedding and become man and wife in all ways."

Coralie turned her back on her husband, feeling the heat radiating from him. She resisted the urge to lean against his strong, warm chest, resisted the urge to turn and beg him to kiss her again. She enjoyed the kissing, but feared the rest of the marriage act. Her fingers plucked nervously at her skirts. "Please, Jordan, I need more time."

Jordan turned away to unload the horse with a harsh curse. A sliver of pain ran through her when she realized she'd hurt him—again. She bit her lip. She didn't mean to—she liked his kisses—but she didn't want him to hurt her, and she knew from her friends that the act of consummation hurt. Listening to Eirica each night had proved to Coralie that they were right.

Coralie set up their tent, then turned to see Jordan sitting on the hard, cold ground, pulling off his boots. She gulped. Her time had run out. There were no more excuses to be given or accepted. She backed away from the tent.

"What are you doing, Jordan?" she said in a squeak, her eyes wide and wary when he stood, shrugging out of his shirt. But when he unfastened his jeans and looked at her, she held her hands out in front of her, warding him off. "Uh, Jordan? Can't we at least wait until dark? What if someone comes?" she stammered.

"No one will come. There weren't any other wagons behind us all day, and those who got here ahead of us are camped closer to the ferry crossing so they can be among the first to cross tomorrow. I made sure we're well away from everyone else." Then he began to shed the new blue jeans her father had given him.

Coralie turned abruptly and stared out over the river, noticing for the first time the small, secluded cove they were in. She was trapped with nowhere to flee. Begging hadn't done any good, so she drew upon anger. "If you think for one moment I'll allow you to do this to me, you've got another think coming, Jordan. I won't allow you to do this. Take me back to my brother," she ordered.

"No, we are husband and wife. You've nothing to fear. I'll be gentle," he reassured her, coming up behind her.

Suddenly she found herself swept off her feet and cradled against her husband's broad, hard chest. Fear of the unknown brought the roar of blood pulsing in her ears.

When Jordan spoke, his voice seemed to come from far away. "How about a bath first?"

Startled, she stared up into his twinkling gaze and realized he was carrying her into the water. "Jordan, I don't want to bathe in the river," she said. "It's too cold."

Jordan chuckled. "I'll warm you up," he promised, pushing his way through the fast-moving current until he was waist-deep in the water. Coralie tightened her hold around his neck. She struggled to remain above the gently swirling river tugging at her skirts.

"Let me heat some water and bathe in the tent. You can bathe in the river."

"Uh uh, I've waited too long for this. We'll bathe together."

Jordan lowered them both, keeping his arms tight around her. Coralie barely had time to grab a breath before he dunked them both under. As they surfaced, the scream died in her throat, and she sucked in her breath against the cold water swirling around her. Jordan shook his head, sending droplets of water flying.

Coralie held up her hands to block the droplets of water. Stepping back, she slipped under. Jordan grabbed her and pulled her to him. "Now, doesn't that feel better?" He grinned.

Sputtering and choking, Coralie didn't know whether to scream or cry. The current tugged at her ruined skirts, trying to pull her back down. She was forced to grab hold of her husband for balance. Jordan held up a small sliver of soap and began to work up a lather.

In spite of her anger, she was mesmerized by her husband's loving gaze. She stood still when his fingers moved over her face, gently washing away the dirt and grime. Next he lathered her hair and neck, turning her so he could reach each strand of her hair and massage her whole head. Coralie closed her eyes to avoid the stinging soap and found herself awed by the gentleness of her husband's touch.

"There, now rinse yourself, Corie. I've got you. I won't let you drown."

Coralie sank into the swirling water and rinsed the soap from her hair and face. When she surfaced, she wiped the water out of her eyes and glared at her husband, unwilling to admit that she did in fact feel much better.

She tried to return to the bank, but Jordan refused to budge. "I'm cold, Jordan, let me . . ." Her voice faded when he rubbed the cake of soap across his hair-covered chest, his bulging arms and the two-week-old growth of stubble on his jaw. Coralie sighed with pleasure when he ran his slick hands over hers, soaping her hands.

She buried her fingers amid the lather-covered dark hairs covering his chest. Then he dropped the bar of soap into the water. She turned her head to watch the soap sail away on the current like some small boat caught in the rapids. Her resistance fled, floating downstream with it. Giving in to the desire to touch her husband, she moved her fingers in small, ever-widening circles, smoothing the soap across the wide expanse of his sun-darkened skin.

Jordan sucked in his breath, and she pulled her hands away, afraid that she'd done something wrong. He looked as if he were in pain, but he guided her hands back over the

139

erect nubs of his nipples. "See what you do to me with just your sweet touch." He groaned.

Coralie licked her lips and eyed her handsome husband. "Jordan, do you think you could kiss me again—like you did before? I did like it."

Jordan pulled her close, his hands threading themselves through her tangled mass of wet blond hair. She moaned and fell against him, giving herself over to his knee-weakening kiss and heated caresses, and didn't even protest when he yanked her skirts over her head and dropped the ruined material into the river to be claimed by the greedy current swirling around them. She didn't care. An aching need filled her, overriding all her fear of becoming a woman.

And this time, when he reached down to take her full, creamy breasts in his hands, she leaned into him. Then he claimed her lips once more, his hands moving around to grip her buttocks as he pulled her into the cradle of his hips. Hot waves of longing washed over her when she felt his hard, pulsing heat.

Jordan scooped her up into his arms and waded out of the river. His eyes, hot with love and desire, promised greater pleasures, but when he reached the entrance to the tent, he stopped and stared down at her, as if afraid she'd changed her mind. Coralie lifted one hand to his cheek. "I love you, Jordan. I'm ready to become your wife," she whispered, sealing her fate.

Chapter Ten

Early the next day, the emigrants were ready to cross the Kansas River. Wolf snapped orders until the wagons were lined up at Pappan's Ferry Crossing long before the first sign of daylight. Joseph and Louis Pappan ferried emigrants and their wagons and oxen across the Kansas River for six-plus dollars per family.

He threw himself into the hard work of lowering the wagons by rope down the steep banks to be loaded onto boats, which consisted of two canoes bridged with poles. Each boat held two wagons and ten to twelve oxen. Once they reached the other bank, double teams were required to pull the wagons up and away from the river. The crossing took all morning. When the last wagon was loaded, Wolf stood on the bank of the Kansas River, hands on his hips and feet spread. The loud protests of cattle drew his attention downstream. James and Jordan were herding them into the water.

As soon as the last of the cattle and horses were safely across, Wolf led the wagons upstream to a relatively quiet spot far from the crossing confusion, then stopped, giving the emigrants another day to rest. The men tended to their animals; then a few took off on foot to try their hand at hunting, while the rest sat around smoking their pipes or napping. But for the women, there were endless tasks that needed doing, the most time-consuming being the laundry. Anne and Eirica knelt at the stream with piles of soiled garments. Kerstin and Hanna knelt beside their mother, soaking the clothes in the river.

Jessie and Coralie joined them, their arms full with not only their own soiled clothing but also that of their brothers. Coralie had also volunteered to do Rook's wash in return for cooking lessons. The women grimaced at one another as they plunged their hands into the ice-cold water. Word spread that the women were doing laundry, and before long the single men in their party had shown up with bundles of dirty clothes. The men, abhorring the idea of doing woman's work, offered good pay to Eirica and Anne to do theirs.

As the day wore on, Jessie found herself watching her sister-in-law. She couldn't believe the overnight change. This morning Coralie had returned to camp wearing a pretty calico dress of cream and blue, the same style worn by the other two women, and on her feet, she wore brand-new boots. Jessie hid her grin. Never had she thought to see the day when Miss Priss dressed in plain, everyday garb.

Beside her, Coralie stood and shook out her skirts. "Look how wet and muddy my skirt is," she wailed.

Jessie and Anne rolled their eyes at each other and watched Coralie move to a less muddy spot before plunging her hands back into the water to scrub one of Jordan's shirts. "Well, some things haven't changed," Jessie murmured with a soft chuckle.

Eirica bit her lip to keep from laughing. She called out to Coralie, "Don't worry, Coralie. That dress'll wash and be as good as new."

That brought on another groan. "I never want to see another dirty piece of clothing again. How can there be so much? Look at my hands. They'll never be the same again," she finished sadly, staring at her hands.

"Welcome to the real world, Corie," Jessie said, wiping a stray curl off her forehead. She stared at her own hands. Between the harsh soap and the cold water, they all suffered with red and raw hands. Silence fell. Jessie hid her grin, knowing it would be only a matter of time before the complaints started up again, but for all her griping, Coralie did her fair share. Not once had she tried to weasel out of it, and that alone amazed Jessie. She sneaked another glance at her sister-in-law, noting her flushed cheeks and her eyes sparkling with a hint of some inner knowledge.

Jessie sat back on her heels when the last of the clothing had been rinsed. This time it was she who groaned as she stretched the kinks from her aching back. Together she and Coralie carried the wet clothes to a group of trees, where Jordan and Elliot had strung lines of rope. When they were through hanging the clothes to dry, Jessie moved to help Eirica and Anne finish theirs. Her jaw dropped when Coralie silently joined her. She'd assumed that once she was finished, Coralie would hightail it back to her tent. But without complaint, she began the process all over again, assisting Anne, which left Jessie to help Eirica with the children's clothing.

Much later, the last load was hung out to dry. Eirica rubbed her lower back. "Thank the good Lord that's done," she said with a moan.

The others echoed her sentiment. Jessie was just going to suggest putting on some water for coffee or tea, but Jordan came up behind Coralie.

"If you ladies don't mind, I'd like to take my wife for a walk before dinner." Coralie blushed and smiled shyly at her husband. Hand in hand, the couple left.

Jessie and Eirica looked at each other and grinned. Jessie shook her head, confused. "I can't believe the change in her. What did Jordan say to her last night? She's even wearing the clothes he bought for her."

Anne laughed. "Oh, Jessie, it's not what he said; it's what he did."

This time it was Jessie who turned pink from the neck up. Raised in a household of men, she wasn't totally innocent of what went on between a male and female, married or not. "But Anne, they've been married over a week. Are you saying they've not, uh, you know . . ."

The older woman grew solemn, her blue eyes serious. "I think your sister-in-law feared the marriage bed, but seeing her today, I think it's safe to say that your brother convinced her that there's nothing to fear.''

Eirica broke in, her tone wistful. "She's lucky, so very, very lucky to have a kind and gentle husband. Not to mention being surrounded by her family,'' she finished, her voice dropping to a mere whisper.

Jessie bit her lip and lowered her gaze to Eirica's hand, which rested on the gentle swell of her abdomen. "Oh, Eirica, I wish there were something I could do,'' she dared to say aloud. She wanted to put her arms around Eirica's shoulders, but she didn't dare in view of the others.

Eirica straightened and shook her head. "It's not your problem, Jessie. You've helped a great deal just by listening and being my friend. Back home, Birk never allowed me have friends of my own, but here, on the trail, he can't do much to prevent it.'' Her eyes filled with tears. "I'll treasure each day and pray that when we get to Oregon, we can find some way to remain friends.''

A lump formed in Jessie's throat, and she reached out to squeeze the other woman's hand. "Don't worry; we'll always be friends,'' she whispered, averting her gaze from the fading bruise on Eirica's cheek. She wished there were a way to get back at Birk for some of the pain he'd inflicted on his wife.

Jessie realized her wish several days later when she was out walking along the river to get away from Wolf's bothersome presence. Heading upstream, away from the long line of wagons camped along its banks, she followed the beckoning cool, blue river. Though she was tempted to stop and bathe, she didn't dare. She'd have to wait until dark, and even that was becoming risky, as she'd discovered last night.

Luckily, she'd already dried and dressed when Wolf had come strolling out of the darkness. That close call had sent her heart into a panic, and as she'd fled back to her wagon, she could have sworn she'd heard him laughing. There was something else that disturbed her: his smile and easy banter.

Rounding the bend, she stopped when she noticed a lone

man bathing in the river. She turned away to give him his privacy, but stopped when she recognized the angry, muttering voice. Dropping down to her hands and knees, she crept forward. Yep, it was Birk, and he was drinking. She watched him toss his flask to the bank and stifled a groan, knowing he'd likely return to his family drunk.

Staring at his clothes, she plotted. Perhaps she could take his clothes and delay his return—but then she discarded the idea. It'd just put him in an even nastier mood. She glanced at the sun's position to gauge how long she'd been gone. That was when she spotted it—a hornet's nest—high up in one of the cottonwood trees at the water's edge. Her gaze shifted from the hornets back to Birk, and she bit her lip to still the gurgle of laughter that threatened to spill forth. Even as she wondered if she dared, she was pulling a slingshot from her back pocket.

Her eyes narrowed when she remembered Eirica's bruised cheek and the finger-sized bruises she'd seen on four-year-old Alison's arm that morning. Yes, she dared. Searching the ground for several small stones, she kept an eye on Birk, waiting until he ducked his head beneath the water. Taking careful aim, she fired three rocks in rapid succession. She heard his cries of pain echo past her as she fled.

On day sixteen, the emigrants arrived at Alcove Springs. Jessie stood below the rocky ledge of the falls. Above her, clear springwater spilled over the brink, falling ten feet to splash into a large pool at her feet. Behind the waterfall, she spotted a dark alcove carved into the rocks. Reaching down, she dipped her fingers into the pool and shivered. It was icy cold. She quickly abandoned the idea of trying to get behind the falls to explore, and instead opted to soak up the beauty surrounding her.

The spring was heavily timbered with oak, cedar, ash and a few other trees green with the delicate color of spring. Around the rocky pool, lush grass mingled with a profusion of wildflowers. Color bloomed everywhere, lending a romantic aura to the setting that her fingers itched to commit to paper. Bending down, she picked a small yellow flower. Twirling the thin stem gently between thumb and forefinger, she inhaled the sweet scent while staring into the pool at a large rock with a name and date etched into its surface.

Despite the warmth of the day, she shivered. Like most emigrants, she'd heard the horrible story of the Donner party. At least James Frazier Reed's mother-in-law, Sarah Keyes, had been spared the horrific winter her party suffered when they became stranded in the Sierras. At the age of seventy, she'd died here of consumption. Traveling with them, Edwin Bryant had given the springs its present name, while another member of that ill-fated Donner party, George McKinstry, had carved the name above the brink of the fall.

Jessie forced thoughts of the Donner party from her mind, grateful that Wolf, for all his hateful ways, was an experienced guide who tolerated no lolling about. He set a hard pace, and she, for one, could fully appreciate it after this reminder. Her gaze swept the area, absorbing the historical surroundings. After climbing the small hillside, she stood over the ledge, watching the water spill downward. The sun warmed her as she lowered herself to the ground and sat, half-hidden by the branches of an ash tree growing ten feet below her.

Tipping her head back, Jessie sighed with contentment. In the last week they'd traveled over the gently undulating prairie past St. Mary's and Scott Springs, covering a hundred and sixty-six miles in sixteen days. She yawned. Being able to sit and do nothing felt so good, but it also left her feeling guilty. She felt bad that neither Anne nor Eirica had the luxury of much free time with her husband and children. They were kept busy every minute of their day. Even when they rode in the wagons, their time was put to good use as they knitted winter sweaters and mittens or mended torn shirts. She'd even caught Anne mixing bread dough so it could rise while they traveled.

Jessie brushed a fly from her nose. But whether married or single, with or without children, there was one task that fell to the uprooted women. They were recorders of life and

146

death. Each day, the number of graves passed was noted in their diaries, and sometimes, if the markers were legible, the names of the unfortunate souls might also be written in the daily entry. And the same went for births. Just yesterday Anne had assisted in the birth of a baby boy.

But always birth seemed shadowed by death. Jessie recalled two rock-covered graves of children that she and Eirica had passed earlier that day. Eirica had grown quiet, hugging Ian to her breast as they walked past the tiny mounds of earth that gave testimony to the harshness of trail life. Jessie recorded their names in her diary, and suspected Eirica would do so also.

Pushing the depressing thoughts from her mind, she leaned back on her hands, her chin pointed toward the sun as she let her mind wander. It was easy in this idealistic, romantic place to imagine being alone in the secluded pool below to bathe and frolic in the dark, mysterious waters, surrounded only by lush greenery. Flipping over onto her stomach, hands propped under her chin, she frowned and watched a small bee buzzing at some wildflowers near her elbow; then she picked up a small rock and tossed it over the falls. It landed in the pool with a splash, shattering the perfect stillness of the water.

As she watched the rippling rings in the water grow larger, moving ever outward from that one small disturbance, she felt as if Wolf were a rock that someone had dropped into her life. Each day the ripple of awareness grew, leaving her confused, disturbed by her thoughts and feelings for the wagon master.

Ever since the night he'd relieved her from guard duty early, he'd become much friendlier. Anxiety rumbled through her, but she wasn't sure why. Plucking a blade of grass, Jessie chewed it and contemplated the changes in Wolf's attitude. During their first week on the trail, he'd found fault with whatever she did, but during this last week, he'd quit criticizing her and no longer piled on the extra chores. But he hadn't stopped watching her. In fact, the more she thought about it, the more convinced she was that he watched her more. Her brow knitted with confusion. Why? What had changed between them? An unpleasant thought occurred to her. Did he know?

The thought that he knew her secret didn't sit well with her. Her fingers nervously picked at the grass as her mind raced with the possibilities. After a few minutes, she discarded the notion. She just couldn't imagine him remaining silent. But then, why was he being so nice to her? Every time she turned around, there he was with a helping hand—which astounded her.

From cold and aloof to warm and friendly. It just didn't make sense. She closed her eyes and dropped her head to her fisted hands, confused and unsettled by Wolf's strange behavior—like last night, when he'd ordered her to demonstrate her knowledge of knots. She groaned as she recalled his insistence on teaching her a new knot. Wolf's method of teaching involved lots of close contact: working shoulder to shoulder, his long fingers guiding hers as he taught her the squaw knot. When she'd mastered it, he patted her shoulder in a manly gesture of encouragement.

She grew warm just thinking about his hard, lean body so close to hers. This new attitude toward her was driving her to distraction. What was she going to do? A helpful and friendly Wolf was torturous, far worse than when he barked out orders. While it was nice to have him off her back, she wished he'd go back to being mean and obnoxious. That she could handle!

"What is wrong with me?" she asked herself, torn between her conflicting emotions. It was times like this that she missed her ma. She had so many questions about what was happening inside her. Her brothers would think her crazy if she started talking about weak limbs, shortness of breath and a racing heart. And sometimes her stomach fluttered at the very thought of Wolf. Just thinking about it brought on a familiar ache. "Stop thinking of him," she commanded herself, willing her racing pulse to calm. This was ridiculous nonsense, pure and simple.

When she heard the sound of someone whistling, she lifted

her head, grateful for any diversion that would take her mind off Wolf. Edging closer to the ledge, she glanced down, then gasped and dropped her head back to the ground, praying that the tall grass concealed her presence from the very man who haunted her thoughts. She slowly inched back from the edge. The last thing she wanted right now was for Wolf to see her here, away from camp, where they were alone. She didn't trust herself or her feelings for him, especially as she had no trouble envisioning them together, hidden from the world behind the falls below. Her lashes fluttered closed, and in her mind's eye she saw him: his golden brown hair dark from the water, his eyes bluer than the sky above and his lips as soft as his chest was hard.

Her breathing quickened and her eyes shot open, filled with dismay and longing. Her heart raced, and she wondered just what it was about the wagon master that drew her like a bee to a sweetly scented bloom. Each day he intruded into her thoughts, her dreams, and now even her fantasies.

Life would be considerably simpler if it were still Elliot who held her heart, but it wasn't. The dream of one day becoming his wife and the mother of his children—miniatures of their easygoing father—no longer held any appeal to her. Since leaving home, she acknowledged that her feelings for Elliot had been no more than a young girl's starry-eyed first love. What she'd taken to be love had faded into a strong friendship. And while she still considered Elliot handsome, his looks paled beside the formidable and frustrating White Wolf.

The silence broke through her thoughts. The cheerful whistling had stopped. Was he gone? Jessie scooted forward, peering through a small bush. "Oh, my God." She gasped, her eyes growing wide as she gulped air into her burning lungs. Wolf stood below her—gloriously naked!

Jessie squeezed her eyes shut, but of their own accord they opened to feast on his muscular and sun-baked backside. From the broad shoulders down to lean, tapered hips, he presented a magnificent sight. But it was that one narrow swath of pale skin, the tight slope of his buttocks, that sent blood crashing through her veins like rapids churning down a river. Her face grew hot, and a hard, tight ball of desire seemed to seize her stomach.

With agonizing slowness, she watched him enter the pool of water until it lapped at the bottom of his buttocks. She must have made some sound, however slight, because he suddenly turned and faced her. Jessie closed her eyes against that most private part of him, but not fast enough. She'd caught a glimpse.

And unfortunately that one small peek was enough to take her breath away. How foolish she'd been to think she was immune to the male body! She backed away. She had to get out of there, but it was too late. She'd been spotted. When Wolf called her name, she nearly died of embarrassment.

"You sleeping up there, Jess? Water's fine if you want to come down for a dip." Jumping to her feet, Jessie fled.

Wolf's laughter drifted over the pond. Oh, it was so perfect, he thought with a shake of his head. If Jessie had been thinking clearly, she'd have realized that men and boys washed or relieved themselves together on a daily basis. She'd given herself away and hadn't even realized it! Her flight also told him that she wasn't immune to him. She was attracted, all right, and he planned to make full use of that.

What a stroke of luck that she'd been up there. He waded over to the falls and let the steady stream of water wash the trail dust from his body. As the cool water hit his skin, pangs of guilt assailed him, but his fury at being so thoroughly duped quickly overrode any misgivings.

His pride still smarted. By observing the emigrants carefully, he'd ascertained that everyone but the Nortons knew the truth. He figured that the only reason Hugh and Rosalyn didn't know was because they kept to themselves. Well, he'd show Jessica Jones. He'd teach her the folly of pretending to be something she wasn't. His plan to make her uncomfortable in her role of a boy was going better than he'd hoped. Each day he made it a point to have some sort of physical contact with her, and it was succeeding beyond his original hopes.

He knew she was battling her attraction to him, that the pretense of being a boy was becoming harder with each passing day—exactly as he'd planned. "This'll teach her a lesson," he declared, wading out of the pond. His smile faded as he grabbed his clothes and stared down at himself. Trouble was, he too was paying a price for indulging in his little game of revenge. Just her gaze on him had been enough to stir him, forcing him to sit in the water quickly to hide his swelling erection. His mind might deny his desire, but his body couldn't.

After donning his buckskin pants, Wolf rested his hands on his hips and shook his head, sending droplets of water into the air. He was disgusted with himself for slipping under her spell despite his intention to remain aloof. His gaze narrowed. He didn't like this feeling of impending doom, of helplessness—not one bit.

He'd sworn to guard his heart against a woman's wiles, and before Jessie he hadn't had any trouble maintaining the cold and forbidding demeanor he so carefully adopted around all women. But Jessie was like no other woman he'd ever met. Something about her drew him against his will. Despite her impulsiveness and her tendency toward wild and mischievous behavior, he knew he'd pegged her wrong that very first time he'd seen her from Lolita's window. From Elliot, he'd learned of the long-standing feud between Jessie and Coralie.

Over the last two weeks, he'd also discovered that Jessie harbored a kind and generous nature that was apparent in all the little things she did each day, like giving rides to the young Macauley children or spending time with the Svenssons' girls, who openly adored her. Even Wahoska, who had no use for most humans, had fallen under her spell. In the evenings, the wolf could usually be seen dogging her heels, despite her dog's resentment.

Wolf rolled his shoulders, his gaze narrowed. Her temper was her biggest flaw, and he had shamelessly used it to build the barriers between them. Ah, it felt good to know which strings to pull. Getting her riled was easy, and watching Rook or one of her brothers hold her back gave him immense satisfaction. A soft laugh broke forth as he conceded that Jessie Jones was a feisty, spirited filly.

Wolf stared up at the sky, then gave the treetops careful consideration. Another soft laugh escaped. Yep, she was spunky, all right. He just had to make sure he stayed away from trees with hornets' nests. Macauley had been stung so severely, he'd been forced to remain in the wagon, swollen. Wolf shook his head, recalling Birk's screams as he'd run into camp naked, red welts covering his body. After he and Rook had seen to the man's stings, Wolf had gone to the river to retrieve Birk's clothing. While there, he'd found three rocks on the pile of clothes and spotted the holes in the nest above.

Someone had deliberately riled those hornets, and by the pleased smirk Jessie had worn the rest of the evening, Wolf knew she'd found a way to exact revenge on Eirica's behalf.

Wolf finished dressing. If he were smart, he'd keep his distance from her, deliver the whole damn bunch of Joneses to Oregon, then get the hell out of there, but deep inside he knew he couldn't. A twig snapped behind him. Whirling about, cursing himself for being careless, Wolf wrapped his hand around the hilt of his knife. It was Rosalyn, standing behind him. He should have known it'd be her. She made it a point to try to come upon him whenever he was alone. Wolf hid his displeasure and resheathed his knife.

"Why, Wolf, what are you doing here all by your lonesome?" she cooed, her voice low and seductive. "What a shame you've already bathed. I could have washed your back for you." She ran her fingers up and down his chest.

Wolf grabbed her fingers and squeezed, noting that her eyes were filled with desire as she stared at his bare chest. "I've told you before, Rosalyn, I don't mess around with married women. You don't interest me. Get it through your head." Ignoring her harsh, indrawn breath, he removed her hand and walked away, his vest and moccasins gripped in one hand.

Chapter Eleven

Jessie bit back a yawn as she and Rook repacked the wagons. In between handing Rook the supplies, she nibbled on a hard biscuit and drank her coffee. Lifting the half-empty tin cup to her lips, she grimaced. It was stone cold. She poured the remaining coffee out onto the ground and stared up into the bleak, early morning sky. Her gaze swept across the wide expanse above them, noting the dark, roiling clouds that were heavy with the promise of rain.

"Why the rush, Rook?" she asked, handing him the empty coffeepot, then bending down to pick up a sack. "We only have a mile to go to reach the Big Blue." Receiving no answer, she tossed the sack of hard biscuits into the wagon.

"Hey, watch it," Rook shouted, poking his head out the back.

Jessie winced. "Sorry. Didn't know you were still in there."

"Dang foolish young'uns," Rook muttered.

Jessie yawned again and leaned against the side of the wagon, listening to Rook mutter to himself. Tuning him out, she rubbed her eyes. She hadn't slept well, and it was all Wolf's fault. Her dreams had been punctuated by visions of his golden, sculpted body. Never in her wildest fantasies had she imagined that the sight of a naked man could affect her so. The memory of him standing below her in the pool left her breathless, even in the light of the new day.

She remembered how the sunlight caressed his tight buttocks, gleamed across his broad back and rock hard chest. But what left her feeling weak-kneed was the memory of the dark golden curls that arrowed downward to surround his male member. She'd been raised with three brothers, so the male body held no secrets for her. But before yesterday she'd never really given much thought to *that* part of a male body. At Coralie and Jordan's small wedding, many of Coralie's friends had whispered behind gloved hands all the horrors they'd heard about the wedding night, but Jessie hadn't paid much attention to their silly chatter.

Unlike her sister-in-law, Jessie looked forward to discovering the secrets between a man and a woman. She imagined how it might feel to touch and explore his firm, heated flesh, and she longed for him to kiss her. She groaned, her head falling back against the canvas of the wagon, her cheeks suffused with heat.

"Hey," Rook shouted, sticking his head out the back. "You gonna hand me up the rest of the stuff or not? What's with ya this mornin'? Quit yer daydreamin'. We's got work to do," he ordered, nudging her head from inside the wagon.

"All right, all right," she grumbled, feeling out of sorts. "Here, take this." She handed him the lantern, then kicked dirt over the small firepit and poured a bucket of water on top of it for good measure. "Why the rush this morning?" she asked for the second time, tossing the remains of her biscuit away.

Rook climbed down from the loaded wagon. "See them clouds?"

Jessie glanced up and shrugged. "So? Looks like rain. Won't be the first day we've had rain. What's that got to do with anything?"

Rook shook his cold and empty pipe at her. "If it's gonna storm here, then you can bet it's gonna be stormin' upriver— if it ain't already. The Blue rises fast. If we don't cross afore the storm breaks, we might find ourselves stuck here for a long while, waitin' for the water to go down. Now, enough talk. Git them oxen hitched."

White Wolf

The sun was barely peeping over the horizon when the wagons rolled the short distance toward the north fork of the Big Blue. When they arrived at the crossing, Jessie drew Shilo to a halt and stared at the sight before her in open-mouthed amazement. The Big Blue was a large, deep river. Gnawing at her lower lip, she dismounted. Unlike at the Kansas and Vermillion rivers, there was no one to ferry them across. They'd have to ford the swirling waters on their own.

But staring into the steely gray sky, Jessie worried that it was already too late. Leaf-laden branches whipped to and fro in a mad frenzy and churned the river to a foamy white. She glanced at Rook doubtfully. "Are you sure it's safe to cross?" Her eyes grew wider as she tried to take in all the noise and confusion. They weren't the only ones trying to cross before the storm broke.

Mules brayed, oxen lowed and women and children screamed. Adding to the profusion of chaos came the sound of the men cursing and swearing in several languages. Rook patted her on the shoulder. "Don't worry none, lass. We'll git across jest fine. Let's git lined up."

Jessie held Shilo by the reins, watching anxiously as a small party of six wagons proceeded to cross. The wind howled and ripped at the canvas covers, rocking the wagons. Three wagons had already made it across, and the fourth one plunged into the water. She glanced around, noting other wagons camped along the banks, not anywhere near ready to cross as men sat around finishing their meals. She lifted her nose to the wind, inhaling the aroma of bacon. Her belly rumbled in protest. "They got to fix a hot meal," she grumbled beneath her breath.

Rook heard her. "Aye, they did, but I reckon they won't make it across afore the river swells. Looks like we's goin' next."

"Oh, fine. Lucky us," Jessie mumbled, not sure she wanted to go through this. Suddenly she needed reassurance from her family. "I'm going to find Jordan and see how Coralie's doing." Just as she turned away, shrill screams rent the air.

155

She jerked around just in time to see that the wagon in the river had fallen prey to the strong winds and relentless current. Helplessly, those on the banks watched the overloaded wagon tip over. Choruses of screams came from both sides of the banks and rose in volume. "Oh, my God," she cried in horror, her gaze glued to the middle of the river, where three young children and their mother clung to the inside of the sinking wagon. There was no sign of the father.

Jessie forced her way through the onlookers gathered at the bank. Already several men on horses were swimming toward the fear-stricken family.

"Stay put," Wolf ordered, plunging in on horseback. Jessie held her breath when she saw him reach out and grab two of the children. Someone else grabbed the mother and the third child. When Wolf reached the bank, sobbing relatives took the children from him. The mother and other child joined them, but the father was nowhere in sight. Men fanned out along the river bank.

Jessie sat frozen with fear. She stared at the wagon, but it was too late to save it. The greedy current carried most of the lighter items downstream. The oxen pulling the wagon had drowned, unable to free themselves of their yokes. A shout from downstream brought a hush over the crowded banks. Jessie couldn't hear what was said, but word quickly spread that the man had been found alive. A wave of relief rushed over the emigrants.

Jessie rejoined Rook. He laid a comforting hand across her shoulders. "Don't fret, now, lass. They's safe. Damn fools, overloading them wagons with heavy furniture."

"But what will happen to them, Rook?" Her voice was husky with emotion. She'd seen that family several times along the trail and knew they were all related, traveling together, the young and old, all with the common goal of starting a new life in California.

Wolf came up behind her, heard her question and stopped. "Unfortunately they will continue on, blinded by dreams of becoming rich. But not, I hope, before they unload some excesses from their other wagons."

He stared at her, his gaze hard and unrelenting. "Forget them, Jess. Only the tough and prepared survive. Remember that the cowards never started, and the weak die along the way." With that bleak forecast, he rode off.

Jessie stared, openmouthed. "How horrible! What a mean thing to say," she said, trembling with the aftershock of the disaster. "That man and his family nearly drowned!"

Rook patted her on the shoulder. "Life is full of tragedy, lass. Ya listen ta him. He might be an arrogant bastard at times, but he knows what he's doin'. Them folk are fools and are lucky no one drowned."

The strong winds ripped across the water and tore through leaves and branches, causing the limbs to twist, bend and tangle together. Several wagons turned away, their owners fearful of the impending storm and the near loss of life. But not Wolf. He knew this was no small spring shower but a full-blown storm. They either crossed now or waited a week or more for the waters to recede. Bellowing out commands, he ordered the removal of all wagon covers, including the hickory-slat frames, in order to lessen the saillike effect.

After witnessing the disastrous scene earlier, each man, woman and child hastened to obey his orders. The dangers and harsh realities of what was in store during the coming months weighed heavily on all. And though it wasn't too late to turn back, no one voiced such a suggestion. The call of the promised land beckoned, giving them the strength to meet the challenge at hand.

Each wagon was lowered by rope down the bank, and the Oregon-bound emigrants crossed the gravel-bottomed river in grim silence. Prayers were said and thanks given for each wagon that made it across under Wolf's expert guidance. Once the wagons were on the other side of the bank, their canvas covers were quickly replaced. Water barrels and canteens were checked and filled, as there was a good chance they wouldn't find another drinkable source of water until they reached the Little Blue.

The skies opened up, and fat drops of rain pelted the earth. The downpour blinded man and beast, but still they continued. Wolf exchanged his stallion for a fresh mount and issued orders to start swimming the cattle and horses across. After dozens of trips into the water he was chilled to the bone, but there was no time to stop and warm himself—the water had already risen past the booted feet of the men on horseback. His voice rose to join with the others as they urged, shouted, swore and flicked their whips over the heads of the wild-eyed, brawling cattle.

By the time the cattle and the remuda had been driven across and counted, the rain was falling in a steady downpour. When the final count came in, Wolf was thankful that he'd lost only a few head of cattle. He gave the signal to move on. Both men and beasts were weary, but he pushed onward. Originally he'd planned to take another much-needed day of rest after crossing, but now he wanted to get away from the angry-looking river. Hunched over the neck of his horse, he rode ahead, searching for a sheltered place to camp.

That night, the cold, wet and miserable weather made an evening fire impossible. The emigrants were forced to settle for another cold meal and damp clothing. The contrary weather stayed with them through the next day as well. It didn't storm hard enough to force a halt to the traveling, but it was wet enough to make their lives miserable as they plodded on.

With the abundance of rain, a new problem arose. Wagon after wagon mired down in the thick, oozing mud of the prairie. Precious time and energy was spent double-teaming the oxen to break the wagons free. Tempers grew short and nerves were frayed. On the third consecutive day of wet weather, Wolf was forced to stop early when an axle on one of the Svenssons' wagons snapped.

It was early afternoon, and a small patch of blue streaked across the sky to dispel some of the gloom that hung over the group of weary travelers. He frowned when he noticed another bank of dark clouds looming on the horizon. There would be more rain. Angry voices rose behind him. He closed his mind to the squabbling as wagons were corralled and oxen unhitched. Running one hand over his jaw, he stared out across the open prairie and spotted a small herd of antelope in the distance. He stroked a finger down his nose. A plan took shape. He found Rook. "I'm going out to hunt. Fresh meat should perk spirits up around here."

Rook puffed on his pipe, then nodded. "Mebbe we should have one meal for all and git Lars and them Jones boys to play some music to lift spirits. If you takes care of the huntin', I'll organize the rest."

"Good idea." Wolf slapped Rook on the back, then caught sight of Jessie walking toward them. He watched her run slender fingers through her hair, fluffing the curls to form a cloud of ebony softness that surrounded her elfin features. With difficulty he hardened his heart to the pull of the woman before him, but it was getting harder to resist her.

"Oxen unhitched, Rook," she announced, interrupting his dark thoughts. When she saw him, she stopped and turned away.

Wolf narrowed his gaze, then grinned. She'd avoided him ever since his dip in Alcove Springs, and due to the adverse weather and the resultant problems that had plagued the wagon train, he'd been forced to concentrate on other matters. But perhaps it was time to pick up where he'd left off.

"What's that no-good grin fer?" Rook demanded.

Wolf raised his left brow. "Think I'll find out just how good a hunter your young protégée is." He walked away, ignoring the old man's sputters of protest. Molding his features into a stern and forbidding glare, Wolf called out to her.

"Got a job for you, *boy*."

Jessie made a face, her eyes wary and her voice cross as she asked, "What?"

He bit back a grin and pointed. "See them antelope yonder?"

When she nodded, he continued, "We're going to get us one."

"We," she choked out, looking around for an excuse not

to go. "Maybe you should ask Rickard or Bjorn to go. I've still got chores to do, and I'm tired."

Wolf knew she was tired from her late-night wanderings with Eirica. The two of them often strolled at night now, many times without talking, until Eirica tired enough to return to her family and sleep. Neither woman knew he was always nearby in case of trouble.

Wolf wasn't willing to risk a repeat of the last incident. Now he made it his business to learn about the wagon trains they came across. The man Jessie had whipped was part of a small party of seedy-looking men heading for California.

"The Svensson boys are busy, and your other chores can wait. Time's awastin'; let's go."

Jessie's green eyes filled with a combination of fear and excitement. Wolf wondered which would win. He didn't have long to wait. She turned wide, innocent eyes on him. "I've never hunted anything so big. I'd just scare them away."

He coughed to cover a laugh. What a lie! She was a good hunter. He suspected that the only reason she hadn't killed anything bigger than rabbits or prairie chickens before now was because she didn't have time in the evenings to preserve any uncooked meat from a larger animal.

Suddenly he found himself looking forward to the hunt. Not just the hunt, he realized with a jolt. Every predator knew the fun was in the chase, and the closer he got to closing in on her, the weaker his anger was. He had to force himself to remember his purpose. "It's lucky for you that I'm willing to teach you. Let's go."

Left with no choice other than that of making a scene, Jessie fetched Shilo and followed Wolf. Watching his hair stream behind him, she bit her lip. What was he up to now? His motives for taking her hunting were questionable, but the thought of having fresh, hot meat with supper overcame her feeling of unease.

Wolf led them in a wide circle, staying downwind of the prey. When he stopped and dismounted, she followed suit.

"We'll go the rest of the way on foot to keep from spooking them," he whispered.

Jessie nodded. Hunting the larger animals out in the open prairie wasn't easy, which was her main reason for sticking to the smaller game. On horseback, the small game were easier to scare out of hiding, shoot and retrieve. She snapped out of her musings when Wolf removed his shirt and vest, leaving her with an up-close view of his broad, muscular chest. "What are you doing?" She gasped.

Wolf glanced down at her, then put his hands on his hips, drawing her attention downward to his lean, hard belly and the soft mat of golden hair that shot past the small round indentation several inches above the waistband, then disappeared beneath the material of his hip-hugging breeches.

Jessie missed the knowing grin spreading across his face. "The white of my shirt stands out. Now I blend in with my surroundings." He looked down at his buckskin breeches and moccasins. "My people usually hunt in far less. Just a breechclout in the summertime," he said, running his thumbs along the inside of his waistband as if it constricted him. His eyes sparkled with mischief. "Feel free to do the same, but hurry," he ordered.

Jessie closed her open jaw. "I, uh, my clothes are dark. They'll do just fine." She wore a dark pair of woolen trousers and a loose-fitting brown shirt.

Wolf shrugged, then crouched low to stalk the herd. "Stay low and close to me."

She breathed a sigh of relief when he turned, presenting her with a view of his back. Taking several deep, restoring breaths, Jessie clutched her scattergun to her chest and followed. She imitated his low crouch and stayed close. Jessie quickly discovered the perils of being close to White Wolf. With her following downwind of him, his scent washed over her, tempting her to get closer than she should. And if she'd thought his bare back was any less appealing than his hair-covered chest, she was mistaken. Her gaze locked onto the rippling motion of his muscles dancing a slow waltz from one side to the other.

She forced her gaze downward, away from the naked, rock hard flesh, then moaned softly, mentally cursing the man for wearing soft, supple leather that molded itself to his firm backside like a second skin. Then she recalled what he'd said about wearing only a breechclout. Visions of him wearing a narrow piece of hide held to his waist by a leather thong danced before her. Thanks to that night at the pool, she had no trouble envisioning those smooth buttocks barely concealed by a flap of animal skin. Just what she needed, she thought, another wildly sinful vision to haunt her dreams.

Her heart knocked against her ribs, her blood warmed and she had to fight an overwhelming need to reach out and touch him. She tried to think of something else, tried to fight her attraction to this man, but it did no good. White Wolf possessed some secret, vital power that drew her to him. When Wolf stopped suddenly, she crashed into him and would have fallen had he not reached back to catch her around the shoulders. Heat from his fingers burned through cloth and into skin, traveling upward to flood her face with color.

"Careful, Jessie; watch where you're going. No daydreaming allowed," he admonished, a twinkle in his sky blue eyes.

Flushing hotly, she shoved away from him, wishing he'd let her bounce off him to land in the grass. Now she had to rid herself of the feel of him. Luckily he started forward, giving her time to regain her composure and concentrate on her role. They were only nineteen days out of Westport. She didn't dare chance his discovering her deception. Wolf stopped again. This time she came to a halt well behind him. Still crouched, he went down on his stomach, letting the tall green grass shield him from the antelope. He motioned to her to do the same. As soon as she joined him, Wolf crawled forward. Jessie held her breath and followed.

Peering over the top of the grass, she saw that the antelope were within firing range. She propped her shotgun in front of her and made a face, wishing defiance hadn't made her grab the wrong rifle. There was no way she was going to be able to make a kill with her scattergun. Not wanting to ruin their chances of fresh meat for supper, she decided to fire her gun after Wolf did so the hunt wouldn't be jeopardized.

Wolf propped his elbows on the wet ground, held his rifle up and took aim at the unsuspecting animals. Then, surprising her, he took her scattergun away and gave her his rifle. "This here's a Sharps rifle, good for killing larger game, especially buffalo. Try it; see how it feels. Your shotgun is better suited for small game," he whispered.

Jessie groaned. She knew that; she'd left hers behind purposely to discourage Wolf from making a habit of taking her hunting.

Taking his rifle, she sighed in appreciation of the sleekness of the wood. She held her breath to still the tremors that raced through her. It was up to her to make the kill. She lifted the rifle, sighted a large antelope and prepared to fire, but Wolf stopped her, his hands closing over her arms.

"Here, push your elbows in, like this," he instructed, his breath tickling her ear. Wolf encircled her body with his, his chest half-resting on her back, his arms pressed against hers as his hands positioned hers. Jessie closed her eyes and tried to steady her erratic breathing, but the musky pine and sunshine scent of Wolf sent her senses spiraling. Wolf's face nearly rested against hers. If she turned her head even a fraction, she'd find her lips close to his.

"Don't move. As soon as I let go, fire at the one nearest us."

Closing her eyes, she sighed with relief when Wolf moved away. Her ear still felt the heat of his lips as his every breath warmed her. Biting her lower lip, she sighted the animal once again. The large beast lifted its head, sniffing the air.

"If you miss, the herd will scatter and be gone in seconds," Wolf warned, his breath fanning her outer ear.

Jessie ignored the coldness of the air washing over her back where just moments ago there'd been warmth. Her hands trembled, but pride came to her aid. She didn't know what game he was playing, but if there was one thing she was good at, it was hunting. Fine. She'd show him. Taking her time, she focused all her energy on the movements of the herd as they grazed. Slowly and deliberately, she sighted another larger antelope a bit farther away, then squeezed the trigger. When the shot rang out, the herd scattered, bounding out of range within seconds, leaving one lying still on the ground.

Each family dug into their stores to fix a special dish to contribute to the impromptu potluck. Over a meal of spit-roasted meat, hot corn bread and apple pie made from dried fruit, the bickering and fighting of the last few days gave way to laughter, stories and high spirits. Standing in the shadows, Wolf stewed. While he was glad his idea for a feast had brought back the air of camaraderie needed to get these people through the difficult journey, his own mood worsened as he observed the cheery sight. When Lars pulled out his fiddle and the Jones family dug out their mouth organs, he turned to leave.

A soft *woof* drew his attention downward. Wahoska eyed him, then looked to the half-empty plate in Wolf's hands. Wolf glared at his uneaten meal. Even his appetite had fled. Setting the plate down for the wolf with a snort of disgust, he strode away, leaving the bright fires and merry music behind as he headed back toward the cattle.

Walking across the dark prairie, he went over in his mind the disastrous afternoon. His plan to tease and torment Jessie had backfired on him but good. Touching her today had been a mistake. A big one. When he'd covered her body with his, her sweet scent had sent desire racing through him.

Just one touch had been enough to stoke his burning embers, but when her hair—those baby-soft curls—caressed his cheeks, he'd nearly taken her fully into his arms to kiss and love. He groaned just recalling the irresistible urge he'd had to run his tongue around the pink swirls of her ear when he'd leaned down to whisper to her. And watching her swallow nervously at his closeness had struck a vibrant chord in him. It'd taken all his will to resist touching his tongue to the pulsing hollow of her throat. That she was just as affected had made it worse.

Picking up a large rock, he tossed it as far from him as he could. If only he could rid himself of his growing attraction to Jessie Jones as easily. "Why her?" he asked the star-studded heavens above. "It's not as though she's baby-doll beautiful like her sister-in-law, and she certainly isn't well rounded like Lolita." But he didn't want someone like Lolita. He wanted a woman who wasn't afraid to take him on; he wanted neither a woman obsessed with her looks nor one who flaunted herself. He wanted someone who greeted each day with a zeal for living—he wanted Jessie. He wanted to wake up and see those eyes first thing each morning—those innocent-looking green eyes that were the mirror to her soul.

They twinkled with humor, flashed with devilment, grew wide with innocent wonder, and—his favorite emotion—they sparked like green fire when she was angry. Like his black stallion, Jessie Jones had spirit, and her streak of fierce independence rivaled that of his wolf. Like the animals who walked the *Maka*, she had a core of wildness. Unafraid of hard work or the challenges that came with taming a new land, she belonged; she was of the earth. Wolf stopped and stared toward the western sky with mounting frustration. He had no room in his life for a woman, not even one who was a good shot! He'd been left speechless when she'd handed him back his rifle and stalked out to claim her kill.

Once again, he recalled the conversation he'd had with Striking Thunder the morning after Jessie had come at him with fists raised in righteous anger. Had he met his match in a woman? He shook his head. No! He refused to even consider it. He wouldn't lose his heart to any woman, but especially not to an emigrant traveling to a new territory with her family—a family important enough for her to lie in order to go with them.

He steadfastly ignored the differences between Jessie and Martha, seeing only that both women had put their families above all else—which was exactly what he had to do: put his family, his people, before his own personal wishes. Pushing all thought of the two women from his mind, Wolf strode over to the feed wagon and found his bedroll. Laying it out, he lay down on top of the blankets, fighting images of a woman with ebony curls and green eyes.

In the dark predawn hours, Wolf awoke to the distant roll of thunder announcing the arrival of yet another storm. Instantly alert, he tossed his bedroll into the feed wagon and mounted his horse. He woke those not already on guard duty, ordering them to saddle up. Riding out toward the cattle, he cast worried glances up into the black clouds. Nearing the herd, he saw the animals on their feet, milling about restlessly. In a low, soothing voice, he positioned everyone around the cattle and then prayed like hell they didn't stampede. The difficult crossing of the Big Blue combined with the storms of the last few days had left the cattle edgy.

The thunder grew closer, louder. His fear of an impending stampede grew. The Jones brothers continued to play soothing tunes on their mouth organs while others sang soft ballads, but it wasn't calming the cattle. They bawled anxiously. Thirty minutes later, the first flash of lightning zigzagged across the dark sky, followed by a crash of thunder. His gut tightened and his worst fears were realized when the herd spooked and surged into the blackness of the night—toward the corralled wagons less than a mile away.

Disturbed from her restless sleep, Jessie sat up and glanced around in confusion. Cocking her head to the side, she listened, hearing the distant rumble of thunder. Frowning, she lay back down. It was the arrival of the storm that had startled her awake. But then she felt the trembling of the earth beneath her and realized that the roar that filled the air wasn't caused by thunder. Swallowing her fear, she grabbed her rifle and a Colt Manhattan cap and ball five shooter that belonged to Jordan and bolted out of the wagon.

Jessie fired the Colt into the air, signaling danger. Men poured out of their tents and ran toward her. She turned to Rook. "Stampede! If the cattle are headed this way, we've got to change their direction. Have the men shoot into the air to frighten them away." While Rook shouted orders, Jessie jumped onto Shilo's bare back and rode away from the corralled wagons, praying the cattle weren't headed for them.

Her hopes sank when the thundering hooves grew louder. She peered into the darkness, but the shadows of the storm clouds overhead obscured the gray light of the approaching dawn. A bolt of lightning raced across the sky, giving Jessie her first glimpse of the dark, roiling mass bearing down on her. Her heart hammered with fear. She slowed Shilo and lifted the rifle.

Pointing it skyward, she pulled the trigger, signaling Rook that the cattle were headed right for them. Behind her, the sound of shots filled the air and mingled with the roar of thunder and hooves. It did nothing to slow the herd. Tossing the rifle down, she wrapped the horse's mane around her left hand and urged Shilo forward.

With her right hand she aimed the pistol at the ground in front of the approaching animals. She fired, but the lead steer refused to budge from its course. Pulling her hand up slightly, she took aim again and fired. She breathed a sigh of regret and relief when the animal went down, taking several of the frightened beasts with it as they faltered and fell.

The herd still surged forward, bellowing in fright, but the confused cattle veered slightly to one side as several more fell. That slight slowing was all she needed. She rode toward the herd, coming up alongside the stampeding mass. She fired the remaining bullets into the air to keep them from resuming their course. Forcing several steer farther to the right, she singled one out for a new lead. To her relief, the surging mass followed him.

Even though the herd had turned, she continued to yell and scream, making as much noise as she could to keep the animals running away from her and the vulnerable wagons. She chanced a look over her shoulder and gave a cry of relief when she spotted two riders gaining on her. Her brothers and the rest of the hands had finally caught up with the herd. Only when she was sure someone was coming to take her place did she veer to the left, turning Shilo back toward the wagons to let the others take over and finish forcing the cattle into running a wide circle that would eventually be tightened until the animals ran themselves out.

Suddenly the sky lit up as a bolt of lightning streaked out of the clouds and plunged to the earth. The air sizzled and the ground shook. Shilo reared in fright. Jessie tightened her hold, but the mare's back was too wet and slick for her to get a firm hold. She screamed as she felt herself falling.

Wolf rode hell-bent-for-leather. The emigrants were in danger. He had to turn the herd. When he heard shots coming from up ahead, he breathed a sigh of relief. Rook had alerted the emigrants to the imminent danger. Gaining on the lead steer, he spotted a shadowy figure riding in from the left, firing into the frightened cattle.

He watched several animals go down, which caused a few cattle in the lead to veer slightly. It was all he needed. Raising his hand, he fired into the air, shouted and forced the herd to continue to the right. The herd continued to form a wide circle as flashes of lightning lit up the sky. Glancing over his shoulder, he saw that the other hands were spaced out behind him, forcing the beasts to the right with their whips and gunshots. It was then that he noticed one rider gaining on him, yelling and pointing to the rider who was still fighting to keep the lead steer going to the right.

Wolf couldn't hear James, but it was obvious he was upset. He glanced at the rider in front of him. He didn't know who it was or how he'd gotten ahead of him, but given the rider's size, he'd bet it was Shorty. But then a flash of light from above revealed a slim figure on a black horse. His pulse pounded in his ears. There were only two black horses in this group: his and Jessie's.

In that brief, heart-stopping moment, he realized she'd saved the corralled wagons from destruction, and it was Jessie who even now continued to put her life in danger by riding dangerously close to the herd to keep them on the new course. Digging his heels into his mount, he leaned over and urged the horse faster. Closing the distance, he was determined to get her the hell out of there. He was right behind her when she glanced over her shoulder and pulled away, leaving the job to him. Wolf felt a small measure of relief.

But his relief was short-lived when another flash of lightning crashed to the earth. The ground shook. In horror, Wolf watched Jessie's horse rear. Terror, stark and vivid, stabbed him. Cursing beneath his breath, he urged his horse faster, leaning to the side of his Indian-trained mount, fighting his own grip on the slippery animal's back. Just as she lost her grip and slid off her horse's back, his hand shot out and plucked her out of midair as if she were nothing more than a rag doll. Regaining his seat, Wolf rode away from the madness with Jessie half sitting, half lying across his thighs. His heart hammered painfully in his chest, and his blood boiled with anger with the realization of how close she'd come to losing her life.

Jessie struggled against him. "Shilo! Go back."

Furious, Wolf glanced down at her, his jaw clenched so tight it hurt. He came to a grinding halt and glared down at her. "Forget the damn horse!" he shouted. "You nearly got yourself killed, you fool!"

Jessie pushed against him and slid to the ground, landing on her backside in the mud. Wolf jumped down and stood above her, making no move to help her to her feet. The rain fell steadily, soaking them to the skin. In silence he watched her jump to her feet and wipe her hands down her pants.

"What the hell did you think you were doing out there?" he shouted above the noise of the storm overhead.

Jessie tilted her chin at him. "Don't shout at me, Wolf. I did what had to be done, same as anybody—" The crash of thunder overhead drowned her out.

Wolf narrowed his eyes and advanced, pointing an accusing finger at her. "I told you to stay away from the cattle, and I meant it! I should beat you to within an inch of your life for pulling a stupid stunt like that. And as for your horse—figures you'd think more of her than you do yourself!"

A swift flash of anger swept across her features. "I knew

what I was doing," she threw out, taking a couple of steps away from him.

He took one step to her every two. "You nearly got yourself killed, you fool," he shouted, his voice as cold and lashing as the rain pelting them.

"But I didn't," she replied, her voice low and taut with emotion.

His gaze traveled up her slim figure and latched onto her rain-soaked long johns. The wet top plastered against her small breasts revealed pouty tips straining against the thin material. That reminder that she was a woman, a woman he could no longer deny he was falling in love with, unleashed his anger.

He shoved his hands on his hips and leaned close. "Yeah, but I'm responsible for each and every person on this wagon train. Now I know why your brothers wanted to leave you behind. You're a damn nuisance. You don't follow orders worth a damn. If you weren't a damn woman, you can bet I'd take a whip to your backside for disobeying orders."

Wolf's words hung heavy between them. They stood toe-to-toe, oblivious to the thunder and rain, oblivious to all except the sparks arcing between them. His eyes narrowed with satisfaction when Jessie's jaw dropped. She took another faltering step back, and he pursued.

"You know?" she said in a croak.

Wolf smiled, a wolfish smile that boded ill. He glanced pointedly at her chest. "I know."

Jessie glanced down and gaped at the revealed shape of her small breasts. She covered herself with her arms, but it was too late. Her tongue flicked out to lick lips wet with rain. Lightning slashed the heavens, thunder drowned all sound, and like the cattle who'd bolted in fear, Jessie turned tail and ran.

Chapter Twelve

Thunder rumbled from massive charcoal gray clouds scrolling and colliding across the night sky. The sonorous noise mingled with the howling of the wind and Wolf's angry shouts. Jessie ignored all of it as she pushed herself through the turbulent storm. Fat drops of blinding rain pelted her, but dealing with nature's tantrum seemed far safer than facing Wolf's fury.

Risking a fearful glance over her shoulder, she gasped. Her heart slammed against her ribs. He was close. So close that when the sky exploded with flashing light, she could see the angry flare of his nostrils and feel the dark fury emanating from him. Desperate, she feinted sharply to the right to avoid capture, but the water-saturated earth gave way beneath her bare heels. She cried out, her arms flailing wildly as she sought to regain her balance. But she fell, skidded across the slick earth and came to a dizzying and painful stop on her back.

Groaning, Jessie sat up and wiped the mud and water from her face. She blinked until her vision cleared, then cringed. Wolf stood above her, feet planted apart, hands on hips, and his eyes were narrow slits of fury. Licking her lips, she grimaced at the taste of mud, then tried to sit. Wolf stopped her escape by dropping to his knees to straddle her. His hands pinned her shoulders to the wet earth. "Let go," she shrieked. Her heart hammered frantically, and she struggled, but escape was futile. Staring into Wolf's glittering eyes,

Jessie knew she was doomed. Her day of reckoning had arrived.

Seconds merged into agonizingly long, silent minutes. Above her, Wolf's chest heaved with every breath, his nostrils flaring with each intake of air. Against her will, her gaze locked with his, and she nervously bit her lip. Fear mingled with injured pride. No one intimidated her in this manner. She was wet, muddy and cold. And to top it off, the rain falling into her face made it hard to see. Anger rose to the surface. Jessie drew strength from that anger and renewed her efforts to free herself. She wasn't ready to admit defeat—yet.

Taking Wolf by surprise, she twisted her hips and bucked, sliding her mud-slicked body out from under his. But he was fast. He grabbed a fistful of her long johns. On their knees, they struggled, but Wolf was stronger. He shoved her back down beneath him and pinned her legs beneath his. Desperate, she aimed her fists and connected with his cheekbone, beneath his right eye. A hiss of breath and the tightening of his lips were the only signs that she'd caused him any pain. Quick as lightning, he fell on top of her, his chest hard against her unbound breasts. The feeling shocked her into submissiveness, allowing him to grab her wrist.

"You little hellion! Damn it, be still!"

Jessie renewed her efforts to free herself. Her free hand eluded his and splattered him with a handful of mud, but she didn't have a prayer against his strength. He easily captured her other hand and pinned both her wrists above her head. Breathing heavily, she glared up at him. Each assessed the other's anger.

Wolf grinned, a devilishly evil grin that let her know more than words that he was in full command. She was at his mercy. "You've got some explaining to do. What the hell were you trying to do out there, get yourself killed?"

Jessie stared at him, caught in the trap of his silvery blue gaze and his savage beauty. Fear snaked a path up her spine. Oh, Lord, she thought, he's mad as a peeled rattler. In the shadows of the stormy night, Wolf looked every bit the savage Indian.

He spoke, his voice dangerously low. "Now, talk. What the hell do you think you were doing out there? We'll save the lying to me part for later." Wolf released her hands and sat up, crossing his arms across his chest.

Shielding her face from the rain, Jessie breathed a sigh of relief. Having Wolf, half-naked, lying on top of her had made it nearly impossible to think clearly, and she needed a clear mind to deal with the tough and formidable wagon master. The wind whipped over her, chilling her. Now she wished he would lie back over her. When his arms and thick shoulders had circled her she'd felt safe, protected.

She frowned. Safe was not something she should have felt, given the circumstances, yet she had. She tried to shake off the conflicting emotions. How could she like him? He was so darn infuriating! She was ready to tell him so when he settled his hips intimately over hers. The words died in her throat.

His buttocks were rock hard as they pressed into her woman's mound, sending waves of heat trailing from the juncture of her thighs, up through her belly, through her pounding heart and into her face. Biting her lower lip, she was shocked by the sensation. A strange ache filled her, centering on that part of her where he sat. Closing her eyes, she fought the urge to move her hips beneath his. A loud crash of thunder startled her, reminding her of where they were. The ground trembled beneath her. She was wet, the rain pelting her face. She didn't like the feelings he aroused in her. "Let me up, Wolf. I need to get back. My brothers will be looking for me."

Wolf sat above her, dark and forbidding, golden strands framing his face. Water beaded on his lashes, dripped from his chin, and near his jaw, a muscle jumped. The rain did nothing to lessen the aura of danger surrounding him. He shook his head, sending water flying. "Your brothers deserve to worry about you. Might teach them a lesson where you're concerned. That was one hell of a stupid stunt. I'm of a mind to send the lot of you back to Westport.''

Wolf's words pierced her heart. A thread of fear slid down her spine. Would he really kick them out? She thrust out her chin. She'd fight him. She'd done what had had to be done, and despite his anger over her deception, she didn't regret keeping her family together. She'd do it again in a heartbeat. Her gaze narrowed. And when it came right down to it, it was *his* fault she'd been forced to lie, forced to assume the role of a boy. Her temper rose in conjunction with the storm.

She glared up at him. ''This is all your fault, White Wolf. You can kick me out, but you can't stop me from following.''

''My fault? You and James lied to me. That alone is grounds for banishment.''

Jessie's eyes grew wide. The fight left her. If Wolf kicked them all out, they wouldn't have enough provisions for the remainder of the trip. They'd purchased only enough for Elliot and Coralie, as Wolf had promised to provide the rest as part of the deal. ''You can't do that,'' she gasped.

''I can. Your brothers signed a contract agreeing to abide by my rules. By allowing you to come, they knowingly broke the contract.''

Jessie narrowed her gaze. ''And if you hadn't hired them, offered pay and free passage to Oregon, they'd never have considered leaving me behind.'' She refused to allow him to place all the blame on her shoulders. She calmed her voice, hating to beg, but there was too much at stake for pride to get in the way. ''What difference does it make if I'm their sister? You even said families belong together. Besides, I've done my fair share of work and haven't been any trouble.''

Wolf snorted and lifted his brow. ''That's a matter of opinion, but that's not the point. You made a fool of me, Jessie. I don't like being made a fool of, especially by a damn woman.''

In a quick and unexpected move, Jessie shoved Wolf off her and jumped to her feet. ''You lout! That's all you care about, isn't it? You don't care about anyone else. All you care about is your damn pride and your damn rules. Well, you're not going to play God with me and mine.'' Even when Wolf stood to face her, Jessie didn't back down.

She poked him in the chest with one finger. "You're nothing but a big, mean bully, White Wolf. I thought Indians prided themselves on honor, but you have none. You're a vile varmint, a no-account scalawag—''

Wolf's hand snaked out, and he pulled her roughly to him. She slammed against the wall of his chest. Before she could object, his mouth crashed down on hers with a fierceness that rivaled the storm playing out over their heads. His mouth moved possessively over hers. Jessie's emotions whirled in time with the winds whipping around them.

She'd dreamed of his kisses, but in her dreams they'd been chaste, impersonal—a far cry from the hard demand of reality. Before she could even think of protesting, the savage intensity of his kiss faded. Tenderly, his hands cupped each side of her face. His moist mouth softened, warmed and explored hers with slow thoroughness, coaxing a moan from deep in her throat.

All anger fled. There were only the two of them, each caught up in their own private storm of desire. Jessie leaned into Wolf, eagerly giving herself over to his mastery. For the first time, she felt like a desirable woman and gave in to the urge to explore. Unclenching her hands, her fingers moved against his hard, firm flesh, learning the feel of him.

Taking her time, she explored, pausing briefly to rub her thumbs over the small brown nipples beaded from the cold and her touch. She moved upward in her exploration, her palms resting briefly on his broad shoulders before sliding along the taut ridge to the thick cords of his neck. Her fingers dug into heated flesh as she hovered between the desire for more and a fear of the raging emotions storming through her. But feeling the wet heat of him, she moaned. She wrapped her hands around his neck.

This was what her dreams had lacked: passion. Heat. Mind-numbing desire. His touch, his scent and the taste of his mouth on hers heightened her senses and assailed her with new sensations. From the tips of her fingers down to her bare toes, she felt alive, beautiful.

Her blood sang with pleasure even as her mind ordered her to end this sweet torture. But how could she end something that felt so good, so right? She closed her eyes. Her lips parted on a sigh as she gave herself up to the sweet pleasure of her first true kiss.

Wolf's lips suckled hers, his tongue tracing just inside her mouth before his mouth slanted over hers to claim her once again. Instinctively, her fingers moved upward and gripped the back of his head to hold him tightly as she answered the primal call surging through her.

Long, breathless moments later, Wolf drew back, allowing her to swallow great gulps of moist air into her starved lungs. Jessie opened her eyes and stared up into his heavy-lidded gaze. In the darkness, she was unable to see his expression. She didn't need to. She felt the emotion in the trembling of his fingers caressing the sides of her face. Her own eyes went wide with the wonder of the kiss.

This man, so hard, unyielding and demanding in his expectations of those around him, had somehow slipped unbidden and unwanted into her heart. He'd claimed the part of her that she'd kept hidden, and Jessie knew she could never belong to anyone else. Was this love? What they'd just shared was so right, so perfect, it had to be. A fierce sense of protectiveness swelled within her breast. The intense feeling startled her. Wolf, of all people, didn't need or want protection—especially from her.

But over the last few weeks, she'd glimpsed many hidden facets of White Wolf. He could be soft-spoken and gentle around the women, watchful over the young children, firm yet respectful toward the men, never asking more of them than he himself gave. And what she most enjoyed was his playful manner when he wrestled with Wahoska and Sadie—whenever he thought no one was watching—or the infinite patience he showed in training his stallion.

In the dark of the storm, Jessie felt Wolf's chest heave as he pulled gulps of air past his parted lips. Staring up at him, she licked her own kiss-swollen lips. Protective wasn't all she felt right then. Lifting one hand, she fingered his rain-darkened hair. The strands fell forward, clung to his neck and outlined the strong line of his jaw.

Her hands slid back down over his bare, glistening torso. Beads of water ran past bulging muscles, tunneled through the mat of curly hair before disappearing beneath the waist-band of his pants. Jessie returned her gaze to his, her tongue snaking out to lick the rain from her lower lip. She wanted another kiss but wasn't sure how to go about getting it.

Wolf groaned, his eyes following the movement of her moist, pink tongue. His fingers raked through her wet curls and tenderly stroked the sensitive flesh behind her ears. That act of gentleness, so at odds with his anger of moments ago, was her undoing. She needed more, wanted more, had to taste more of him. She pulled on his shoulders. "Kiss me again, Wolf" The tip of her tongue flicked out to taste a droplet of water that beaded on his upper lip.

Wolf gave a hoarse cry. "This is madness."

Jessie wrapped her arms around his neck as his lips claimed hers once again, but while the first kiss had started off savage as the prairie storm, this one started slow, a low-burning flame. His lips touched the corners of hers with the gentleness of a butterfly's caress as it flitted from one bloom to another. Then his tongue darted out to lap the drops of water from her skin with a sweetness of which she'd not thought him capable.

The gentle teasing quickly became a torment. She lifted her head, pressed her lips hungrily to his, silently begging for something more—something substantial, something to fill the hunger that gnawed deep within her. Wolf deepened the kiss. The sweet teasing turned to demanding passion, a man's primitive need to explore and conquer. Her lips moved with his, enslaved by his mastery.

Kiss for wild kiss, she met his stormy assault with her own fierce desire until it became impossible to distinguish leader from follower. The wind whipped into a frenzy. White, jagged streaks flew across the sky, followed by the crashing of thunder that reverberated through the air and shook the ground. But neither Wolf nor Jessie noticed. They were caught up in a passionate storm of their own making.

Wolf lifted his head to the cooling caress of the rain against his hot skin. He groaned, then exhaled deeply. He had to stop. He hadn't meant to kiss Jessie, not like this. All he'd intended was to shut her up, and perhaps frighten her a bit in retaliation for scaring ten years of life out of him earlier. But when those emerald greens had flashed with fury, he'd been sucked in, unable to resist. And after that first sweet taste, he'd been lost to the attraction he'd tried so hard to deny. Jessie Jones was so damned desirable. And when she was angry, she was irresistible.

Once more he lowered his head. Just one more taste, one more sweet, chaste kiss, he promised himself. His lips touched hers, lightly, briefly, then closed over hers. But as soon as her lips moved, parted, it wasn't enough. He needed more, had to have more. His tongue snaked out to lick the inside of her lower lip. He moaned when her lips responded, parting further with an innocent sigh. He ran his tongue over her lips, pushed the tip of his tongue through the small space between her teeth.

"Open your mouth, sweet Jess," he whispered, his voice thick with desire. When her lips opened to allow him admittance to the sweetness hidden to him, he slid inside, into the warm, moist cavern of her mouth. A low, guttural sound rose deep in his throat. Never had he tasted such sweetness, such innocence. Her tongue shied away, but slowly, patiently, he coaxed her, taught her, and soon their tongues were twining, mating with desperate need.

With a little coaching, a whispered plea, she followed his retreat, and hesitantly her tongue entered his mouth. Immediately his lips closed around her and suckled, his moan blending with hers as her needs grew to match his. Then he took her lips in one more long, searing kiss that left them both gasping for air. The wild hammering of her heart, the softness of her breasts against his chest, sent desire, hot and heavy, arrowing a path of fire from his belly to his groin. Wolf wanted all this woman could offer.

She who handled teams of oxen and hunted with skill. The woman who stood up for the weak and fearlessly protected those she cared about, disregarding her own safety to save those she barely knew. This woman had stoked the dying embers of his heart into full flame, something no one else had been able to do since Martha's betrayal.

His eyes flew open. Betrayal . . . lies . . . deceit. Wolf tore his lips from hers. How could he forget so quickly? So easily? She'd lied to him. Lied to keep her family together. She'd put her needs over truth—as Martha had done when she and her family had welcomed him with open arms. It was only later that he'd discovered his real appeal had been his experience as a guide. The truth, discovering that *his* fiancée, was already promised to another, had left him distrustful of the opposite sex.

And now he'd nearly fallen into the same trap. Had he learned nothing? Calming his ragged breathing, Wolf vowed not to succumb to Jessie's sweet innocence and fiery passion again. It could only lead to heartache. He ignored the pang of regret this decision left in his heart. It was better this way.

For long moments they stared at one another wordlessly. The harsh sounds of their breathing seemed loud in the sudden lull of the storm. Jessie blinked rapidly, her eyes filled with a combination of wonder and desire. Wanting nothing more than to take all she offered in her gaze, he hardened his voice.

"You're a fast learner, Jessie, but don't think a few kisses are going to get you off the hook. You lied and used me to further your own purposes." Wolf expected his words to send Jessie into another rage, but they didn't. Instead, hurt replaced the desire in her eyes. His gut tightened painfully. Damn. He didn't want to care, yet he did.

Her hand lifted toward him, then fell helplessly to her side. "Please, Wolf, don't take this out on my brothers. It wasn't their fault. It's mine. I'm sorry that I deceived you, truly I am, but I would have done anything to go with them. Please let us continue to Oregon.''

Wolf lowered his brows. ''Anything? Does that include kissing me?'' Hurt sharpened his voice. The thought that she'd responded to his kisses only to keep him from kicking her and her siblings out burned a hole in his gut.

Jessie took a step toward him, her fingers bunched into tight fists. ''How dare you suggest that I'd—that I would—'' Her voice broke suddenly, and she turned around to hide the tears running down her face.

Wolf heard her muffled sob and swore. Guilt nipped at him as he recalled that James had turned down his initial offer to drive Able's cattle. Not wanting to lose Able's most experienced men, he'd made his next offer to James far too tempting for the other man to refuse. James would have been foolish to turn it down. He sighed, envisioning the difficulties that lay ahead. There was no way he'd abandon this woman and her family to the unpredictable whims of the trail. Besides, he needed James and his brothers. He would see to it that they reached Oregon safely, no matter the cost to himself. And the cost would be high. Jessie wasn't a cold-blooded schemer as Martha had been. But on some subconscious level, he knew she could hurt him, devastate him.

He now acknowledged that with Martha it had been a case of wounded pride. With Jessie he feared for his heart, and as much as he wanted this green-eyed witch, he wasn't free to pursue his own happiness. Saddened by the sense of loss, he sighed. ''You and your brothers will continue on one condition.''

Like the sun coming out after a storm, Jessie's expression brightened. ''Do you really mean it? I'll do anything, I promise.'' She bit her lip and waited.

Wolf tipped her chin up with one long, lean finger. ''Careful what you promise, young Jess.'' Before she could give in to the angry words he saw in her eyes, he stepped back. ''Here's the deal. You'll do as I say and don't, I repeat, don't ever put your life in danger like you did tonight. I'm warning you here and now that if you ever pull another stupid stunt like that, I'll put you over my knee and give you the spanking James should've given you a long time ago!''

Jessie's eyes narrowed with resentment. "I did what I had to do, Wolf, and would do so again. If I'd truly been a boy, you wouldn't be upset," she accused.

Wolf studied Jessie. Her eyes flashed with emotion, but her lips still trembled. She was a wild she-cat, but beneath her spit and fire he saw the vulnerability she tried so hard to hide. He just couldn't remain angry any longer. She was right. She'd done exactly what he or any of the other men would have done. His lips twitched and he shook his head. "You never give up, do you, Jess? Let's get one thing straight: I'm the boss. What I say goes. Agreed?"

Jessie didn't look happy, but she nodded. "Now can we go? I'm cold and bone-tired."

Wolf grinned a sly grin. "Maybe you'd like to thank me with another kiss, Jess? Or should I now call you Jessica?"

Jessie scowled. "Jessie or Jess is fine, and you've had enough kisses already. I'd rather have the extra chores, thank you," she stated primly.

Wolf threw back his head and roared with laugher. "Wise choice, *Jessica.*" He grew serious as he ran the pad of his finger down her wet cheek. "Fear me, beautiful Jessica, for I want more from you than a few kisses. Heed my warning and keep your distance."

Jessie's eyes widened with comprehension when he released her. "Wolf?"

He turned back, lifting one brow at her mischievous grin. She stepped close, placing her hands on his shoulders. Standing on tiptoe, she pressed her parted lips to his. When he did nothing, she slanted her mouth over his and kissed him until his groin tightened. White-hot shards of heat seared him. He shuddered, then felt her lips curve over his. She nipped his lower lip none too gently, then stepped back, leaving him to deal with his longing. "Maybe you'd better keep your distance as well," she suggested smugly, then stalked away, swaying her hips unconsciously.

Wolf watched her go, his hands planted on his hips.

Damn! He should never have kissed her. He knew better than to play around with innocent virgins. He let out a piercing whistle. When his horse came trotting out of the stormy darkness, he mounted, rode up to Jessie and held out his hand. She reached up and placed her hand trustingly in his. She was foolish to trust him. She was an innocent, he reminded himself. Wolf knew an unreasonable urge to wipe out her smug, self-satisfied look—both for her sake and his. ''Not a bad kiss for a virgin, but I prefer my women experienced—like Rosalyn. Now, the things she can do with her tongue . . .''

Jessie gasped. With regret, Wolf watched her eyes flare with resentment, denial and anger, but before she had a chance to lambaste him, he pulled her up behind him, then sent his mount into a full gallop toward the wagons.

The night had grown silent; the thunder of the storm had gone. When they neared the circle of wagons, two riders rode out to meet them. Wolf stopped. Jessie's brothers had come to find her. She jumped down. Wolf followed, ignoring her reproachful glare. He tried to convince himself that it was better this way. He had nothing lasting to offer her. Someone like Elliot would be better for her. However, the thought of another man kissing her or taking what he wanted for himself left a bitter taste in his mouth.

James and Jeremy dismounted and ran to their sister. ''You all right, Jess?''

''Yeah, I'm fine,'' she replied, her voice tight with suppressed anger.

''Wow, Jess, you did that real good. Didn't she, James?'' Jeremy slapped his sister on the back, his eyes wide with pride.

James rocked back on his heels. ''Scared me good, Jess, but ya did good.'' Wolf's fury grew with each bit of praise they sang. How dare they encourage the very behavior that nearly killed her? His hands clenched as he relived those moments of horror. If James had taken Jessie in hand long ago, she wouldn't be such a wild tomboy, wouldn't be the feisty woman to whom he was in danger of losing his heart to.

182

He stormed over to James and slammed his fist into his jaw. "That's for lyin' to me and putting your *sister* in danger, you bastard. Her name is Jessica. Use it, and while you're at it, start treating her like a woman." Wolf mounted his horse rode off.

Chapter Thirteen

Slivers of sunlight streaked through the flimsy mantle of clouds to kiss the waterlogged earth. The warmth and light lured the emigrants from their damp shelters. Within minutes, the seemingly barren prairie teamed with life. Birds of all sizes, shapes and colors flitted about, calling to one another as they preened themselves in the warm rays. Prairie dogs emerged from burrows tunneled twelve feet beneath the matted green grass to scamper, play and sit on their haunches. Their high-pitched *yek, yek, yek* rang across the prairie as they scolded the group of emigrants camped nearby.

By noontime, the last of the gray clouds were gone, leaving a blazing sun set against a bright cobalt blue background. Traces of wispy, cotton white clouds drifted lazily by, while far below, tendrils of steam rose from wagon covers, tents and clothing to ascend toward the heavens. Weary men, women and children eagerly embraced the new day, which held the promise of being fair and warm. They were grateful to see the end of the stormy weather that had plagued them since crossing the Big Blue and were thankful that none had been seriously hurt in the confusion of the terrifying stampede.

Inside her wagon, Jessie shivered in her damp clothing. She wished she had something dry to put on, but everything she owned was damp from the previous days of rain. Drawing her damp quilt tightly around her shoulders, she shifted her position to take advantage of the rays of sunlight filtering into the wagon. Sneeze after sneeze racked her body. She grimaced and blew her nose. She'd come down with a damn cold after last night.

Alison, Kerstin and Hanna ran past. Sadie followed, barking at the exuberant children as she chased them. Jessie stared out into the gleaming-wet prairie, amazed that just a few hours could change the landscape so dramatically. Puddles of water, chunks of churned-up earth and grass, along with a dozen dead cattle, were the only reminder of last night's close call.

Just thinking about those hair-raising, terror-filled moments gave Jessie the willies. She never wanted to go through another experience like that! Then she recalled her confrontation with Wolf. A sigh of longing escaped. Closing her eyes, she relived the soul-searing kisses they'd shared. Her cheeks grew warm just thinking about Wolf's kiss and what he'd done with his tongue. She sighed and ran her fingers over her mouth, imagining the firmness of his lips, the rough texture of his tongue as it mated with hers. Her breathing grew erratic at her thoughts, and waves of heat washed over her, warming her from the inside out.

She clasped her hands across her breasts and felt their hardened tips. Her body instinctively yearned for what it knew Wolf could give her, but if he had his way, she'd never share any of those wondrous feelings with him again. An empty void opened in her heart. Somehow she had to convince him that she, Jessica Jones, was woman enough for him. But when she recalled his comments about Rosalyn's kissing abilities, she felt sick inside.

How could she compete with that woman? Rosalyn had the kind of curves men liked. Jessie's hands fell back into her lap. Sticking her head out the back of the wagon, she glanced around. Her gaze found and narrowed on Rosalyn.

As usual, the Nortons and their driver were off by themselves. Rosalyn mounted her horse and rode off toward the cattle—toward Wolf. Imagining Wolf kissing *her* the way he'd kissed Jessie last night sent a surge of furious jealousy whipping through her. The pencil in her hand snapped. Startled by the depth of her emotion, Jessie stared at the two pieces, then stuffed them into a pocket sewn into the inside of the canvas cover.

With her chin resting on her fist, she stared glumly outside, forced to admit that Wolf was free to kiss anyone he liked. That thought settled like a hot rock in her belly. Previously she'd refused to examine her feelings for Wolf too closely, refused to acknowledge that it went beyond attraction. But after last night, she could no longer deny that she was falling in love with a frustrating and formidable man.

There was no wrapping Wolf around one's pinkie. With Wolf, it would be all or nothing, and she wanted it all. "This is ridiculous," she muttered. "So he kissed me. Big deal. Fine. Forget him, 'cause he isn't interested in you. Not looking like you do, anyway." If only she had some nice dresses to wear, or had long, flowing hair.

She ran her hands down her chest and sighed deeply as all hope faded. "What you need is more, lots more," she grumbled. There wasn't a chance in hell that she'd attract Wolf. Not with Rosalyn and her generous hourglass figure prancing around in front of him.

But he'd kissed *her,* a small voice full of hope echoed in her head. She grimaced. So what? She knew enough about men to know a kiss didn't mean squat. Jessie shoved the memory of her first kiss into a special place in her heart, then forced her attention back to her journal.

Even though her mind felt fuzzy and her body ached, she was determined to finish committing the account of the stampede to the pages of her journal. Her pencil moved across the page, adding line after line of neat script until her fingers cramped in protest. Flexing her fingers, Jessie closed the book with a snap. She'd finish the account later. It wasn't as if she'd forget those harrowing events anytime soon!

Though she felt tired, drained and weak, she was too restless to remain confined. Jumping out of the wagon, she winced in pain. Her tailbone was bruised from the fall she'd taken last night. She leaned against the wagon, soaking up the warm rays. Around her, the camp bustled with activity as each family unloaded their wagons to air them out. Jessie glanced inside hers and made a face. The inside reeked of mildew, and she too needed to unload everything to allow the fresh air to dry the dampness that lurked in every nook and corner. A small breeze swept across the prairie. Jessie shivered, then sneezed.

"Thought I told ya ta stay abed this morning, lass."

Startled, Jessie opened one aching eyelid to see Rook standing in front of her in worn buckskin trousers and a plaid shirt that had seen better days. He narrowed his eyes. She groaned. His body might be timeworn, but woe to the fool who though his mind had dulled. There wasn't a sharper mind around than his—as they'd all learned over the last twenty days.

"Well?" he demanded, his bushy brows drawn together.

Jessie eyed the noon sun and sent him a sassy grin. "I did. It's well past noon." But when he only gave her his don't-mess-with-me look, she wrinkled her nose in distaste. "Come on, Rook. It's damp in there. I need to air it out and dry my bedding. Smells too."

Rook harrumphed and jabbed his unlit pipe at her. "Don't ya go gittin' all sassy with me, lass. I'll git one of them boys to take care of it. You finds yoreself a dry spot and sit. You're not ta lift a finger today, and that's an order."

Jessie grinned when Rook stalked away, his voice booming across the prairie as he shouted for Alberik and Nikolaus Svensson to lend a hand. It didn't matter whether the boys were busy or not. If Rook wanted something done, no one stood in his way, and after last night no one else would mind either. Her brothers had come to check on her first thing that morning to make sure she didn't get any grief over her deceit. They'd made it clear that the Jones clan stuck together.

However, it was unnecessary. Most of them had long ago determined her gender, and all morning, her fellow travelers had stopped by to praise her quick actions of last night. She grimaced. All but Rosalyn and Wolf, anyway. Rosalyn's husband, Hugh, had mumbled something that had sounded vaguely like thanks when he'd passed her earlier, but his wife had pointedly ignored her.

Jessie set her jaw, refusing to allow the woman's surly attitude to sour her mood. But thinking of Wolf left her feeling depressed. Even though he'd been furious at her for risking her life, the least he could do was come check on her! And the way she felt right now, she'd even welcome his high-handedness and anger. It would give her an excuse to argue with him. Now that her secret was out, she didn't have to worry about drawing attention to herself.

Her emotions seesawed. While part of her was relieved that Wolf wasn't around to give her grief, still she felt neglected. Clenching her jaw, she told herself she was glad he was keeping his distance. Who'd want the company of a hard, stubborn, frustrating man like him anyway? She'd be better off setting her sights on someone like Elliot, who was gentle and kind. But her lips curved downward and moisture gathered in her eyes.

But she wanted Wolf. Wanted and needed whatever he'd give her. After last night she knew she'd never be able to settle for Elliot or anyone else. The shared kiss with Wolf was forever etched in her mind, heart and soul. She wanted it all—or nothing. Frustrated and angry at his stubbornness, she kicked a stone.

"Sakes alive, Jessie. You nearly hit me," Anne said in a startled voice.

She sent the older woman a sheepish smile. "Sorry, Anne. Didn't see you."

Anne clucked her tongue. "You look downright tuckered out."

Rook joined them with Alberik and Bjorn in tow. He issued orders for them to clear out Jessie's wagon. After heaving himself inside the wagon, Rook glanced down at her and jerked his thumb over his shoulder, silently ordering her to leave.

Anne grabbed her arm. "Come with me, Jessie. I'll fix you a nice cup of tea. You look like you could use one. The boys will take care of your wagon."

Sighing with relief that she didn't have to exert energy she couldn't muster, Jessie fell in step with Anne. Though she was too tired and depressed to visit, a cup of hot tea sounded heavenly. "Don't go to any trouble. It's just a little cold."

Anne clucked with motherly concern. "We need to find a nice warm spot for you to sit in. Too bad the wood's too wet for a big fire. I'm lucky my Lars was able to get a small one going just to heat water. Good thing too. Need the water for Rickard."

Jessie watched Anne put on another kettle of water and frowned. Rickard had been injured during the flurry of shooting last night. "How's he doing? Rook said he'd been shot. How bad is it?"

Anne put her arms around Jessie's shoulders and guided her to a box, then gently pushed her down. "Not bad. The bullet passed through his calf. He'll be up driving me crazy in no time."

"Honest?"

"Honest. The boy's too ornery to stay abed long." Anne smiled reassuringly. "Now, you just sit there while I fix you a cup of my grandmother's special herb tea. It'll soothe your throat."

"Jess, is that you out there?" a boyish voice called out. "Ma, is Jessie here?"

Jessie craned her neck toward the wagon. She wanted to see for herself that her young friend was going to be all right. "Do you think it would it be all right if I said hi to him?"

Anne glanced heavenward when her son continued to call for Jessie to come see him. "Well, I guess it wouldn't hurt— but only for a minute. Just don't get too close with your cold. Maybe if he sees with his own eyes that you're truly all right, he'll settle down. He's been hankering to talk to you all morning."

Jessie grinned and went to the front of the wagon. Hopping onto the wooden tongue, she peered inside. Rickard struggled to a sitting position. Levered above his bed, his leg rested on a pile of pillows and bedding. A white bandage covered his left shin. "I'm here. What do you mean by getting in the way of a bullet, you ninny? Don't you know better? You're supposed to dodge them. Who hit you?"

Rickard smiled sheepishly and fingered the edge of his bandage. "Um, I guess I did it to myself. The gun just went off all by itself, and, boy, was Pa mad. I'm not supposed to touch his guns 'cause I'm not real good with them."

Jessie rolled her eyes. She was fond of Rickard. He was several years younger than she and was eager to learn the things she knew, like hunting and using a whip. Looked like she'd be adding gun-handling to his education. "Tell you what, when you're up and about, I'll teach you the *proper* way to use a gun—if it's all right with your parents."

His eyes grew wide. "Really? Damn, you sure know how to do lots of exciting things."

"Rickard, you mind your mouth in the presence of a young lady."

"Yes, Ma. Sorry, Jessie." Rickard's apologetic demeanor fled when Anne left them alone. With his eyes shining with anticipation, he leaned forward and lowered his voice to a conspiratorial whisper. "I wish I were you, Jessie. I ain't gonna be no farmer. I'm gonna learn to use my whip as good as you and shoot too. You were great last night," he said. "Is there anything ya can't do?"

Jessie sighed. In Rickard's eyes, she was just one of the boys. Surprisingly, it didn't bother her. In fact, she kinda liked having someone look up to her. She stuck her head inside the wagon so Anne wouldn't hear her. Grinning, she confided in a conspiratorial whisper, "Yeah. I can't sew worth a damn." They burst into giggles.

"You fool!" An angry voice behind her interrupted them. "Risking your life isn't enough? Now you're trying to catch your death running around sick."

Startled by Wolf's voice, Jessie jerked around and fell from her perch. Strong arms reached out and caught her. She jerked out of Wolf's arms and scowled up at him. "I'm fine," she lied, her voice ending on a croak. Truthfully, she was beginning to feel downright awful, but she wouldn't admit it to *him*.

Wolf glared at her. "Rook says you're ill."

"And it's all your fault for keeping me out in the rain last night," Jessie shot back, her chin jutting out.

She tried to push past him, but he blocked her exit. Hands on her hips, she sent him a look of contempt. "It should relieve your mind to learn that I don't take sick often, so don't worry that someone else will have to do my share of the work."

Wolf stepped forward, forcing Jessie back. His blue gaze sparked with fury. "I don't give a damn about your chores. The trail is unforgiving to those in poor health, so you're going to return to your wagon and stay there for the rest of the day—tomorrow too, if you're not better." Scooping her up into his arms, he headed for her wagon.

Though there was nothing Jessie wanted more, she struggled. "Put me down," she said angrily, embarrassed to have everyone watching them. Even though her secret was out, she didn't like the attention they were drawing.

Wolf ignored her. "You still take your orders from me," he reminded her. His eyes narrowed. "Don't forget the contract James signed."

"You're nothing but a big bully, Wolf," Jessie said in a croak, laying her head on his shoulder, too worn out to argue with him. Her head had started to pound painfully, exhaustion blurred her vision and she was cold.

The anger vanished from his eyes, replaced by an amused glint. He grinned. "You wound me, Jessica. You didn't think I was so bad last night when you kissed me." His eyes darkened as he stared at her lips.

Jessie's flush deepened. "Go kiss Rosalyn. She's more

190

than willing. The two of you deserve each other,'' she shot back.

"Tsk, tsk, Jessica. Temper, temper.''

Jessie's mood darkened when he called her by her given name again. Jessica was a prissy name, a name for someone who wore frilly clothes, fancy hats and slippers. She wasn't that type of person and never would be. The thought hurt. Her temper flared. "My name is Jessie!'' She was proud of the haughty disdain in her voice, but the effect was lost when she went into a sneezing fit. She groaned in pain. Her throat was on fire.

Wolf tightened his hold. "Serves you right. Now maybe you'll shut up and do as you're told.'' When they reached her wagon, Wolf dropped her to her feet and removed the back gate to the wagon.

Jessie glanced inside. It was empty, except for some fresh dry bedding that Rook had scavenged from somewhere. Suddenly Jessie wanted nothing more than to crawl between the covers. As if he knew how tired and weak she felt, Wolf put his hands around her waist. He lifted her and sat her on the edge of the wagon bed, then removed her boots. She blinked in surprise. "What are you doing?''

Boots in hand, Wolf stared at her with undisguised amusement. "Making sure you stay put for the rest of the day. Now get under those blankets and sleep.''

Speechless, she stared at Wolf, torn between anger at his gall and pleasure that he cared. She narrowed her eyes. Anger was the safer emotion. Just because he now knew she was a woman didn't mean he could up and run roughshod over her. Tipping her chin, she flashed him a look of utter defiance. "You just love to play the big, bad bully, don't you? Well, take my boots, but you can't make me sleep if I don't want to.'' Though it was childish, she crossed her arms in front of her.

When she just sat there staring at him, he lifted his hand to her face and ran the back of his fingers down her flushed cheek, his calm gaze holding her glazed one. "Stubborn to the end, eh, Jessica? Listen well, then. When I take on a responsibility, I do my job, no matter what it takes. Seeing you and every member of this wagon train to Oregon safely is my highest priority. If you won't get under those covers on your own, I'll put you there myself.''

His blue eyes gleamed with devilment. ''And if you don't stay put, I'll just climb in with you and see that you stay in bed, even if it means sharing your bed to keep you there. Of course, if you're real cold, there's nothing like sharing body heat to warm a person.''

Jessie gasped and swallowed nervously. Just the mere thought of him sharing her bed chased away the chills. She felt her cheeks flush. ''You wouldn't!''

''No?''

He would. Of that Jessie had no doubt. He'd do it just to humiliate her and embarrass her in front of everyone. She whipped her head around with a huff of displeasure and scrambled inside. Pulling the warm weight of the quilts over her shoulders, she thumped her pillow and lay down with her head facing the back of the wagon so she could watch the activities if she wanted to. She refused to look at Wolf. He might have won this battle, but there'd be others.

Then Wolf did something that shocked her. He reached out and fingered one tightly curled lock of hair, rubbing the softness between his thumb and fingers. ''By the way, Jessica Naomi Jones, your brothers may forget you're a woman and treat you like a younger brother, but not me.''

Jessie narrowed her eyes. ''Who told you my name?''

Wolf shrugged. ''Does it matter? I like the name Jessica. It's beautiful. Like you.'' He then turned on his heel and strode off, leaving Jessie with her mouth wide-open and a glow of warmth and happiness spreading through her as she snuggled contentedly beneath the blankets.

Wolf wasn't sure if he was annoyed or amused. Jessie's outrage whenever he addressed her by her full name amused him, satisfied his wounded male pride. But her shocked expression when he'd told her she was beautiful annoyed him.

It confirmed that, raised by her brothers, she had no idea of her worth as a woman.

He stopped and stared out into the steaming prairie. And she *was* beautiful, with her mischievous gamine's grin, bright, lively eyes, kind heart and wild spirit that drew him to her. Something tickled his arm. He glanced down and saw a single black strand caught in the curly hair on his arm. He plucked it off and curled it around one finger. He sighed. Her hair was so soft, and he loved the way it framed her face and drew attention to the smattering of freckles across her nose and cheeks.

He stared out across miles of prairie, the bright green grass reminding him of her mischievous eyes when she had something up her sleeve. Little did she know her eyes were so expressive. They were a mirror to her soul, luring a man into their depths. And her lips. Against his will, he recalled the feel of her soft mouth, the taste of her and the womanly softness of her body pressed against his hard maleness. He drew in a deep, ragged breath when the blood pooled in his groin. No, there was no doubt about it. Jessica Jones was one hell of a woman, and she scared him senseless.

Forcing thoughts of their passionate kiss from his mind, Wolf resolved to keep his distance. Jessie was an innocent, and though he knew she wasn't out to use him as Rosalyn was, he feared she could hurt him far worse than Martha had. There was no place in his life for a woman, especially one who was high-spirited and who took perverse joy in challenging him. He rejoined his men, feeling thoroughly depressed.

The trail followed the Little Blue River; water, wood and grass were plentiful and the days were uneventful—paradise compared to the first three weeks of travel, with their difficult river crossings and rainy days. The emigrants were once again filled with hopes for the future as they continued up the pleasant valley of the Little Blue, heading for the famous Platte River.

By now the homeless emigrants had adjusted to life on the trail and considered themselves seasoned travelers. But even with their newfound confidence, not a day went by that they weren't reminded of the hazards of trail life. The hundreds of hastily dug graves along the rutted trail were constant reminders of the fragility of life.

Early morning of day twenty-three found Anne, Eirica, Jessie and Coralie staring down at a grave that had survived the ravages of time and nature. Jessie and Anne cleared out the choking weeds while Eirica and Coralie gathered armfuls of wildflowers to lay beside the grave site of one George Winslow, who had died June 8, 1849. It made no difference that the man was unknown to them; their need to pay their respects was stronger so far from civilization.

A shrill whistle sounded, signaling that it was time to roll. They hurried back. Coralie grabbed a long, thick walking stick from her wagon. She'd been surprised when Rook had presented it to her, along with an offer to teach her how to cook and build her own fires.

Coralie smiled to herself, pleased with the way things were going. Pride filled her as she thought of the meal she'd cooked for Jordan last night. It had been nearly perfect. Only her bread had been burned and Jordan had pretended not to notice that. Ready to begin another day's march, she took her place next to Jessie, wishing Jordan didn't have to watch over a bunch of stupid cows all day. She missed her husband during the long, tedious trek.

Admiration filled her as Jessie cracked her whip and steered the oxen into line. Because of Rickard's injury, Jessie had taken command of the team. Coralie was glad. It gave her someone to talk to during the day, as Anne and Eirica were usually busy with their children.

The very idea that she actually enjoyed her sister-in-law's company seemed so strange. She smirked. If only Becky and Sarah could see them now. Who'd have ever believed that she and Jessie would actually become friends?

Their truce had turned into mutual admiration and respect. Gone was the fighting and feuding. She no longer taunted Jessie for looking like a boy, and Jessie shared her knowledge and helped her whenever she needed it, which was pretty often. She chuckled softly. Her father would be so pleased. *He'd* always liked Jessie. She had a letter full of news to mail when they reached Fort Kearny, and she wished she could be there when he read it.

Jessie turned her head. Her voice still held a hint of her cold. "What's so funny, Coralie?"

Stretching her arms overhead, Coralie yawned. She still didn't like getting up so early. "I was thinking about us, the way things used to be."

"Oh."

"Doesn't it seem strange, Jessie? After all those years of us fighting, now to be friends?" She held her breath, praying Jessie wouldn't deny their friendship. For some reason she really wanted it to be true. She admired her onetime nemesis and envied her abilities. She frowned briefly. What good were all the social graces that she'd spent years perfecting?

When Jessie didn't answer, she licked her lips nervously. "We are friends, aren't we?"

"Yes, Coralie. We are definitely friends." The corners of Jessie's lips curved upward in a mischievous smirk. "I kinda miss things the way they were, though. Gotta admit, it wasn't boring between us."

Shuddering, Coralie jabbed Jessie in the ribs. "I for one don't miss it. You were pretty awful. I still don't know if I can forgive you for ruining my pretty pink dress. It was my favorite." She wrinkled her nose. "And ridding myself of that horrible stench—"

Jessie swatted the lead ox and pulled him back into line when he veered to the right. "Ah, but Coralie, you looked so pretty sitting on that manure pile—like icing on a cake."

The two women stared at one another; then both burst out in giggles. "You're incorrigible, Jessica Jones, but I forgive you. I wasn't very nice, either."

Jessie bent down, pulled a blade of grass from the ground and stuck it between her teeth. "What's done is done, Corie. It's what's ahead that counts. You're not so bad."

Coralie for once did not object to her newest nickname. In fact, she kind of liked it. It meant she was accepted. Up ahead, Elliot was having trouble with one of the oxen. Her mouth dropped open when Jessie thrust the leather leads into her hand.

"Here, hold these."

"Jessie, wait. I can't—" But Jessie was gone, leaving her to grip the reins gingerly. She eyed the oxen nervously. "Nice cows," she muttered, keeping as far from the lumbering beasts as possible. Glancing over her shoulder, she saw Anne walking between Kersten and Hanna, who were herding the four sluggish milk cows in front of them. In one hand Anna held a slate and was busy writing. Each morning she insisted on conducting lessons. Sometimes Jessie helped.

Up ahead and to the left, Eirica trudged behind her wagon, holding Ian by the hand. The toddler wore the sweater his mother had just finished knitting. Coralie grimaced. Both Eirica and Anne were trying to teach her how to knit, but so far their efforts had failed dismally. Even her sewing skills were far beneath the talents of these women. Faced with her lack of useful skills, Coralie felt depressed. She was useless. What good would she be in a new land where homemaking skills were required for survival? Her steps slowed. The oxen followed suit. She dreaded Oregon. She didn't want to disappoint Jordan, and she feared his love would turn to contempt. She pressed a hand to her middle. She could live with anything but that.

"Why the glum face, Corie?" Jessie asked, returning.

Coralie handed over the leather leads and thrust her stick into a small hole in the ground. "You're lucky, Jessica."

Jessie raised her brows. "Oh?"

"Look at you. You can do it all. Drive the oxen, hunt for food and cook decent meals. Even stampeding cattle didn't scare you. But what good am I? I'm not even pretty any-more.'' She sniffed. ''My clothes are plain, I'm always dirty and my skin is turning brown! I even have freckles!'' she wailed. Staring at her hands, Coralie voiced her worst fear. ''I won't have anything to offer Jordan by the time we reach. Oregon. I'll be so ugly he won't want me anymore.'' Her voice fell to a whisper.

Jessie started to laugh, then sobered when she realized Coralie was serious. She turned and walked backward. ''Come on, Corie. Don't you think you're being too hard on yourself? You're not ugly. You're still the prettiest woman around, even in boots and calico.'' She leaned close, her voice confiding.

''Besides, I know my brothers. I'll bet Jordan likes your freckles.''

Coralie looked skeptical. ''Then why hasn't he said any-thing?''

''Because, you ninny, if he had, you'd just start to bawl.'' She winked. ''Don't forget, I know you too.''

Coralie narrowed her eyes and stared hard at Jessie to see if she was just funning with her. She relaxed when Jessie seemed earnest. ''Really? You're not just saying that, are you?''

''Really.'' Jessie turned back around to snap the reins to keep the oxen moving.

Coralie felt better, but she still worried over the changes in her life. ''Well, that doesn't help me with the rest. I don't know how to make cloth, knit or even sew, let alone all the other stuff I've heard the pioneers have to do just to sur-vive.''

Jessie rolled her eyes. ''Come on, Coralie, don't borrow trouble. Jordan knew that when he asked you to marry him. And besides, by the time we reach Oregon, we'll have time to build only one house for all of us, so for the first year or so, we'll be living together.''

''And you'll help me?''

Jessie hooked her arm through Coralie's. ''I'll make you a deal. You teach me all that lady stuff—you know, how to dress nice and do my hair, after it grows out—and I'll teach you how to manage three—no, make that four—men living under one roof.''

Coralie brightened and grinned happily. ''Deal!''

Three days later, the pace slowed to a crawl as the emigrants encountered their first real bottleneck along the trail: the Narrows. On one side of the trail the Little Blue flowed, and on the east bank, tall rugged bluffs rose high above them. The trail became so narrow in places, the wagons were forced to proceed single file.

By afternoon, the emigrants made camp when it became clear that they wouldn't make it through the Narrows before nightfall. In the morning, they continued on with their journey, and soon after leaving the Narrows behind, the emigrants said farewell to the Little Blue and trudged over the sandy hills that separated them from the Platte River.

The night before reaching the Platte, Jessie sat in front of the dying embers of the fire, thumbing through her guidebook for information on the famous river. She held the pages up to the lantern beside her and scanned page after page. To her disappointment, there wasn't much mention of the famous river. When Rook joined her, she turned to him. ''Rook, did you know that Platte is French for *flat*?''

Rook grunted and lit his pipe. Jessie smiled, well used to his ways. He'd talk when good and ready; then there'd be no shutting him up. ''Is it really as flat as everyone says?''

Settling himself on his box with a block of wood in one hand, his knife in the other, Rook went through his nightly ritual of smoking his pipe. After several minutes, he stuck the stem into the corner of his mouth, then stroked his beard.

''Ah, so now ya wants to know 'bout the Platte, eh, lass? Well, it's true. Flatter 'n' a pancake, she is. The river is like none other. Floats bottom-side up. Not more 'n' a couple inches deep in some places, yet it's a mile wide.'' With his smoldering pipe clenched between his lips, he whittled over the fire. The slivers of wood fell into the flames and caught fire.

Wolf stepped from the shadows surrounding them. "My people call the river *Nebraska*. It means weeping water."

Jessie held her breath, and her heart fluttered with pleasure when he stepped into the flickering light. It was obvious he'd just come from bathing in the river. Rivulets of water dripped from his long hair and rolled down his bare chest. He hunkered down in front of the fire and held his hands out to the warmth of the glowing embers.

Drops of water slid from his shoulders and hit the fire, sizzling loudly, sending wisps of steam rising from the pit. Mesmerized, Jessie stared at his profile. She watched the soft glow of light flicker and dance along the hard planes of his face, chasing away the concealing shadows and softening his hard features.

Her gaze devoured the long, thick lashes shielding his eyes, the gentle slope of his nose and the relaxed set of his full lips. Even his jaw seemed less harsh in the firelight. Desire unfurled deep inside her, but Wolf seemed oblivious to it—and her, she thought sourly. In fact, it seemed as though he'd forgotten her presence entirely as he engaged Rook in a discussion of the coming day. A wave of frustration hit her. He spoke to her only when necessary. And no matter how many excuses she found to speak to him or to see him, she hadn't been able to break down the barrier he'd erected between them. Her heart ached with deep disappointment.

At her side, Sadie growled. Wahoska sauntered into their midst, taking his place beside Rook. Jessie glanced down in annoyance. The animals' animosity toward each other seemed to symbolize that between her and Wolf, a fact she meant to change. "Hush, Sadie," she commanded, her voice low and husky. During a lull in the men's conversation, she addressed Wolf. "I talked to James tonight. He thinks we'll reach Fort Kearny tomorrow."

Wolf's gaze snapped to hers. "We'll be camped within

three miles of the fort by nightfall.'' That said, he went back to staring into the glowing embers.

Jessie swallowed a groan of frustration and ignored the speculative glances Rook threw her way. She tried again to engage Wolf in conversation. "Before we leave in the morning, I'm going to go see Susan Hail's grave."

"Best do it early—before chores. We leave at daybreak."

Encouraged, Jessie sighed, resting her chin on her drawn-up knees. "What an incredibly sad and romantic story. Imagine her poor husband burying her, then returning all the way back to St. Joe to fetch a headstone and bring it back here in a handcart." She watched Wolf from beneath her lashes. No response. Her lips tightened and her gaze narrowed. Some sense of devilment prompted her to ask, "Do you suppose it's true that she died drinking water poisoned by Indians?" That got a response.

Wolf whipped his head around, sending drops of water flying. He stood and glared down at her. "More likely she sickened and died from drinking water polluted by too many people and animals camped too close to the water supply," he snapped. Planting his hands on his hips, he frowned. "Don't you have something to do besides talk our ears off? If not, why don't you be a good girl and head off to bed?"

Stung, Jessie stood toe-to-toe with him. "I'm not a child to be ordered to bed, White Wolf." Her chin jutted out. "Seems to me that you're the one who's touchy as a teased snake. Maybe you should take your own advice and find the nearest hole in the ground to slither into."

Picking up her lantern, she turned to leave. "Just in case I'm too busy with my *chores* in the morning, I'll go see Susan's grave now. She's sure to prove better company than you!"

The two men watched until the moving light faded, swallowed by the darkness. "Ya gonna let her go off alone in the dark, lad?"

Wolf glared at his old friend and shrugged. "She can take

care of herself. Don't know why she carries a whip. Her tongue can rip shreds off a person without even trying.''

Rook sent shavings of wood flying. ''Reckon you're right. Jess ain't no fainthearted town gal who needs a man to protect her from trouble. The lassie'll be fine out there by herself.''

Wolf snorted and shrugged his vest on. ''Reckon she'll cause the trouble!''

Rook calmly wielded his hard blade against the soft wood. ''Ya riled her on purpose, lad. Don't think I can't see what's goin' on b'tween the two of you. I gots eyes, ya know. They may be old, but they's not blind.''

''Now you're the one talking crazy, old man. She's nothing but trouble.'' Wolf paced in front of the fire, shadows dancing around him. After a few minutes, he took off into the prairie.

Rook grinned and shook his head. Those two were the most stubborn people he knew. He eyed the two animals left behind. They faced one another, low growls coming from both throats. He sighed. ''Reckon you two should settle your differences as well.'' He went to the wagon and returned with two meat-covered bones. Sitting, he called each animal to him, holding a bone out to each. The dog and wolf snapped up their bones, eyeing each other before plopping down—one on either side of Rook—to gnaw their unexpected treats. Neither animal was willing to leave in case the other was offered more prime scraps.

Chapter Fourteen

Wolf donned his vest, feeling like a heel. For days he'd done his best to avoid Jessica Jones. It was for her own good. He'd tried to convince himself that he was protecting her from hurt and disappointment, but deep down he knew better. By keeping his distance, he was shielding his own heart from pain.

The love in Jessie's emerald green eyes scared him because he knew there could be nothing lasting between them. To pursue her meant commitment, something he longed to give but couldn't. And he knew her brothers well enough to know he'd have to deal with them if he hurt their sister. The Jones siblings were close, tight-knit. He was no longer angry at being deceived. Part of him even admired their courage, all in the name of staying together. All he had to do was think of his own siblings. There wasn't anything they wouldn't do for each other.

Yet, because of his family, his commitment to the People, he couldn't remain in Oregon, nor could he expect Jessie to return with him when his future was uncertain. Come spring he'd return to his cabin, his horses and his lonely existence. The thought left a hollow ache in his heart.

Slowing when he neared the faint glow of Jessie's lantern, Wolf crouched down in the tall grass to watch over her and make sure she returned to camp safely. He plucked a blade of grass and closed his eyes, allowing his mind to see what his eyes couldn't in the blanketing darkness. To his right, bedded down half a mile away, cattle lowed. Behind him came the quiet murmurs of emigrants preparing for bed. And from somewhere in front came the sound of crying.

His eyes snapped open and sought the woman he feared he was losing his heart to. The flickering lantern revealed that she was still crouched beside the grave, sobbing. She was right. He *was* snakeheaded. It was *his* problem that he wanted her so badly he couldn't sleep, couldn't concentrate on his job. With a sigh of defeat, Wolf went to her.

Standing behind her, he opened his mouth to apologize, but no words came. Her heartbroken sobs ripped holes in his gut and left him reeling for breath. He stared at his hands, wanting nothing more than to reach down and gather her into his arms, but they fell uselessly to his sides. He feared if he touched her he'd do more than offer comfort.

Jessie didn't move, didn't acknowledge his presence, but judging by the set of her shoulders she knew he was there. Tension thickened the air. Wolf hunched down and tentatively laid his hands on her shoulders. Beneath his fingers, she shook as she continued to cry. Swearing, he let his hands follow the taut line of muscles to her neck, then back down as he sought to soothe and comfort.

Wolf lost track of time as he knelt beside her. Finally her sobs subsided to an occasional hiccup. When she spoke, her voice was low, husky with emotion. Reaching out, she lovingly traced the lettering on the headstone.

"June second, 1852," she whispered sadly. "Her husband must've loved her an awful lot to have gone to so much trouble to preserve her final resting place so everyone who passes by will remember her. I wonder if she knew how lucky she was to have found a love so strong that even in death she wouldn't be forgotten."

He felt her shudder. Staring down at the top of her bent head, he fastened his gaze on the back of her neck where her silky black curls had fallen aside. He twirled the fine strands around his fingers; then his hands slipped beneath the dark curtain of hair and slid forward to her face. He felt the wetness dripping from her chin and closed his eyes against the pain that cleaved his heart in two. Tenderly, he stroked her tears away with his thumbs.

She glanced over her shoulder and her haunting green gaze captured his. His insides squeezed. When she spoke, he had to lean close to hear. "I'm sorry, Wolf. It's not your fault. I'm too boyish. Men want women who are beautiful—like Coralie—or they want someone like their mother, someone who will cook, clean and bear children."

Her chin came up. "That's not me. I'll never be able to stay home and cook and sew all day." She waved her hands. "Look at me. I don't wear my brothers castoffs because they're all I have. I wear men's trousers and shirts because I'm not comfortable wearing a dress." Fresh tears welled. Wolf watched her fight them back. Her jaw tightened and her nostrils flared. "I know and accept that I'm not woman enough for a man like you." Her lower lip trembled despite her brave words.

"Oh, hell." Wolf pulled her against him, turning her so she sat in his lap. Rocking her, he smoothed the hair from her face. *"Ceye·sni yo.* Don't cry, Jessica. Don't do this to yourself. You were right. I'm a low-down, rotten snake. There's nothing wrong with you. It's not your fault," he murmured.

The dam holding back her tears broke. "Look at me, Jess," he whispered, using the nickname he knew she preferred. She shook her head, hiding her face in her hands. Wolf cupped her chin in one hand, forcing her to look at him.

She stared up at him, her eyes luminous in the moonlight. He wiped the tears away. "What's this about your not being woman enough?" She sniffed and tried to look away, but Wolf held firm.

"It's true. I don't blame you for wanting Rosalyn," she said.

Wolf sighed and pulled her closer. So much for trying to keep his distance. When the soft curve of one breast brushed against his arm, he nearly groaned aloud. "You foolish girl, I've never kissed Rosalyn Norton. Nor do I plan to kiss her, or do anything else with her. You are much more of a woman than she. You have what it takes to live anywhere and survive. Not everyone can do that, Jess. You should be proud to be a strong woman.''

"But you said—''

Wolf silenced her with a finger pressed against her lips. "Don't remind me. I know what I said, but it wasn't true. I wanted to make you mad so you'd stay away.''

"But why?''

Wolf drew a deep breath, his nostrils flaring as he struggled with his emotions. "Listen to me, Jessica. I'm not the right man for you. You need someone who can make a commitment, someone who can stay in Oregon and marry you—like Elliot. You don't need a half-breed who doesn't know what he wants in life. You need—''

Jessie turned in his arms, rising up onto her knees, her eyes filled with longing, her lips full and inviting. Her fingers slid up and over his shoulders until she caressed the back of his neck, bringing her face close to his. Her warm breath rolled across his lips. She sighed. "What do I need, Wolf? Show me what I need.''

Unbridled desire flooded him. He'd never wanted anyone or anything as much as this green-eyed enchantress. Her lips, full, pink and lush, tempted him. Her breath, innocently alluring, drove all his hard-won resolve from him. Closing his eyes, he drew a shaky breath. Pain sliced through him. Refusing her was sheer torture.

He wanted nothing more than to stroke the moist flesh of her inner mouth with his tongue and savor the sweet scent of her. Passion raged inside him, but he held back, afraid of frightening her with the enormity of his desire. His hands framed her face, held her captive as his gaze roamed over her features, seeing the ghost of pain and rejection in her eyes.

"Please, Wolf, show me how to please you,'' she pleaded. Her lips trembled, and the green of her eyes swam in a pool of despair.

Wolf crushed her to him, unable to deny either one of

them what they both wanted and craved. He thrust his tongue past her parted lips, taking her with a savage need that rocked him to the soul. A low groan rose up in his throat.

He tried to draw back, to go slowly and gently, but Jessie would have none of it. Her arms wrapped around his neck, and she held him to her, her passion matching his as her tongue snaked out to tease and torment his.

Their mouths mated as they each relearned the feel, texture and taste of the other. Locked in each other's arms, they fell to the soft bed of grass. Jessie lay sprawled across Wolf under the bright canopy of stars and moonlight. Wolf showed her with his lips what he needed while his hands stroked the gentle sway of her back and inched down to grip her buttocks, pulling her against him for one brief moment before rolling her beneath him.

When he pulled away, Jessie stared up at the man she was falling in love with. The soft grass pillowed her head, and her mouth burned from the heat of his kisses. More. She wanted more. Her eyes begged him to return to her. Wolf lowered his head once again, his lips searing a path along her jaw and down her throat, pausing to linger at the hollow he found there.

A shiver of anticipation ran through her when his fingers feathered down the center of her chest, then splayed over her belly. When his hand brushed the underside of her breast, her breath caught in her throat. He cupped the slight mound of firm flesh, and the warmth of his palm caressing her left her gasping and clutching his shoulders. A throbbing ache began between her legs. "Please, Wolf," she said in a whimper. Her voice ended on a husky gasp when his fingers kneaded one cloth-covered nipple, bringing it to a hard, throbbing peak. Her breast swelled in its eagerness for his loving attention. In that moment, Jessie felt like a woman.

He unbuttoned her shirt, the brush of fingers warm against her bare skin. Need, want, and desire now warred with embarrassment and shame. She stopped him, pulling her shirt closed. "Wolf—"

His lips moved over hers. "I want to see you, Jessica. I

need to see you,'' he whispered, his lips meeting hers in a brief, teasing caress.

Eyes wide, she caught her lower lip between her teeth. "I'm not much of a woman there, Wolf," she confessed, her voice small, filled with uncertainty.

Wolf laughed, the sound soft, not unkind as he traced the curve of her jaw. "Sweet Jess. What I felt was very womanly. Trust me."

Shy and uncertain, she stared up at him. "Okay, but your vest goes first."

Wolf sat up, his gaze holding hers, but before he could shed the softened deerhide, Jessie rose to her knees and pulled the garment from him, then splayed her fingers out over his chest. Her unbuttoned shirt parted to reveal creamy, smooth skin.

Jessie's fingers threaded a path through the furry mat of springy curls that begged to be touched and caressed. To her surprise, he shuddered when her fingers rubbed his nipples. Moving her hands upward over the hard planes of his chest, she stroked the breadth of his shoulders, then leaned into him, bringing them flesh to flesh, hardness meeting softness. Jessie's head lolled back as she reveled in the rough texture abrading her sensitive flesh.

Wolf moaned and shoved her shirt down her arms. When her breasts were bared to his hungry gaze, he gripped her waist with both hands and slid his lips down the side of her neck, leaving a trail of heated flesh in his wake. One arm supported her from behind, while the other drifted down to stroke her belly, moving ever upward. Slowly he bent her over his arm until golden moonbeams revealed her aroused flesh to him. His fingers, rough and callused, caressed one rosy peak.

Jessie cried out. Her fingers dug into his arms as waves of new and wonderful sensations swirled through her, leaving her weak and giddy. Then she was lying on the ground, his mouth warm and wet as it closed over one straining breast. Her back arched as he licked, laved and worshiped until she feared she'd burst.

When his lips pulled away and moved to her other straining nipple, the night air brushed over her moist skin, making her shiver with awareness. Again his tongue stroked and teased before his lips closed over the tight bud, drawing it into his mouth to suckle. Jessie gasped, her hands tangling in his hair. "Don't stop," she begged, moving restlessly under him.

Wolf groaned and lifted his head for a brief moment before resting his forehead against her desire-flushed skin. "God, Jess, we've got to stop. Now." When she protested, he laid a finger against her lips. "Trust me. If we don't, I'll take you right here, right now."

He sat and stroked her pale flesh one last time before he closed her shirt. "You're beautiful, perfect," he said, his voice thick with need as he came back down over her to take her lips in one last searing kiss. His fingers twined with hers to keep her from wrapping her arms around his neck. Then he stood and pulled her to her feet. Jessie stared up at him, bewildered. Why didn't he take what she offered? But before her insecurities had a chance to surface and taunt her, Wolf took one of her hands in his.

"Do you have any idea how much I want you, Jessica Jones?" He placed her hand against the bulge in his pants. "Feel how much I want you. Don't ever think you're not woman enough for me. But I can't do this—we can't do this. You're starting a new life in Oregon, and I can't stay to be a part of it. I must return home to my people and the responsibilities there."

Jessie lifted a hand to his stubbled jaw. "I could go back with you," she whispered, ignoring the sharp pang of sadness that washed over her at the thought of leaving her family.

A cloud passed overhead, shadowing them in a cloak of darkness. Wolf closed his eyes, grateful she couldn't see the moisture gathering in his eyes. So sweet were her words, but the stakes were high, too high. Somehow Jessie had broken through his defenses and unearthed the lonely man he'd become.

Since childhood, he'd been forced to walk his path alone, belonging to no one and nothing. Until now, that part of him had been kept buried in a cavern deep inside. But now loneliness rose through the many fissures and threatened to surround and suffocate him.

He'd been a fool to give in to his desire to kiss her, to touch her silky skin. Pain twisted his gut. He placed his hand over hers, sandwiching her fingers against his rough chin. Full of regret for what could not be, he shook his head. "No, your life is in Oregon with your family." With one last caress of her face, Wolf rolled to his feet and pulled her up to him. "Someday, my sweet Jess, you will find a man worthy of you." Stepping back, he turned and left her.

Jessie watched his silhouette fade into the black shadows. Her heart pulsed out of control with each breath that tore from her. Tears streamed down her cheeks, and she pressed her hand to her heart. "I have found the man for me," she whispered into the still night air.

Far away in a small Miniconjou village, Star Dreamer slept. Dreams and visions chased one another behind her closed eyelids until they blended together, making it impossible to separate the two. A smile curved her lips upward at an image of her brother, Wolf, kissing a green-eyed woman beneath a star-studded sky. Then her vision blurred, their forms misting, becoming indistinguishable, but she felt the mix of strong emotions that surrounded the two lovers. With certainty, she knew this woman would someday be her sister.

Suddenly she felt something else. Hatred, dark, menacing and evil. Cold, bone-deep and frightening in its intensity, it held her in its icy grip. She was helpless to do anything but watch as a jagged bolt of fury fell between Wolf and the woman, tearing them apart. She tried to call out, to warn them of the danger, but couldn't. Her brows drew together, and her head rolled from side to side as she fought the dream. She didn't want to see this. Didn't want to know things. But the vision held her, forcing her to watch future events unfold.

Star stopped fighting when she realized her brother was in

danger. She had to help him, but try as she might the shadowed form of evil remained faceless until it too faded. This time she tried to hold on to the dream, learn more. But it was over. She woke bathed in sweat. Lying on her back, she willed herself to stay calm by taking deep, even breaths as her grandmother had taught her.

Tears gathered in her eyes. How she wished for her grandmother's comfort and words of wisdom. She turned her head and stared at her husband, needing to talk to someone about the visions that haunted her. Each revealed a bit more, but not enough for her to understand.

Two-Ree slept soundly. Lifting her hand to wake her husband, Star Dreamer hesitated, then let her hand drop back to her chest. What could she tell him? Her visions remained too hazy. After a long time, she turned onto her side, but didn't close her eyes.

The following day the emigrants reached the south bank of the Platte River, referred to as the Coast of Nebraska. By the day's end they arrived at Fort Kearny, the "Gateway to the Great Plains." The mood drifting on the breeze was one of relief and cheer. The emigrants had traveled over three hundred miles in a month's time. Travelers who knew each other by sight if not by name came together to share their joy and jubilation.

Women went from wagon to wagon, trading their excesses for goods they'd fallen short on, while men grouped together to trade stories. Soldiers, many of them no more than young boys, homesick and eager for news from home, rode across the prairie to welcome the travelers and spread the word that their fort boasted a storehouse, post office, laundry, blacksmith facilities and a crude hospital. Invitations to share a meal and company were made and accepted.

Jessie, Eirica and Coralie walked a short distance to get a better view of the fort. The four-acre fort presented a drab, squalid and homely appearance, with its ramshackle collection of sod, sunbaked adobe and a few wood-framed buildings. Eirica was disappointed by the sight. She'd expected something much grander.

"Look. There's the flag. Hard to believe we're still on American soil. It's so different."

Eirica glanced upward and beheld the flag, bearing stars and stripes, waving proudly in the breeze. The sight didn't reassure her. She still felt as though she were standing on foreign land. She turned in a slow circle. Spreading out up to a mile from the fort, circles of white-topped wagons littered the prairie. "There must be hundreds of wagons out here."

Coralie clapped her hands, her voice high with excitement. "Oh, I do hope this means there's going to be a dance tonight."

Jessie grinned and rolled her eyes. "Don't worry, Corie, with this many people, there's going to be a lot of celebrating and visiting going on. Come on, I'd best get back to help with the chores." The three women walked back to camp.

After supper, music from fiddles filled the air, luring everyone to an evening of visiting and dancing except Eirica. James stood in the shadows of the corralled wagons and silently watched her pace back and forth. She stopped every so often to scan the night-shrouded prairie, and when she did, the delicate features of her profile were bathed by moonlight. He sucked in his breath. Even rounded with child, she was beautiful.

Her golden-red hair hung down her back in one long twisted rope and her hands rested on her abdomen. As soon as he'd learned from Jessie that Eirica had stayed behind, he'd decided to come and make sure she was all right. He didn't like the idea of her being left alone.

Her husband was drinking with his buddies and on an evening when drink flowed heavier than normal, James worried that Birk would return too drunk to heed the warnings Wolf had given him. James couldn't allow him to beat Eirica again, but how could he prevent it? His forehead creased with worry. He could only hope that Birk would drink himself into a stupor and pass out somewhere on the prairie. That gave him an idea. He grinned. It was perfect.

Just as he was about to leave, he noticed that Eirica seemed to be in pain. Surely, she wasn't in labor. He mouth went dry. He had no idea where to find Mrs. Svensson. Stepping out of the shadows, he cleared his throat softly and waited for Eirica to acknowledge his presence. She glanced at him, looking skittish, ready to bolt. He didn't want to frighten her, so he stopped a fair distance from her and removed his hat. "You have nothing to fear, Mrs. Macauley. I came to find Jessie," he lied, "and couldn't help notice that you seemed to be in pain. If the babe is coming, I can fetch help. Your husband, I believe, is visiting with a group of men bound for California."

Her gaze met his for one brief second before dropping to the ground. She clasped her arms in front of her. Her voice was a carefully controlled whisper. "What a kind way of saying my husband has found someone to supply him with more spirits so he can get drunk, Mr. Jones."

James stepped closer and like a startled doe, she glanced up, her eyes wide with fear. He smiled gently. "You are correct, Mrs. Macauley. And judging by the way those spirits are flowing, I'd be very surprised if he found his way back to camp tonight."

Eirica laughed, but the sound held no humor. "Fear not, Mr. Jones. My husband will find his way. He always does," she said, her voice quavering with the fear she couldn't suppress.

James felt helpless. There wasn't anything he could do and it didn't sit well with him. As head of his household, he was use to being in control, making decisions and protecting his loved ones. The thought of this woman being left to the mercy of an abusive husband with no family to intervene left a sour taste in his mouth. Frustration ate at him. How the fates must be laughing at him, he thought glumly. How ironic that a woman who was so attractive to him was married to an abusive husband.

He pursed his lips and glared at the heavens for their cruel jest. Turning to leave, he realized she was still rubbing her belly. Concern overrode his other emotions. Clearing his throat, he asked, "Should I fetch Mrs. Svensson?"

Eirica turned back to him and shook her head. "No, the babe is fine."

An uncomfortable silence fell and James knew he should leave. Birk would be angry if he should see them talking. He replaced his hat, tipped the brim toward her, then strode away. Mounting his horse, he rode until he found a soldier he'd talked to earlier who agreed to slip a bit of sleeping powder into Birk's drink. After watching the man head off to where Macauley was carousing, James rode a short distance away then stopped. Pulling his mouth organ from his shirt pocket, he played softly, comforted by the knowledge that Eirica would be safe from her husband's abuse tonight.

Chapter Fifteen

At daybreak, Jessie and Rook drove four oxen into the fort to have their worn shoes replaced. While Rook saw to the animals, Jessie explored the fort. Walking across the parade grounds, she noticed uniformed men coming and going from several wood-framed buildings. She assumed the structures were the officers' quarters and their offices, and that the enlisted soldiers occupied the sod or adobe buildings.

Threading her way through the crowd, she spotted the tiny post office. Inside, she handed over a packet of letters. Most were addressed to Orvil Baker or Coralie's friends, but one was destined for Eirica's parents, hidden in the pile without Birk's knowledge. Jessie left the post office. A cloud passed in front of the sun, raising the gooseflesh on her arms. Hugging herself to ward off the morning chill, she stewed over Eirica and her troubled marriage. How could Birk be so mean as to forbid his wife any contact with her family?

Birk's possessiveness and mistreatment of his family infuriated her and seemed to grow worse with each mile they traveled. Jessie wished there were something she could do, but it truly didn't seem her place to do anything straightforward.

She chuckled as she basked in the success of her latest scheme. It had been so easy to bribe a young soldier into giving Birk a flask of whisky doctored with a few drops of laudanum. Laughing out loud, she ignored the smiles sent her way. Her plan the night before had worked wonderfully. So well, in fact, that Birk had passed out on the prairie and had to be carried back to their camp by Lars and his sons. The sun came out from behind the clouds as if sharing her glee.

"Hey, pal, you've got a wicked look about you. What have you been up to, Jessie Jones?"

Jessie whirled around and saw Elliot and Coralie coming toward her. Arching her brow and schooling her features into a mask of innocence, she shrugged. "I'm not up to anything, Elliot. Just checking the place out while Rook gets a couple of the oxen reshod. Hey, look. They have a store too. Think I'll see what they have."

Elliot shook his head. "Nice try, brat, but I know that look. You've been up to your old tricks again."

Jessie opened her mouth to deny it, then grinned. "You wound me, Elliot. What possible trouble could I get into here?"

Rolling his eyes, Elliot cuffed her gently. "You don't really want me to list all the things your devious little mind could cook up, do you? We'd be here all night."

They laughed. Elliot tipped his head to one side. "You left the Adamses' wagon early last night. My dancing wasn't that bad, was it?'' he asked, a twinkle in his eyes.

Jessie felt a nostalgic stab of longing. There was a time when she'd have given everything she owned to achieve the closeness she and Elliot now shared. Unfortunately, she'd outgrown her girlish infatuation for the handsome blond man, leaving her to pine for a stubborn wagon master too blind to see how well suited they were. She sighed to herself. Life would be so much simpler if it *were* Elliot who held her heart. But not nearly as exciting, an inner voice whispered, bringing to mind thoughts and sensations that sent heat rising in her cheeks.

Unwilling to let her thoughts ruin her outing, she winked at Coralie and shook her head with mock disappointment. ''Just wasn't the same without any of Mrs. Applegate's pink punch.''

''Brat.'' Elliot reached out and yanked her hat down over her eyes. ''Seriously, Jess. Is everything all right?'' he asked, his eyes shadowed with worry.

Staring into Elliot's sky blue eyes, seeing the brotherly concern, Jessie had the uncomfortable feeling that he knew of her feelings for Wolf. She stared at the tips of her toes. ''Yeah, things are fine. Just fine. I was just tired last night.''

Coralie shifted and fanned herself. ''Can we get moving? It's hot out here.''

Elliot grimaced and laid a casual arm around Jessie's shoulder. ''Want to walk back with us? We've already been in the store.''

Jessie shook her head. ''Thanks, but I should check with Rook and see if he needs help.''

She waved them off and headed for the storehouse. Inside, it was cool and crowded. Emigrants lined the wooden counters, their purchases piled in front of them. Wandering around, she stopped at a small barrel filled with bags of colored beads.

Thoughtfully, she grabbed one and opened it, fingering the cool glass beads. They were for trading with the Indians, but she knew two little girls who'd love them as well. She chose one for Alison and one for Lara, then took her place at the end of the counter to await her turn. While waiting to pay for the beads, Jessie let her gaze travel around the room. Shelves loaded with supplies lined three walls, while the fourth wall had been designated as a message board. Bits of paper fluttered in the breeze from the open door. Jessie scanned them. Most were notes letting family or friends know the writer had made it this far safely; others gave news of the trail ahead passed from wagon train to wagon train. Sadly she also noted the death announcements. Her gaze skimmed further to several Wanted posters.

"Morning, Jessie," Anne called out, pushing through the throng of browsers to join her.

Jessie turned away from her study of one poster, which showed sketches of two men and a woman. "Mornin', Anne. Isn't it a wonderful day?"

The other woman grinned and smothered a laugh behind her hand. "Sure is. I trust the laudanum did the trick."

She returned Anne's conspiratorial wink and giggled as she paid for the beads. "Sure did. Worked like a charm. Why didn't I think of it—"

"I didn't realize you were ill yesterday, Jessica."

At the sound of Wolf's deeply concerned voice, Jessie choked on her glee and went into a coughing fit. Strong hands thumped her enthusiastically on the back. She waved Wolf away and, with eyes watering, glanced over her shoulder.

Wolf lifted a brow. His eyes gleamed, boding ill for her. Of all the people to run into, he was the one person she needed to avoid at all costs. Though she was fast losing her heart to him, she was smart enough not to want to invoke his fury. No matter his feelings toward her, he was still White Wolf, wagon master.

Thinking fast, she hugged her purchases to her chest and shrugged. "Hmm, not really. Just had a bit of an achy head, but I'm fine today." With relief, she noticed that Anne had finished paying for her supplies. "Umm, well, we should go. Getting kinda crowded in here." Jessie and Anne scurried out into the sunlight, leaving Wolf to await his turn to pay for his purchases.

The two women quickened their steps across the compound, hurrying toward the open prairie. Jessie glanced over her shoulder, feeling guilty for abandoning Rook. There was no sign of Wolf. She breathed a sigh of relief. If he found out what she'd done last night, he'd be furious. Just when she thought she was free and clear, Wolf caught up with them and positioned himself between her and Anne. Jessie swore under her breath. Her heart sank to the toes of her boots. She knew him well enough to know he wasn't there to engage in idle chitchat.

Sure enough, he turned to Anne. "You don't mind if I speak with Jessica alone, do you, Mrs. Svensson?"

She and Anne exchanged nervous glances. Jessie stopped and blurted, "Oh, shucks, I forgot. I'm supposed to meet Rook when he's through and help him with the oxen." She spun on her heel.

Wolf grabbed her arm and swept her away from Anne, who headed back to the wagons. "I think Rook can handle the oxen. This won't take but a moment. One would think you didn't want to be with me, hmm?" His gaze slid to her lips. "Not the impression you gave me the last time we were alone."

Jessie gulped. She had the horrible feeling Wolf was playing with her, as if—but no, he couldn't know. She'd been careful. "Don't be silly." She forced a laugh.

Wolf continued pleasantly, "Everyone seemed to have a good time last night. Did you?"

She slid him a look from the corner of her eye. "Sure. Met a lot of nice people."

"Didn't stay up too late, did you?"

Jessie feigned a yawn. "Guess I stayed out too late. But no crime in that. Today *is* a day of rest." Her voice challenged him. "In fact, maybe I'll take a nice long nap before suppertime."

Wolf nodded. "True. No need to get your dander up." He slid her a sideways glance. "You're not the only one tired today. Mrs. Macauley's husband is still abed, and it's past midmorning. Perhaps if he's not awake when we get back, I should make sure he's all right.''

Jessie bit her lower lip and drew it into her mouth with worry. ''Ah, I don't think that's such a good idea, Wolf. He must've drunk an awful lot last night, so maybe it'd be best to let him sleep it off,'' she suggested, keeping her eyes trained on the uneven ground.

Desperate to get away, she pulled her arm from Wolf's grasp and quickened her steps. ''James said you're selling a few head of cattle to the soldiers, so I won't keep you.''

Wolf laid his arm across her shoulders, preventing her escape. ''How considerate of you, but I've already finished my business. I'll just escort you back to camp. No telling what shady characters are hanging about. Wouldn't want you to run into Zeb, now, would we? Scarred his face but good with that whip of yours,'' he commented casually.

Jessie's jaw fell. Neither she nor Eirica had ever mentioned running into the drunken man to anybody. When she'd learned that he was traveling, she'd kept a low profile, making sure he didn't see her when their trains passed one another.

Before she could explain, Wolf lifted a brow. ''Well talk about that one later. Let's talk about your more recent activities.''

''How 'bout not,'' Jessie mumbled.

Wolf ignored her and continued thoughtfully, ''I spoke to James earlier. Seems he was a bit worried to find Birk still sleeping. His unexpected concern over a man he despises made me curious, so I asked him why he cared.''

He paused dramatically. ''To my surprise, he confessed to drugging Birk's drink last night with laudanum.''

Jessie stopped and stared in disbelief. ''James did what?'' Her voice ended on a squeak, and her mind raced. Surely she hadn't heard right. James, her straitlaced, never-do-wrong brother, had drugged Birk?

''You heard me.'' Wolf rested his hands casually on his hips. ''Now mind you, his intentions were good; something about wanting to make sure Birk slept through his drunken stupor and didn't beat up on Eirica. Very clever of him, wouldn't you agree, Jessica?''

"Sounds like it worked," she muttered, wondering where this was leading. But she knew. Somehow he'd found out that she'd done the same thing. She sighed in defeat and thrust her chin out. It wouldn't do any good to continue the charade. She glared at him, daring him to take her to task. "It served him right," she said under her breath. "How'd you find me out?" She kicked a stone.

Wolf lifted a brow, his mouth set in a grim line. "About the incident with Zeb or that you drugged Birk's drink?"

Jessie screwed up her face. "Both." Resigned to his anger, she waited.

Wolf put his hands on his hips, his features grim. "Let's take Zeb first. I saw the whole thing. Before I could step in and take care of him, you were there with your whip. Nice piece of work. Of course, I followed him once I saw that you were taking care of Eirica. Added my own warnings to yours and have kept my eye out for him and his buddies since.''

Jessie swallowed hard. "You followed him—"

Wolf startled her by slashing the air with one hand. "No one threatens or harms those under my protection. *No one*."

Oh, lordy, here it comes. Jessie braced herself.

"And as for last night, I saw Birk drinking with Zeb and his pals and found it particularly interesting when a soldier joined them with a flask just for Birk. Heard them laughing when the soldier said some lady sent it. Of course, I had to wonder who this lady was.''

Jessie groaned, but Wolf continued, his voice conversational, yet she heard the thread of fury and disappointment underlying his words.

"Curious, I followed the soldier." A gleam came into his eyes. "I convinced the lad that it was in his best interest to tell me what was going on.''

"Convinced? His best interest?" Jessie repeated in horror. She cringed at Wolf's smug expression.

"Not to worry, Jessica, dear. I didn't touch him. Didn't need to. He figured out on his own that it was wise to tell me what I wanted to know. He was only too happy to spill his guts. But can you imagine my surprise when he described you as the one who paid him to deliver the bottle?"

His voice hardened. "Didn't take much to figure out you'd drugged Birk's drink, as apparently James had done. Hearing you and Anne only confirmed it."

Jessie bit her lip and focused her attention on the row of fringe sewn into the yoke of his buckskin shirt. She supposed he'd traded his vest for a more conventional shirt because of the visit to the fort. "Don't blame her. If she hadn't given it to me, I would have gotten it elsewhere."

Wolf stepped close and gripped her chin, forcing her to meet his furious blue gaze. "Jessica, be careful. Birk Macauley's not a man to play games with. While he may or may not deserve it, it's not your place to punish him. Are you willing to accept the responsibility of his death? He could have died."

Jessie swallowed hard, her face paling, her eyes wide. "You don't think—"

"No, he won't die. He's just sleeping—deeply—but you and your brother are lucky. What if, God help us, others had done the same thing?" Wolf released her, stepped back and folded his arms across his chest.

Jessie narrowed her eyes. "I didn't think anyone else would do it too."

"You were lucky, as you were with the hornets. Men have been known to die from that many stings."

Jessie winced. Wolf knew all. She didn't know how, didn't want to know. She dug a toe into the sandy soil. While it hurt to have Wolf angry with her and disappointed in her, she didn't regret what she'd done. Well, maybe just her impulsiveness. She clasped her hands behind her back and looked him in the eye. She'd done what she'd thought needed to be done. She wouldn't apologize for that. "It was never my intention to harm Birk. I just wanted to lay him up, keep him from beating on his wife and children."

"I know. You've got one hell of a good, caring heart. I can't fault you for that. Just be careful. I don't want to see you hurt." With that admission, Wolf walked away, leaving Jessie to stare after him.

Leaving Fort Kearny, the emigrants headed up the broad, sandy track along the left side of the Platte River, following the Great Platte River road. Seven days after leaving the fort, they came to Cottonwood Spring. Wolf dismounted and stretched his arms over his head. He drew in deep, relaxing breaths, then studied his surroundings.

He'd hoped to gain a few more miles before stopping, but even he'd had more than enough of the dry, dusty and sandy trail. He led his horse to the spring. Though it wasn't much more than a seep in a gully, it boasted the best-tasting water since Alcove Springs.

He eyed the old riverbed, following the curve up toward Cottonwood Canyon, and made a mental note to remind Rook that the nearby ravines were filled with scrub cedar. The slight breeze lifted his long hair off his shoulders, soothing his hot, dry skin. It was blessedly cool, thanks to the tall cottonwoods. His horse, Black Shadow, lowered his head and drank greedily, which meant the spring was untainted.

Wolf followed suit and cupped the cool water in his hands, drinking deeply, then splashed some of the soothing liquid over his face. With his thirst quenched, he sat back on his heels to enjoy the quiet. There were only a couple of wagon trains camped nearby, but before dusk, at least two others would catch up to take advantage of the water supply.

"Is the water good, Wolf?" a low, husky voice inquired behind him.

Wolf stood. His lips tightened when Rosalyn sashayed up to him and caressed the gaping edge of his vest. Damn the woman. Every time he went off by himself, she managed to intrude. Did she spend all her time watching him? His nostrils flared. She certainly didn't understand plain English, and he was growing weary of fending off her unwanted advances.

He plucked her fingers from his vest. "Help yourself, *Mrs. Norton.*"

Rosalyn's eyes darkened with restrained fury, but in the blink of an eye, it was gone. She stepped in front of him. "Oh, Wolf, I thought we agreed to drop the formality. The name's Rosalyn." Her lips formed a pout, and she fluttered her long lashes at him. "Please, Wolf, won't you say my name just once? It's not so hard."

Her fingers dug into his arm like an eagle's razor-sharp talons. "Just say Rosalyn," she purred. Two fingers walked up his chest. "You must be so tired after sitting in the saddle all day. I can make you feel so much better."

Wolf stepped back, frustrated that Rosalyn refused to take no for an answer. "You don't have anything I want. Now, if you'll excuse me." He had to get away from her. His patience was near an end, yet he held on tightly to the reins of his temper.

But Rosalyn wasn't going to be put off any longer. She lunged forward and wrapped her arms boldly around his neck. "Oh, Wolf, I love it when you turn fierce. Though I do wish you'd stop worrying about Hugh. It's so trying. He won't mind, you know. He has man problems, and this trip is so long and boring. You and I could amuse each other."

Her voice dropped to a seductive whisper. "If you're too tired, I'll do all the work. I love to ride." Her dark eyes glazed over with passion, her full lips parted and her bosom heaved as her breathing grew erratic.

Disgust ran through him when she boldly rubbed her full breasts against him. He reached up to pull her arms from him but she refused to let go. She pressed her lips to his and moved her pelvis against him. Clamping his lips shut, he shoved her away. "Mrs. Norton, I'm warning you for the last time to keep your distance. My men may not care that you're married, but I do."

Rosalyn's gaze hardened. "And if I weren't married?"

Weary of the game, Wolf ran a hand through his hair, his temper taut, ready to snap. "It's a moot point, Mrs. Norton. Go back to your husband."

Rosalyn ducked her head and stared at the front of his pants. She reached out and stroked him. "Oh, Wolf. You don't have a problem down there, do you? I'm really, really quite good."

She grabbed the waistband of his trousers and giggled, a false sound that grated on his nerves. But before he could dispense with her, he saw Jessie standing in the deep shadows. Her hands were jammed onto her hips, and from the look of her, she was furious. When Rosalyn slid her hand into the waistband of his blue jeans, Jessie's right hand dropped. He swore beneath his breath when he saw her go for her whip. He tried to disengage the Norton woman's hands, but before he could, the sound of rawhide snapped at Rosalyn's back.

Rosalyn squealed and jumped behind Wolf.

Jessie stepped out of the shadows into the sunlight. "I believe Wolf has refused your services, Rosalyn. Why don't you be a good whore and ply your trade elsewhere." Her eyes were spitting green fire.

Rosalyn narrowed her eyes and stepped in front of Wolf. "Why, you little bitch. You're just jealous because you don't have anything to offer a man like Wolf."

Wolf groaned when he saw Jessie's fingers tighten on the handle of her whip. He was so disgusted with Rosalyn Norton, he was tempted to leave her to Jessie. But no matter how angry or disgusted he felt, he didn't dare.

Never had Jessie she felt such an all-out consuming rage as when she'd come upon Rosalyn and Wolf. It hadn't taken long to figure out that Wolf had no interest in the woman, but jealousy reared its ugly head.

"At least I'm no lickfinger. Now, you heard the man, *Rosalyn*" she mocked. "Don't want to be greedy, do you? According to the gossip one hears at mealtime, you *are* quite the bed warmer, so take your whoring ways where they're appreciated." She smirked. "If I recall rightly, tonight is Duarte's turn."

Rosalyn sputtered, her face a furious red. "How dare you

interfere? Do you really think Wolf is going to be interested in some flat-chested little girl? Why don't you go practice flirting on the youngest Svensson boy? He's more your type. Now get outta here and mind your own business," she said, the air whistling through the gap in her front teeth.

Jessie's answer was to bring her arm overhead and send the rawhide zinging forward. Wolf lunged and yanked Rosalyn out of the whip's reach. The balled ends snapped a mere inch from her nose.

She stumbled backward, tripped over a rock and fell, landing in a heap on the ground, her bonnet hanging from her neck.

"If you persist in goading Jessie, you're a fool, Mrs. Norton. This is your last warning. If you continue to cause trouble, you and your husband are out."

Jessie watched Rosalyn frantically replace her bonnet and tie the ribbons. Curious, she stared at the other woman's hair. She had light-colored roots. She shrugged and forgot about it when Rosalyn got to her feet and flounced off. Smug with her victory, Jessie couldn't resist one last taunt. "By the way, *Rosalyn*, there's nothing wrong with any of Wolf's parts." She stepped close to Wolf and patted the parts in question. "They work just fine." She snickered when Rosalyn screeched out a long string of curses.

Wolf grabbed her hand in a crushing hold. "Jessica Jones, you minx. Did you have to add that? Now she's going to think we've slept together."

Jessie shrugged and turned to face Wolf. Standing on tiptoe, she kissed him firmly on the lips, slipping her tongue inside for a brief, teasing touch. He groaned. She pulled back, satisfied. "So? There's many miles between here and Oregon. You want me and I want you, but you're just being stubborn. We're well suited. Your heart knows it, and soon your mind will admit to the truth." She clipped her whip to her belt.

Before he had a chance to launch into another lecture, she looked him in the eye, a small grin tugging at the corners of her lips. "Wolf?"

"What?" He sighed.

Her eyes gleamed with mischief and shifted to the obvious bulge beneath his buckskin trousers. "I don't think there's anything wrong down there." Chuckling, she sashayed off, confident in her ability to arouse him, and patient enough to wait for him to come to his senses.

Chapter Sixteen

The landscape continued to go through major changes. Tall green grass undulating across vast, open prairies gave way to short brown grass and endless sandy soil. Sagebrush, thin-bladed yucca plants and prickly-pear cactus took the place of the tall cottonwoods, and rattlesnakes replaced songbirds. Dried buffalo chips became the fuel for cooking, and even the air they breathed seemed different.

Since leaving Missouri, they'd climbed steadily. The air was thin and dry, chapping their lips and causing their wagon wheels to shrink and crack and the axles to squeal. The sun burned bright, its fingers of light racing across a cobalt blue sky, beckoning man and beast onward, bringing them ever closer to their goal.

Wolf rode ahead of the wagons, scanning the sandy ground for rattlesnakes. He took note of his bearings and nodded in satisfaction. Despite earlier problems with one wagon losing a wheel, they'd traveled a fair distance, making up lost time by going through the low, sandy O'Fallons Bluff where, once again, the trail had bottlenecked, forcing wagons to proceed single file. But rather than losing time waiting,

Wolf had led his wagons across a three-mile detour up and over the rolling sandy hills toward one of the crossing sites of the South Platte.

Many of the wagon trains had crossed back at Fremont's Ford, a fork of the Platte River. One fork became the South Platte, which ran a southwestern course, and the other fork became the North Platte, running northwest toward Fort Laramie. Wolf preferred the lower California crossing, so he'd continued along the left side of the South Platte. He studied the position of the sun, gauging the amount of travel time left in the day. He'd hoped to reach the crossing by nightfall.

Glancing over his shoulder, he grimaced at the sight of the oxen plodding forward, tongues lolling, eyes glassy. The animals were nearing exhaustion and couldn't go another five or six miles. They had to stop, and soon. A sudden blast of hot air blew sand into his face, forcing him to raise an arm to shield his eyes. Black Shadow shifted beneath him and pawed the ground restlessly, drawing Wolf's attention. "What is it, boy?" he crooned, automatically soothing the horse with a pat to the withers.

Then he saw it—a dark, cloudy mass rising in the distance. Standing in his stirrups, he stared at what looked to be another thunderstorm. But when he lifted his eyes upward, his gaze encountered clear blue skies as far as the eye could see. Another dust storm? Frowning, he dismounted and knelt, keeping a firm hold on the reins. Then he felt it, a tremble in the earth.

"Damn." That dark, roiling mass was no storm. It was buffalo. A large herd, judging from the way the dust rose like some tornado to obscure the horizon. He jumped back in the saddle and rode hell-bent-for-leather toward the wagons.

"Williams, circle. Wheel to wheel. Oxen in the center," he shouted, letting all know by his instructions that this was an emergency. "Elliot, see that everyone leaves their oxen yoked, and tie all horses and cows to the back of the wagons." Wolf rode on. Black Shadow lengthened his stride, closing the distance separating wagons and livestock. Wolf issued orders to halt the cattle and wind them into a tight circle, then traded Black Shadow for Lady Sarah and rode for the wagons.

Jessie stood next to her oxen, dimly aware that the tired beasts leaned into one another, panting with exhaustion. She glanced at Rook when Wolf raced by, this time riding bareback on his Indian-trained mount. "What's up?" she asked, fearing an Indian attack. Rook didn't answer, his attention focused on the western horizon.

She groaned when she saw the widespread darkness. "Not another storm! I'm not through mending the holes in the canvas covers from that last hailstorm," she grumbled, remembering the large stones of ice that had torn through the covers and bruised their animals.

And if the rain and hail weren't enough, the dust storms were the worst, wreaking havoc by driving the fine, dusty soil into wagons and tents, coating everyone and everything.

"Not another storm, lassie," Rook said, planting his hands on his hips, his bushy white brows lowered.

"Then what—" Suddenly it dawned on her. "Buffalo." She whipped her head around and stared at the mounting dark clouds. But before she could comment, Wolf returned, a rifle slung over his shoulders.

"Buffalo headed our way. I want every man to arm himself. Same drill as with the cattle stampede, but do not shoot until I give the command."

Birk swaggered forward. "Wait a minute. You tellin' us we can't shoot them beasts?"

Wolf lifted a brow. "That's what I said. Got a problem with that, Macauley?"

"Yeah, I do. Heard them hides bring good money, and fresh meat would be welcomed by all. Man has a right to feed his family," he challenged. Murmurs of agreement broke forth.

"There must be thousands of them. What's the harm in shooting a few?" Alberik Svensson asked.

Jessie and Rook exchanged grimaces. Wolf's hard gaze seared the crowd. "Start shooting into that herd and you risk

227

scattering them. You willing to risk turning these wagons into firewood, Mr. Svensson?'' His voice was low, taut.

Nineteen-year-old Alberik backed down under the scorn of the older man and received a hard thump on his back from his father. ''The boy is young, Wolf; he'll follow your instructions, won't you, boy?''

Alberik nodded sheepishly.

Wolf turned back to Birk. ''You got anything more you want to say, Macauley?''

Wolf's scornful question turned Birk's face red. Jessie bit her lip at Wolf's disrespectful address. Birk backed off, muttering vile curses beneath his breath when he realized that he'd lost the support of the crowd. Wolf ignored him and continued issuing instructions.

Minutes later, everyone ran off to carry out Wolf's orders. The men took up their positions a short distance from the wagons with guns clutched in their hands. Women and children scurried to gather dried chips and start hot-burning fires outside the circle of wagons in the hope that the lead buffalo would steer clear of the fire and smoke.

''Rook, keep an eye on things here. You know what to do,'' Wolf said.

Rook nodded and took off, his bowed legs moving as fast as his bulk allowed. Jessie ran after Wolf and grabbed his arm. ''What about me?''

''I don't suppose you'd tend the fires with the rest of the women.''

''Not on your life,'' she said, her heart racing with excitement. ''Not when I'm a good shot, better than any man here.'' She held her breath, waiting for his answer.

Wolf studied her for a moment, then nodded. ''Get your rifle and come with me. Better that you're where I can keep an eye on you.''

Ignoring his stinging comment, Jessie ran to her wagon. Right now she didn't care. He could insult her all he wanted, so long as she got a closer look at the herd of buffalo headed their way. Her blood thrummed with excitement as she gathered her rifle and extra ammunition.

228

Back on Shilo, she nudged the horse forward. Passing the Nortons' wagon, she heard Rosalyn yelling and swearing at the two men. She glanced over her shoulder at the strange couple, surprised to see a pouch of double-eagle coins spilled on the ground near the horses. Sammy and Hugh were frantically scooping up the twenty-dollar gold coins.

Jessie halted Shilo. A look of loathing and disgust crossed her features. They were trying to save themselves. She wheeled Shilo about and rode up to the back of the wagon. "Wolf gave orders to *everyone,* Rosalyn. We all stand to lose everything if we don't work together!"

Startled, Rosalyn whirled around and glared at her. Hugh and Sammy stopped loading their horses to turn guilty eyes to Jessie. They grabbed their guns while Rosalyn adjusted her bonnet. "I'm not losing everything I've worked for," she said with a snarl. "You go save the day!" Her eyes filled with malice. "You and I aren't through, Jessica Jones. No one makes a fool of me." She left the wagon and secured a packet in an already bulging saddlebag.

Jessie narrowed her gaze, wondering what it was about this woman that nagged at her. It was almost as if they'd met before, yet she knew they hadn't. Throwing the trio a look of loathing, she rode off to join Wolf. Dismissing the troublesome Nortons from her mind, she rode alongside Wolf toward the buffalo. When they were within half a mile, he halted. She nudged Shilo close and whispered, "What do we do now?"

He glanced down at her and pointed. "We watch and wait. They're running south. As long as nothing frightens them into changing their course, they should pass right before us."

Jessie bit her lip as the dark mass grew. The ground trembled beneath them. Both horses pawed the ground and shook their heads, but neither panicked. Then before she knew it, the great brown beasts were plunging into the river. Out they clambered, resuming their run, lumbering past. Jessie was thankful to see that Wolf was right. They were keeping to their southerly course.

A tremor of fear ran through her. What if the animals

shifted course? Could they outrun them on their horses? And what about the rest of their party at the wagons? She bit her lip. Wolf's hand closed over hers. She stared at him, finding comfort in his brilliant blue gaze.

"Relax, Jessie," he said, raising his voice above the roar. "We're fine."

"There're so many." Her eyes widened, and a sense of wonder filled her. The buffalo were massive, with their large heads, humped shoulders and shaggy manes. Their thick, furry hides were tattered with remnants of last winter's coat, which hung in shreds and flew off into the air. Coughing, she drew her shirt over her mouth to keep from breathing in the hair and dust.

The animals came within a quarter mile. Snorting nervously, they shifted their brown eyes toward the humans, who sat quietly. Jessie wrinkled her nose at the smell of the wet beasts. Thick, choking gusts of dust rolled toward them in waves that clouded everything.

"Quite a sight, isn't it? There's nothing like seeing a herd of buffalo on the run. They'll destroy everything in their path."

Jessie shuddered, grateful they weren't in the herd's path. She leaned close to Wolf. "What do you suppose caused them to stampede?"

He shrugged and drew her close. His breath tickled her ear as he replied. "Hard to tell. Could have been anything. A storm, fire, snakes, even hunters. Whatever. Once they spook, they'll run for hours." He held out his hand. "Give me your reins."

Puzzled, she handed them over and was surprised when Wolf swept her off Shilo and positioned her in front of him. He wrapped his arms around her waist. She glanced at the buffalo nervously. "What if we have to make a run for it?"

"Relax. We're not in any danger. See, they've veered slightly to the west."

Jessie shielded her eyes from the brightness of the sun. "Shouldn't we let Rook and the others know?"

He nuzzled her ear. "Rook knows the drill. Two shots

mean to take action. He also knows this can go on for hours. We'll stay here, just in case the herd splits and changes course.''

Jessie snuggled against Wolf's comforting strength, her hands resting on top of his. They sat in silence. Nothing felt more right to her than sitting here with the man she loved. An hour passed, then two, then three—yet there still seemed to be no end in sight. The sun disappeared beyond the horizon. As the fierce ball of fire gave way to the relief of cool twilight, the sandy-bottomed river became a winding stream of shimmering liquid gold, matching the golden brown hues of the land until the fierce ball of fire gave way to the relief of cool darkness. Still the buffalo came.

''How much longer?'' she whispered, wiping the dust from her tearing eyes. Never had she seen such a large herd of animals.

Wolf ran his hands through her hair, then pointed. ''There's the end.''

Sure enough, she made out the thinning of the herd.

''We can return now.'' Wolf tightened his hold around her waist, then turned her around, his gaze on her mouth.

Jessie ran her fingers over the edges of his vest. ''Thank you for today. It was wonderful. I'll never forget it.''

Running a finger down her dusty cheek, he kissed the tip of her nose. ''You're pretty amazing, Jessica. Does nothing scare you?''

''You do.''

His fingers slid to the back of her neck. His lips lowered to hers. ''That makes two of us, sweet Jess.''

Eagerly anticipating his kiss, Jessie sighed and closed her eyes, but the kiss never came. Confused, she glanced up. ''What's wrong?''

''I can't, Jessica. Lord knows I want to take all that you so innocently offer, but I can't. I can give you only these few months and no more. That's not enough. You deserve so much more than what I have to offer. My duty is to my people.''

Jessie stared at him. ''I don't understand, Wolf. What duty?''

Wolf closed his eyes, his mouth pinched, nostrils flared. "I don't know. I sure as hell wish I did. That's why I can't take you back with me. I have nothing to offer you. Not even the promise of tomorrow."

"I don't want promises, Wolf. I want you. Whatever your duty is, we can do it together." She watched him. His eyes grew bleak, and she caught a glimpse of haunting pain. His hands lifted to her face.

"Jessie—"

The sound of gunshots startled them. Jessie jumped off the horse and grabbed her rifle from the scabbard hanging from her saddle. Looking for the danger, she saw men on horseback riding after the buffalo. The loud cracks of gunfire split the air. "Wolf, look!"

He swore. The reason for the running buffalo was now clear. Hunters. The riders had caught up with the tiring beasts at the end of the stampeding herd. Bellows of fear and rage mingled with shouts of triumph filled the night air. Jessie cried out in dismay when several animals fell. For the first time, the thought of hunting made her sick. She looked to Wolf, but he'd turned away. From the tense line of his shoulders, she knew he was upset too.

Frustrated, she mounted Shilo and followed him back to their group. She had come so close to breaking through the barrier he'd erected between them. Pensively, she studied him. His shield was firmly in place. Somehow, some way, she'd find a way through those barriers. She would convince him that whatever his duty was, she could help.

After the stampede and the emotional scene with Jessie, Wolf longed to ride away and find some peace and quiet, but after he had refused Birk the use of a horse to go after the buffalo, the man had been trying to cause unrest among the travelers. Wolf feared an outright fight between the men if he left. Dropping his bedroll, he gave each man a hard stare, silently commanding them to ignore Birk Macauley and go about their business. While waiting for tempers to settle, he decided to get one last distasteful chore out of the way. Rook had informed him of the Nortons' refusal to follow orders. It was something no wagon master could afford to tolerate. The very life of each man, woman and child depended on everyone's following orders.

Long, angry strides brought him to where the couple and their driver sat hunched around a fire. He towered over them, fisted hands on hips. "Ignore my orders again and you'll find yourself out on your own. Survival out here depends on everyone pulling together." His voice deepened with cold contempt.

"I suppose that brat squealed," Rosalyn said with a sneer.

Wolf was taken aback by the rage in her dark eyes. He vowed to watch her. It was obvious Jessie had made herself another enemy with her whip.

He held Rosalyn's gaze until she looked into the fire. "*Rook* informed me that the three of you refused to follow orders. Do it again and you're out." He stalked away, silently cursing. How was it he'd ended up with so many problems in one small wagon train?

The aroma of coffee drew him to the fire. He poured a cup, suspecting it was going to be a long night. His weary gaze sought Jessie. She and Rook had started the meal preparations. Beside her, Coralie was kneading dough. She'd taken to helping Jessie and Rook whenever Jordan was on guard duty. He allowed himself an amused smile. Now, there was a woman who'd gone through a dramatic change since the first day he'd seen her sitting in the wagon, dressed in her finery.

Shifting slightly, he leaned against the wagon and watched Rook. His friend was in his element as boss, mentor and father figure as he tested the bread dough, checked the firepits that Elliot had dug, then helped Jessie carry a large kettle of water over to the smoking fires. The foursome worked well together, and it was clear his friend had taken Elliot and his sister under his protective wing along with Jessie.

Wolf was happy to see his old friend content. After years of grieving and feeling guilty, Rook had found peace and a replacement for the family he'd lost. No one deserved it more, and he was glad now that he'd agreed to the trip. Good *had* come of it. But with the good had come the unexpected.

He turned his brooding attention to Jessie. In the pale light of dusk, her hair hung in wet ringlets. It was longer now, though when the strands dried they'd curl and frame her face, lending her a soft, feminine look that trousers and shirts couldn't hide, especially now that she didn't have to conceal the fact that she was a woman. Her shirts weren't so baggy, and she wore her trousers cinched at the waist, revealing her slim figure and slightly flared hips.

He ran his hands through his own dust-coated hair, eager to go wash and change, yet he didn't want to leave. He could have stood there forever, watching her, loving the way her face glowed as she talked or used her hands so expressively. The gentle sway of her hips when she moved left him trembling. His gut tightened. What was he going to do about her? What were his own feelings? He felt ill. He tossed the coffee aside, mounted and rode off, giving Lady Sarah her head.

But thoughts of Jessie stayed with him. Not many women would have sat so quietly, so patiently and fearlessly, while experiencing such an awe-inspiring event as a buffalo stampede. But then Jessie wasn't most women. What other female would ride into the path of stampeding cattle or come to a man's aid when he was set upon by a strumpet?

A reluctant smile tugged at his lips. Jessica Jones was a study in contradictions. Bold and brash—full of confidence, ready to protect and defend those around her one moment—then young and naive, lacking self-confidence in her desirability as a woman the next. He never knew what to expect—and that was part of her charm. He loved her whatever her mood.

He came to a halt when the unwanted truth hit. He loved her. Though he'd tried to shield himself, she'd pierced his armor and stolen his heart; she was a true warrior worthy of his love. Wolf closed his eyes and drew in deep, even breaths to calm the racing of his heart.

She was right. They *were* well suited. More than just

suited. They fit, like a knife to its sheath. She was his other half, and with her he felt complete. And earlier, while watching the buffalo, she'd understood his reverence toward the animals and shared it. Longing for love and a need to belong skimmed the surface of his heart, refusing to be buried. Yet because of his people, he was destined to walk alone.

Wolf silently cursed his supposed gift: knowledge. Sure, he had lots of knowledge, had even been sent to a fancy college, but what good was his education? How was he supposed to use it? His grandmother had known, but when he'd asked how and what he'd do for their tribe, she'd only shaken her head, telling him to be patient, that the spirits would reveal the truth when the time came. That had been fifteen years ago.

He was no closer to the truth now, which left him stewing like a kettle of fish. Until he knew what was expected of him, he had nothing to truly offer Jessie. What if he had to go off for months on end and couldn't take her with him? His stomach clenched when he remembered returning to Rook's cabin to find his friend's family had been murdered. How could he go off and leave Jessie to fend for herself in a place where there were no neighbors, only the occasional trapper or contingent of soldiers?

His lips compressed grimly. Too many of them were little more than criminals or layabouts. They thought nothing of raping women, Indian or White. He drew in a deep breath and released it slowly. No, he could not promise something he might not be able to finish. Until he knew his future, he was destined to walk his path alone.

After a late supper, Jessie headed for her wagon, first stopping at the canvas latrine. The landscape had no trees for cover, so Rook and Wolf had fashioned a tent to be placed over a hole in the ground as they traveled over barren prairie. By the time she reached her own wagon, her head ached from built-up tension. She was tired and depressed. The evening had been a disaster.

Birk had returned from a walk with a flask of whiskey. With each sip he'd grown more vocal, ranting and raving about everything under the moon. While everyone tried to ignore his bad mood, it was nearly impossible to ignore his meanness directed at his family. Even now, she heard him still shouting at Ian to shut up. His yelling only made matters worse, for the baby cried louder.

Jessie leaned her forehead against the wagon's canvas side. Why didn't someone do something? How could everyone just let it go on? Her features tightened. When she reached her wagon, she heard muffled crying. Looking inside, she saw little Alison Macauley. Swearing beneath her breath, she hoisted herself into the wagon. "Alison? Honey, what are you doing in here?" Scooting on her knees down the narrow aisle, she reached out and pulled the trembling child to her.

Alison threw her thin arms around Jessie's neck. "I don't want to go back! Pa's angry. I want to stay here with you." The little girl sobbed.

Jessie patted the four-year-old's back and tried to soothe her. She wished she could keep Alison for the night, but she knew Birk would never allow it. "Listen, sweetie, your mama must be worried over you. How about if I take you back and tuck you into bed?"

Alison's grip tightened, making it hard for Jessie to breathe. "No!"

Jessie's heart ached at the stark fear in that one word. She vowed that for this night, she'd find a way to keep Alison from her father's rage. "Okay, sweetie, I'll go talk to your mother."

Pulling the girl's arms from around her, she unrolled the blankets and tucked her in, running the backs of her fingers down the child's windburned cheeks, wiping away the tears. Leaving the wagon, she fastened her whip to her belt and headed for Eirica's tent. When she arrived, Birk was drinking from a flask held in one hand. In his other beefy hand, he held his screaming two-year-old son.

Eirica was crying. "Birk, please. Give him to me. He's

sick. Let me put him to bed. I'll quiet him, I promise." She reached out and tried to grab Ian.

Birk shoved her away with his foot. "Shut up, woman. I'll deal with him. You's spoiling the brat." He tossed down his flask and shook his son hard.

"I said shut up, boy!" Ian continued to scream hysterically. In an effort to get away, he let his small body go limp, but Birk hauled him back up and shook him again. "Shut up, I said!"

This time Eirica grabbed her son. "Stop it, Birk. You're going to hurt him."

Birk slapped her with enough force to knock her to the ground. Enraged, he dropped Ian and raised a fist. Eirica crawled over and covered her baby's body with her own.

"Git the hell away from him, woman. I ain't gonna have a crying, sniveling brat for a son. He'll listen to his pa or else."

Horrified, Jessie stepped forward. That was it. She couldn't stand any more. A quick glance around confirmed that the others were also on the verge of interfering. "Leave them alone, Macauley!" she shouted.

Birk glared at her. His pale, bloodshot eyes turned to hard beads of hatred. "Go 'way, girlie. Mind yer own business. My family's my business, not nobody else's," he said with a snarl.

His expression turned defiant as others flanked Jessie. To make his point, he kicked Eirica hard in the ribs. "Git up, woman, and git yourself to the tent. I'll deal with you later."

Eirica lifted her head, her eyes wide and pleading. Tears streamed down her face. "Please, Birk you've been drinking. Leave us alone." Another kick to her side silenced her.

Lars, Elliot and Jordan stepped forward. "Leave off her," Jordan ordered.

In a blind rage, Birk reached down to grab a handful of Eirica's hair. He yanked her to her feet and raised his hand to strike.

Jessie snapped her whip and sent it darting forward. It wound around Birk's wrist, preventing him from hitting his wife. "You're not going to hit her anymore," she said, her voice shaking with anger. "We've had enough of your bullying."

Birk grabbed the rawhide still wrapped around his arm. He flung Eirica from him, then yanked the whip from Jessie's hand. "You'll be sorry, girl."

Suddenly she found herself on the other end of the rawhide as Birk sent it snapping toward her. He was drunk, and his aim was off. She jumped to one side. Behind her, she heard the others shouting. Just as Birk drew his arm back, someone snagged her around the waist and hauled her out of the whip's stinging reach.

"Why does it not surprise me to find you smack in the middle of this?"

Startled, Jessie glanced over her shoulder. She cringed at the sharp crack of the whip, but Wolf's body shielded hers. He raised an arm to protect his face as Birk sent the whip forward again. The rawhide caught him on the arm.

Silence fell. Jessie held her breath. Never had she seen such deadly violence in a person's eyes. Wolf set her aside and stepped forward, feet planted apart, arms hanging loose and fisted at his side. His voice dripped with promised violence.

"You want to fight, Birk, fight me."

Birk threw down the whip, lowered his head and charged forward with a roar of fury.

Chapter Seventeen

Wolf measured Birk's rage-filled charge, then stepped neatly to one side, sticking out one booted foot. Birk flew through the air and landed hard on the dusty ground. Crouched, Wolf waited. His blood boiled, and he shook with rage. The drunk bastard would pay for attacking the woman he loved. His fists clenched and unclenched. Birk stumbled unsteadily to his feet.

"Come on, you bastard. Afraid of taking on a real man? Or can you only lift those hands of yours to helpless women and children?" Wolf goaded. Birk came at him.

"You dirty half-breed." He charged, swinging his fists at Wolf.

With his knees slightly bent and his body attuned to the drunken man's every move, Wolf feinted to the right and avoided one meaty fist while slamming his own into Birk's soft belly. The two men converged. While Birk had a weight advantage, Wolf's finely honed body moved with lightning quickness. A blow to his midsection bent him over. But despite the pain, he welcomed the chance to expend his anger, his frustrations, in this physical fashion. Pent-up desire also found release in a well-aimed punch to Birk's nose. With a grunt of satisfaction, he watched the blood spurt. "That's for beating on your woman and son." A kick to Birk's belly sent the man skidding across the ground and into a wagon, and Wolf advanced. "That's for messing with Jessie."

Birk tackled him around the knees. The two men rolled

across the ground, fists slamming into flesh, forcing the on-lookers to jump out of the way. Grunts, groans and curses mingled with cheers and shouts of encouragement from the male emigrants and the cries of the women. One of Birk's fists clipped Wolf on the jaw, snapping his head back. Birk took advantage of Wolf's dazed condition and slammed his paunchy body down onto him. Wolf's lungs emptied with a whoosh. Forcing his eyes to focus, he saw Birk's fist poised for another punishing blow. Ignoring the pain in his jaw, he surged upward, plowing his own fist into Birk's belly.

Birk doubled over. Wolf added a quick right-handed jab to the man's bloody face and sent him sailing backward. Wolf rolled to his feet, rubbing his jaw, his breath coming in short, harsh, gasping swallows. He rested his hands on his knees and waited for Birk to move, but he was out cold. Wolf lifted his head. A hushed silence fell over the group, broken only by the hysterical crying of children. "It's over. You can all go about your business." After a moment, every-one moved away.

Wolf staggered over to Eirica and hunched down in front of her. She sat, white faced, clutching her sobbing son tightly to her breast. Jessie stood beside her, holding Lara. Alison clung to her leg. "Are you all right?"

Eirica ran the back of her hand over her eyes and wiped the tears away. She nodded but didn't meet his gaze.

Wolf glanced at Ian. "What about the boy?"

Anne answered, sparing Eirica the effort. "He's bruised and scraped. It looks like he also has an earache. I've got some powders to help ease his pain."

Wolf nodded, then turned back to Eirica. She reached out and clutched his sleeve. Her voice shook with despair. "I can't take any more. He's going to kill the children or my baby."

"You can leave him," Wolf suggested gently.

Fresh tears appeared. "He won't let me go."

"Do you want to stay with him, Mrs. Macauley?"

Eirica took a deep breath and shook her head. "N-no, I-I have t-to think of my babies. But how? He'll never let me leave." Her lashes lifted, her gaze beseeching him to help her.

He couldn't refuse. "I can offer you and your children protection until we reach Oregon. Once there, though, you'll have to decide what you want to do. I told Birk to lay off the beatings. Now he must face the consequences of ignoring my orders. As of tonight, he's out." A hush fell over the group.

James stepped forward. "Eirica and her children are welcome to share our wagons and supplies. We have plenty."

Jessie handed Lara to her brother and went down on her knees. "Please, Eirica, say yes. We're all your friends, and we can help you make a new start."

Eirica stared at Jessie, then at James, then scanned the concerned faces around her. Wolf waited. If she refused to leave her husband, he'd have no choice but to abandon her to Birk's cruelty. Birk was out. The man was too violent and unpredictable.

Finally, Eirica nodded. "Thank you, Jessie," she whispered, her voice raw. "I got my pride, but nothing matters more to me than my babies. For them, I accept." She stood. Alison and Lara ran to their mother. "But I will repay you for your kindness."

Both James and Jessie acknowledged her statement with a nod. Wolf suggested they help her fetch whatever she wanted from her wagon before Birk regained consciousness.

Early the next morning, Jessie left the wagon circle, hoping a brisk walk would clear her mind of last night's events, which had haunted her dreams. But no matter how fast she went, she couldn't outrun the images of Birk slamming his meaty fist into Wolf's face. She'd seen countless fights, had indulged in her share with the kids in school and even with her own brothers, but she'd never witnessed one involving the man she loved. Unlike the common street brawls in Westport that drew crowds of cheering bystanders, the fight between Wolf and Birk hadn't been exciting. It left her feeling weak-kneed and sick. She never wanted to witness anything like it again, even though she was grateful for the outcome.

By the time Birk had come to, his wagon and tent had been moved apart from the others and he'd been placed under guard. Birk had been furious, and his shouts and threats had kept them up most of the night. Jessie stopped short of a small rise in the terrain and stared up at the pale blue sky. "What's done is done. I just hope he stays away," she muttered, knowing full well he wouldn't. And what of Wolf? Was he all right? Had Birk seriously injured him? By the time she'd gotten Eirica and the children settled in one of their tents and gone looking for him, he'd left the camp.

Perhaps she should head back and find him. Already the heat was stifling. It was going to be another unbearably hot day. Using her hat as a fan, she waved it in front of her face. A cloud of black birds circling a short distance away drew her attention. Curious, Jessie jammed her hat back on and ran toward them, kicking small rocks and pebbles out of her path. When she topped the rise, the stench of rotting flesh slammed into her.

Her head snapped up. She stared, horrified at the sight before her. Spread out as far as the eye could see, hundreds of dead buffalo lay beneath the relentless sun. Some were skinned and gutted; the majority were not. Birds of prey moved among them, picking at the ample amounts of flesh left by the nighttime scavengers. She covered her mouth with her hand. Nausea threatened to choke her. Recalling the serenade of howling wolves during the night, Jessie now understood why there seemed to have been more than normal. They'd come from miles around to feast on the spoils of wasteful hunters. It also explained why Rook had ordered Sadie tied up for the night.

Gagging, she turned away, unable to bear the rotten stench or sickening sight. She stumbled a few feet, then bent at the waist, fighting the roiling of her stomach.

A shadow fell across her, and strong fingers shoved her to the ground, forcing her head between her knees. "Breathe slow and deep, Jessica."

Wolf. Jessie groaned in mortification, embarrassed to have

him see her like this. "Go 'way." She moaned.

"Hush. Breathe. Slow and deep."

He stroked her hair until her stomach calmed. Lifting her head slowly, she glanced at him through watery eyes, grateful she hadn't humiliated herself by being sick. "What a waste," she cried. "All that for sport?" She pressed a fist into her unsettled stomach. She moaned as another wave of nausea swept over her, brought on by the smell of carrion.

Wolf pulled her to her feet, picked up her hat, which had fallen off, and led her away. When they were out of range, he stopped, keeping her encircled by his arms. "No matter how many years I spend living the white man's life, I cannot understand this senseless killing. Killing driven by fun, not necessity. The amount of meat back there would last my people the whole winter, not to mention the warmth the furs would have provided."

Hearing the sadness in his voice, Jessie lifted her head. She gasped when she got her first good look at him. "Oh, Lord, look at your face," she whispered, reaching up to run her fingers tenderly over his swollen jaw and the discolored area covering one cheek. Her gaze roamed and lingered on a cut over one eye, and his split lip. This was her fault. "Oh, Wolf. I'm so sorry. I shouldn't have interfered. James told me not to, but I couldn't help it—"

Wolf silenced her with a finger across her lips. "Not another word, Jessie. You did what you had to do. I did the same."

Though Jessie agreed, and felt a warm glow at his praise, the sight of his swollen face pained her. "But your face . . ."

"My face will heal. Now, if you're feeling better, we'd best get back."

Standing on tiptoe, Jessie tenderly pressed her lips to a small cut at the corner of his mouth. "All right. I've got some salve that will help."

Wolf waved her concern away. "There's no time. I want to get under way before Macauley wakes and causes more trouble."

Determination narrowed Jessie's eyes when he refused to

look at her. He was trying to put distance—both physical and emotional—between them. She jammed her hands onto her hips. She'd have none of it. Somehow, some way, she'd prove to him that they were meant to be.

"Fine. We'll leave as soon as I've tended to your injuries." Walking off, she didn't turn to see if he followed.

The signal to roll came by whispered words instead of the usual piercing whistle. Jessie followed the wagons, leading Shilo, with Alison and Lara in the saddle. Lara, sitting in the front, reached down to pluck nervously at Shilo's black mane. Neither child spoke. Normally mornings were a time of laughter and good cheer, as all were rested and eager to continue, but not today. The mood enveloping the party was one of solemn dread. Voices were hushed, and nervous glances were directed toward the lone wagon sitting off to one side.

No one wanted Birk to awaken. None wanted to witness the rage he'd surely display when faced with the realization that he was being left behind with only his wagon, supplies and oxen. Jessie kept a wary eye on the white-topped wagon as, one by one, they rolled forward. Quiet commands replaced the customary crack of whips as drivers urged the oxen onward. Gunner and Leroy, both big, brawny men with crooked noses and thick, beefy arms, remained behind to allow the emigrants a head start before Birk followed.

Breathing a huge sigh of relief when they made it with no sign of trouble, Jessie turned her attention to the trail before her. In front of her, Rickard swatted the rump of her oxen. Male pride had made him reclaim his duties. When he glanced back, she waved. He grinned at her, then drew his arm back, sending his whip zinging over the heads of the oxen. Jessie smothered a laugh at his showing off. But when she noticed that he was still limping, she furrowed her brow. However, experience with her brothers kept her silent. She knew any show of concern on her part would be met with a careless shrug.

Coralie hurried to her side, her blue eyes shadowed with

worry. Jessie marveled over the changes in her sister-in-law. Though she still acted the spoiled rich girl on occasion, each day brought on a new maturity. Overnight it seemed, she'd become a loving and caring woman. Just a few short months ago Coralie would have worried only over herself and her fancy dresses. Now she fussed like a mother hen.

"What's wrong, Corie?"

"Oh, Jessie, Eirica's hurting bad. Pale as a ghost and just looks awful. You don't suppose it's the baby, do you?"

Jessie glanced over her shoulder. Her sister-in-law was right. Eirica looked on the verge of collapse and was favoring her right side. "Not the babe. Cracked ribs, I'll bet." She stopped. Eirica limped up to them, and Jessie and Coralie silently took their places, one on either side of her.

After the cattle were under way, James left Jordan in charge and rode out to check on Eirica and her children. His lips tightened as he fought off an almost uncontrollable urge to go back to her bastard of a husband and make sure the man was in no condition to follow for many days, but he didn't. Justice would be served, but not by his hands. When he reached the squeaking and creaking caravan of wagons, he slowed. They were spread out side by side so no one would have to suffer walking through great clouds of dust. Passing the Svenssons, he tipped his hat and nodded at Elliot. When he spotted Eirica, he spurred his horse forward.

Coming up behind the three women, he heard Ian crying. Jessie was carrying him, patting and rubbing the youngster's back in a soothing manner. The sight suddenly struck him as being so right, so natural: her cuddling a toddler in her arms. It dawned on him how good she was with young children. Why had he never seen that motherly side? In that moment, James finally admitted that Wolf had been right. He'd never seen his sister as a grown woman.

Sighing deeply, James vowed to talk to Jessie soon and apologize for not admitting she'd grown up. He drew up alongside the women, worried when he noticed that Ian was fighting Jessie, leaning toward his mother. A quick glance at

Eirica confirmed that she was in no condition to walk, let alone carry her son. Dismounting, he took the baby from Jessie's arms and handed her the reins. Ian immediately settled, his bright blue eyes wide as he stared up at him. "How's he doing?" James asked.

"Cranky, but no sign of fever today," Jessie answered, moving away to make room for him. His pulse jumped. That put him right next to Eirica.

"And you, Eirica?" he asked, noting the pale, pinched look to her face.

Eirica's startled gaze flew to his. Her cheeks turned pink at his free use of her given name. James hid his grin. She was so proper, he'd done so purposely, hoping to put some color back into her face. She opened her mouth, then shrugged.

"I'm doing well, Mr. Jones. I'll take Ian. You must have other duties that require your attention." She pressed a hand to her side, her breathing shallow.

James knew from watching her that her ribs were bruised, maybe cracked. "The boy is fine, and no, I have no other duties at this moment. You and your children are under my protection. As the head of the family, I take my responsibilities seriously."

Eirica sighed and shook her head. "I don't want you to think me ungrateful, Mr. Jones—"

"James, if you don't mind, Eirica. With two brothers, I'll find it a lot less confusing if you use our first names."

"As I was saying—James—don't think me ungrateful, but you needn't worry about me and mine. The children and I will manage on our own. I do appreciate your willingness to share your food and being able to store my mother's things in your wagons. I will repay you when I'm able. Some of my mother's fine linens, china and silver should fetch a tidy sum in Oregon."

James nodded, refraining from telling her that he would not take her money or allow her to sell her prized possessions to repay a debt. He knew she had her pride, but the only thing he wanted was her happiness. One genuine smile was worth more than anything he could buy. But he had a problem: she was understandably wary of him. He'd have to go slow.

Eirica stumbled over a hidden rock and cried out in pain.

"Damn," he swore beneath his breath. Reaching out with one hand, he caught her gently around her shoulders. When she regained her balance, he handed Ian back to Jessie. "Woman, you're in no condition to walk. Why aren't you riding in the wagon?"

She took several shallow breaths, then grimaced. "No, thanks. I'd rather walk."

James stared at the wagons ahead of them, noting how they bumped and swayed. He took the reins back from Jessie. "Ride, then."

Shaking her head, Eirica pointed to his saddle. "I can't."

James tipped his hat back, frustration showing in his features when he realized that with her skirts, she needed a sidesaddle. Determined to ease her suffering, he mounted and held out his hand. "Then you'll just have to ride with me."

The emigrants reached the lower California crossing at noontime, and by late afternoon the last wagon was hitched with ten yoke of oxen. Wolf led the last group into the swollen and raging snow-fed water of the South Platte River. Crossing at an angle, he forced the oxen downstream. Men plunged in after the wagon to keep it moving. Sand gave way beneath the wheels, jarring the wagon something fierce, but he kept the oxen moving. Wolf knew that if they stopped for even an instant, the wheels would bog down. Reaching the middle of the river, he turned the oxen upstream to finish the crossing.

By the time all the wagons were safely on the other bank, the oxen were exhausted. Each yoke had been double and even triple teamed, used and reused to haul all nine wagons safely across. They would go no farther with their loads. He gave the go-ahead to make camp, then kept watch for Birk, who likely wasn't that far behind. They'd had a two-hour start, but Birk would catch up to them before the night was over.

Sure enough, four hours later Birk's wagon came into view. Even with the fading light and the half-mile distance between them, Wolf could see Birk beating the oxen with his whip, urging them to go faster. Wolf stayed at the edge of the bank and waited for the man to reach the river.

"I've come for my family. Ya ain't got no right to take them," Birk yelled.

Wolf heard the hush behind him when it became apparent that Birk planned to cross with only three yoke of oxen. Although he despised the man, he had no desire to see him drown. He cupped his hands around his mouth. "Don't be a fool, Macauley. It's too dangerous to cross in the dark. Wait until morning. I'll have some men help you."

"No good, you damn half-breed. I'm coming for what's mine." Yelling vile curses, Birk jumped onto his wagon tongue and lashed the backs of his oxen with his whip, sending them protesting into the dark, swirling river.

Chapter Eighteen

Listening to her husband's shouts, Eirica wrapped her arms around herself. Fear slid up and down her spine. If Birk got his hands on her, he'd kill her. She shook.

"Don't worry, momma," Alison whispered. "Pa won't hurt you no more, will he, Jessie?" The need to be brave warred with fear as Alison looked at Jessie.

Jessie knelt down and hugged the little girl. "No, sweetheart. No one will hurt you or your momma ever again. Now, stay here and watch over Lara and Ian. I'll be right back.'' Jessie turned away but Alison's trembling voice stopped her.

"Aren't you gonna take your whip?"

Alison's frightened question penetrated the fog of fear that held Eirica in its grip. She stared at her young daughter then straightened. It wasn't Jessie's place to protect her children. It was hers. She drew a deep breath. Even though she was grateful for Jessie's help, sooner or later, she'd have to take a stand. It might as well be now. Birk was her problem and her children were her responsibility.

"That won't be necessary, Alison. Wait here with your sister. I'm going with Jessie."

"No, momma, he'll take you away," Alison screamed, grabbing hold of her mother's skirts.

Eirica bent down. "No, sweets, he won't. Now, look at me." She waited until Alison's frightened blue gaze met hers. "Dry your tears, no more crying. You and I must be brave from now on. We can't let others do our talking. I must tell your Pa that we won't go back to him. Now, be strong for your ma." She turned away before she lost her courage. Falling in step with Jessie, they went to the edge of the river and peered into the murky darkness.

When she saw Birk trying to cross on his own, fear chilled her heart and paralyzed her. If he came after her, there'd be trouble between him and Wolf. She'd felt so guilty when she'd gotten a good look at Wolf that morning. The oxen faltered but Birk refused to let up on the whip. When he spotted her, he shouted angry curses. She nearly turned tail and ran but remembered her own words to Alison and stood firm.

"—yer mine—" she heard him call. "I'll make ya sorry—comin' for you—"

Her resolve strengthened when he shook his fist at her. She took a deep shuddering breath and stepped forward, the water lapping at her shoes. "You won't harm me or my children ever again, Birk Macauley," she shouted.

He shook his fist at her. "Yer mine, woman. Them brats

is mine. I'll take them from you. A man's got a right to his children.''

Eirica fell back, the pain caused by his words like a blow from his fist. Jessie's arm slipped around her shoulders. Eirica turned away, her moment of bravo gone. "Oh, Jessie. He'll do it. He'll take the kids from me.''

"He won't get close enough, Eirica. He's just trying to frighten you.''

Another voice joined in. "He'll have to go through me and every man here.''

Eirica turned to see that James had joined them. She swallowed her fear, again feeling safe and protected. She fought the feeling. "Mr. Jones—'' A sudden cry rose from the bank. Whirling around, she saw that Birk's oxen had stopped in the middle of river.

"Macauley, you god-damned fool. Keep the oxen moving,'' Wolf yelled, plunging into the fast-moving stream. Lars, his sons, Elliot and James followed. But before they reached Birk, the wagon wheels lodged, sinking deep into the quicksand-like bottom. The oxen bellowed as the current smashed against the wagon.

Maddened, Birk shouted and swore at them, but it was too late. The wagon was mired. The water continued to swirl around them. The oxen thrashed and bellowed in fright. Men from the bank reached the animals and unyoked them as their struggles were rocking the wagon back and forth. Wolf tried to reach Birk who clung to the front of the wagon but before he reached him, a large piece of wood caught in the strong current slammed into the back wheel. Horrified, Eirica watched Birk disappear into the murky waters.

For the next two hours, Eirica paced the bank, waiting, watching and wondering. When Wolf and the men finally returned, wet and weary, she ran to them. At the slight shake Wolf's head, she turned away, dazed and shocked. Arms cradled her shoulders and led her to the fire. Cold and numb, she sat, staring into the flames, her thoughts rolling like a tumbleweed. Birk couldn't swim. He was gone. Gone for good. She was widowed. Alone. Safe. Safe from his beatings.

Shivering, she moved closer to the fire. Her eyes burned, and her head ached, but she felt no sorrow. No joy. Nothing. Sitting for hours, unable to eat, unable to talk, she tried to dredge up a bit of sadness, an ounce of compassion—something—anything—for the man who'd been her husband and the father of her children. But all she felt was an overwhelming sense of relief that she was free. It made her feel guilty and scared.

She was so far from her family, alone in a strange land and heading for the unknown. A spray of sparks from the fire popped and floated before her. Watching them drift back to the earth, she rubbed her stomach. She had three children and one more on the way. What was she going to do? How would she provide for them? She had no training and no skills, except those of a farmer's wife. Eirica glanced over her shoulder at her wagon. Maybe she didn't even have a wagon. A fire flickered nearby, providing extra light for the Jones brothers who were trying to repair two of the wheels while Jessie and Coralie dealt with the wetness inside.

Panic rose within. How would she survive? It didn't matter that she'd left her husband that morning and was already on her own. Somehow, his death made it different, more final. She now faced a different kind of fear, a different type of loneliness. With Birk gone, there was no reason for anyone to help her, or offer protection. These men and women had their own survival to worry about. She dropped her head into her hands.

Wolf joined her. "I'm sorry, Mrs. Macauley. We did our best."

Eirica stood. "I thank you and the others for your efforts," she whispered, staring at her hands as she wrung them in her lap.

Wolf took hold of her fingers. He rubbed them until they warmed. "You'll make it. You're a strong woman."

Startled, she stared up at him in disbelief then shook her head. "No, I'm a coward. Jessie's strong, but not me. I allowed the father of my children to beat them. I should have been stronger but I wasn't. I failed them."

Wolf shook his head. "The white man's world places a woman under her husband's dominance. A woman and her children belong to the man. What he decides to do is law whereas with my people, the tipi and all within belong to the woman except for a warrior's possessions. If the wife chooses to divorce her husband, all she has to do is set his belongings outside. She doesn't lose respect. My people revere women and children.

"Today, you took the steps needed to divorce yourself from a husband who had no honor. You choose to protect yourself and your children by stepping off the path Birk walked to go your own way. Those actions took courage. Now you must be stronger for the way turns rocky. You must continue on your chosen path, drawing strength and courage at each fork. The direction is yours and only yours to choose."

Looking into the wagon master's serious and compelling gaze, Eirica felt the first stirring of hope. Could she do it? She glanced once more at the men working on her wagon. Pride and the desire to be in charge of her own destiny replaced her crippling fears. She stood and smoothed her skirt. In her present condition, Eirica knew she would still need help and could live with that. She squared her shoulders. But as of now, she would take charge of her life. Never again would she bow to the domination of a man.

"I thank you for your words of wisdom, Wolf. I believe there is much to be done before the new day. And I would be pleased if you dropped the missus and called me Eirica." With head held high, she walked away, feeling a weight lifted from her shoulders.

The next morning, Jessie and Rook started up California Hill. The steep terrain between the south and north forks of the Platte River was pitted with imposing ruts, making it a long and arduous climb. After climbing for what seemed like hours, they reached a high plateau. Wolf pushed them onward, allowing only a short rest. By midmorning of the following day, they reached the end of the plateau, a high tableland between the South and North Platte rivers. Jessie tied Shilo to the back of her wagon, then joined Eirica and her two girls at the edge. Ian was asleep inside.

Jessie stared down at Windlass Hill and beyond. The steep land descended into the ravine that formed Ash Hollow, the gateway to the North Platte Valley.

"Oh, Lord," she whispered, staring at the wreckage littering the hillside. Splintered wood, torn canvas and other debris bore testament to the risks in descending. Coralie waved her hand in front of her face. "I'm so tired. That climb yesterday did me in. I do hope we're stopping for the day."

Jessie grinned. "Don't think so. Looks like the fun's not over yet." Though it was a bit mean of her, she couldn't help teasing her sister-in-law. "But not to worry, Corie. It's all downhill from here."

"Oh, good—good Lord," Coralie said in a squeak, her tone changing to one of horror as she glanced down the hill. "We're not going down that, I hope." She pressed a hand to her heart.

Rook patted her on the shoulder. His blue eyes twinkled and he winked at Jessie, who was trying not to laugh at Coralie's horrified expression. "Yep, lass. Only way down. But jest wait until we get to Ash Hollow. I figure ya gals will love that place. Pretty as a picture."

Coralie stepped back, arms crossed. "Well, I'm not going down this way! Surely there's a much safer way."

Jessie shook her head. "Nope."

Narrowing her eyes, Coralie pushed out her lower lip. "This isn't funny, Jessica. The wagons will never make it. They'll be smashed to pieces."

Jessie took pity on Coralie. "We'll be all right, Corie. Don't start fretting. Won't be that bad." Secretly though, Jessie had her doubts. How in the world would they descend this slope?

James joined them, with Ian still sleeping in his arms.

"Here, Eirica. Jessie's wagon is first in line. We need you to take the boy."

Eirica held out her arms. "Lord help us," she said. "It looks straight down."

James peered over the edge. "Whoo-ee, that it does. What a ride." Whistling, he headed back to the wagons.

The three women stared at one another. "Men," Coralie grumbled. "Trust them to think this a lark."

Rook coughed. "Reckon we'd best get outta the way. Gonna take the rest of the day jest to get them wagons down this hill."

Jessie watched him go, rolling her eyes when she noted the spring in his step. Standing to the side, she watched James lead her wagon to the edge. Her heart hammered. Surely the wagon would plunge down the hill and break into a thousand splinters. Thinking of her ma's rocker, Bible and china, Jessie decided to unload them and carry them down— but it was too late. The men were already tying everything down in the front of the wagon so nothing could fly out on the descent. Then the oxen were unhitched, leaving only the wheel yoke in front. Brakes were set, and hind wheels were locked with a chain attached to the body of the wagon. Last, a log chain was wrapped around the wheels to cut into the ground. "Oh, be careful," she bade her brothers.

James and Jeremy hitched the remaining oxen with their heads facing the rear of the wagon. Silence fell as long lengths of rope were tied to the wagon and all available men took up their positions, the ropes wound around their gloved hands. "I can't look," Coralie said, turning away.

Eirica grabbed Jessie's arm and they watched the scene unfold with bated breath. The oxen in front were urged onward, and the oxen in the rear were pulled along. Unaccustomed to this sort of treatment, they bellowed in fear and rage and tried to resist the downward pull, slowing the wagon's descent. But even with all the precautions, the men holding on to the ropes were dragged down the deeply pitted hill. They dug in their heels, arms straining to hold on to the ropes, their voices loud. It seemed to take forever before the bumping and jarring wagon finally came to a successful stop. Jessie released her breath. "Come on, Coralie, Eirica. There's not much we can do here but watch and worry with our hearts in our throats." Anne and her daughters joined them, and together they slowly descended the steep hill. By the time Jessie reached her wagon, the oxen had been re-hitched in their correct positions. The chains and ropes were unfastened to be reused on the next wagon. The men trudged back up the hill.

As Jessie was taking up the reins to continue on toward Ash Hollow, someone shouted her name. Turning, she saw Rickard limping toward her. His face was pale, his lips pinched with pain and his limp pronounced. He reached for the reins but she held them away. "Why don't you wait down here to help after the wagons are lowered? I'll go on ahead."

Scowling, Rickard grabbed the reins. "I'm fine."

"Boys," Jessie muttered. "Always trying to prove themselves."

Rickard flicked his whip at the oxen. His hazel eyes suddenly twinkled. "Like you don't, huh, Jess? Heard Jordan talkin' 'bout the time you went to that social all dressed up fancy and landed yourself in the punch bowl."

Hands on her hips, Jessie glared at him as he walked away, whistling. Coralie snickered behind her back. Jessie whirled around and narrowed her eyes. Where once Coralie would have run screaming from that look she now stood her ground, her own blue eyes glittering with laughter.

"He has you there, sister dear." Coralie linked their arms together. "Now, come on. Let's go. I don't want to be anywhere near this spot when they lower the next wagon."

Still smarting under Rickard's retort and the remembered humiliation she'd suffered at that long-ago social, Jessie decided a few words with Jordan were in order. "You go on ahead. I'll stay here and help."

Coralie grabbed Eirica and Anne by the arms. "Come on, ladies. I can assure you we don't want to be anywhere near here when Jordie comes back down."

Biting back her own laughter, Jessie watched the three women walk away, giggling. How well her sister-in-law knew her.

With California Hill, the high tableland and Windlass Hill behind them, the wagon train followed the Oregon Trail down into the deep ravine between the North and South Platte rivers. Tired and thirsty, Jessie ached all over from repeatedly climbing up and down the hill. She stopped to rub her knotted calves. For once, she'd been the one to fall behind.

Spotting a large boulder, she gave in to the temptation to sit and soak up the wonderful cool breeze washing over her. After weeks of traveling across the hot, dusty, barren land of the Great Platte River Road, it was sheer heaven to be surrounded by the lush greenery and cool shade provided by the fifteen-foot-high ash trees that gave the six-mile-long plain known as Ash Hollow its name. Hearing the sound of a horse behind her, she put her hand on her whip and turned. She relaxed when she saw it was only Wolf.

"Tired, Jessica?" he asked, stopping his horse in front of her.

"Yeah, I am. That hill was unbelievable. My poor legs may never be the same."

"You didn't have to make all those trips back and forth to help, you know." He glanced around. "Where's your horse?" he asked.

Jessie grimaced and continued to work the tight muscles. "Rook's got her. Are we stopping here for the night?"

"Just up ahead a bit farther. Come on, hop up behind me. Your brothers are bringing down the cattle."

Too tired to argue, Jessie took his hand and placed her booted foot on his. She swung up behind him and wrapped her arms around his waist. Giving in to the luxury of being so close to him, she laid her cheek against his shoulder. Wolf stiffened but didn't say anything. Black Shadow picked his way through the picturesque wooded canyon. Content and happy, Jessie absorbed the beauty of the unexpected paradise. Surrounding them, white cliffs frowned down on them and fluffy clouds floated across the hazy blue backdrop like graceful swans on a pond.

Blue-gray sagebrush ran along the white sands and up the slopes of the bluffs, and everywhere she looked, there were beds of blooming flowers growing in wild profusion. But the most amazing and delightful sight of all was the splash of wild pink roses everywhere. She sniffed. The air was heavy with their sweet perfume. "It's so beautiful, Wolf. Have you ever seen a more glorious sight? They should've named this place Rose Valley. I could stay here forever."

Wolf turned his head to answer. Suddenly only a mere breath separated their lips. Jessie and Wolf stared at each other, lost in the romance of their setting. The horse stopped with a snort and took advantage of the pause to nip at the tender green shoots growing along the trail.

Shifting in his saddle, Wolf tipped her chin up with his fingers. His thumb dipped into the shallow dent there. The blue of his eyes deepened. "I'm looking at a far more glorious sight. In your eyes I see the green of this valley, and here"—he stroked her lower lip—"are lips as soft as the pink rose petals." He slid a finger between her lips. "And sweetness, Jess? Do you know what I taste when I kiss you? Honey. Sweet nectar."

Jessie groaned when his lips brushed hers. His sweet, poetic words sent shivers of delight through her. They were unexpected, beautiful. Her heart pumped with the promise of his kisses. Her lips parted, eager, inviting, hungry.

Wolf accepted the invitation. His mouth was warm and soft as he kissed her with a passion that left her breathless. She was filled with dreamy intimacy when he thrust his tongue into her mouth. Her fingers tangled in his hair. She moaned in protest when he ended the kiss. But when his mouth trailed downward, blazing a path of searing heat down her throat to the soft hollow where her heart pulsed with need, she tipped her head back, giving him full access.

"And here, my sweet Jess, pulses the sweet scent of your body: sunshine and morning dew, sweet innocence and wooded spice. You are the rose in this valley, my love. So potent are you, I want to say the hell with the consequences and take what you so willingly offer.''

"Oh, Wolf," Jessie pleaded, staring into desire-laden gaze, "kiss me, like you did before."

He stared into the dark jade of her eyes before crushing her to him. His mouth closed over hers, his tongue thrusting inside, finding no barriers, only welcome sweetness. Her passion matched his. Her tongue found his, and she took as much as she gave, demanding entrance to his mouth.

Back and forth they dueled, each seeking, retreating, thrusting. Their mating grew frantic. He pulled her across his lap, his hands roving the gentle curves of her body while his mouth loved hers. Her soft moans were music to his ears. Blood pooled and gathered in his groin. He pulsed with need. Damn the consequences. He had to have her.

She moaned. "Please, Wolf, don't stop this time."

The sound of her breathy voice brought him back to awareness of their surroundings. He didn't want to stop, but now was not the time to . . . Cupping her face between his hands, he gave one last, lingering kiss, then lifted his head. His thumbs caressed her cheeks, following the trail of freckles across her nose. "I can't deny myself or you any longer," Wolf whispered, his voice hoarse with desire. "Tonight, sweet Jessica, I'll come for you."

She stroked his jaw. "Truly?"

He grabbed her fingers. "Be sure."

Emotion filled her. "I'm sure."

With a quick kiss, he moved her behind him once again. When they reached their camp, he helped her down. Before she walked away, he called her name softly. "Jess, be sure this is what you want. I can't make promises, except that once we're alone, there'll be no turning back." With that he kicked the horse into motion and returned to help James with the livestock.

Jessie finished putting away the pans and utensils she and Rook had used for the evening meal. A soft whine drew her attention. She glanced around and saw Sadie sitting beside the wagon, her tail wagging. Dropping to her knees, she scratched the dog behind her ears. "Where have you been, Sadie girl? I was getting worried about you." Sadie's response was to lick Jessie's hand, then lift her muzzle to swipe her tongue across Jessie's face. "All right. You're forgiven. Just don't disappear like that again."

Sadie barked once, then stood, peering beneath the wagon. She barked again, this time softly. To Jessie's surprise, Wahoska's pale, furry body emerged from the shadows. He answered by licking Sadie behind her ears. Unbelievably, Sadie accepted Wahoska's nuzzling. Jessie removed her hat and tossed it into the back of her wagon, but Sadie ignored it, preferring the wolf's attentions.

Shaking her head, she grinned at the two animals. "You must have it bad, Sadie, to ignore my hat. About time the two of you patched up your differences." She watched Sadie lift her muzzle to the wolf's. "You'd better watch out, girl. He's as unpredictable as his master, even if he does tolerate a collar."

Wahoska turned from Sadie and barked, jumping up to plant his large forefeet on the back of the wagon. His nose pointed upward as he sniffed the air. Tail wagging, he turned his pale blue gaze onto Jessie. Jessie rolled her eyes. "I take it the pair of you are hungry?" Both animals answered with eager whines. "All right, here you go. Rook sure spoils the two of you."

"Me, spoil them varmints? I'm jest keepin' 'em from fightin', that's all," he said, joining her. He stuck his pipe between his lips and glowered at the tails wagging in greeting.

Jessie ducked her head to hide her grin as she set two tins of fatty scraps on the ground. Glancing around, she saw that everything was neat and put away. There was nothing more for her to do, so she went to her wagon and unrolled her bedding under it. But it was too early to retire for the night. Leaning against the wagon, she crossed her arms in front of her and stared at the darkened sky. Stars twinkled, and the moon glowed. Around her, families readied themselves for bed. Nervous anticipation filled her.

Would Wolf really come? Could she go with him, knowing that at the end of the trail he'd leave her? Jessie sighed. Yes. Not only could she, she would. She'd take whatever he offered. She just wished she knew why he was so adamant that they had no future. Why was he so against taking her back with him? The thought of never seeing Wolf again left an ache deep in her heart.

But loving him meant she'd have to leave her brothers to go to his home. There in the quiet of the evening with the wind caressing her skin, she felt torn between love and family. True, the thought of leaving her brothers, of maybe never seeing them again, was hard to bear, but she'd found the man she loved and wanted for her husband. The man she wanted to father her children. To have what her dreams promised, she'd have to trade one family for the promise of another—leave one family to start a new one.

Jessie knew that given the choice, she'd gladly go with the man she loved, that this was what life was about. She belonged with Wolf. Jordan had Coralie, and if she weren't mistaken, James was sweet on Eirica. Soon her brothers would each be engrossed in their own lives, as she should be. Somehow she had to find a way to convince Wolf that this was the way of things. They belonged together. She frowned. He'd spoken of duty. But duty to what? She couldn't fight an enemy she didn't understand. And somehow, deep inside, she knew that this was the key.

Rook's tuneless whistling drew her attention. He sat before a fire, whittling as he did each evening. Her eyes narrowed. Rook knew Wolf better than anyone. With purposeful strides, she headed for the fire. She sat across from him, elbows on knees, chin resting on her fisted hands as she tried to find a way to broach the subject.

"All right, lass. Spill it. What's got ya bothered?"

Jessie grimaced. So much for easing into it. "You know Wolf pretty well, don't you?"

One bushy brow lifted. "As well as anyone, I s'pose. Quit beatin' 'round the bush, lass."

"Wolf says he's duty bound. What does that mean? To what?"

Rook laid down his knife and hunk of wood. "Ah, lass. Would it be that I could tell you."

Jessie sat forward. "Please, Rook. I need to know. I won't say a word, I promise."

Rook lit his pipe, and blue smoke rose into the air. "It's not that simple. He don't know. Nobody knows. That's his problem."

Her shoulders slumped. "I don't understand."

Rook chewed on the end of his pipe, his eyes glazing as he stared into the glowing embers. "Let me tell ya a story. Ya know that Wolf's part Sioux?"

Jessie nodded, holding her breath. "I met his brother, Striking Thunder."

"Yes, well. Wolf's the second son. He was born jest minutes afore his twin sister."

"He has a twin?" Jessie realized there was much she didn't know about Wolf.

Rook lowered his brows. "Don't go interruptin' me every five minutes, lass, or we'll be here all night. Now, where was I?" He drew on his pipe. "Ah, yes, he has a twin sister. Now, Wolf's grandmother, she had the sight. Could see the future. She foresaw that these twins, one boy, one girl, would each possess a gift that would serve the People.

"Star Dreamer discovered hers early on. She inherited the sight from her grandmother. Wolf's gift is knowledge. He was even sent away for schooling." Rook fell silent and resumed his carving.

Though Jessie sensed there was much more to the story, she knew he'd said all he was going to. She thought about what Rook had told her, and Wolf's frustration the day of the buffalo stampede. Her voice was soft. "He still hasn't figured out his role, has he?"

Rook sent slivers of wood into the fire. "No, lass."

His tone, one of sadness, told her more than the words

themselves. She stood, ready to return to her wagon. She had a lot to think over.

Rook called her name. "Jess."

Surprised, she glanced over her shoulder at him. Seldom did he call her by name, preferring *lass*.

"Sometimes the Lord works in ways we don't understand. Sometimes the answers we seek are there afore us but we's too blind to see."

Jessie cocked her head. "Do *you* know what he should be doing to serve his people?"

"I'm tellin' ya to keep an open mind and heart, lass." Rook stood. "Mebbe you's the answer."

They fell silent. After a while Jessie returned to her wagon. As she slid beneath her quilts, her mind raced with what she'd learned from Rook. Though she'd felt all along that they were well suited, did that mean they were meant to be? She frowned. The thought that there was a higher power behind her love for Wolf made her a bit nervous. She knew nothing about Indians, had nothing to give them. All she was good at was farming and tending livestock. Even her talent at hunting or in using her whip would mean nothing to them.

Rook had told her a bit about Wolf's cabin and horses. Now, that part of his life she knew she could embrace. What could Wolf's duty be? One thing was for sure: meant to be or just suited, she had to help him find out before the next spring or he'd leave Oregon without her.

She turned onto her stomach to wait for Wolf. Her pulse quickened in anticipation, and at the same time, a sense of panic set in. What would he expect of her? She knew nothing about pleasing a man. Would he find her lacking? Could she go through with it?

One part of her, the emerging woman, longed for nothing more than to have him take her away and show her what it meant to be loved by the man who held her heart. And she did love him, did want to be with him. But another part of her feared the union, feared the unknown. Grimacing, she ran a hand through her hair; the curls were longer and not so tight now, and they framed her face.

Voices faded, fires burned down and soft snores filled the air, but Jessie remained awake. Switching to her side, she stared at the night sky through the spokes of the wheel. The stars hung against a deep backdrop of midnight blue. As her gaze followed one bright dot to another, she was reminded of the long, painful nights that had followed her parents' death. Months after losing them, she'd leave her bed in the dead of night and sneak out into the yard while her brothers slept. With tears blurring her vision, she'd let her gaze roam across the dark heavens until she found the two brightest stars among the countless shiny lights.

Jessie had been only eight when her secure world had shattered, and she'd held firm to the belief that those bright, twinkling lights above were her ma and pa watching over her. She'd stand out in the cold of the night until one of her brothers woke to lead her back inside. Jessie frowned. What made her think of that after all this time? "Must be because so much is changing—I'm changing," she mused, once again finding two stars side by side that shone brighter than any of the others.

"Oh, Ma," she whispered, "how I wish you were here to guide me. It may be wrong for me to go with Wolf if he comes for me, but I love him." Jessie closed her eyes, feeling so very alone. If Wolf came, she'd take whatever he offered and deal with the rest later.

A while later, a soft whisper broke the stillness of the night. "Jessie?"

She crawled out from beneath the wagon. Holding her breath, she peered into the darkness to see Wolf standing near the wagon tongue. In the dark he looked like a pagan god, with his hair flowing down to his shoulders. His vest was parted, baring his bronzed chest to her hungry gaze. She stepped close, stopping only a breath away. Her heart hammered with equal measures of fear, anticipation and excitement. Wolf reached out, his hands gentle as he cupped her chin.

"Are you sure?" His voice came low, a hum drifting on the breeze.

Jessie nodded and stared up into his shadowed face. His features were blocked but for the glint of his eyes.

"I can't make you any promises, Jess."

"I know," she said softly as his lips lowered to hers.

His lips lingered for an all too brief moment; then he pulled her into the deep shadows. When they reached his horse, he mounted and pulled her up across his lap, cradling her against his bare chest. "Where are we going?" she whispered, snuggled against him. She nuzzled her cheek against his warm skin.

"You'll see," he replied, staring down at her.

His gaze held hers. "I want you, Jessica Jones." He groaned, kissing her roughly. He deepened the kiss, his passion fierce. His hand roamed over the gentle swells of her breasts. Then he lifted his head, his breathing labored. She buried her head against his shoulder and gasped. "Wolf, you make me feel so strange. I don't know what's happening, but you're the one who makes me feel this way." Tendrils of fear returned.

Wolf slid his lips along her neck, his breath hot and heavy. "Don't worry, sweet Jess, I feel the same way. You make me feel things that none other has."

His words reassured her. The two of them fell silent, passing several other sleeping camps. At the base of the eastern bluff, Wolf dismounted, helped her down and secured his horse to a tree. Then he took her by the hand. Together they climbed the steep hillside. Jessie glanced down. Darkness floated up to her. She couldn't see, but she knew they were pretty high above the ground.

Wolf turned and grinned. "It's a surprise. Come on, it's not much farther."

"What's not much far—?" Her voice broke off when Wolf pulled her behind some thick bushes. When she saw the dark void before them, her eyes grew wide. "A cave," she said, excitement ringing in her voice.

"Wait here," he commanded. Leaving her at the entrance, he disappeared inside.

Within minutes, faint light dispelled most of the gloom.

When Wolf called out to her, she stepped inside and gasped. Along one wall, several squat candles flickered, sending shadows dancing on the walls and ceiling. The faint light revealed a thick pile of blankets spread across the floor near the side of the cave. A tantalizing aroma wafted toward her, and she sniffed the air.

Stepping forward, she peered into the shadows. Her breath caught in her throat as she stared at dozens of wild pink blooms scattered across the floor, ridding the air of all mustiness.

She stooped, picked up one of the wild roses and held it to her nose. Her gaze flitted around the cozy confines of the cave, then back to him. She was touched, incredibly overcome by his thoughtfulness. First sweet words, and now an action so romantic she had to sniff back the tears. Flickering candles sparkled in his eyes, revealing the love he felt but hadn't put into words. She realized that behind the hard outer shell lay a deeply sensitive man. Somehow he'd known of the soft, romantic part of her heart that she'd never revealed to another soul.

"This is incredible. I don't know what to say."

Wolf stood in the middle of the bedding. Shadows danced across his features. "Don't say anything." He held out his hand.

Chapter Nineteen

Wolf waited. Love welled inside him as he watched the emotions play across her features. The last of her hesitation fled and she joined him in the middle of the bedding.

"It's beautiful, Wolf, the candles, the roses. So romantic. I can't believe you did this for me," she whispered.

He saw the moisture in her eyes and lifted her hands to his lips. Taking the rose from her grasp, he caressed her cheek with it. "The candles are so I can see you when we make love and the roses remind me of your beauty."

Jessie laughed nervously. "I'm more tumbleweed than rose."

"That, sweet Jess, is where you're wrong." He pulled a petal from the blooming bud. "The rose has layers of petals that bloom separately, yet make the rose the beauty it is. And despite the sharp thorns to protect it, it's fragile." To demonstrate, he crushed the petal between his thumb and forefinger.

He dropped the rose and cupped her face between his hands. "You're my rose, Jess." His smile turned wry. "Sometimes a thorn in my side, but always my beautiful, wild rose. So many layers, so fragile inside, that I fear I will hurt you." He groaned. "You shouldn't have come." He closed his eyes as if in great pain.

Jessie slid her arms around his neck, afraid he'd change his mind. Pressing herself against him, she wove her fingers through his hair, sliding them through the long, silky golden locks. "Oh, Wolf. I had to come. Don't you know that when you crush a rose petal, its scent fills the air with a sweetness all its own?"

Standing on tiptoe, she offered up her lips with a softly spoken plea. "Kiss me, Wolf. Teach me and love me. I want so much to please you." Taking matters into her own hands, she pulled his head down and ran her tongue over his parted lips. "I want you. All of you."

Wolf couldn't refuse her. He claimed her mouth, plundering the lush fullness with demanding mastery. When her lips parted on a hungry sigh, he thrust his tongue inside, taking her with a savage intensity that only grew.

Her heavenly taste, the luring texture of her—he couldn't get enough. The kiss went on, lasting for an eternity, yet it was not enough, never enough. His blood pumped, heated as though buffeted by the hot winds of the prairies. His lungs burned, and with a gasping need for air, he tore his mouth from hers.

Together they drew in ragged breaths. Her desire-glazed eyes pleaded, begged for more. She ran her tongue over her lips, luring him. His head dipped; his tongue flicked out to stroke her lower lip. But rather than deepening the kiss, he slowed the pace, wanting to take his time, needing to savor and cherish every moment of their loving. Jessie followed his lead. She caressed the back of his neck and sucked his lower lip. Taking turns, they teased, explored and learned the taste of each other.

Wolf loved the feel of her, the scent of her, her soft moans and gasps that filled his ears. But it wasn't enough. Against her lips, he whispered, "I want to see you, sweet Jess, all of you." He unbuttoned her shirt, the backs of his fingers skimming the soft flesh hidden from his eyes. Shards of pain stabbed his lower region.

Control became a battle: mind over body. Wolf ignored his urges to drive himself into her. With infinite slowness, he drew the moment out, touching her with teasing strokes until she moaned and lifted her hands to help him. He clutched the edges of her shirt in each hand and stopped her with a deep kiss. "Let me undress you, slowly, layer by layer, petal by petal, until the very heart of you is exposed." His lips sought the soft, silky skin beneath her jaw. Her head tipped to one side.

Jessie sighed, her eyes fluttering closed. He pressed his lips to each eyelid. "Open your eyes, Jess." When she stared up at him, he slowly pushed her shirt off her shoulders, letting her see his hungry gaze slide down and feast on the gentle slope of her breasts. The cool night air brushed her pale skin, beading her dusky peaks. An answering pull echoed deep in his groin. His fingers feathered over her small globes of milk white flesh. Soft as the night breeze, he caressed her, molded her small, pert breasts to fit into his palms.

She smoothed her hands up and down his chest, grazing his nipples with her fingertips. "Don't stop. Please don't stop." She arched into him.

Her words deepened his desire, set his body on fire with need. His fingers wandered downward, teasing her flesh as he slid her pants down her hips.

Fingers dug into his shoulders as he knelt before her and removed her boots and pants, leaving her revealed to him. Her legs shook; his fingers quivered. With tantalizing slowness that threatened to shatter his control, he glided his palms back up the length of her silky thighs, roamed over her hips and circled around to cup one pale cheek in each hand. "Perfect," he whispered, leaning forward to plant a searing kiss to the smooth alabaster skin of her abdomen.

Jessie whimpered when his tongue laved the inside of her navel. The sensations he aroused in her made her forget her embarrassment over her nakedness. His fingers smoothed back up her spine. She arched her back, her fingers clutching the sides of his head. Her knees buckled, refusing to support her. She slid down before him. With each loving stroke of his fingertips dancing over her fiery skin, her insides trembled and melted into pools of longing. She wanted him, wanted to see and touch him.

Her hands searched for the fastening at his waist, but he

stopped her. She moaned in frustration. "Please, Wolf."

"Not yet, sweet Jess." He groaned. "We have all night."
He swallowed her protests, his kiss mind numbing and bone
melting. He rolled onto his back, drawing her on top of him.
His hands skimmed up and down her back, then lower to
knead her buttocks and pull her tightly against him. He
rocked against her, the buckskin straining over his arousal—
rough, yet soft.

She responded, circling her hips to meet his thrusts. Heat
throbbed between her legs. Her cries turned to soft whimpers.
Finally, on an anguished moan, he rolled over and stood, his
heated gaze holding hers as he shoved his buckskin breeches
down past his lean hips and stepped out of them. Rising to
sit on her heels, Jessie held her breath. Starting at his ankles,
she lifted her gaze, noting the strong muscles, the fine dust-
ing of golden hair that gleamed in the soft light. She drew a
deep, shaky breath as she gazed at him. His hands rested on
narrow hips, and his spread feet left her with a wonderful
view of his thick thighs.

When she dared, her gaze rose still further. She gasped,
her eyes widening with undisguised delight mixed with little
tremors of fear as she stared at his breechclout and his swelling desire, which pulsed against the leather flap. When his
hand went to the leather thong at his waist, she shook her
head, her voice low, hoarse with need. "Wait. Turn around."

Wolf grinned but did as she bade—ever so slowly. Jessie
thought she'd faint. Oh, God, he was sinful in that thing. The
narrow strip of cloth didn't quite cover his rock-hard buttocks. She licked her lips. Her fantasies were nothing compared to the real thing. On her knees, she leaned forward,
her fingers reaching out to trail up his thigh and disappear
beneath the hide. Her hands encountered firm, heated flesh.

He turned, growled, and yanked off the hide breechclout,
then fell to his knees and took her back into his arms to kiss
and caress her. Where he touched her, she touched him.
When his tongue left her mouth, hers entered his. Flesh to
flesh, man to woman, they twined together, rolled across the

bedding, seeking satisfaction but finding only a greater craving.

Jessie's cries mingled with his harsh moans. He eased her back onto the silky-soft fur beneath her and covered her with his rock-hard length. She clutched his shoulders, loving the feel of his hard, bulging muscles beneath her fingers.

"*Skuya*. Sweet." His lips nipped and teeth scraped the tender skin of her neck. She shivered, craving the warmth of his mouth against her skin.

Without releasing her lips from his, he pressed himself to her, his chest hard against hers, crushing the swollen mounds of her breasts, abrading the sensitive tips with his silky curls. She shifted slightly, lifting to greet his pelvis as he settled into the cradle of her hips. He pulsed against her, turning her blood to liquid need.

Shadows danced along the cave walls, and the scent of melting wax mingled with rose-perfumed air and heavy desire. Wolf lifted himself up on one hand and used the other to cup one side of her face. "So beautiful," he whispered, trailing his hand down her neck.

Jessie arched her back when he fondled one candlelight-bathed breast, running the pads of his fingers over her straining nipple. But when he lowered his head, his lips closing over the aroused flesh, she gasped and gave herself over to his loving. The blood pounded in her head as his tongue laved, flicked and suckled the hard bud. She moaned, waves of pleasure radiating outward and downward. Her hips moved restlessly beneath his. The feel of his engorged length pulsing against her throbbing flesh ignited a deep, piercing ache that spread upward, then settled deep in her belly. With each heartbeat, each pulse, the ache grew, tugged at her, sent her hips undulating frantically beneath his.

Wolf reared up, his features contorted in pain. "God, Jess. I want to take it slow, go easy."

Jessie thrashed beneath him. "Wolf, please—I ache—I need . . ."

Wolf slid partly off her and skimmed his hand over her

flat belly. "Easy, sweet Jess. Let me show you what you need."

Jessie sucked in her breath when his fingers combed through her nether curls, finding and fondling her intimately. A wave of uncertainty came over her and she stiffened. Closing her eyes, she held her breath, unsure of the intrusion of his fingers as they slipped further between her damp folds to caress her aching womanhood.

His lips tickled her ear, nipping at the lobe. "Relax, Jessica. Relax and let your body feel." Quickly Wolf's fingers worked their magic. Her fear and uncertainty fled, replaced by a new tension. "Oh, Wolf," she cried, reaching out to hold on to him, feeling all control slipping away. Her hips jerked frantically under the firm pressure of his fingers as he continued to rotate them in ever-quickening circles.

"That's it, sweetheart. Just let yourself go. Let me bring you to fulfillment." Wolf slanted his lips over hers, swallowing her soft cries.

Jessie gasped and moaned against his mouth, unsure what he meant, but it didn't seem to matter. Her body knew. A tremor started deep within her and rushed to the surface with the force of a summer storm. Onward and upward she spiraled. Suddenly she stiffened and shuddered. Her cry of wonder filled the small cave, and she gave herself up to an indescribable joy as she soared toward the heavens in a brilliant explosion of light.

Wolf's murmured reassurances brought her back slowly. Moments later she lay there, savoring the feeling of incredible satisfaction he'd left her with. "Oh, Wolf, I've never . . . I didn't know . . . It was wonderful," she said softly, finally finding the courage to look at him.

Wolf shook his head slowly from side to side and smiled tenderly even as his body urged him to find his release. He fought the urge. Tonight was for Jessie. He wanted to go slowly, to make it last. "The best is yet to come, my beautiful rose."

He kissed her deeply, his fingers gentle on her overly sensitive flesh as he brought her back to the brink of release.

When he sensed she was close, he moved over her and nudged her legs apart. Her knees fluttered open, inviting him to sample her pleasure. He poised himself at her entrance, his face a mixture of pain and pleasure.

"I can't wait any longer, Jess. I need you, but I don't want to hurt you." He moaned.

Jessie cried out, her hips seeking him. She reached up and pulled his mouth to hers. Her legs wrapped around his hips, drawing him to her. "I'm already hurting, Wolf." She whimpered, lifting herself until her damp heat touched the tip of him.

Wolf groaned, and with one powerful thrust, he breached the thin barrier of her maidenhead and buried himself in her moist sheath. Jessie's fingers dug into his back, and his lips moved over hers to swallow her cry of pain. He wanted to stop, to hold back the forces that drew them to this point. He wanted to wait until she adjusted to him, to his size, but he couldn't. He'd waited too long and could no longer control his frantic thrusts. "Jessica," he cried out. But he needn't have worried. Jessie met him thrust for thrust until together, as one, they gave themselves over to the wondrous turbulence of ecstasy.

Tossing and turning in the rose-scented cave, Wolf dreamed of his grandmother, becoming once again that frightened, ten-year-old boy summoned to the deathbed of a loved one. Immersed in his dream, he felt the pain, the fear. His grandmother hadn't been just a loved one. She'd been special. She'd known things, seen things, and when she'd spoken of them, they came true. It was a gift that both fascinated and scared him. Already his twin sister, Star Dreamer, was having visions.

So he stood outside his grandmother's tipi, listening to her harsh breathing and racking coughs, afraid, yet torn by his need to see her.

"Come here, grandson," she whispered.

Wolf slipped into the tipi she'd shared with Hawk Eyes, his grandfather, who'd died two winters before. "You wanted to see me, *Uncheedah*,'' he'd asked, trying hard to keep the wobble from his voice. He took her hand, trying so hard to be brave, but when he felt the coldness of her grip, heard the rattle in her chest with each breath, he wept. She couldn't die. He needed her. His grandmother understood him. She knew he was different from his siblings and the other braves.

"No tears, child. My time is near. You must listen now."

He bit his lip to still the trembling. "No, Grandmother. You must get well. I'll get the *Wicasa*. I'll fetch Father." He tried to pull away, but her fingers tightened on his wrist with unexpected strength.

"No! Golden Eagle has done all he can. I've spoken to your parents and to Star. Now I must speak with you before I leave this world." Seeing Eyes went into a coughing fit that shook her thin frame.

Fearing her time had come, Wolf glanced over his shoulder and saw his mother standing in the doorway. Her nearly white hair hung loose around a face wet with tears. Only later would he wonder if her tears had been for her mother-in-law or the news of his grandmother's last vision, which would change his life forever.

"You must listen to me now, grandson. You have a difficult path to walk, but it is one you must take." Each breath became a gasp. "Our future is uncertain. You must leave. Develop your gift. Knowledge. That is the gift you will one day give back to the People. I have seen this. . . ." Seeing Eyes stopped, her chest rising and falling as she gasped for air.

Wolf knelt and smoothed the graying black hair from his grandmother's face. "What do you mean, *Uncheedah?* One day I will be a great warrior as my father and grandfathers. I will help protect our people and stop the white men from taking what is ours." His young voice had rung with such conviction.

"No, child. You are of two worlds. You must use the knowledge of one world to help the other."

"What do you mean?" Her breathing grew faint. Wolf

held her hand to his cheek. "*Uncheedah*! Don't go. I need you here."

Seeing Eyes opened her eyes briefly for one last loving look. Her voice grew strong. "There will be another who will understand you, grandson. Together you will help the People. This I have also seen. You must go to the white man's school. Learn all that you can. . . ." Her voice faded and a smile blossomed over her face even as her dark eyes glazed over.

"Hawk Eyes, my husband. I am ready," she whispered with her last breath.

"No!" Wolf shouted. He awoke with a start, bathed in sweat. Sitting, he rubbed his hands over his face to rid himself of the remnants of his dream. He glanced around. The candles were pools of molten wax. A few still burned, dispelling total darkness. He lay back. Why had he dreamed of his grandmother's passing after so many years?

Beside him, Jessie lifted her dark head. "Wolf? Are you all right?" Her eyes were wide with concern. He pulled her back to him, pillowed her head against his shoulder and nuzzled his cheek against her soft black curls. For long moments he lay there, breathing in her comforting scent. When he'd calmed, he spoke. "It's nothing, just a dream."

Jessie slid her hand up his chest and cupped his jaw. She tilted her own head so she could see him. "Do you want to talk about it?" she asked.

Wolf closed his eyes and shook his head. "No. The past is past."

"Yet it still haunts you today."

Her voice wrapped around him, loosening some of the anger and bitterness encasing his heart. With his eyes fixed on the rough surface of the ceiling, Wolf spoke of his grandmother and of her dying words. He'd meant to stop there, but like a festering wound opened to drain, he told Jessie things he'd never told another soul. He shared with her the loneliness of a boy sent away from everything he knew into a strange, alien and hostile world. Five hellish years during which he'd been punished every time he'd spoke his native tongue, whipped each time he left his bedroom without wearing proper white man's clothing, or failed in his studies.

Jessie listened as he spoke of the summers when he was allowed to return to his people for a few short months before being sent back to the missionaries. And how he'd endured it all because he wanted so badly to help his people. When he grew silent, she rose up on one elbow and smoothed her fingertips over his lips. "I'm so sorry. No child should go through what you did. They were wrong to treat you so."

Wolf wanted to believe her, but he also still believed his grandmother's dying words. Then he remembered her telling him he would find another who would also help his people. Could this person be Jessica, the woman he loved? Did she hold the answer to his future? He reached up and ran his fingers down the softness of her face.

Sighing, he pushed the thought from his mind, ordering himself not to be foolish. What could she do? She couldn't prevent the white man's invasion. She couldn't wage war against the soldiers. No matter how well she could shoot, she was still a woman—a woman vulnerable in a savage land. Images of Rook's dead wife were enough to banish his impossible dreams. Until he discovered where his future lay, he would remain alone. Lonely.

The thought depressed him. He took hold of Jessie's wrist, kissed each fingertip and drew her down to him. His voice was low, hoarse. "Enough talk of the past. Nothing can change it."

Chapter Twenty

Jessie woke to the feeling of something tickling the flesh below one ear. She groaned. Her body felt stiff, tired and sore. She swatted at the nuisance, then settled back to sleep. The irritant moved to her lips, then to the tip of her nose. She slapped at it, but it was gone. It returned, this time caressing one cheek. Her nostrils flared as she caught a whiff of roses. She opened her eyes.

Wolf lay beside her, leaning on one elbow, his hand cradling his head. With his other hand he twirled a pink blossom across her cheek, down her throat and over her breast, an artist painting her skin with its sweet scent.

Jessie wasn't awake or coherent enough to appreciate the tenderness of the action. She only knew she didn't want to wake up. Her eyes blinked rapidly, then closed, the lids too heavy to hold open. "Oh, Wolf, tell me it's not morning already." She groaned, turning onto her stomach, seeking sleep.

Wolf caressed the back of her neck and ran the soft petals down the indentation of her spine.

"No, *Wi* has not yet shown her face, but we must return to camp before the others wake."

Warm lips nibbled at her earlobe. With a sigh, she turned and welcomed the warmth of his body covering hers. How many times during the night had they turned to each other to make sweet, gentle love? Three? Four? She had no idea and didn't care. She pouted. "Do we have to? I like it here."

Wolf drew her lower lip into his mouth. With sweet tenderness, he deepened the kiss. Her heart-beat sped up, and all tiredness fled when his fingers slid down her body. He broke the kiss and grinned down at her. "Perhaps we can stay a bit longer." His finger slid into her.

Jessie arched her hips, seeking his touch. "Oh, yes, Wolf."

The heel of his hand pressed against her. She throbbed and grew moist.

Wolf whispered against her mouth, "What do you want, Jessica?" He parted her legs.

Jessie bit him gently, then arched up, pressing her damp folds to his pulsing flesh. "You, Wolf. All of you."

He groaned and entered her slowly, considerate of her tender flesh, but Jessie was beyond feeling any pain beyond a burning need for release.

"God, what you do to me, woman. I need you, sweet Jess."

Her lips closed over his. "Then quit talking and love me."

By the time they left the cave, the stars had already faded. Wolf brought his horse to a halt a short distance from their camp. Neither moved. Jessie didn't want the night to end. She reached up and caressed his face, running her fingers over a day's worth of stubble. "Why do you shave every day? Why not just grow a beard like most of the other men on the trail?" she asked.

"My people do not grow hair on their faces," he replied simply.

Jessie understood. He had the ability to grow a full beard, but if he did, it would be one more reminder that he didn't fit in with his people.

"You must return now, before the others wake." He gave her one last lingering kiss, then helped her down.

Jessie stared up at him, reluctant to walk away.

"I'll come for you tonight," he promised.

Content for the moment with his promise, Jessie watched man and beast fade into the purple shadows. She yawned and made her way quietly to her wagon and crawled into her bedroll. Surprisingly, she fell asleep immediately.

From the shadows, a tall, lanky figure emerged and released Sadie's collar. "Okay, girl, you can go to her now." When the dog curled up with her mistress, he turned away, his green eyes shadowed with worry.

Pleasantly tired from her night in the cave with Wolf, Jessie slid the needle through the canvas one last time then surveyed her stitches. "Not a bad job," she grinned. After replacing the wagon cover, she glanced at the mid-morning sun and stifled an impatient sigh. Now what? All her chores were done. Why was it that when you most wanted time to pass quickly, it dragged? Sadie emerged from beneath the wagon, stretched and yawned. Then she plopped down, her muzzle resting forlornly on her front paws.

Jessie laughed softly. The dog missed Wahoska. Just as she herself missed Wolf. "I know how you feel, girl. We're a pair, we are. I'm afraid it's going to be a long day." Closing her eyes, Jessie leaned against the sun-warmed canvas. Images from her and Wolf's night of loving replayed within her mind. A spark of desire low in her belly grew, radiating upward and outward, sending tingles of remembered pleasure up her spine. She wanted Wolf, wanted to feel his hands roam her body and yearned to experience once again the incredible pleasure brought about by his clever fingers. And the thought of touching him, feeling his velvety hardness, seeing the pleasure pain in his features as she stroked him, sent her blood pulsing with need. So lost in her fantasies of the night to come, she didn't hear Sadie's warning growl.

"Dreaming of your lover, *Je-ssss-ica*?"

At the sound of Rosalyn's harsh voice, Jessie straightened. Her eyes narrowed. "None of your concern, *Rosalyn*." Unwilling to get into another showdown with the unpleasant woman, Jessie strode past her.

The woman reached out and grabbed her by the arm and arched one brow. "Wonder what your brothers would say if they knew their baby sister was laying with a 'breed?'' Rosalyn's eyes shone with hatred.

Jessie shook off the claw-like fingers. Why couldn't the woman just leave her alone? The voice of reason told Jessie to leave, that the woman was all bluff, but she couldn't risk having her carry tales. Jessie couldn't let her brothers learn of her relations with Wolf. Well, two could play this game. She eyed the woman, deliberately letting her gaze roam insultingly up and down the other woman's body. Her lips twisted. "If I were you, I'd be more concerned with my own affairs. Seems like you have enough troubles of your own without borrowing more."

Rosalyn froze. She stared at Jessie through slitted eyes. "What do you mean?"

Unable to resist taunting the hateful woman, Jessie smirked. "Can't be good for your ego to have a husband who prefers to spend his nights with his hired hand instead of his wife. It must have shocked you, being newly married and all." She paused, taking measure of the rage building in Rosalyn's eyes. "No wonder you're so desperate for male company. But to bed Sunny?" Jessie shuddered delicately. "The man's got no teeth."

Rosalyn let her breath out in a long drawn out hiss. She advanced, one small hand clenched, the other buried beneath her apron. "Why, you little tramp," she spat. "You're spying on us!"

Amused now, Jessie rolled her eyes. "Really Rosalyn, I've better things to do. As for knowing about your husband, we all have eyes in our heads. And those of us who sleep outside can't help but see Hugh and Sammy sneak off into the night."

Rosalyn took several deep calming breaths. Her brown eyes gleamed with intent. "You seem pretty observant. What else do you know 'bout us?"

Shrugging, Jessie eyed her. "Talk at meal times does get interesting." She grinned and hooked her thumbs over the waist of her jeans. "But rest assured, no one seems to hold it against you. After all, Wolf's men are more than willing to warm your bed at night, except my brothers, of course."

"Why, you . . . I'll teach you to mess with me." Rosalyn advanced on Jessie. Her apron fluttered and a gleam of metal flashed.

A low rumbling growl sounded. Sadie moved between the two women, her teeth bared, her shoulders hunched and fur raised. Rosalyn took a hasty step back. Sadie followed, her body crouched to spring.

"Sadie!" Jessie snatched the dog by the rope collar with one hand while her other hand hovered near the hilt of the knife strapped to her belt. Did Rosalyn have a knife? And if so, was she fool enough to pull it? While Jessie wasn't as good with a knife as she was with a gun or whip, she knew how to protect herself with one.

The dog strained to be released. Menacing growls filled the air. Daisy backed away slowly, her hand coming out empty from beneath the apron. Jessie breathed a sigh of relief.

The sound of Wolf's voice rang out. "What's going on here?" He approached with Wahoska beside him.

The wolf brushed against Rosalyn's skirts, and the woman jumped back with a squeal.

Wolf glanced from Rosalyn to the animals. Wahoska added his growls to the dog's. "I asked a question."

Rosalyn moved close to Wolf. She fluttered her eyes and gripped Wolf's arm. "Oh, Wolf, I'm so glad you're here. I was just walking past, minding my own business and for no reason, Jessie turned her dog on me," she accused in a tearful voice. She wiped non-existent tears from her eyes and chewed on her lower lip.

Jessie's jaw dropped. "I did not," she returned hotly. Her finger stabbed the air in front of Rosalyn. "You're the one who came over here to start trouble. Sadie was just protecting me."

"That dog is a menace," Rosalyn sniffed. "She should be tied up!"

"You're the menace and a liar besides," Jessie shot back. Now she wished that Rosalyn *had* tried something on her. If she'd pulled a gun or knife, she'd have gotten kicked out of the wagon train and they'd all be rid of her and her trouble-making.

Wolf held up his hands. "I've heard enough. Mrs. Norton, I've told you once before that I won't tolerate troublemaking. Sadie wouldn't be carrying on like this unless you threatened her mistress."

Rosalyn gritted her teeth and narrowed her eyes, all pretense of tears gone. She turned on Jessie. "You! He's only taking your side so he can get you back into his bed," she hissed, then stalked off in rage.

Jessie released her hold on Sadie, her heart racing. Should she tell Wolf that Rosalyn had nearly attacked her? No, she decided, she'd deal with the woman herself. It would only be her word against Rosalyn's, anyway. She patted her own knife and vowed to make sure it was on her person at all times—and her whip.

"You okay?"

"Yeah, I'm fine."

"Be careful, Jessie. You've made yourself another enemy."

She shrugged, her eyes narrowed. "I can handle her. She's just a two-bit tramp."

Wolf stared after Rosalyn. "Just be careful, Jess. Don't get cocky. And you let me know if you have any more problems."

Jessie sighed but agreed. There *was* something dangerous about that woman. The feral gleam in Rosalyn's eyes had warned her that things between them weren't finished. But she didn't want to worry Wolf, so when Jeremy joined them, she brightened her voice. "We're going to go check out the springs. Want to come?"

Wolf shook his head. "No. I've got things to see to."

Jessie and Jeremy left camp to explore Ash Hollow with its many springs. They headed for the rocky bluffs on the east side. She slid her brother a worried look. He was quiet, too quiet. "What's wrong, Jeremy?"

Jeremy glanced at her, his pale green gaze troubled. Stopping, he grabbed her by the shoulders and stared into her eyes. "Do you know what you're doing, Jess?"

A tremor of unease slid up her spine, but she schooled her features into a bland look. "What do you mean, Jeremy?"

"Don't play dumb with me, Jess." His features turned stern, making him look a lot like James. "After my watch was over last night, I came into camp to raid some of our supplies."

Jessie groaned. "You and your stomach!" Inside, she winced and waited for Jeremy to start yelling at her. It was apparent that he knew about her and Wolf. How was she going to bluff her way out of this one? He knew her too well for her even to attempt to lie.

"Don't try to change the subject, sister dear. I was worried when I found your bed empty. I searched all over for you but couldn't find you. Figured you and Eirica were out walking. So I waited. Imagine my surprise when I saw you return with Wolf. You're playing a game that could get you hurt."

Jessie sighed. "It's no game. What I feel for Wolf is real."

"Like your crush on Elliot all these years?"

Jessie grimaced, then resumed walking. He fell into step beside her. "No, this is no crush. I love him, Jeremy. I want to be his wife, have his children. I'll go where he goes. Funny coming from me, wouldn't you say? Here all I wanted was to go to Oregon, and now I don't want to stay." She sniffed, perilously close to tears.

Her brother laid an arm around her shoulders. "Good God, Jess. You've grown up on this trip. I don't know if I can handle my baby sister sneaking off in the night with a man. You're liable to get hurt."

Jessie stared up into his pale green gaze and grimaced. "And what if I'm already hurting?" She reached out and put her hand over his. "I love him, Jeremy."

Jeremy ran his fingers through his hair and shook his head sadly. "Somehow I always knew that when you fell in love, nothing would stand in your way. But Jess, I don't see Wolf settling in Oregon."

She released her breath in a long, deep sigh. "I know." There was nothing more to say.

Jeremy pulled her into his embrace. "Why'd ya have to grow up, Jess?" After a few minutes of emotional silence, they resumed walking.

Jessie hugged her brother, then stepped back with a troubled sigh. She was glad he knew. She needed to talk to someone, so she told him briefly what she knew of Wolf family and his commitment to his tribe. "One way or another, I'm going back with him." Her voice hitched. "No matter how hard it will be to leave you, James and Jordan, I have to."

"I know, sis, I know. Things will work out." Brother and sister stared at one another quietly.

Jessie knew Jeremy wouldn't tell James or Jordan about her and Wolf. James would have a fit, and Jordan's temper would cause him to do something foolish, like engage Wolf in a fight.

"Cheer up, Jess. I can always get my shotgun and make Wolf marry you."

Jessie stopped abruptly. His lips curved into a grin, but his gaze was dead serious. Her hands went to her hips and she sent him a hard glare. "Jeremy, promise me right now that you won't interfere."

Jeremy cuffed her lightly on the chin. "No promises, Jess. There's lots of time to convince Wolf to do right by you. Come on, I heard the lower spring is the best of them all, and I've got some news to share with you. Seems Elliot may have found himself a girl."

"Truly?" she asked, her eyes wide with shock. "Okay, Jeremy. Start talking," she ordered.

Golden Eagle leaned against his backrest. Across from him, his son did likewise while speaking of a small herd of buffalo roaming nearby. His attention wandered when White Wind, White Dove and Star Dreamer entered the tipi. Watching his wife's graceful movements, Golden Eagle marveled that even after twenty-eight winters, their love was still strong, his need of her a driving force. Even now, his fingers itched to undo her long white braids and comb through the thick ripples.

He smiled to himself. Their love was meant to be. She was his life, had held a part of his heart even when she'd been a young child called Sarah, the daughter of a trapper who had lived peacefully alongside the Indians. When her stepfather died, leaving her to the care of an evil guardian, she'd run away to search for the Indian father she'd never known. The spirits had led him to her. He'd fallen in love with her, but they could not marry, as he was pledged to Wildflower, daughter of White Cloud. It had been a long and arduous journey, but they had overcome all, as had their love.

Over the years, White Wind had given him five children, but, sadly, one had died during its first winter. As she reached up to hang one of her parfleches, his gaze roamed over her trim figure and pale white braids. Her hair had once been white-blond. With age it had whitened.

His attention shifted to his daughters. White Dove spoke softly to her mother. At nineteen she was his youngest, his pride and joy. She'd always been beautiful, first as a baby, then as a child, but now that she'd become a young maiden, her beauty worried him. She had many suitors, though she didn't seem to be in any hurry to choose a mate. He didn't mind. As long as she remained unmarried, she was still his baby.

He rolled his shoulders, attempting to scratch an itch on his back. He loved quiet evenings visiting with his family. What more could a warrior ask of life than to be surrounded by those he loved? The women would talk and gossip, while the men planned the new day and his grandchildren filled his tipi with love and laughter. Ah, all was as it should be—except . . . it was quiet, too quiet. He lifted a brow. Where were the children? And Star's husband, Two-Ree?

Alarm ran through him when he caught the solemn glances passing between the three women. Instead of sitting with their beading or quilting, they stood off to one side. He felt uneasy. Leaning forward, he addressed Star. ''What is wrong, daughter? Your husband and children have not come with you. They are well?''

She kept her eyes trained to the ground. ''My family is well, my father.''

Golden Eagle leaned back. Star refused to look at him, which meant she was troubled. ''Come. Sit by me.'' He also motioned for Dove and White Wind to join them for a family meeting.

Star came, careful to pass behind her brother as she made her way around the fire to sit beside him. Normally the women sat on one side of the fire, the men on the other, but Golden Eagle enjoyed being surrounded by his wife and daughters. As he looked upon them, he admitted with a certain amount of arrogant pride that his womenfolk had never acted typically of Indian women. When everyone was seated, he waved a hand. ''Look at me, daughter.''

Star Dreamer did. In her dark eyes, he saw what he'd expected: fear and uncertainty, which meant she'd had troubling visions. He knew she fought her gift of sight, one passed down from his own mother. And when the visions left her looking haunted, they boded ill. He kept his features impassive. Inside, a knot of dread took hold. ''Tell me of the visions,'' he commanded, becoming not only her father but her chief.

Star looked to her mother. When she received an encouraging nod, she spoke, her voice soft, hesitant. ''They come nearly every night.'' Her voice shook. ''My brother who travels across the *Maka* has found his mate, and in her, he will at long last find the peace he seeks.''

Golden Eagle lifted a brow, pleased by the news but confused. ''These visions do not sound bad, daughter.''

Hugging her arms around herself, Star Dreamer continued. ''Darkness surrounds them.''

''Wolf is in danger?''

She glanced at him helplessly. ''I don't know. I can't tell, but darkness surrounds him and a woman.''

Golden Eagle made no comment. He motioned for her to continue. She closed her eyes and described a beautiful place filled with many roses. "There is great happiness and joy in this place. I feel the love this woman and Wolf share, yet each is sad."

Star pressed her fingers to her lips and lifted her weary gaze. "There is darkness ahead of them. They go to a place where there are many soldiers and many wagons. It is there that the evil spirits wait." Her eyes glazed over.

"Darkness. It will destroy them."

Father and son exchanged glances. Striking Thunder spoke. "The time is right for my brother to be at a place the whites call Ash Hollow. If that is so, the place where soldiers gather must be Fort Laramie."

Star buried her head in her hands. "How I hate seeing things that others do not!"

Golden Eagle laid a hand on his daughter's shiny black head. "No, my daughter. Your sight is a gift from *Wakan Tanka*. You have been honored by your grandmother. Remember this."

"But it's so hard," she whispered. White Wind reached over and drew her daughter into her embrace.

Striking Thunder turned to his sister, his eyes filled with curiosity. "The woman you see in your visions, does she also dress as a boy and have eyes the color of the spring grass?"

Star glanced up, surprised. "Yes," she nodded. "She is the one."

Striking Thunder recounted his meeting with the spirited girl. He told of his curiosity, of following her back and witnessing her attack on Wolf and what had followed.

"We will go to this fort," Golden Eagle decided, reaching for his quiver of arrows and the Sharps rifle he owned. It would take many days of hard travel to reach the fort at the same time as Wolf. He prayed they would arrive in time.

Star Dreamer's gaze softened. "I see her so clearly in many of my visions."

Thinking over his daughter's words, knowing her visions to be true, Golden Eagle whirled around. "Have you seen their children?" he asked. If she had, then there was hope.

Many of her visions, like her grandmother's, were warnings of things to come, and if the vision were heeded, the outcome would be favorable.

Star Dreamer shook her head helplessly. "I see children, my father. Many children: Indian boys and girls, but I'm not sure if they are theirs or not. There are just too many of them."

Frustrated by distance and uncertainty, he spoke to his son. "Choose six of our best warriors. We leave when *Wi* shows her face."

White Wind stood. "I am also going."

Before Golden Eagle could object, his two daughters stood and moved to flank their mother. Dove reached up behind her and took down her own bow and a quiver filled with arrows that she'd made herself.

"*We* are going," she corrected, speaking for all three.

The two men groaned, but Golden Eagle knew it was pointless to argue. Besides, his daughters had been taught well how to take care of themselves. They never ceased to be a sore spot among many of the younger warriors, who felt shamed when White Dove's arrows always hit their mark. "There is much to be done. Let us prepare."

Chapter Twenty-one

Wolf held the emigrants over in Ash Hollow for a few days of blissful rest. On their forty-ninth day since leaving Westport, they hitched up once again. All were reluctant to leave the wooded valley. However, they knew must press on.

On the third day after leaving Ash Hollow, the emigrants passed Courthouse Rock, four miles south of the Oregon Trail. Rising above the flat plains, the massive monolith and its smaller companion to the east called Jail Rock were, from what they'd heard, only a taste of impressive landmarks to come. If they looked fourteen miles to the west, they could see a tall column of rock rising from the flat plains to soar up into the heavens. During the next day of travel, they grew closer to the landmark. Wolf led them a couple miles off the trail, toward the spiraling tower to forage. Already they were well into June, and the grass that grew beside the trail was gone.

He gave the signal to make camp and rode back to see to the cattle. Before they could be driven out to feed, they had to be watered in the North Platte River, which they'd followed since leaving Ash Hollow. Dusk was settling when he returned to camp. He grabbed the plate of cold food Rook had set aside for him and leaned against the back of the wagon to eat. Between forkfuls of dreary plain beans and rice, he rolled the tiredness from his shoulders and scratched his back against the wooden side of the wagon. He was tired, sweaty and gritty with the day's coating of dust. Now he wished he'd taken the time to bathe in the river, even if it'd been crowded, with no secluded bathing areas.

His brows lifted. Tossing his empty plate aside, he stared out at Chimney Rock. He grinned in anticipation. If he recalled correctly, there was a small stream several miles beyond that rock that continued down to Courthouse Rock before joining the North Platte River. Folding his hands across his bare chest, he closed his eyes, envisioning the area as he'd last seen it. If memory served him right, there was also a small branch of that stream that flowed toward the landmark, ending in a nice, hidden little cove. Was it still there? Untying his horse, Wolf mounted. He glanced around the camp, searching for Jessie.

Jessie left camp sick at heart. Two little girls in another caravan had taken sick and died that day. They'd come across the grieving family earlier. She, along with the others, had gone to their burial. Damn. It wasn't fair. She kicked at the sandy soil, sad and angry at the senseless loss of life. Those two sweet girls had often tagged along after Kerstin and Hanna when their families' wagons were traveling close to each other. They, along with their quiet young mother, had even joined Anne and the girls for combined lessons. Head down, Jessie kicked at a rock in her path.

"Hey, ow, watch it," an indignant voice called out.

Jessie glanced up and grimaced. "Sorry, James. Didn't mean to get you."

He hugged her. "I know, Jess. I know."

She drew a shuddering breath. "They were so healthy the last time we saw them at Ash Hollow. They came over nearly every day to play and visit. How could it happen so fast?"

James ruffled her hair. "Just happens, that's all. No reason. No blame."

Jessie stared out into the darkness. If it happened to them, could members of their own caravan sicken and die without warning? And her brothers? Wasn't this precisely why she wanted—no, needed—to come with them? As if reading her mind, James patted her shoulder.

"Nothing's going to happen to any of us, Jess."

She nodded but kept her fears to herself. "Think I'll go for a walk. I need to be alone."

"All right, but be careful. It's getting dark, and there's lots of prairie-dog holes and rattlers."

"Not to mention those sword-plants," she added with a wry grin. She had scrapes and cuts from them. With a half salute she left the noise of the camp behind. After an hour of aimless wandering, she heard the sound of an approaching horse. Turning, she recognized Wolf on his stallion. She stopped and waited. When he drew up alongside her and held out his hand, she took it, swinging up behind him.

He sent the horse galloping forward. Jessie laid her head against his shoulder, letting tears of grief flow. She didn't question where he was taking her. She didn't care. She just needed to be with him. He stopped just below Chimney Rock and pulled her around onto his lap. He held her until her storm of weeping passed. With one finger, he tipped her chin up. "Better?"

Jessie sniffed and nodded. "I don't know what's wrong with me. I'm not the weepy sort, you know." She tried to turn away, embarrassed, but Wolf held her close.

"It's been a long day." His fingers smoothed the moisture from her skin. Wolf clucked, and Black Shadow moved onward. "I know something that will make you feel better."

She'd thought the landmark was his destination. "Where are we going?"

His smile was full of secret promise, and she settled against him, knowing he wouldn't tell her. She smiled wistfully when she remembered the rose-scented cave they'd made their own. It would always hold a special place in her heart. Not only had she discovered the joys of becoming a woman there, but she'd also discovered a romantic side to Wolf. Since leaving Ash Hollow, he'd been able to come for her only once. But to her delight, each evening when she returned to her wagon, she'd find evidence of his love: a flower or a carved bit of wood or even a pretty stone waiting for her. And even though he still wouldn't discuss the future, he surely knew after the closeness they'd shared that this bond between them was meant to be.

Wolf sent his stallion farther away from fires, tents and wagons.

Jordan and Elliot clambered up Chimney Rock, grunting and groaning as they fought for hand and footholds on the steep surface. "This is as far as I'm going," Elliot shouted. He watched in amazement as Jordan pushed upward and carved their names into the soft, sandy rock.

"Come on up; the view is fantastic," Jordan called.

Elliot chanced a glance down and closed his eyes. Feeling slightly faint, he inched his way down, though he had to admit that the view was indeed something else. The sun had dipped below the horizon, leaving golden streaks to fade from the sky as the grayness of dusk wiped out all color. Far in the distant horizon, he noted dark clouds moving toward them.

From his great height above the prairie floor, Elliot drew in a deep breath and marveled over the countless small fires burning across the prairie like flickering fireflies. Clouds of smoke rose to stretch across the prairie, billowing upward to obliterate the moon and stars, leaving a layer of haziness to drift over the river. But enough was enough. He was more than ready to plant his feet back on solid ground. "I'll wait for you down below, Jordan. Don't know why I let you talk me into this." Staring out at the North Platte River for one last look at the view, Elliot felt a silly, love-besotted grin come over him.

She was out there, just a few miles back. He closed his eyes with a sigh. Mary Beth, with her long, silky brown hair, eyes the color of cinnamon, and a shy giggle. He'd meet her at Ash Hollow. Her father was a preacher, and they were going to Oregon to start a new church with a large number of their congregation. With a sigh, he wished there were more time for courting on the trail.

He was a third of the way down when he heard what sounded like crying. Moving slowly, he inched his way around the base of the spiral, searching for the source. His brows drew together when he saw a horse far below him with two riders. The man held a sobbing woman in his arms.

He wondered if they were the couple who'd lost their two daughters that day. But just as he was about to turn away, something familiar about the woman drew his attention. Taking another long look, Elliot nearly fell from his high perch. That was Jessie sitting across Wolf's lap. What was she doing way out here? And why was she crying?

A boot tapping his head nearly sent him plunging to the ground. "Hey, you fall asleep down there, Elliot?"

"Jordan, look below. Isn't that Jessie with Wolf?"

Jordan moved down until he clung to the rock next to Elliot. Brotherly concern etched lines into his face. "Looks like, but what's going on?" The horse and rider rode off.

Jordan made his way down as fast as he dared, leaving Elliot to struggle on his own.

Elliot hoped nothing was wrong.

Jessie glanced around her when Wolf halted his horse. She didn't see anything special. She shrugged. Maybe he'd just brought her way out here where they could be alone. He struck a match and lit one candle so he could see where to spread the blanket he'd tucked behind his saddle. That was when she heard it: the sound of burbling water reached her ears. Taking the candle, she held it out and peered into the darkness. She gasped with pleasure when she saw the secluded cove hidden by overgrown vegetation.

Wolf slid his arms around her waist from behind her and kissed her just below her ear. "Join me, Jessie," he whispered.

Jessie groaned with desire. "What if someone comes?" She still found it disconcerting to make love in the open.

"It's secluded, and unless one knows it's here, finding it in the dark would be nearly impossible." He turned her, framed her face between his hands and planted tiny, teasing kisses on her lips, flitting away before she could kiss him back.

She wrapped her arms around his neck and shivered with desire. When she felt his lips move down to the sensitive flesh beneath her jaw, her head fell to one side, giving him complete access. "Oh, yes, Wolf."

When his lips moved up to claim hers, all her pent-up worry and frustration surfaced. Suddenly she couldn't wait. Wolf's tender, slow pace wasn't enough. Her need was too great. She pulled at his vest. "I need to touch you, see you— all of you, Wolf."

Wolf stepped back and shucked off his vest, leaving only the glowing moonlight to bathe his golden skin. Then he made quick work of the ties to his buckskin breeches and stepped out of them. He stood before her, gloriously naked, strong, sure and hungry for her, yet he waited for her to make the next move.

Jessie stared at him, all of him. The sight of him was all it took for the sharp throbbing to start at the apex of her thighs. Heat radiated up and outward. She closed the distance between them, feeling bold, empowered. During their brief snatches of loving, Wolf had been the one in control, the one to set the pace. But not now. Not tonight. This time it was her turn. Her fingers gently raked his skin from his shoulder down to his nipples. She eased her thumbs over the tiny nubs, caressing them to hard points. Wolf sucked in his breath and bent his head to hers.

"Uh-uh." She grinned, giving him a gentle push away. "My turn." Bending her head to first one, then the other dark brown disc, she tasted him, licking and laving and suckling, paying homage to him as he'd done countless times to her. When she felt a deep shudder pass through him, she knew it pleased him. And knowing she pleased him set her own desire humming. With her tongue and lips, she blazed a trail downward and teased the hollow of his navel until Wolf let out a rumbling moan and pulled her back up.

"God, Jessie, you have no idea what you're doing to me." He groaned, his fingers tangling in her hair as he tried to end her tormenting explorations.

Staring at the sheen of sweat covering his body, Jessie teased her fingertips lower. "Yes, I do." And holding his smoky blue gaze with hers, she reached down and took the hard length of him in her hand. She licked her lips and stroked him gently from root to tip.

He trembled, pulsing with need. Her own body responded. Heat and moisture gathered between her legs, and an ache for what he could give her settled low in her belly. Tearing her gaze from his, she glanced down and saw a single drop of dew beaded on his very tip. She smoothed it away, marveling at his velvety softness. But when her fingers cupped him, he tipped her face up, holding her firmly between his hands.

"No more." He groaned. His lips came down on hers, hard, hungry and demanding.

Jessie wrapped his long hair around her fists and pulled

his head to her, meeting him kiss for frantic kiss. His hands tugged her shirt from the waist band of her trousers, his lips nipping along her jaw and glided down her throat. She arched forward, her head lolling back.

Wolf blazed a trail down past the pulsing hollow of her throat. Each button gave way and revealed smooth, pale skin for his lips and tongue to tease and taste. Her shirt fell to the ground, and his hands lifted to cup her pale breasts. She gasped when his fingers feathered lightly over the erect nipples. "So beautiful, so ripe. I'm going to taste you, sweet Jess, all of you."

He bent his head, his lips closing first over one beaded nipple, then drawing the other one deep into his mouth. Jessie shuddered as the throbbing in her center increased. She moved her hips in invitation, feeling the tension growing between her legs. "Please, Wolf, I need you," she pleaded, rubbing herself against his hardness.

"Not yet, *kechuwa*," he murmured. Quickly he undressed her, tossing her pants away. She stood before him, clothed only in starlight, and as she'd done to him, his tongue stroked in and out of her navel, swirling in and around the tiny indentation.

Jessie cried out when she felt his tongue trail lower, setting the sensitive nerve endings of her belly on fire. But when his lips pressed against the tight nest of curls that hid her damp womanhood, she stopped breathing. Her fingers tangled in his golden brown hair. His hands gripped her buttocks, pulling her even closer to allow the tip of his tongue to slip between her folds and stroke her sensitive bud. She shuddered and her knees quivered under his sensual assault. Resting her weight on hands that gripped his shoulders, she jerked her hips against his mouth.

"Wolf, oh, God, I can't, not like this," she cried, feeling herself growing tighter with the need for release.

"Yes, my wild rose. Let me feel your release against my mouth. Let me taste you. Do it," he begged, his voice thick with desire. "Now!"

The choice was taken from her when his tongue flicked

against her in earnest. Her hips jerked, keeping pace with Wolf's velvety strokes until spasm after wonderful spasm rocked her, sending her soaring to a wondrous, shuddering ecstasy. Gasping for breath, she fell against him. Wolf lowered her to the blanket and leaned over her. "I love you, Jessie," he cried. With one thrust, he ignited the flames of their passion, sending them both soaring through the heavens.

Wolf cradled Jessie against him in the water, his arms resting just beneath the swell of her breasts. He rubbed the top of her head with his chin. Neither spoke, each content to savor the sweet afterglow of their loving as the water gently lapped against them. The buzz of insects grew as the air around them cooled. In the distance a lone howl echoed. Above them the moon beamed indulgently.

He tightened his hold on the woman who each day was becoming more important to him than ever. He'd never felt so content, so satisfied with life as he did right at that moment. After making love on the bank they'd moved into the water and made love again, her need as great as his own. Even now, the memory of her legs wrapped around his waist, the water surrounding them, surging against them—wetting her breasts, turning them into sleek, pale mounds—made him want her all over again.

He stared up into the twinkling heavens and felt a twinge of sadness creep in as he finally admitted to himself what he'd ignored, put off, and refused to consider. Not only did he love Jessica Jones, but he didn't think he could live without her. The acknowledgment tore deep. Whatever he chose, with her or without her, someone was bound to get hurt— her or him. Yet how could he marry her when his life was filled with uncertainty? More than anything else, at that moment, he wanted Jessie for his wife. Destiny be damned. He wanted happiness, contentment. He wanted forever.

Clouds passed in front of the moon. Why? he grieved. Why this woman? Why now? But the heavens held no answers for him this night. Already the sky had clouded over.

Another prairie storm brewed. With a regretful sigh, he knew it was time to return to camp, but before he could make the suggestion, Jessie stroked him along the length of his arms.

"I love you, Wolf."

Pain tore through him. Loneliness as he'd never known before struck hard. All his life he'd walked alone. Until now. But his love for Jessie didn't change things. He was neither white nor Indian. He was a man who drifted without direction. For a while he'd deluded himself with thoughts that Jessie belonged at his side. Her declaration of love tore a hole in his heart. He recalled the dreams that had haunted him since their first night of lovemaking.

In more than one of them, his grandmother had appeared with Jessie at her side. Secretly, he'd wanted to believe that she was telling him Jessie was the one she'd foreseen so long ago, but now he forced himself to admit the truth. It was his own desire, wishful thinking, and his love for Jessie that made him wish it were so. And though he'd told her that he loved her, meant the words, felt them with all his being, he couldn't promise forever. Not yet. He had to think and plan. "Jessica—"

She turned in his arms and pressed her fingers against his lips. "I'm not asking you to make promises," she said softly. "All I want is to be with you. When spring comes, I'm going home with you."

Wolf stroked the side of her face, wishing it were so simple. "Jessie, if you leave Oregon, you may never see your brothers again. The life I live is harsh, primitive. There's nothing there. Just a cabin. No town."

Jessie's eyes flashed with anger. "Do you think so little of my feelings as to believe I care? It's *my* choice. One I'm perfectly capable of making. I know what I want, what I feel. We belong. I love you and you love me. That's all that matters. Your family will become my family. Your home, ours."

"Jessie, listen to me. There's more to it."

"No! Tell me that you *don't* love me, Wolf," she demanded. "Tell me you lied when you said you loved me."

She stared at him, waiting for him to say the words or deny them.

His hand lifted. He couldn't lie to her. "Jess," he whispered, "you know I love you." He ran the back of his fingers along her jawline. "Words, however sweet, sincere, and earnest, don't change anything. Until I know what it is that I must do, I'm not free to make promises. Come spring I'll return, alone. It's better this way." Wolf put her aside and left the water to gather his clothes. He was afraid that if he remained close to her, he'd give in as his heart urged him to do.

Jessie's voice stopped him. "Better for whom, Wolf? You or me? Who are you seeking to protect? There's no reason why *your* mission cannot become *our* mission."

Wolf dressed—tempted—oh, so tempted—to say the hell with family, his and hers, and keep her at his side. He hated the thought of hurting her, yet the thought of losing her left a dark void deep inside. Fully dressed, he turned. She had dressed during their long silence, and she stood before him, her back rigid as she stared out into the night. "Come, Jessica. It's time to return."

"Fine. Go ahead. I'll walk back."

Wolf went to her and turned her to face him. He closed his heart against the tears trailing down her cheeks. "Jessie, I don't want to hurt you. God knows I love you. But I don't have anything to offer you."

Jessie leaned into him with a desperation that tugged deeply at his conscience. She reached up and cupped his tightly clenched jaw. "Oh, Wolf, you're so wrong. All I need is you and your love. Nothing else matters." Wolf put her aside and drew upon every ounce of control an Indian warrior possessed. "It matters to me."

Whirling away from him, Jessie grabbed the blanket, tossed it over her shoulder and stomped off. "Fine. If you're going to be stubborn about it, I'll just have to find a way to convince you. Rook once told me that if it's meant to be, it will be. I'll prove it to you." She said over her shoulder.

Wolf watched her go, an inexplicable feeling of emptiness

assailing him. Sadness and regret speared their way through the wall he'd once built around his heart, shattering it, leaving him open, raw and bleeding. Damn it, he needed her. His chest tightened; his eyes burned. He took a step toward her, then stopped, letting his hand fall back to his side. It was better this way. Jessie reached his horse and mounted. With a defiant glare, she kicked the spirited stallion into a gallop and left him to walk back. Wolf rubbed his hand over his face and watched until the shadows of the land swallowed her from view.

She'd breached the last of his walls. They'd crumbled around him, releasing all past bitterness and hurt. He closed his eyes. Raw, exposed and vulnerable, his heart bled, scrambled to fortify itself, but there was nothing left to rebuild his defenses. The solitary man inside rebelled. He no longer wanted to walk through his life alone. He'd tasted heaven, and now he'd been tossed into hell. And he worried that he'd never be able to leave her. He headed for the cattle. Surefooted, he skimmed over the rough terrain as he ran, nostrils flaring, fists clenched and trickles of sweat running down the sides of his face. But no matter how hard or fast his feet pounded the ground, two simple words echoed over and over in his mind: *we belong.*

James laid out his bedroll, yawning as he shucked off his boots. Climbing beneath the coarse woolen blankets, he stared up into the cloudy sky and frowned, praying for the storm to hold off until morning. Nearby, Jeremy snored and snorted in his sleep. Jordan, he assumed, was with Coralie. He was happy things had worked out between them. He thought of Elliot, who was head over heels in love with Mary Beth. A sigh of contentment washed over him. It looked as though there might be another wedding by the time they reached Oregon.

James turned onto his side. Of course, if he had his way, there would be two weddings. He loved Eirica—loved her and those children so bad it hurt. But the woman was cussedly stubborn. Oh, the other day she'd accepted help—with the oxen—but otherwise she kept her distance. During the day she walked with Coralie or Jessie, and if he came around in the evenings, she ducked into her tent with the children. Grinding his teeth together, James sat up, one knee bent toward the sky. How could he convince her that he was not Birk, that he, James Noah Jones, would never hurt her or her children? How was he to prove himself if she wouldn't give him a chance?

All he wanted was to help her, ease her burden. She deserved to be taken care of. And who better than the man who loved her? Long used to taking care of his siblings, James felt at home in the role. Why wouldn't she allow him to take care of her? He huffed out a breath. Why'd he have to go and do something stupid like fall in love? Life was a whole lot less complicated without woman worries. But before he had a chance to dwell further on the affairs of his heart, he heard the rapid approach of a rider.

Resigned to having to ride out to deal with some problem with the herd, he stood and waited. To his surprise, Jordan came to an abrupt halt. "James, we gotta talk," Jordan shouted. "Wolf's been bedding Jessie, and he ain't got no intention of doing right by her. What are we going to do—"

James held up one hand. "Now, hold on, Jordan. What the hell are you talking about?"

"Wolf is bedding Jessie. I saw them." Jordan slammed one fist into another. "No one uses Jessie like that and gets away with it."

Narrowing his eyes, James knitted his brows. He'd suspected Jessie was sweet on the wagon master, but *bedding* him? "You sure about that?"

Jordan swallowed and looked uncomfortable. "Yeah, saw them comin' out of this secluded pond. They were arguing. Heard him giving her some cock-and-bull story about not making promises. He's using her. He's using our baby sister."

James paced. "Damn." He liked and respected Wolf. But Jordan was right. No one treated their sister like some common saloon girl. She was ruined now. What if she got with child? The thought chilled him.

"Can't see why she loves the bastard," Jordan said.

James lifted a brow. "Just like she couldn't see how you could love Coralie?"

Jordan lowered his brows. "That's different."

"No. I can see why she does, and if she loves him she'll have him, one way or another."

"How, James? How are we gonna make that bastard do right by Jessie?" Jordan paced, smacking his fist into his palm.

James smiled grimly, bent down, and picked up his rifle.

"Hot damn," Jordan shouted.

"What the hell is going on?" Jeremy demanded, joining them, having been awakened by Jordan's shout. He stared at the gun in James's hand.

Jordan turned to him, his face red with rage, his voice deep with determination. "A wedding. Get your gun, little brother. We're gonna have ourselves a wedding."

Chapter Twenty-two

"Looks like trouble, boss."

Wolf turned from Shorty to see the three Jones brothers riding toward him as if the devil were nipping at their heels. He glanced around quickly but saw nothing amiss. The cattle were bedded, the horses grazed contentedly and all his men were going about their business. Mounting Black Shadow, he rode out to meet them, fearing trouble at the wagons.

But as soon as he saw the fury in Jordan's expression and

the heavy frown on James's overly serious face, he knew they'd somehow discovered that he was sleeping with their sister. Instinctively, he knew it hadn't been from Jessie. He met Jeremy's apologetic glance and grimaced inwardly. Nor, apparently, had it come from Jeremy. Wolf dismounted and braced himself.

James stomped over to him and spoke first. "Wolf, we've come to—"

Jordan launched himself from his saddle and flew at Wolf. In a blur, the two men skidded across the ground. "You damned bastard!" Jordan swung his fist.

The blow caught Wolf just below the jaw. Stars floated behind his eyelids. Dimly he heard Jordan egging him on, telling him to get up and fight. His own anger and frustration rose. If they wanted a brawl, who was he to argue? He returned the punch. Fists flew, and grunts filled the air as they rolled close to the prancing hooves of the nervous horses.

James and Jeremy yanked them apart. "Damn it, Jordan." James yelled, shoving his brother aside. "I said I'd take care of it. Now, leave off."

Wolf rolled to his feet and warily faced James and Jeremy.

Jordan staggered toward his grazing horse and returned, gripping a shotgun that he leveled at Wolf's chest. "No one uses our sister."

Wolf lifted a brow. "You going to shoot me, Jordan?"

"Don't think I won't, you no-account bastard. No one hornswoggles me and my brothers. You're gonna marry my sister. By force, if necessary."

Wolf's jaw dropped. He snapped it shut. "A shotgun wedding? And if I refuse?"

James stepped between Wolf and Jordan before fists started flying again. His voice remained low, controlled. "Answer one question for me, Wolf. Do you love her?"

Crossing his arms, Wolf took the measure of Jessie's eldest brother. Though it was dark, there was no mistaking the man's fury in his glittering gaze. Wolf almost wished he would come at him and lose the control that held him in check. "That's between Jess and me, James."

James narrowed his eyes. His fists clenched, and he took a step forward. Catching himself visibly, he backed off. "It don't matter. You'll do right by her or answer to us."

Wolf couldn't fault the three men flanking him. After all, were he in the same place, he'd be just as concerned. He waited a heartbeat, then spoke honestly. "Jess knows how I feel about her. She knows the score." Guilt assailed him. She might have come with him willingly, but she'd been an innocent. She deserved better.

Jordan jabbed him in the chest with the rifle. "Jess ain't old enough to know better. You took advantage of her. You'll marry her or else."

Wolf lifted a brow. "Did she send you?"

Jeremy looked uncomfortable. "She don't know we're here." That earned him a glare from his brothers.

Arching one brow, Wolf addressed James. "And what if she doesn't want to marry me?"

"She ain't got no choice." Jordan said. "She ain't gonna have no baby out of wedlock. You two are going to marry, tonight." He tightened his grip on his rifle for emphasis.

Wolf didn't think this the time to tell James he'd rounded up some Queen Anne's lace to keep her from becoming with child. He glanced at Jeremy, who, so far, had remained conspicuously quiet. "Do you think Jess will thank you for this?"

Jeremy shrugged but looked uncomfortable. It was clear he stood united with his brothers, no matter what his personal feelings were. Deciding to put an end to the standoff, Wolf spoke to James. "My feelings for Jessie are mine, but yes, I love her. There are reasons I can't marry her. She knows why, even if she doesn't understand or agree. It's for her own good that I ask you to think of her. She's better off remaining in Oregon with her family. She'll be safer."

James considered his words. "But will she be happier?"

Wolf's silence was answer enough.

James folded his arms across his chest. "If Jessie wants you and loves you, then, by God, you'll marry her. Jeremy, fetch Jess. Jordan, go fetch that preacher. We'll wait here."

Wolf watched the two brothers ride off. Anger speared

through him. *Marriage!* A shotgun wedding. Damn, he should have listened when his instincts warned that this family was trouble. Of all the possible events he could have foreseen, this was not one of them. And though he could simply refuse, honor wouldn't allow it.

"You'd better treat her right," James warned, his voice vibrating with fury.

Wolf lifted a brow and indicated the rifle Jordan had tossed at James. "You and I both know that if I refuse to marry Jessica, you won't shoot."

James dipped his head. "True. But you're an honorable man. You'll marry her."

Wolf sighed. It was true. In truth, he admired Jessie's brothers for looking out for her.

They were well within their rights to feel as they did. If he'd caught a warrior bedding White Dove, he'd have reacted in the same way.

No. It was his own fault that he was in this predicament. He should have stayed far away from Jessica Jones, but he hadn't been able to, and he didn't regret it. Except that now she'd ultimately be the one to pay the high price for their loving.

Jordan returned a short while later with a harried, disheveled man in tow just as Jeremy rode in with Jessie. The minister, obviously awakened by Jordan, shifted uneasily from foot to foot. A gust of wind tore through Wolf's long hair. A storm was brewing, and if he knew Jessica Jones, the elements wouldn't hold a candle to her fury. She wasn't going to be any happier at her brother's interference than he was.

Jumping off the horse, Jessie ran forward, confused and worried. Jeremy had refused to tell her anything except that her presence was needed. She glanced at the subdued group. Why were her brothers and Wolf out here? She scanned the gathered assembly while Jeremy hung back. She stood between James and Wolf, looking from one to the other. "What's going on, James? Why all the secrecy? Jeremy said you wanted to see me. Wouldn't tell me—"

Her voice broke off when she saw Jordan pointing his gun at Wolf. Worry replaced confusion. Had her brothers found out? "Wolf?"

His gaze slid from hers to the darkening clouds gathering overhead.

"Got good news for ya, Jess. Wolf's gonna marry you," Jordan announced, his voice grim. His lips curved in a satisfied smirk.

Shock held her silent for a long moment. Then full realization dawned. "Are you out of your mind?" she shouted. "What kind of joke is this?" She glared at her eldest brother.

James stiffened. "It's no joke."

Jessie glared at the three bearded faces before her. "You can't be serious." She laughed hollowly, but no one denied it, including Wolf, and when she recognized Mary Beth's father standing to one side, her panic grew. They were serious. Dead serious.

This couldn't be happening. She swung around to Wolf, noting his stoic expression and his deceptively calm stance. But the muscle working near the base of his jaw signaled the true state of his emotions. "You're not agreeing to this, are you?" she asked in disbelief.

He lifted one brow and indicated the rifle. "Your brothers are calling the *shots.*"

Jessie glared at Jordan. "Put that gun away, you lunkhead." When he lowered the muzzle to the ground, she jabbed James in the chest. "Stop this nonsense right now, James Noah Jones. This is none of your concern."

Jordan whipped her around. "Like hell! When somebody beds our sister and takes advantage of her innocence, he deals with us."

Jessie walked stiffly over to Jeremy and punched him square in the belly. "You promised not to tell, Jeremy Ezra. You said you'd let me handle it. How could you do this to me? We're not even halfway to Oregon yet. I had lots of time."

Jeremy gasped and backed away, holding one hand out to ward her off. He pressed the other to his stomach. "Don't go blamin' me, Jess. Jordan came across you and Wolf at that pool tonight.'' Pandemonium broke forth. James and Jordan launched themselves at Jeremy, demanding to know why he hadn't said anything.

Jessie turned her back on her brothers, furious with the lot of them. They were going to ruin everything with their damn interference. She rubbed her temples with the tips of her fingers, trying to find a way out of this mess. She glanced at Wolf. He looked disgusted. ''Wolf—''

He took her by the upper arm and led her to the minister, who looked on with bright interest. ''You boys can fight it out later,'' Wolf called over his shoulder. ''Let's get it over with.''

Jessie yanked out of his grasp. Surely he wasn't going to go along with this absurd wedding? ''Wolf, you don't have to do this. They can't make us marry,'' she said, her voice quavering. Her eyes pleaded with him. ''Do you really think they'd shoot you if you refuse? We'll both refuse.'' Chills ran up her arms. She wanted Wolf to accept her as his help-mate because he loved her and wanted to spend the rest of his life with her, not because her hot-tempered brothers forced him into it.

Wolf lifted his chin, his blue eyes filled with pride. ''No. We'll marry. It's the honorable thing to do. Your brothers are right to demand it.''

Tears stung her eyes. She wanted to run, to hide from the cold resolve in his gaze.

Honorable thing to do. A hollow pang hit her stomach and left her reeling. *I don't want honor,* she wanted to shout.

Wolf pulled her to his side. The preacher started the ceremony. His voice droned on, lifting in volume as the wind kicked up. Miserable, Jessie watched the dark clouds roll in. They echoed the grim, foreboding silence surrounding her. Beside her, James and Jordan stood, hands clasped behind their backs. Jeremy stood at Wolf's side.

She sneaked a glance at her husband-to-be. He stared straight ahead, his jaw set and arms crossed. Where had the tender, sensitive man gone? Tears threatened. This was her wedding day. Where was the happiness? The words of love? The secret smiles and giddy rushes of warmth? She rubbed her arms. All she felt was cold despair. This wasn't what she had wanted. Yes, she wanted Wolf, wanted to be his wife. But not like this. The first crack of thunder boomed. Beside her, Wolf frowned and motioned for the preacher to hurry. Her heart sank. He couldn't wait to get it over with so he could leave.

A jab to her ribs startled her. Beside her, James whispered "Say, 'I do.' " Jessie bit her lip and glanced at Wolf. All she'd wanted was his love. Had her brothers' interference killed it? In a whisper, she sealed her fate. And when it was all over, Wolf, at the insistence of her brothers, pulled her close for a chaste kiss. Then he issued orders for everyone to return to their posts. Watching him stride off without a backward glace, Jessie felt all her hopes of him accepting her into his life shrivel until they lay in a corner of her heart.

After a week of no rest, Wolf halted the emigrants after only six hours of travel, near a massive bluff on the south bank of the North Platte River. For many of the emigrants, Scotts Bluff was one more grand display of nature that helped lessen the boredom of the endless flat prairie. In awe, they stared at the bluffs, which resembled immense fortifications with their many bastions, towers, battlements, embrasures, scarps and counterscarps. The wagons circled, and the never-ending round of chores began anew. Jessie eagerly embraced the hours of hard work that followed. It helped keep her mind off her fight with Wolf and their mockery of a marriage. Everyone knew of their wedding, and many knew the reasons.

As she had for the last two days, she took on more chores than normal. And if by chance she finished early, she found other tasks that didn't need doing but did them anyway, just to wear herself out. The last thing she wanted was to lie awake wondering if Wolf would come to her during the night. But he hadn't come near her since the minister had pronounced them man and wife. Right after the kiss that had sealed their vows, the skies had opened up, pelting the wedding party with hail the size of small stones. She grimaced. It was a sign that boded ill for a marriage that really wasn't a true marriage yet.

Depressed that Wolf refused to acknowledge their marriage or share her bed, Jessie spent the afternoon checking equipment, then baking biscuits to restock their supply of bread for times when they couldn't cook a hot meal. She even tried her hand at making pemmican from a recipe Rook taught her. The men enjoyed chewing it during the day when they were riding. She grimaced. It sure beat chewing tobacco. That was one habit she found disgusting.

When the sun began its showy descent, Coralie and Rook joined her to start the evening meal. Jessie forced thoughts of Wolf from her mind. Together they worked, the only sound Rook's gruff voice as he continued instructing her sister-in-law. Several hours later, long after the hired hands had left and the kettles and fry pans had been scrubbed clean, Jessie took her own plate of food and sat down. She stared at it with disinterest.

Jordan and Coralie walked past. Her brother held his wife close. She giggled softly. They were so happy, and that depressed her. Not that she wished them ill, but their joy in each other was a painful reminder that so far her own marriage was a disaster. When Jordan glanced over at her, she turned her back on him and forked a bite of beans and bacon into her mouth. The food was tasteless and hard to swallow past the lump in her throat. She tossed the plate down.

Rook lifted a brow. "I'm sick of beans," she grumbled, watching Sadie lick the plate clean. Sadie glanced up with soulful brown eyes, asking for more. "You're getting fat, girl," Jessie scolded. The dog whined softly and gave her mistress a quick face washing with her tongue, then trotted off to lie beside Wahoska. Sighing heavily, Jessie stared morosely out into the black cloak of night, feeling an echoing bleakness deep inside.

"How long you gonna hold on ta yer anger, lass?" Rook plopped down onto an old stump he'd fashioned into a seat and guarded zealously so no one would chop it up into firewood. As usual, he was whittling a piece of wood.

She shrugged. "They interfered where they had no business."

"They love ya, lass. Can't blame 'em fer that."

Tears threatened once again. It used to be that only fights with her brothers could reduce her to tears. For a fleeting moment she wished things could return to the simple, everyday life she'd once known, but then she'd never have fallen in love.

When Rook cleared his throat, she glanced at him. "Maybe, maybe not," she answered. "They should've talked to me first. They're always making decisions that affect me without asking. It's wrong. I'm old enough to handle things my own way."

Rook lifted his brow and resumed his whittling. "Well, now, what's done is done. You make yer peace with them, and soon. It's tearin' ya apart, and don't ya be denyin' it."

Jessie sent Rook another pained look. She drew her knees to her chest and rested her chin on one fisted hand as she watched Rook whittle away at the wood. "I know they meant no harm, maybe were even trying to help. I'll settle with them soon." She gave a weak grin. "They can suffer just a tad more."

"That's my lass. Now, off to bed with you, and don't you worry none 'bout Wolf. He's a stubborn cuss, but he'll come around. Just be patient."

She hugged Rook. He'd become more father than friend. "I hope you're right."

Rook lifted a brow. "Course I'm right. Now off with ya. Give an old man his peace afore bedtime."

Star Dreamer shivered despite the warm nighttime breeze sweeping across the land. Nearby, her parents and siblings slept. How she envied their ability to sleep. She longed to fall into a deep, soothing sleep, but it wouldn't happen. The visions were growing stronger, more frequent as they neared the white man's fort. The brief flashes of color and emotion haunted her day and night, But those she could handle.

What troubled her now was the cry. Wrapping her arms around her knees, she rested her forehead on her warm leggings, wishing for her husband's comforting arms. But Two-Ree was on guard duty near the hobbled horses. She cleared her mind, concentrating on the sounds of the *Maka*: the chirp of insects, the brush of rodents scurrying through the night and the gentle sound of water slapping the bank of the nearby stream. For a time, it worked. Then, unbidden, it came.

The cry of a child. Star Dreamer shuddered, and a low, guttural moan escaped from her tightly clenched lips as images flashed across the lids of her eyes. And she was frightened by what she saw: the green-eyed woman and a child in the clutches of an evil two-headed form. When strong hands closed over her shoulders she cried out. The tender words of her husband reassured her as he drew her into his embrace and held her securely while she cried noiselessly. Nearby, Striking Thunder rose to stand guard. He met the worried gazes of his mother, father and sister, none of whom were asleep.

Chapter Twenty-three

Jessie kept her gaze trained on the ground to avoid the blinding glare of the sun bouncing off the sandy prairie. Clouds of dust hung in the air, and it was stifling hot. In short, it was another miserable day on the trail. She sneezed, then choked on the thick waves of dust that rose from the prairie. The square of calico she held to her nose did little good.

Swatting at an annoying insect crawling on her arm, she grimaced when dust rose from the long sleeve of her shirt. Over the past week she'd been forced to wear the same blue flannel shirt and woolen pants. First their group had been assaulted by a dust storm, which left a thick layer of dust everywhere. Then two days later a rainstorm turned the dust to clinging mud. She was at least grateful that her woolen pants offered protection against the heat of the sun's rays and the sudden drops in temperature at night. After leaving Scotts Bluff six days ago, they'd followed the trail through Mitchell Pass which was more popular than the older Robidoux Pass.

Coralie fell into step beside Jessie, then nervously looked behind them. "You don't think those Indians will follow us, do you?" Yesterday they'd stopped for the night a few miles from the Grattan massacre site and were visited by a large band of fierce-looking Indians.

Jessie shook her head. "Wolf says there's nothing to fear." The evening had been fraught with tension, made worse by whispered reminders of the massacre that had taken place nearby several years before. Though Wolf tried to reassure everyone that they had nothing to fear, fear nonetheless ran high. He'd finally divided the men into groups to rotate guard duty and had even remained on hand to keep a close eye on things. She'd hoped he would come to her, but he hadn't. Depression fell upon her.

Coralie leaned close and lowered her voice. "Those Indians seemed so savage. Wolf gave them some cattle and horses. He bribed them not to attack us, didn't he?" She shuddered and drew a shaky breath. "I heard Lars and Rook talking about that massacre. It sounded like it just happened," she babbled, throwing worried looks over her shoulder.

Jessie hooked her arm through her sister-in-law's and squeezed, putting her own troubles on hold to reassure Coralie. "Quit stewing, Corie. Rook told me they didn't give Wolf any trouble. Seems they're also Sioux Indians. As for the massacre, that happened a couple years ago. Some soldiers tried to arrest several Sioux Indians for killing and eating a stray cow that belonged to a Mormon emigrant.''

Coralie bit her lip. ''But the Indians killed the soldiers. I heard Rook telling the story last night. Only one soldier made it back to Fort Laramie before he died. Rook said the Indian chief also died.'' She wrung her hands in front of her. ''I'll sure be glad to reach Fort Laramie. After all that horrible noise those savages made last night, I just know I won't sleep unless there are soldiers nearby.''

''Come on, Coralie. We're safe enough,'' Jessie said, giving her a gentle shake.

Morning gave way to afternoon. Jessie relieved Rickard to give him a break. In the wagon train, both man and beast plodded along the vapid trail, shuffling through sand a foot deep, kicking up clouds of dust that lingered in the air, making it hard for Jessie even to see the wagon in front of her.

During the hot afternoons, it wasn't unusual to see men sitting or standing on the wagon tongues, nodding off or resting with their hands planted on the rumps of the oxen. But at some point, someone would swat their oxen halfheartedly and remind the sluggish beasts to keep moving.

Up ahead, Elliot grumbled those very same words to his team.

Without glancing up, Jessie mechanically repeated the words, then jerked her head up to listen for Rook, who walked behind her. This daily form of prairie telegraph amused her. Commands were repeated up and down the long line of wagons from one man to another. Sure enough, she heard Rook's admonishment—''Get up thar''—his voice as sluggish as the oxen. Jessie would have grinned, but she felt too tired and lethargic. Instead she grimaced, a wave of depression and regret overcoming her, stemming in part from lack of sleep and partly from the man riding ahead of them on his big black horse.

She lifted her eyes, her gaze straining through the clouds of dust for a glimpse of her husband, but she didn't see him anywhere. Since becoming man and wife, they hadn't exchanged more than a few polite words at mealtimes. A dull ache of hopelessness spread through her. How she missed him—missed the secret smiles and the stolen kisses they'd shared behind the wagons or shielded by their horses. Her body felt bereft of their sweet lovemaking in the darkened prairie.

And now that she didn't have them, those stolen hours beneath the stars seemed all the more precious. But what she missed most was what followed their loving. Sated, cuddled together, they'd talked late into the night, about everything and nothing. Her shoulders slumped further. Wolf was still angry, and she didn't blame him. His pride had taken a beating. She smacked her fist into her palm. Damn her interfering brothers. She took a calming breath, then regretted it when she choked on dust. Coughing, she dropped back to the rear of the wagon and uncovered the water barrel. Filling the tin cup hanging on the inside, she drank the tepid water. Though stale, it relieved her parched throat. She resumed her place beside the lumbering oxen.

Coralie left Elliot's side. "Elliot's not very good company right now." She pouted. "This is so boring! There's nothing to do all day but walk and stare at a bunch of scraggly bushes."

Jessie rolled her eyes. Though her sister-in-law had matured, some things hadn't changed. Of course, not so long ago she herself would have made a snide comment back to her, so Jessie supposed she too had matured. With fondness in her voice, she spoke to Coralie much as one would talk to a young child. "Where's your knitting?" she asked.

Coralie threw up her arms. "Ruined. It's just ruined. I've dropped five stitches and can't get them back on the needle, and now they've unraveled too far down. I'll never learn to knit," she wailed, moving over to the wagon tongue. She sat, securing her skirts around her legs so they wouldn't get caught in the wheels.

Jessie bit back a laugh as she watched Coralie scoot as far from the rumps of the oxen as she could. She was practically hugging the wagon front. "It takes time, Coralie. Be patient.

You'll learn. Why don't you take it to Anne tonight? She can help you straighten it out."

"Coralie, I'd be happy to give you a hand tonight after my babies are asleep," Eirica said softly. "Do you mind if I join you? The children have finally fallen asleep."

"You know you're always welcome, Eirica, but shouldn't you be resting also?" Jessie asked, eyeing the rounded belly that clothing no longer hid.

Eirica wrinkled her nose. "Don't you start in on me, Jessie. Having your brother constantly nagging after me to ride or rest is quite enough, thank you," she said primly. She glanced over her shoulder as if watching out for James.

"He cares for you, Eirica."

Eirica shook her head. "I'm just an added commitment he took on because he thinks he's obligated to." She shrugged. "Don't get me wrong. Your brother is a good man, but he doesn't need a ready-made family. He deserves a nice young woman and a chance to start his own family, and I need to prove to myself that I can take care of me and mine."

Jessie heard the thread of wistfulness in Eirica's voice but wisely kept her mouth shut. James loved Eirica; there was no doubt in her mind of that. She could see it in his eyes. But Eirica had to discover it on her own. After all, she knew firsthand what well-meaning interference could do. Silence fell. It was just too difficult to talk with the choking dust. Coralie jumped off the wagon tongue with a disgusted squeal when one of oxen added his share of the cow patties to the prairie.

Wolf alternated between riding ahead of the wagons and keeping an eye on the livestock, even though he didn't anticipate any trouble from the band of Lakota Brule Indians who had paid them a visit last night. So far the emigrants had dealt mostly with the Pawnees who held the territory along the Platte River on the other side of Scotts Bluff. They were for the most part curious and friendly, seeking to trade or to beg food and clothing when they wandered into camp. But the Sioux Indians who'd visited last night, with their striking colors of paint slashed across their cheeks, foreheads and chests, had not been out for friendly trade. They had eyed the horses and wagons with malevolent intent.

But once they'd learned that Wolf was of the Miniconjou tribe, son of Golden Eagle, the mighty warriors had welcomed him as brother. The Brule, Miniconjou and Hunkpapa, his mother's tribe, all belonged to the Teton branch of the Sioux. But despite Wolf's Indian blood and their respect for Golden Eagle and Striking Thunder, they still expected payment for crossing their land. The bargaining went on for hours. He'd finally agreed to a dozen head of cattle, two horses, flour, tobacco, a sack of coffee, a battered coffeepot and some calico shirts brought along for trading purposes. In return, the warriors agreed not to harass any more wagons that summer.

He stifled a yawn. Red Hunter and his warriors had deliberately carried on late into the night with their shrieks and yells, forcing Wolf to stand guard—to keep the emigrants from overreacting and doing something foolish. He drew abreast of Rook, who was riding his horse.

The old man lifted bushy brows. "How long ya gonna keep that lass of yours waitin', lad?"

Wolf rolled his shoulders. 'Not your concern, old man."

"Well, now, I reckon when two people can't sleep at night, it affects everyone. That girl is as tired as you, and you're both techy." He fell silent a moment. "Weren't her fault, ya know."

"Makes no difference. You know how it is. What kind of life can I offer her?"

"Ya know, lad, ya might see more if ya open yer eyes. Sometimes the answers we seek are right there afore us." With that, Rook dismounted and took his place beside his oxen.

A few hours later they were within sight of Fort Laramie. Wolf rode ahead and located an area along the Laramie River with ample grazing. As he stared out at the fort three miles off in the distance, he decided they would remain there for a couple of days. Every man, woman, child and animal needed a break from the monotonous, strenuous days of travel. Between heat, exhaustion and the tensions within his party, morale had fallen to an all-time low. The oxen also needed extra rest to regain their strength before continuing onward. When the wagons caught up with him, he announced his intentions.

The gloomy mood lifted. The emigrants cheered and laughed as they formed their wagon circle. Instead of following his usual pattern of riding out to help with the herd, Wolf sat on his stallion and watched Jessie unhitch her oxen, check them over and turn them loose to graze.

His wife. He sighed. What was he going to do? Neither of them could continue this way much longer. The strain was telling on both of them. Over the last few days, he'd spent many hours thinking about his marriage. Was it possible to make it work? He envisioned her in his life, sharing his cabin, visiting with his family. He thought of his mother, of her desire to see him settled. Yes, she'd approve.

He spent most of each summer with his people. Dove would be pleased to have a sister-in-law who shared her love of a good hunt. He remembered how the buffalo massacre had upset Jessie, and he knew she'd approve of his people's method of hunting, of taking only what they needed and wasting nothing. He tipped his head back. He had no doubt she could handle the harsh life, and, knowing Jessica, she'd thrive on it.

She was strong, brave, resourceful and smart. And not only was she a fast learner, she was a good teacher. He knew that she helped Anne and Eirica with the schooling of their children, taught Rickard to use a whip and was giving the older Svensson boys shooting lessons. He grinned despite the grimness of the situation. She'd even taught Shorty a thing or two on the art of spitting. Amazing. His wife a champion spitter. Again the word rolled through him. His *wife*. She was his. He thought of Jessie telling him that together they could work to help his people. It looked as though there was no choice. He would never leave her alone and defenseless now.

His grandmother's words came back to him. He cleared his mind and heart and opened himself to the voice of the spirits. Peace stole over him as he examined his feelings for Jessie and the place she held in his heart. She fit there, as if she'd been meant to fill that void within him. His doubts fled. The dreams were right. Jessie was the one, the key. Together they'd form a team. Wolf squared his shoulders. He loved Jessica Jones with all his heart, and regretted the time lost due to his battered pride. Lighter at heart, he decided to pack enough supplies for two days and take her away into the mountains so they could be alone. He'd tell her what was in his heart and confess his love.

But what if she'd changed her mind? What if she didn't love him anymore? Had he killed her love? That small, niggling doubt set his stomach to churning. Just then she turned and stared right at him. The wind lifted her hair and blew it around her face. His fingers twitched with the urge to brush it away, and when her lips parted, his gut tightened. He fought the temptation to sweep her into his arms and take her away right then so he could lose himself in her sweet loving. Instead he yanked on the reins and galloped toward the herd of cattle. He had supplies to gather.

Jessie watched her husband ride away as if a herd of demons were nipping at his heels. She smiled with satisfaction. It meant he wasn't as cool and unaffected as he pretended to be. But that knowledge did her little or no good. She still didn't know how to repair the damage her brothers had caused. She went in search of Rook. "Do you need me this afternoon?" she asked.

He glanced up from unloading one of the wagons. "Don't reckon I'll need ya till dinner. What are ya planning, lass?"

Jessie shrugged. "Just going to explore. I need some thinking time."

Rook sent her an understanding look. "Watch your step out there, and don't be gone long."

Jessie grabbed a canteen from her wagon and stuffed some

dried meat into her pockets. She contemplated riding but remembered she'd have to cross the Laramie River. From what she'd heard, there was a footbridge, but she wasn't sure it would hold the weight of a horse and rider. She decided to walk the three miles. It would give her time to think. Sadie ran after her, looking at her expectantly. "No, girl, you stay here."

Glancing over her shoulder, she saw Jordan and Jeremy approaching. Head held high, she showed them her back and set off for the fort. She heard her name called but ignored it and tamped down her feelings of guilt. She knew Rook was right: her brothers did love her, had done what they'd thought best. She realized she wouldn't be able to stay mad at them much longer. Though her anger had faded, she wasn't quite ready to let them off the hook. They needed to learn their lesson too. She'd gone only a few paces from the wagons when Alison ran up to her.

"Where you going, Jessie? Can I go too? Please?"

Jessie stopped and bent down. "I'm going to visit the fort, Alison. How about if I take you for a ride when I get back? I'm walking, and it's a long way there and back."

"But Jessie, I'm bored. Lara and Ian are asleep, and mama is visiting. There's nobody to play with. Hanna and Kerstin are with the horses. I can walk. I'm a good walker. Please?"

Jessie shook her head. How could she say no to that earnest, pleading face? When her gaze fell to Alison's bare feet, an idea came to her. The child's birthday was in a few days. She would take her to the fort and purchase a pair of shoes for her. "All right. But we have to ask your ma first, and you have to promise to stay with me and be good."

"I will," Alison promised, reaching up to take Jessie's hand.

As they passed the Nortons' wagon, a low growl made Jessie turn around. Sadie had followed them and stood, hackles raised, teeth bared at Rosalyn.

"Call off the dog, Jessie, or so help me, I'll shoot it," Rosalyn warned, her voice rising.

317

Alison stepped forward, filled with all the righteous anger that a four-year-old could muster. "You can't shoot her. She's nice and you're mean."

Rook, hearing the commotion, popped out. "What's goin' on?"

Jessie sighed. "Sadie's showing her good taste in judgment again." Jessie waved at the dog. "Better tie her up for a bit, Rook. Never know what kind of varmint she might get it into her head to hunt." Jessie smirked when Rosalyn marched off in a huff.

Rook's lips twitched, but he grabbed Sadie by the scruff of her neck. "And what are ya up ta, li'l lass?" he asked Alison.

Alison jumped up and down. "Me and Jessie are gonna go see the fort."

Jessie watched Rosalyn stalk away, then turned to caution the little girl. "Only if your mom says it's okay. Now, let's go ask her. Thanks, Rook."

He muttered something, stuck his unlit pipe between his lips and dragged Sadie to the wagons. Eager to go, Alison pulled Jessie over to where Eirica and Anne were sitting. Jessie knew she wouldn't get much thinking done, but she didn't really mind. She enjoyed Alison.

When Alison bestowed the same soulful pleas on her mother, Jessie and Anne exchanged amused looks. Eirica glanced at Jessie. "Are you sure you want to take her?" she asked.

Jessie laughed and glanced down into the little girl's wide, anxious gaze. "I'm sure. We'll have fun. Ali's never been to a fort before. She'll learn lots of new things, right, pumpkin?"

Alison nodded, her eyes bright and pleading.

Eirica wrinkled her nose and smoothed her daughter's hair. "You be a good girl. Do as Jessie tells you and stay close. No wandering off."

"Yes, Mama!" she said.

"Well, then, perhaps I will go lie down for a bit." Eirica

kissed her daughter good-bye and headed for her tent.

Jessie took Alison by the hand, and together they skipped toward the fort.

"She's still huffed at us," Jordan said glumly. "And Corie's still mad at me too."

"Yeah, Jess is riled as a rattler." Not to mention that Eirica wasn't speaking with him either. *Women! Try to help them and they turn on you.* James flexed his shoulders and stared at his brothers.

Jeremy took off his hat, slapped it against his thigh and faced his brothers with his hands on his hips. "Well, what did ya expect? You piled on the agony between her and Wolf. They both got more pride than a dog has fleas. Did you really think forcing them to marry would make everything all right? I told ya she'd be downright angry."

James stared at Jeremy. Jeremy had been against the forced marriage, had been the only one of them confident that Jessie could deal with Wolf on her own. He exhaled loudly, wishing he'd listened to his youngest brother. Damn, when had Jeremy grown up and become so wise? He felt old and foolish suddenly. Soon his siblings wouldn't need him. Digging his hands deeper into his pockets, he kicked Jordan to get his attention. "Jeremy's right. We owe her an apology. She knows her own mind. We ain't got no right to make her decisions." Glum silence met his pronouncement. Then a new voice brought them out of their contemplations.

"Glad to hear you boys have finally figured that out."

James turned to find Wolf standing behind them. He grimaced and opened his mouth to apologize, but Wolf held up a hand, forestalling him.

"Save it. I'm taking my wife away for a couple of days." Wolf speared each of them with a hard look. "While I'm gone, check the cattle. Cull out the ones going lame or showing signs of weakness, and we'll sell them to the fort. The horses also need shoeing, and we need to stock up on grain." Wolf strode away from the silent and subdued brothers.

Chapter Twenty-four

The Mormon Trail merged with the Oregon Trail at Fort Laramie. The sudden mass of humanity resulted in dust, confusion and noise. Jessie glanced over her shoulder, awed by the long lines of wagons. Their white-topped canvases made a picture of white stripes fluttering across the golden land. Holding tight to Alison, Jessie wove a path around wagons and tents, wandering through throngs of people and oxen in order to reach the fort.

"What are those, Jessie?"

Jessie grinned. "Those, my sweet, are tipis. They are like our tents. That's where the Indians live. Remember the ones who came to our camp last night?"

Alison nodded. "Can we go look?"

"We'll see," she said, and led Alison into the fort with its fifteen-foot-high whitewashed adobe walls topped with a wooden palisade. Towerlike bastions stood at the south and north corners, and a blockhouse had been erected over the main gate. The interior of the quadrangular structure was divided: the corral on one side, and opposite, a large square area surrounded by storerooms, offices and apartments.

Jessie eyed the women and soldiers standing in the doorways of the buildings. She assumed the neatly clad women who wore white gloves were wives of the soldiers, and had learned from Rook that many of the Indian women parading around in calico skirts were hired to do the laundry. Against one of the adobe walls, trappers, dressed in buckskins with full beards and long scraggly hair, smoked and drank, whistled and made crude comments to the Indian women. She led Alison away. Laundry apparently wasn't the only service these women performed.

Alison tugged on her arm, her eyes wide. The little girls head swiveled from one sight to another. "Jessie, there's soldiers with guns an' everything." She squealed. "What are they doin' way up there?" She pointed to the roofs of the buildings.

Jessie knelt and hugged Alison, loving the wide wonder that filled her eyes. "I expect they're on guard duty." Jessie glanced over her shoulder. The backs of the buildings butted up against the adobe walls, which allowed the roofs to serve the dual purpose of being a banquette as well. Though the sights intrigued and fascinated her, much of it was the same as at Fort Kearny: soldiers, people, animals and most of all, all-out confusion. But watching the little girl take it all in lent a freshness to it. "How about if we go find the store?"

Alison nodded and skipped happily alongside Jessie. Loud laughter and raised voices came from one building. It didn't take more than a peek through the door to see that it was likely the enlisted men's bar. Jessie stopped and scanned the area. When she spotted a doorway with women coming and going, she headed for it. Sure enough, it was the sutler's store. "Here we go. Let's go see what they have inside." The interior was crowded with people and merchandise. The shelves were laden, but when she saw the price of coffee, she was shocked. The cost was at least four times higher than back home.

Leading the little girl, she moved to the bolts of cloth and the shelf of shoes. To her disappointment, there weren't any shoes small enough for Alison. "Drat," she muttered. *Now what?* She'd really wanted the little girl to have a new pair. Then she remembered the Indians who'd come to their camp last night. Maybe she could purchase a pair of mocassins— not only for Alison, but for the other two as well. With that in mind Jessie turned to leave, but found her exit blocked by those who were lined up at the counter, piles of purchases sitting before them. She and Alison were well and truly hemmed in. She stooped and lifted Alison into her arms, afraid the girl would get stepped on.

"Is that . . ." The little girl in her arms was pointing to something, but Jessie just wanted to escape the crowded environs.

"Hang in there, Alison girl. We'll get out of here right quick." Jessie watched and waited for an opportunity to snake a path through.

"I tell ya, the bitch is a cold-blooded murderer, and I aim to take her in and see her hanged for her crime."

At the sound of the loud voice, Jessie glanced to her right and saw a large, well-dressed man speaking to an aproned man at the counter. Stuck as she was, she unashamedly listened.

"Name is Vern Portier. I'm sheriff of a small town near St. Louis. This here's a sketch of the woman I'm looking for. We learned she's traveling to Oregon with her brother and maybe another man. The trio robbed a stagecoach a while back and then killed my baby brother. Poor boy had the unfortunate luck to be this woman's husband."

The stranger went on about the crime and how his brother had fallen for the woman's deadly charms. Jessie glanced away, concerned that such talk might upset Alison. She scouted the crowd in front of her and saw a large group of emigrants move forward, then stop when a new wave of visitors rushed through the open door. She tapped her foot impatiently. Still stuck, Jessie tuned back into the conversation of the two men.

". . . name is Daisy, and this here's her brother, Dan Tupper. Don't know this one's name—just a drifter, from all accounts. But Daisy here should be real easy to spot. Gal's a real looker, with blond hair and brown eyes. Have you seen her?"

"Gee, I dunno. We see lots of women in here every day. Can't say as I seen her or not."

The sheriff, tall as a mountain, turned and nearly jammed his elbow into Jessie's nose. "'Scuse me, ma'am," he said before snapping his fingers and turning back to the harried clerk. "Wait, here's one thing. Woman's conceited as they come 'bout her looks but has this one flaw. She has a gap between her two upper front teeth and they stick out somewhat. She hates it."

Jessie could tell from his voice that he was pleased to impart his sister-in-law's flaw. Then her brows drew together. Rosalyn had a gap between her teeth. With a shake of her head and a roll of her eyes, she chided herself. Much as she disliked the woman, crooked teeth did not make her a murderer. Besides, her hair was short and black. She grew still. Or was it? Was Rosalyn's hair really black? She recalled seeing pale roots the day she'd used her whip to chase Rosalyn away from Wolf. Was it true?

"Here's another poster, if you could post it behind you. I'm going to go have a drink. I'll check back later."

The man named Vern turned and squeezed past Jessie. She noticed the badge pinned to his shirt, but by the time she opened her mouth to call him back, he was gone. Slipping to the counter to get a look at the poster, she ignored the angry voices protesting behind her. The poster was gone, and the man working behind the counter was helping someone farther down. She left, shoving her way outside with Alison in her arms, ignoring the grumbling in her wake. Her mind raced furiously. Rosalyn had money. Lots of it. Could she be the Daisy the sheriff was after? Only one way to find out. She quickened her steps. She had to find that lawman.

"Where are we goin' now, Jessie?" Alison wiggled to be put down. "I thought I saw . . ."

"Hush, Alison." Jessie stopped, her mind a whirl. She'd forgotten about the child in her arms. She didn't dare take her into a saloon! She set the girl down and grabbed her hand. "To the post office."

Jessie tried to hurry back to camp, but was slowed by having to carry Alison. The four-year-old had grown tired. Damn, why hadn't she brought Shilo? After studying the poster in the post office, she was positive that Rosalyn was none other than Daisy Portier, and Hugh was her brother, Dan Tupper. It explained so much—like why she and Hugh didn't act like a husband and wife. Also, she now knew why the three of them had so much money, and why they'd been ready to flee the night of the buffalo stampede.

As soon as she delivered Alison back to her mother, she'd go find Wolf. He'd know what to do. Jessie stopped to survey the landscape. Perhaps she should go straight to him now. James could take the little girl back to her mother. "Okay, Ali, you need to walk for a little while."

"Aw, Jessie, I'm tired," Alison whined.

Jessie knelt down, setting the girl on her feet. "Let's go see James and the cattle. He's closer to us than the wagons, and I'll bet he'll give you a ride back. But we have to hurry or we'll miss him."

Alison squealed in delight and skipped ahead, her fatigue gone at the prospect of new excitement. Jessie quickened her pace, her gaze on the cattle in the distance. A sharp bark drew her attention. Sadie ran up to her, the rope lead trailing behind her. "Sadie, you bad girl," she scolded. She was so intent on untying the rope attached to the dog's collar, she didn't hear the approaching horses until Sadie growled and tried to break away.

"Going somewhere, Jessica?" It was Rosalyn—or Daisy, as she was truly named. The woman was leaning over her saddle horn.

Jessie backed up a step and schooled her features into a mask of disinterest as she eyed the threesome. Why were they here? Did they know what she'd discovered? If so, how? Tipping her hat back, she lifted a brow and sent the woman a look of disdain.

"Just taking Alison out to see the cows. James promised he'd let her ride herd with him this afternoon." She prayed they would believe James was expecting them. Swinging her head around, she noted with dismay how far ahead Alison was.

"Well, I'd better go catch up with her." Daisy kicked her horse and blocked Jessie's escape. Gulping back her fear,

Jessie decided to make a run for it. If she ran in the opposite direction Alison had taken, it would leave the little girl free to go to James. There was little chance of her getting lost; the large herd was clearly visible in the distance. Sprinting forward, she didn't get more than a few feet before Dan brought his horse around and Sammy angled his to the side. Daisy blocked the rear. Sadie growled and barked.

"Don't think so, Jessica." Daisy aimed her revolver at her. "Drop the whip and your knife and hold on to that mutt real good or I'll shoot it."

Jessie did as she was told.

"Now, don't be so quick to run off. Looks like we've got some unfinished business to see to. And don't worry none about the little brat. We'll fetch her for you, won't we, Sammy? After all, wouldn't want her to get lost or fall and hurt herself." Daisy nodded to Sammy, who took off after Alison. She then turned her attention back to Jessie, her eyes filled with malicious glee. "When he gets back, we're all going for a nice little ride."

Jessie swallowed her fear and tried to brazen her way out. "What do you mean, your brother? I thought he's—"

Daisy slid down from her horse and advanced but Sadie lunged and grabbed a mouthful of skirt in her teeth before Daisy jumped back. "That dog bites me, she's dead—and you, don't try my patience," she warned. "Dan saw you at the fort. You know the truth, and that means I can't let you go blabbing. You and the girl are coming with us. A little insurance, if you will."

Jessie pulled Sadie close. Sammy rode up with Alison struggling in his arms. His filthy hand was clamped over her mouth to keep her from screaming. Jessie glared first at Sammy, then at Daisy. "Give her to me. If you hurt her, you'll answer to me."

"Shut up, girl. You aren't in any position to make threats. What I say goes, and don't you forget it, unless you want to see the brat hurt."

Jessie's shoulders slumped. "Let her go and I'll go with you."

Daisy sneered and remounted. "Do you really take me for a such a fool? Without the brat, there's nothing to stop you from raising hell and attracting the attention of the soldiers. She goes, and you're gonna tell her we're playing a nice little game and that she'd better be good. Now tell her to keep quiet!"

Jessie stared into Alison's fearful eyes. Tears streamed down the child's cheeks. It made her furious, but she kept her anger under tight control and silently vowed to make them pay for frightening an innocent little girl. She went to Alison and squeezed her knee. "It's okay, sweetheart. We'll play their game and do what they say, and pretty soon you'll be back with your mama. Okay?" When Alison nodded, Sammy carefully removed his hand.

Daisy interrupted. "Let's get the hell outta here. Too many people lookin' this way."

"I want Jessie." Alison whimpered, holding out her hands.

"Stay away, Jessie," Daisy warned, grabbing Alison from Sammy. She pointed at an old wagon tongue lying buried in the tall grass. "Tie the dog, and don't try anything cute or the brat gets it." She held her palm out so Jessie could see the small knife hidden there.

Jessie had no choice, but there was one thing she could try to do. She tied Sadie, and with her back to Daisy, she pulled out the folded poster she'd taken from the post office to show Wolf. Carefully she tucked it beneath the dog's collar, smoothing the long fur over it. Then she allowed Dan to pull her up in front of him on his saddle. He bound her wrists to the saddle horn, then slipped a scratchy poncho over her head to hide her bound wrists. "Sorry, kid," he muttered. He looked somewhat apologetic.

Daisy nodded with satisfaction, then turned to the crying girl in her arms. "Listen to me, little girl. We're going to play a game now. You like games, don't you?"

Alison stuck her fingers in her mouth, her tear-filled eyes never leaving Jessie.

"We're going to go for a little ride. The rules are simple.

You can't cry or make any noise or Jessie loses. You want Jessie to win, don't you?''

Alison didn't answer.

Jessie saw that Daisy was losing patience. She spoke softly, but her gaze never left the other woman's. "It'll be okay, sweetheart. Do what she says. We'll win this game. The good guys always win.''

Daisy laughed. "You got grit, Jessie. You know, if the circumstances were different, I might have found myself liking you. It's just too bad you won't be around that long.'' With that, Daisy led the group toward the Laramie Range.

Behind them, Sadie barked, straining at the rope.

Chapter Twenty-five

Golden Eagle and his warriors arrived at Fort Laramie in late afternoon. Preferring to keep some distance from the unpredictable whites, he stopped several miles from the wagons littering the prairie. "We wait here,'' he announced to his son.

Striking Thunder slipped on a black leather vest and tucked his long braids beneath an old hat. "I will check to see if Wolf has arrived.'' As he rode around the outskirts of hundreds of wagons, noise assailed his ears, and tantalizing whiffs of meals cooked over fires teased his nostrils. Despite the curious and fearful looks sent his way, he kept moving. There were several caravans of wagons with large herds of livestock, but none were Wolf's. He wasn't sure if he was relieved or not. If Wolf hadn't arrived, then that meant there was a chance that they'd be able to protect his brother and the woman from the evil his sister feared.

He was ready to give up when he spotted another wagon circle several miles from the fort with a large herd of livestock a short distance away. He rode toward it. Nearing the herd, he spotted his brother on horseback, speaking to bearded man with black, curly hair. With his knees, he nudged his horse forward, lifted his hands above his head and called out, "Ho, ho, brother!"

Wolf heard the Indian greeting and twisted in his saddle to see his brother approaching. Fearing bad news from home, he raced out to meet him. The two men dismounted. Wolf clasped Striking Thunder tightly. "Why are you here, my brother? Tell me no harm has come to our family or to Ben."

"Our family is well, as are Able and Woodcarver-Who-Lives-in-the-Woods."

Wolf's gut tightened as he studied Striking Thunder. Despite his brother's words, he knew something was wrong; he felt it, saw it in his brother's grave expression. "What brings you so far from our home in the hills?"

"Our sister has had many visions. Danger surrounds the woman who dresses like a boy and has eyes the color of green grass."

Wolf didn't question Striking Thunder about how he knew of Jessie. He didn't need to, not if Star had seen her. Fear snaked up his spine. "Jessica is in danger? From who? Where?"

Just then, James, Jeremy and Jordan joined them. "What's going on?"

Wolf motioned them to silence. "Tell me what you know," he commanded his brother. He listened as Striking Thunder told him of Star's visions. Worry shadowed his eyes. "Let's go. If my wife is in danger, I want her with us. Then we'll go to where our parents wait. I want to speak with Star."

Striking Thunder's eyes widened at the word *wife*, but he didn't ask questions. Wolf was grateful. There would be time

for explanations later. Right now he had to make sure Jessie
was safe. The men rode for the circle of wagons. When they
arrived, Wolf glanced around. There was no sign of Jessie.
Sheer terror filled his heart. Dismounting, he bellowed,
"Rook!"

Rook came running as fast as his short, stubby legs allowed. "What's all the hollerin' fer?" He came to a stop
when he saw Striking Thunder. His bushy white brows drew
together, forming a straight line across his forehead. "What's
wrong?"

"Where's Jessie?" James demanded.

"She went to the fort. Should be back soon."

Wolf paced. "Damn. How long ago did she leave?"

Rook scratched his scraggly beard. "Soon after we made
camp, I reckon."

Eirica joined them. "She took Alison with her. Is anything
wrong?"

Striking Thunder stepped forward. "Who is this Alison?"

James nodded toward Eirica. "Her daughter. If they went
to the fort, they'll be safe."

Striking Thunder shook his head. "No. It's too late. She
won't be there." He stared at the gathering crowd, his dark
eyes fixed on Wolf. "Star Dreamer has heard the cry of a
small child in her visions." He then looked at Eirica. "Your
daughter, is she young?"

Eirica's face drained of color. "Oh, Lord. She's only
four."

Fear snaked through Wolf. Had Zeb caught up with her?
He had to go to the fort. Furious growling came from one
of the wagons. Wolf turned and held his hand up, signaling
silence. Tied to a wagon to keep him from wandering and
being hurt by some fearful traveler, Wahoska paced. His
hackles were raised, and low growls came from his throat as
he stared out into the prairie. Cocking his head, Wolf heard
the distant sound of barking. The wolf lunged, tried to break
free. Glancing around, Wolf looked for Sadie, but she wasn't
in sight. Perhaps the dog was with Jessie . . . He released the

wolf. The animal took off like an arrow. Wolf jumped on his horse and followed. James, Jeremy and Striking Thunder followed. A mile from the cattle, Wolf stopped when he came upon Sadie, who was barking up a storm. Wahoska continued to circle the dog.

"What the hell is she doing tied out here?" Wolf untied the dog and held tight to the rope when Sadie tried to jerk away. "What is it, girl?" He knelt and grabbed her by the collar. A folded piece of paper fell to the ground.

He opened it and stared at the Wanted poster.

James glanced over his shoulder. "Hey, that woman kinda looks like Rosalyn."

Ice coated Wolf's heart as he studied the trio. Though the sketch was grainy, he was afraid James was right. Sadie broke free of his grasp and ran a short distance away. She sniffed the ground and returned with Jessie's whip in her mouth. Wolf clutched the whip. Jessie would never have left the dog or her whip out here voluntarily. Striking Thunder was right. She was in trouble. "I'm going after them."

Striking Thunder nodded. "I will fetch our warriors."

Wolf and the Jones brothers returned to the wagons. Rook met them, and when he saw Sadie, he frowned. "Now what was that mutt doing out there? I tied her to the wagon for snarling at that Norton woman again." He shook his head. "Don't know what's got into that doggone mutt. Likes everyone else jest fine, but that woman brings out the bad in her."

"Yeah, and now we know why." Wolf shoved the poster into Rook's hands and glanced at the wagon belonging to the Nortons. No one was there. "Where are they?"

Scratching his chin, Rook shrugged. "They been gone a couple hours. Looked like they's planning on being gone a couple days. They was pretty well packed."

Wolf felt a sinking sensation in his gut. Now he knew Rosalyn had Jessie, but finding her would be next to impossible among the mass of humanity. He eyed the western horizon, then glanced east. And which way? Would she continue onward or flee in the opposite direction? If he guessed wrong, Jessie could die. While waiting for his brother and the warriors to return, Wolf headed for the Nortons' wagon. The others followed. He pulled the tailgate off.

"Looks like they pulled out," James said, staring at the sacks of provisions that lay scattered, the open boxes and the hole in the bottom of the wagon. Wolf hopped in and felt inside the secret cubby. He pulled out another wadded-up poster and a sack with a hole in it. It had obviously once held gold, for there were bank markings upon it. He glanced around. He handed Elliot the items. "Elliot, take these to the fort. Tell the commander we need help. I suspect the Nortons have taken Jessie and Eirica's girl with them as hostages. We're going to have to split up and check both directions of the trail."

Eirica gasped and stared from one man to the other. She grabbed Wolf by the arm. "How can you be so sure? We should check the fort first. They're probably still there." Her voice rose in pitch. "They *have* to be!"

Wolf forced himself to remain calm. He gripped Eirica's hands and shook his head. "My sister has the gift of sight. Most whites don't believe, but her visions do not lie." He slammed his fist into his palm. "Damn it, this is my fault!" He closed his eyes, deeply afraid, knowing only too well how foolishly fearless his wife could be.

Striking Thunder had arrived. "It does your wife no good to cast blame. We are ready."

Wolf nodded to the line of waiting warriors. He wasn't surprised to see his sisters or his parents. "Let's go. James—"

"I'm going," James interrupted. "Jordan can take over the herd."

"You're not leaving without me, either." Jeremy stated.

Wolf glanced at Jordan, fully expecting him to join in. But he didn't.

Jordan put his arm around his wife. "I'll stay—in case she returns."

Wolf nodded. "We'll split up. Half will go west and the rest will ride back along the trail."

Star came forward, tears streaming down her dusky cheeks. "No." She pointed behind Wolf. "I see trees, thick forests, like the *Paha Sapa* at home."

A surge of adrenaline rushed though his veins. "Elliot, tell the commander to pick up our trail. We're heading toward the Laramie Range." They wouldn't be able to get away. Not from one of the best trackers in all the land.

A cloak of darkness shrouded the three people huddled amidst the tall grass, but Jessie could hear them fighting and see their shadows from where she sat.

"What are we gonna do with them? We can't keep them; they'll give us away. 'Sides, we don't have that much food or water." Dan sounded nervous.

Daisy shrugged, a malicious grin tugging at the corners of her lips. "What do you think?" she said, slanting Jessie a look of hatred. "Kill 'em?"

Sammy spoke for the first time since they'd fled. "Nobody said nothin' 'bout killin'."

"There's no choice," Daisy said with a snarl. "It's them or us. You want to hang?"

"You're the one who done killed your husband. Not us. I ain't never killed nobody, and I ain't gonna start now, especially not no innocent child. Let's leave 'em here. We'll travel faster without 'em. All I want is my share of the money."

"You fool," she spat. "The girl and the brat are our only chance. We'll keep them until I'm sure we're free. Then they go. I'm not leaving them behind to point our direction to Vern. If neither of you can handle it, I'll take care of it."

Dan shifted uneasily. "Look, sis, I'm with Sammy. We can't kill 'em."

Daisy jumped to her feet. "Don't forget who's in charge. What I say goes."

Sammy threw her a disgusted look. "I ain't gonna be no part of it. I'm leaving."

"Leaving?"

"Yeah, I'm out. Keep the money. Ain't worth hanging for murder." Sammy stalked off.

"Damn it, Daisy. You can't do this," Dan pleaded.

"No one crosses me," Daisy spat.

While the trio argued, Jessie had been quietly struggling. The rope binding her wrists dug into her flesh, but at least her feet were unhampered. She wiggled her fingers, forcing the blood to flow to her fingertips. She grimaced. Not that she could go anywhere with her hands bound. If it weren't for Alison, she might have risked sneaking away while they were busy arguing. With it being so dark, there was a chance she could hide in the tall grass—but she didn't dare. While she could handle Daisy's anger, Alison couldn't. The little girl was frightened enough. Jessie would just have to wait for a better opportunity.

Glancing around, she searched for shadows that moved, praying that help would arrive—and soon. Daisy was desperate, crazy. But there was nothing out there but vast blackness. She rested her chin on top of Alison's head, her thoughts tumbling like rocks down a mountainside. Surely Eirica would have alerted Rook or James that they were missing. Had they found Sadie and the Wanted poster? If so, would Wolf know where to look? There were miles to search . . .

Sorrow and regret filled her. All Jessie wanted was to feel her husband's arms around her one last time and to be able to tell him how much she loved him. Alison shifted against her. Jessie caressed the curly red hair resting against her breast. With her bound wrists looped over the child, she held her close, seeking to reassure both of them.

Alison tilted her head up, her small, bow-shaped mouth trembling. "I'm hungry, Jessie," she whispered, sticking her fingers in her mouth.

Jessie still had some dried meat in her pocket from their walk to the fort, but she needed to save it for later. She didn't know when they'd be fed next. "I know you are, sweet. But we have to be brave and wait."

Huge tears welled in the little girl's eyes. "I want my ma."

Jessie hugged her close. This was all her own fault. She should never have taken the girl to the fort, shouldn't have let her pride keep her from Wolf. Keeping her voice low, she spoke softly into Alison's ear, the soft curls tickling her nose. "I know, sweets. We'll see her soon. Wolf will find us. But you mustn't say so to *them*, okay?"

Alison nodded. "Will James come too?"

Jessie smiled tenderly, praying someone would come soon. "Of course he will."

Snuggling back against Jessie, Alison continued to suck her fingers. Her voice faded. "I like James, Jessie. He don't yell or hit Ma."

"Rest now, Ali," Jessie whispered. It saddened her that the little girl had lived through so much violence in her short life. With Alison dozing, Jessie turned her attention back to the threesome. Daisy had caught up to Sammy. Dan shouted something at his sister; then, with no warning, a shot rang out. Jessie jerked Alison against her to muffle her own startled cry. To her horror, Sammy jerked and fell facedown in the tall grass. Daisy turned away, her pistol in hand. Fear as she'd never known chilled Jessie's heart when the woman strode toward them and ordered them to stand.

Chapter Twenty-six

The sun dipped below the horizon, and the pale dusk deepened. A party of warriors knelt near the river, searching for signs of horse tracks. Their quarry had cut back once again. Striking Thunder left the warriors and approached Wolf. "My brother, we have found their trail, but I say we wait until *Wi* shows her face once more before continuing."

Wolf stared out into the wilderness. His brother was in command of the war party, and as leader, he didn't have to consult him. He could halt his own warriors at will. While Wolf appreciated the show of respect Striking Thunder accorded him, he couldn't stop now. They had to find Jessie. He gripped the hilt of his knife. "No, we must continue. They have a three- or four-hour jump on us. They will stop to rest. We won't."

An imposing figure joined them. "My eldest son is wise in his words."

Wolf turned to his father, his allegiances no longer Indian or white. He was a man desperately afraid of losing the one woman he loved. He ran his hand through his hair. "Jessie is out there."

Golden Eagle laid his hand on Wolf's shoulders. "My son, I know what is in your heart. I felt as you do now when your mother was taken from me by her guardian. But you must remember, emotions cloud the mind. They blind you." He spread his hands out. "Look, I say. It is open land. They can see for miles, and should they see us coming, they may

335

panic and harm your wife and the child. Let them reach the sheltering trees and mountains. They will not risk their captives until there is no longer any use for them. Once they are in the mountains, we will be right behind them. There, none can hide from us. The sons of Golden Eagle are the best trackers in all the land. The spirits will shield our presence. We will find them.''

Wolf rolled his shoulders. His father and brother were shrewd as always, and for once he did not resent it. He stared out where darkness cloaked the mountain range. His father was right. Like the wolf after which he was named, his tracking skills were unequaled, even by his own brother. He calmed, himself, burying his emotions, allowing the Indian in him to surface and take command over the worried husband. He would do whatever it took to find his wife. Head held high, shoulders back, he nodded. ''Tell our warriors we ride at the first sign of the gray dawn, my wise brother.''

After unloading Lady Sarah, he wandered out into the dark prairie. Far from the camp, he stopped and lifted his arms high, fingers beseeching the *Mahpiya,* the spirits of the heavens, as he asked that the trial he followed be preserved, guarded from bad weather. He also asked that the spirit of *Mato,* the bear, guard his love and protect her from harm. Then he asked *Sungmanitu,* spirit of the wolf, to preside over the chase and the war party, to lead them in the right direction.

After his prayers, he removed his white man's clothing. He was Wolf, White Wolf, trained warrior. From his pouch, he brought out paints and smeared them across his face and chest, then sat in the tall grass, his hands resting on his crossed knees, palms up, to await the arrival of *Wiyohiyanpa,* the spirit of the east.

Dawn was fast approaching when a unit of soldiers rode out of the fort, toward the Laramie Range. Lt. Col. Hadden Trowbridge ordered the men to spread out and search for the trail of the man named Wolf. He knew it wouldn't take long to find. According to Elliot Baker, the rescue party was large, making it easy to spot and follow them. Vern rode up beside him. "Think we'll catch up to them?"

Hadden drew a deep breath and eyed the landscape with a jaundiced eye. "Oh, we'll catch up. The question you should be asking is whether you'll get your sister-in-law alive. She's kidnapped the wife of an Indian, and they've got a war party on their trail."

"Yeah, but according to Baker, the woman's husband is only part Indian."

Hadden straightened, his gaze narrowing when he heard a shout in the distance. "Don't matter. He's still Indian. Looks like they've found the trail. Let's go." There wasn't a chance in hell he'd catch up to the criminals before the Indians did. If only Elliot Baker had come to see him earlier. But he'd also lost time trying to find Vern and getting his confirmation that these were the people that sheriff had come so far to find. By that time it had gone dark.

Vern wrapped the reins around his gloved hand. "I'd like them alive, Lieutenant."

Hadden sighed. "Me too, Sheriff. Me too." With a yell, he spurred his horse forward.

By midmorning, Wolf and his party were gaining on the "Nortons." The churned-up dirt, broken branches and over-turned rocks were fresher. But now he also knew it was only Daisy and Dan he had to deal with. Earlier they'd found Sammy's body. He'd been shot. Finding the dead body gave rise to a new fear. Daisy was a killer. Dan wouldn't have shot Sammy. Wolf mentally kicked himself. He should have known something was wrong with the trio when he found out that Dan and Sammy were lovers. He'd stumbled across them one night. They hadn't seen him. Truthfully, he hadn't thought anything about it, though it explained why Daisy slept around. But now he feared for Jessie's life. Daisy hated Jessie. He could only pray they caught up with the band before she killed again. He firmed his lips, refusing to en-tertain any negative thoughts.

The three men rode in silence. Flanked by his father and brother, Wolf felt as though he belonged for the first time in his life. He was a warrior going into battle, and those who'd taken what belonged to him would pay.

By early afternoon they entered the forest. The mountains were thickly forested with pines—so thick that from a distance, the mountains looked black. Sometimes called the Black Hills, the range had the same name as the hills back home where his people lived, the ones his people had named *Paha Sapa*. Hills of the Shadow. That, he felt was a good sign. And because the woods were densely packed, the chance for an ambush was great.

Wolf consulted with his father and brother. The warriors could go much faster without their horses and move silently through the dense forest. They would go on foot. The rest of their party would remain here. After asking James and Jeremy to remain with the women—who weren't expert trackers—he slung a quiver of arrows over his shoulder and grabbed his rifle.

Jeremy tapped him on the shoulder. "You still finding signs from Jessie?"

Wolf put his hand on the boy's shoulder. "Yes. Your sister is resourceful." Pride warred with worry. At each stop Daisy made, Jessie managed to leave him some sign, letting him know that she trusted him to come and rescue her. Wolf smiled with grim determination. He would not let her down. He rejoined his father and brother, and they turned to leave.

Jeremy ran up to them, pointing to White Dove. Wolf's sister wore a quiver of arrows over her back. "Why does she go and not us?"

Before Wolf could explain, Dove stepped in front of him. "I am Indian," she said, tossing her braids. "I move with no sound, and my aim is true."

"Yeah, well, you can't shoot as well as I can. If you go, I go." Jeremy stood, feet apart, rifle in hand and a determined glint in his eyes.

Dove tilted her chin. "Your white-man's shoes are heavy and clumsy. They will give away our presence."

Jeremy lifted one foot and pulled off his boot, then removed the other. Toe-to-toe, the two glared at one another.

Wolf sighed. At every stop since leaving Fort Laramie, the two had baited one another, constantly competing. "Enough, Dove. He can go."

Dove's jaw dropped in surprise. "He does not know how to move in the dark. He will step on a twig or allow the moon to cast his shadow."

Golden Eagle held up his hand. "Then you must guide him, daughter. It is his sister who is in danger, and it is only right that he goes if he chooses. You will remain at his side." Then Golden Eagle pulled off his own moccasins and handed them to Jeremy. "Put these on. They will soften your footsteps and protect your feet. My feet are tough and can withstand the forest floor."

Wolf gave the order to move out. Jeremy grinned and fell in step with Dove.

Every bone in Jessie's body ached as the horses picked their way through the forest. Her vision blurred with exhaustion. They were nearing the end of their second day of riding. Had it only been yesterday that she'd gone to the fort? It seemed so much longer. Though she was tired, she didn't dare allow herself to drift off, not after witnessing Daisy's cold-blooded murder of Sammy last night. There was no doubt in her mind that the woman would kill them when she no longer needed them. She had to remain alert and find a way to disarm the evil woman. Her eyelids fluttered closed, but Dan's shout jerked her awake.

Daisy stopped and twisted around in her saddle. "Now what?" she asked, scanning the dark shadows closing in around them.

"We need to rest."

"No, we keep riding."

"Look, Daisy, If our horses drop dead, we'll never make it out of here alive."

Swearing beneath her breath, Daisy dismounted, but instead of sitting, she paced nervously. "Very well. But not for long."

Dan untied Jessie's hands and hauled her and Alison down. She sank onto the ground with Alison still asleep in her arms.

Daisy came over and glared down at her. "Tie her back up," she ordered.

Dan sighed. The length of rope dangled from his fingers. "She ain't gonna go nowhere. Let her be."

"You aren't going soft on me, are you?" she said, narrowing her eyes.

Dan glared back. "What are you going to do? Shoot me?"

Jessie bit her lip and tightened her hold on Alison, fearing Daisy's quick temper. But to her relief, the woman spun around and glared at her. "Don't try anything," she spat. Her foot shot out, catching Jessie in the side.

Jessie gasped in pain. Daisy sneered, then stalked off. A canteen dropped beside her. Glancing up, she stared at Dan. "Thank you," she whispered.

"Best wake the child and let her drink, too."

Jessie woke Alison and gave her some water, then stood and stretched her legs, grinding her heels into the soft dirt floor. She held on to the hope that Wolf was following them. When Dan turned back to them, she felt bold enough to ask, "Are you going to let her kill us?" She kept her voice low so Alison couldn't hear.

Dan frowned. "I don't want to. I'm no killer." He walked away.

Jessie dropped down beside Alison and pulled out the remaining piece of dried meat from her pocket. "Eat quickly, sweet." Alison did as she was bidden, and Jessie used her as a shield to yank another button from her shirt. It was the last one she dared to remove without risking Daisy's suspicion. Tucking her shirt back in, she dropped the tiny button to the ground and tore up some grass. When Daisy ordered them to mount up, she stood and prayed for her husband to hurry. Daisy was edgy, her temper short, and her hard brown eyes were filled with malice.

Jessie watched as Daisy stood, waiting for Dan to finish tying Jessie's hands to the saddle horn. The woman stared off into the darkness, looking uneasy. Dan finished tying Jessie's hands and joined his sister.

"Daisy, let's just leave them here. We'll travel faster if it's just the two of us. You know Wolf is on our trail. You're a fool if you believe otherwise. You can bet when Jessie and the child didn't return, he set up a search. And he'll find the dog. And when he figures out we're gone, he'll check our wagon. He'll know we've got them."

Daisy kicked a rock. "Damn!"

Brother and sister stared at one another. Dan's voice was low, but Jessica heard it nonetheless. Her heart leaped. "We're as good as dead, sis. Wolf won't take kindly to us taking his woman. If we free her, he may turn back. She's all he wants."

"You're the fool. If they find that poster you tore off the wall in that shop, they'll alert the soldiers. That reward my husband's brother posted will have every soldier on our tail. These two go with us. Now, let's go," Daisy ordered.

Darkness settled over the land, providing cover for the warriors creeping stealthily one by one through the trees, wraithlike, blending with the tall, thick trunks. After another hour of slow penetration of the forest, Wolf knew they were gaining on Daisy. It was obvious from the slow, plodding pace of the tracks that the outlaws' horses were nearing exhaustion. Striking Thunder pointed to a broken leaf, hanging by a mere thread. He picked it and brought it to his nose. "Fresh. It hasn't lost its scent or wilted. Our enemy is not far ahead."

Wolf studied the tracks and smiled grimly. They were closing in. With all his willpower, he focused on the hunt, the chase. He could not allow himself to worry and wonder. Keeping to the shadows, the two warriors, equal in height and breadth, slipped from tree to shadow until they heard muffled voices. He gripped his bow. Blood thundered in his ears. They had caught up. He listened intently, hearing the crunch of twigs and dried needles on the forest floor. The kidnappers were still on the move but close. A hand on his arm stopped him.

Striking Thunder shook his head. "We must wait for them to stop and settle or else we risk injury to your woman and the child."

Wolf acknowledged his brother's wisdom. He tipped his head up and sent three long, rolling chirps into the air. His signal was returned by two short chirps. Striking Thunder continued on, leaving Wolf to wait for the rest of their party. His father joined him. "We will attack as soon as they stop." Golden Eagle nodded and laid a hand on Wolf's shoulder. "The spirits are with us."

Striking Thunder emerged from the shadows and joined the huddle. His voice was low, barely audible. "They have stopped to rest. Your woman and the child are tied to a tree. The other woman sits close by with a gun pointed at them. The other white paces." His eyes glittered with disdain. "He is nervous, afraid."

Wolf narrowed his eyes. "As he should be."

Chapter Twenty-seven

It was late; the sliver of the moon was high when Jessie's captors were forced to stop and rest their exhausted horses. Daisy shoved Jessie against a tree and then shoved Alison at her. The whimpering child crawled into her lap; then Dan wrapped the rope around both of them, tying them to the tree. She was tired. So tired. Despair washed through her.

There had to be a way to get free. She leaned her head back against the rough trunk and closed her eyes. A sharp kick to her side jerked her eyes open. Daisy stood over her.

"Thinking of your husband, Jessica?" Her eyes narrowed to furious slits. "I wouldn't hold any hope of his coming to your rescue. Maybe I'll let you live long enough to see him die by my hand," she gloated.

Jessie gave a short bark of laughter. "Ha, you have to see him first. He's Indian. He'll see you long before you even know he's there—and the darkness won't stop him. Indians can see in the dark and move without making a sound." She smiled sweetly. "You know, Daisy, Wolf could be out there right now, and you'd never know it. You haven't a chance!"

Daisy kicked her again. "Shut up."

Jessie gasped against the pain and shielded Alison from Daisy's wrath. She tilted her chin. Maybe she could scare the woman into leaving them behind. "Wolf is going to sneak up on you, and you'll find an arrow in your black heart will be your only warning."

Daisy bent down and smiled coldly. "Maybe I should just kill you now. Dan's right. We'd go a lot faster without you and the brat."

Alison dug her fingers into Jessie, crying hoarsely. Dan moved forward and yanked Daisy away. "Go sit down and rest." He glared at Jessie. Leaning over her, he said, "I don't want to see either of you harmed. Do as you're told, and I'll see if I can convince her to leave the two of you here, but for God's sake, stop taunting her."

Jessie glanced down at the little girl who was crying silently, but there was nothing she could do except hold and comfort her.

White Dove and Jeremy moved through the forest, from tree to tree, from shadow to shadow. The group had split into twos and threes to keep from being spotted. She cocked her head when another signal sounded. Pointing, she indicated the direction.

"How are we going to catch them if they are on horseback

and we are on foot?'' Jeremy asked, leaning forward to whisper in her ear.

Dove stopped and frowned at him. ''Their horses tire. They move through underbrush less easily than we.''

''You can tell that from the tracks?'' Jeremy asked, his voice incredulous.

Dove glared at the tall, handsome man beside her. It angered her, the overpowering attraction she felt for this white—especially as he was no great warrior. ''No more talk.'' She continued on. Another signal sounded, this one different. She changed directions, making sure her unwanted charge stayed with her. After a few minutes she stopped and crouched.

''Have they found them?'' Jeremy whispered, coming up behind her.

White Dove motioned Jeremy to silence and watched her brothers. Leaning to speak into his ear, her voice soft as the wind, she said, ''They are over there.'' She watched Striking Thunder position his warriors simply with movements of his hands and head. When he was done, she reached back to motion to Jeremy that they should move into their positions. She grimaced. Because of her charge, her position was out of the range of the action. Her head whipped around when her hand encountered emptiness. She searched the darkness but found no sign of him. She swallowed her groan of frustration, knowing that if he did anything stupid, she would bear the blame.

Peering intently in the direction Jeremy must have gone, she searched for any shifts in the shadows around her. Her patience paid off when a dark shape pulled away from one tree trunk and crept to another, moving toward the enemy. Keeping low, she followed and grabbed his arm. ''We wait,'' she whispered.

Jeremy shook his head and pointed. ''There they are,'' he mouthed softly.

Dove glanced to where he pointed. From where they crouched, they could see Jessie tied to the tree, her back toward them.

Jeremy pulled a knife from his pocket and turned his head to Dove's ear. "I'm going to cut her free from behind."

Dove started to tell him no, then gasped when she found his lips mere inches from hers. Startled, she drew back, furious at her wayward thoughts. Though she judged him to be around her own age of nineteen winters, he was just a boy—not a man as the warriors in her tribe were by his age.

Jeremy slunk away, blending in with the shadows once more. She went after him, catching sight of the wink of the metal of his blade. She bit her lip. He held his knife in his hand, the blade out, catching the beams of light from above. She held her breath, moving quickly behind him, praying he'd not reveal their presence. Dove was within touching distance when once again he left the concealing shadows and scurried to another thick bush. To her dismay, the knife blade caught a branch and startled a raccoon, which shot out from beneath the bush, scolding loudly.

She rushed forward, but in her haste to stop Jeremy, she stepped on a twig. Horrified, she stopped and looked down as the sharp crack ripped through the silence. This time it was Jeremy who reached out to grab her arm and pull her down into a crouch behind the bush. Silently, they glared at one another, each accusing the other, not daring to move. But when they heard loud voices, each went into action. Dove grabbed her bow and pulled an arrow from her quiver at the same time that Jeremy inched his way to the tree, his knife clutched between his teeth.

Jessie was watching her captors when the twig snapped.

Dan had dozed off but woke with a start. She saw him glance over at his sister, and Jessie saw that she too was listening, her face pale in the moonlight. Just then a raccoon ran out of the brush, making loud, angry noises.

"It's all right," Daisy whispered, to her brother, "it's only a racoon."

Glancing around him, Dan looked uneasy. "Let's get outta here," the man whispered. "It doesn't feel right."

Daisy went still, "You're right. It's quiet, too quiet."

Standing, she pointed the gun at Jessie. "Get the horses. We'll leave them here."

Dan fetched the horses and handed his sister the reins of her mount, then started to ride off.

Jessie stared at Daisy, who hadn't moved. She had drawn her pistol. Sweat beaded between Jessica's breasts, and her mouth went dry. Her heart had already stopped. This was it. She was going to die, and there wasn't a thing she could do. Keeping her gaze on the gun, she braced herself. At this close range, the other woman wouldn't miss. Even as fear filled her, Jessie's biggest concern was the child sleeping fitfully against her. She prayed that Alison would be spared.

"Well, haven't you any last words, Jessie dear?" Daisy asked with a smirk.

Jessie thought fast. She glared at the woman standing in front of her. Her eyes went wide with surprise for a split second when she felt something or someone tugging on the ropes binding her to the tree. Had help arrived? She took a deep breath. She had to stall Daisy. Quickly she schooled her features into a mask of indifference. "You won't get away."

Thankfully Daisy hadn't noticed anything amiss. She laughed scornfully. "Brave to the end. I like that. But now we must go. So long, Jessie."

Jessie watched Daisy's trigger finger as the gun pointed at her. When the ropes loosened some more, she tensed, ready to throw herself to the side.

Wolf swore in frustration when Daisy aimed her gun at Jessie. He motioned for his brother to hold off. It had been a stroke of luck to catch Daisy and Dan dozing, and in just a few seconds it would have been over. He and the other warriors had arrows ready to make their mark. His rifle had been too risky at this distance with warriors surrounding Daisy and Dan. But the raccoon had alerted the quarry to their presence, and now he didn't dare risk having Daisy's gun go off. He kept his arrow centered on Daisy. Beside him, Striking Thunder did likewise, his bow taut.

Dan had ridden off, but Daisy kept her weapon trained on Jessie. Time slowed. Wolf waited, his gaze never wavering. But when he heard the cocking of the gun, sweat ran down his back, and his heart stopped. He was out of time. Daisy wasn't going to leave her hostages alive. Wolf adjusted his aim a bit lower and pulled his arm back. With a silent prayer, he let his arrow fly. It hit Daisy's hand. Two gun shots filled the air. Daisy screamed. Pandemonium broke forth. Warriors poured from the woods, their arrows aimed at Dan, who immediately dropped his gun.

Wolf ran toward Jessie, past Daisy, who lay on the ground, her eyes staring blankly at the canopy of stars. His only concern lay with his wife. She lay huddled and still on the ground. "Jessie, oh, God, Jessie," he cried, his heart lodged in his throat. With a hoarse cry he fell to his knees and rolled her over, pulling Alison from her grasp. He handed the hysterical child to Jeremy, then gathered his wife in his arms. "Talk to me, Jess. Tell me you're unhurt." Desperation laced his voice, and his fingers shook as he skimmed them over her body, searching for a gunshot wound.

She opened her eyes and looked up at him. Her wavering grin was the most beautiful sight he figured he'd ever see. "I'm fine," she said, her voice quavering.

"Are you sure?"

"I think so." She trembled, then fell back against him. Suddenly she lifted her head and glanced around wildly. She struggled in his arms. "Where's Alison?" she cried. "Is she all right? Oh, Lord! She wasn't shot, was she?"

Wolf didn't know. He'd been focused only on her. He looked over his shoulder and met Jeremy's nod. "She's fine. She's with Jeremy and my sister." He held his wife close. They sat for a long time, oblivious to the activity around them.

"If anything had happened to you—"

Jessie brought her bound wrists up and pressed her fingers to his lips. Tears coursed down her cheeks. "I was so afraid I'd never be able to tell you how much I love you."

"I love *you,* Jessica Jones," he said, holding her tight.

"God, I love you. I'm sorry for being such a fool."

Jessie smiled through her tears. "I love you too, Wolf. We've both been too full of stubborn pride." She buried her head in the curve of his neck. "Don't let me go. Hold me."

Wolf cut the rope binding her wrists, then stood, cradling her to his chest. "I'll never let you go. You're mine. My wild rose. So beautiful, so sweet." He kissed her. "You've given my life meaning. Without you I'm no more than an empty shell." He stared down into her eyes. "For better or worse."

Jessie pulled his lips back to hers. "Till death do us part," she whispered.

Neither was aware of the grinning men watching them or the byplay between their siblings as Dove took Alison from Jeremy, telling him that the child needed a woman's touch.

Jessie snuggled, happy and content in her warrior's arms. *Her* warrior. She still couldn't get over the change in Wolf. Her fingers smoothed and played with the curls on his chest. Another grin, wider, appeared when she thought of what he was wearing—or more precisely, what he wasn't wearing. She definitely had to convince him to wear that breechclout more often. Sneaking a look at his face, she marveled at the change caused by a few smears of paint. In the predawn light, he looked every bit as Indian as those warriors around them, and she thrilled to the fact that he was hers. "I can walk, Wolf. You don't have to carry me." She tried once more to convince her husband that she was fine, able to walk on her own. Already the nightmare reality of the past days was fading into what seemed to have been simply a bad dream.

"I will carry you."

"You're just plain stubborn." But her heart warmed to know he was reluctant to put her down. Smiling, she gave in and rested her cheek against his shoulder, finding comfort in the warmth of his bronzed skin. Her gaze traveled over his shoulder, and found Dan, who walked with his hands tied behind his back. He was surrounded by warriors. Jessie couldn't bring herself to look at the horse bringing up the rear. Daisy's lifeless body was slung across its back.

"What's going to happen to Dan, Wolf?"

Wolf hugged her tight. "We'll take him to the fort. It's up to the law now."

Shuddering, Jessie whispered, "He saved us, Wolf. He shot his own sister to keep her from killing us."

"I know." Wolf stared down into her troubled gaze and could find no words of comfort except: "I love you, Jessica Jones."

Her gaze softened. "I love you too," she whispered.

The sun was just peeping over the eastern horizon when the weary rescue party arrived at the makeshift camp. Wolf watched as loud greetings and cheers woke Alison. The little girl, along with his wife, had fallen asleep on the journey back. When Alison saw James, she began crying and held out her arms to him. He took her, and after she calmed down, he coaxed her to eat and drink some water, as she'd had very little for nearly three days.

Jessie woke too. Wolf set her down, and she too ran to her brother. They hugged and cried. Tears flowed freely as each begged the other for forgiveness.

Wolf watched with an indulgent smile. Striking Thunder approached, and Wolf turned to him. "All is well, my brother."

"Yes. All is well."

Striking Thunder grinned. "Your spirit is at peace."

"I have found love. The rest will come. Of this I'm sure."

"I wish you well, my brother. She is worthy of you."

Wolf laughed. All *was* well. "It is I who am worthy of her. You have not seen her in action. She makes Dove look tame."

Striking Thunder laughed and briefly relayed his first encounter with Jessie in Westport. He confessed to following her back to the livery and witnessing the scene that had followed.

Wolf narrowed his eyes. "You knew, yet said nothing to me?"

Striking Thunder shrugged, his eyes gleaming with humor. "It was meant to be."

Laying his arm across his brother's shoulders, Wolf led Striking Thunder away to give his wife time with her family. "Let me tell you a couple of stories, my brother. This trip has not been dull. Then you must tell me about this maiden who has caught your eye. Meadowlark, I believe Dove said? A fine-looking maiden, if I recall."

The two brothers laughed, each extolling the virtues of their women. The mood turned festive, and Wolf decided that they would remain where they were for the rest of the day and night. Both Jessie and Alison needed more rest.

It was there that Lt. Col. Hadden Trowbridge and Vern Portier came upon them. Hadden wasted no time taking Dan into custody. Wolf took him and Vern aside and informed them that Dan had killed his sister to protect Jessie and Alison. He also relayed Jessie's story of how he'd shielded them from Daisy during the past three days. Vern promised to take the information into consideration. Before leaving, Hadden promised to send word to their wagon train that all were safe and on their way back.

That evening there was fresh meat, a huge fire and lots of storytelling. After eating her fill, Jessie leaned against Wolf and sighed. Her stomach was full, she was warm and rested, but mostly she was relieved to see Alison acting more like her old, talkative self. The little girl still kept close to either her or James, but Jessie could tell the Indian women fascinated her. She kept dragging James over so she could talk to them and finger their soft deerskin dresses and exclaim over the fancy beadwork on their moccasins.

Jessie sat with Wolf and his family, and he took his turn to chant and do what he called counting coup. She listened to the storytelling, fascinated by the graceful gestures and rich voices. The moon rose higher, and soon the fire died down. Everyone moved off into the darkness to bed down. Wolf nuzzled her ear and kissed the side of her neck.

"Come with me, Jessica. I want you."

The words sent a thrill down her spine. She'd nearly given

up hope of ever hearing those precious words again. She tipped her head back. "Not as much as I want you, Wolf."

He assisted her to her feet and stared down into her eyes. "You're not too tired?"

Jessie smiled. "I've slept all day. Take me away and I'll prove it."

Wolf swept her into his arms and headed out into the dark prairie.

Five days after being kidnapped, Jessie watched with sadness as Wolf's family prepared to leave. She glanced over her shoulder at Wolf. "I like your family. I'll miss them. It'll be good to see them again next summer."

Wolf kneaded her shoulders absently. "Are you sure, Jessica? Are you sure you can leave your family and return with me? Though how I could let you go now is beyond me. When I think how close I came to losing—"

Jessie turned and stopped his words with a light kiss. Looping her arms around his neck, she tipped her head back to study his stoic expression, knowing that a small part of him still feared she'd change her mind.

"I'm sure. Your family will become mine, and we'll have children of our own. I will always carry my family in my heart, no matter where I go."

Wolf cupped her face in his hands. "I love you, my beautiful rose, my Wild Rose."

Jessie grinned. "I love my Indian name," she told him.

"It is indeed a name that brings honor to this tribe."

Jessie turned when Golden Eagle, her father-in-law, placed his hands on Jessie's shoulders. He'd performed a simple marriage ceremony of his own last night. "You are my daughter now. My family is yours, as your family is ours. Remember this, daughter."

Jessie nodded and, throwing caution to the wind, hugged him. Then it was Striking Thunder's turn. He grinned down at her and tweaked a curl.

"You look much better cleaned up, my little sister."

She rolled her eyes at him when he walked away, then

hugged Dove, delighted to have her for a sister. They had much in common. Finally only Star Dreamer remained. She took Jessie's hands in hers and stared deep into her eyes. When her eyes clouded over, Jessie grew worried, not sure how her sister's visions worked or what to do, but Star Dreamer's gaze cleared.

Star nodded in satisfaction, then leaned forward to kiss Jessie first on one cheek and then on the other. "The answer lies within you." She moved to Wolf and hugged him tight. "Look to your wife for your answers." Then she walked away.

Jessie and Wolf glanced at one another, but before either could comment on the strange advice, the sounds of bickering reached them. As one, they groaned and turned to see White Dove and Jeremy arguing over who was the better shot. Rickard tagged after them, a wide grin on his face, Jessie's Sharps rifle slung over his shoulder.

"I hit four tins to your three," Jeremy stated smugly.

"No, the fourth one fell before you fired," White Dove corrected, her nose in the air. "Even Rickard hit more than you." She sent Rickard a dazzling smile, which made the boy turn red. Jeremy's scowl deepened as the trio joined them.

Shaking her head, Jessie and Wolf exchanged amused grins. All the way back from the Laramie Range, Dove and Jeremy had argued, accusing each other of nearly ruining the rescue. And when Wolf put an end to it, they started competing with each other in other areas, each determined to prove they were better than the other.

Wolf stopped his sister and gave her a hug. "You're growing up, my little Dove. By the time I see you next, you'll be wed."

Dove tossed her head. "When I marry, it will be to a great warrior."

Wolf lifted a brow when she stalked away, her head held high in challenge. "I pity the warrior who tries to claim her heart."

Jessie frowned as she watched Jeremy. For someone

who'd done nothing but bicker with Dove, he was looking downright miserable as Dove mounted her horse and joined her family. She feared another Jones had lost his heart. Too bad nothing could come of it. She put him from her mind and joined the others in their final farewells. Who knew what the future might hold?

Chapter Twenty-eight

Nearly two weeks later, the emigrants stopped to camp near a huge natural bridge of stone in a red-rock canyon to celebrate Independence Day. In her tent, Jessie turned to face Coralie. "Are you sure?" she asked, running her hands down the front of the blue calico dress. Wolf had never seen her in a dress.

"Yes, yes and yes! I've never worn it. It's yours. It even has a matching bonnet—but you don't need that today. Now hold still and let me finish your hair."

"But it's too short to do anything with." Jessie bit her lip nervously and ran her fingers over her hair to feel what Coralie was doing.

Coralie slapped her hands away. "Will you just wait?" She worked silently for a few minutes. "There. It's up. Don't you dare ever cut your hair short again. Now turn around and let me see."

Jessie did as she was told, feeling foolish, yet giddy with anticipation. Coralie had somehow managed to comb her hair into an upswept style with loose curls framing her face. She grinned. It even felt secure.

Anne and Eirica rushed in, breathless. "Are you ready? The meat's done, and everyone's waiting for you two."

Coralie grinned. "Almost." Finding the white apron, she tied it around Jessie's waist. "Perfect, she's ready."

Suddenly doubts assailed Jessie. The dress was tight in the bodice, and she missed the security of having cloth surrounding her legs. What if she fell, or caught the hem on a rock or something? "Maybe I should just change back into my other clothes."

"Oh, no, you don't," the three women cried out in unison.

"Now, come on, Jessie," Anne coaxed.

"You look great. Your husband will be so surprised," Eirica exclaimed.

"Not to mention her brothers." Coralie giggled. "Now, you and Anne go out first." As soon as the two women left, Coralie followed with a grin.

Alone, Jessie worried her lower lip and pressed her hand to her stomach to calm her fluttering nerves. She couldn't do this. They'd laugh at her. But before she had a chance to move, Coralie stuck her arm back inside and pulled her out.

Jessie tipped her chin and followed Coralie the short distance to the waiting group.

In honor of the Fourth of July, Wolf had ordered the killing of several young steers to provide beef for all the groups of emigrants camped nearby. All during the afternoon, each family cooked their favorite dishes. And for dessert, dried fruit came out of hiding. Soon the aroma of baked pies tempted more than one male to get too close—only to have one of the women smack their fingers with a wooden utensil and shoo them away. With over a hundred people milling around the central area where the meat cooked, the noise was intense. Surrounding Wolf were his brothers-in-law, along with Lars and Rook.

"Now, what is keeping them women?" Rook grumbled.

Wolf ignored the comments and the speculation, wanting only to see Jessie. Earlier he'd been ordered out of his own tent by Coralie. He kept his attention on the roasting meat.

"Here they come. 'Bout time," Jordan announced.

"Holy cow, will you get a look at her," Jeremy said, his voice subdued. Suddenly the men around him grew silent.

Wolf wondered what Jessie was up to this time. He turned around, and his jaw dropped. Stunned, he blinked twice, and even then he wasn't sure that it truly was his wife in the pale blue calico dress. A pristine white apron was tied around her waist. His gaze traveled up the long skirt and lingered where the material gathered, emphasizing her narrow waist. His gaze slid up her figure and came to a startled stop.

Wolf was used to her baggy flannels, so the tight fit of the bodice made his heart thrum with desire. The material flowed from a high neckline and skimmed over the swell of her breasts before gathering at the waist. Lifting his eyes, he stared at her hair. Her unruly curls were missing. Some master with a brush had swept her hair to the top of her head and tied it with a matching blue ribbon, letting the longer strands cascade down.

Wolf swallowed. Had he ever noticed her swanlike neck? The delicate curve to her chin? He didn't think so. Not to this extent. She took a hesitant step toward him, her emerald greens wide and uncertain. Then he became aware of the comments around him, of the whistles and calls from her brothers, of the awed whispers from others who'd also never seen this new Jessica, including him. She'd blossomed, truly becoming his beautiful rose. Wolf wanted to keep this magnificent woman hidden from all eyes but his own.

Dropping his fork, he went to her and took her hands in his, bringing them to his lips before stepping back. Holding her fingers tightly, he whispered, "Jessica, you're beautiful."

Jessie smiled hesitantly, then glanced around self-consciously. "Really?" she said softly. "I don't look silly? I feel so strange."

Wolf grinned. "Close your mouth, sweetheart." He whispered. "Trust me. What's happening to a certain part of me is nothing remotely close to silly or strange. Now, come on, let's eat. As much as I'd like to take you right back to our tent and have my way with you, I wouldn't dream of robbing you of the pleasure of seeing your brothers speechless.''

All during the meal and the dancing that followed, Wolf had a hard time keeping his hands off his wife, so much so that he was the brunt of teasing remarks from her brothers and the other men all during the long evening. Finally he could stand it no more. Walking over to where she was dancing with Nikolaus Svensson, he lifted her into his arms and walked away, ignoring the hoots that followed them.

''I was having fun.'' Jessie pouted, staring up into the determined set of her husband's features. A knowing grin curved her lips upward. ''You know, this is getting to be quite a habit of yours.''

Wolf glanced down, seeing the mischievous sparkle in her eyes. ''You witch. You knew what you were doing to me all night, didn't you?''

She answered with another wicked grin. Wolf changed directions. ''Wolf, the tent's over there.'' She pointed.

He grunted.

Jessie wrapped her arms around his neck and rested her cheek on his shoulder, once again forced to be patient. When she heard the sound of water, she knew he was heading toward the rushing stream nearby.

He didn't stop until he came to a thick stand of trees and bushes. Sliding her down the length of him, he lowered his lips. ''This is closer. I can't wait another minute.''

Looking around, Jessie saw that they were hidden at the water's edge. ''Wolf? The ground's wet, and I don't think there's room for us to lie here.''

Wolf fumbled with the front of his breeches. ''Who said anything about lying down? Let me show you certain advantages of wearing long skirts.''

Jessie watched as he freed himself from his breeches. Her heart thudded, and an ache started between her thighs. Suddenly the wet ground didn't matter, nor did anything else. Reaching down, she took him in her hand, loving the velvety feel of him. He stopped her. ''Not this time. My need is too great. Put your hands on my shoulders,'' he whispered, his voice raw with desire.

She did. He lifted her skirts, his fingers arrowing into her moist center. She gasped as he stroked the embers of her desire until she cried out, her need erupting into flames of liquid heat. Then he lifted her, whispering, ''Wrap your legs around my waist.'' With her legs gripping him tightly, he entered her with one hard thrust. Jessie moaned, taking him deeply within her. He moved, his hips thrusting hard, wild and fast. He demanded. She complied.

''No time for slow,'' he said, panting.

Her head fell back in pleasure. ''No,'' she agreed as he took her to the edge of reason. Then with one final thrust, he sent them both soaring.

For a long time afterward, she clung to him, savoring the throbbing feel of him inside her as the stream rushed by and the crickets chirped. Finally he set her back down on her feet and refastened his breeches while she straightened her skirts. Finished, he lifted her into his arms.

''Now we'll go to our tent. That was only an appetizer. I'm ready for dessert.''

That night Jessie slept deeply. She dreamed of children, many children. She sat in a crude log cabin behind a desk. Before her, brown-skinned boys and girls read from books or wrote on their slates. Waking, she sat, mulling over her dream, recalling each scene, each implication. Over the course of the last few months, she'd entertained thoughts of becoming a schoolmarm in Oregon. She discovered she liked teaching Anne's and Eirica's girls. But now she wouldn't be able to teach. Her place was at Wolf's side.

Star Dreamer's words came back to her. *The answer lies within you.* It hit her—the answer. Jessie laughed softly. It was so obvious. She leaned over to Wolf, shaking him awake.

He opened one eye. ''No more, Jess. I'm tired.''

She swatted him on his tight buttocks. ''Wake up, Wolf.

I have the answer. I know what Star Dreamer was talking about.''

Wolf rolled over and rubbed his eyes. "Answer to what?" he asked, his voice groggy.

Throwing herself on top of him, Jessie laughed. "The answer you've searched for. I know how *we* are going to serve your people. It's so simple, so obvious," she announced.

Suddenly wide-awake and alert, Wolf sat up.

Jessie grabbed his hands. "Remember Star Dreamer said the answer lies within me? Before I left Westport I used to help the old schoolmarm a couple days a week in the classroom. On the trail, I've helped Anne and Eirica with the schooling. I'm going to teach the children of your people. That's the answer."

When he didn't say anything, she sat back on her heels. "You said your gift was the gift of knowledge. What better way to help your people than to run a boarding school for your people's children and teach them about the white world?"

Wolf frowned. She saw the protest, the denial in his eyes.

"It will be a place where they can learn both cultures. A place where they can learn English, but speak Lakota, a place where they can learn to read and write and practice their Indian skills. We'll board them through the winter and teach them; then in the spring they can return home to be with their families until the next winter."

Wolf's expression went from dismay to thoughtful consideration. Then he grinned. "The school will be a place where they are free to be Indian while learning what they need to know to survive as the white man moves into our territory."

Jessie rested her palms on Wolf's shoulders. "We can do this together."

Wolf pulled Jessie back down and snuggled her close. "Together, my Wild Rose." Long into the night they talked and planned, until sleepiness began to slow words and thoughts. "It seems so far away," she murmured, thinking that they still had to reach Oregon, stay the winter, then spend the summer traveling back. It would be at least two years before she'd be able to start her school.

"The time will go quickly. Besides, I don't think I'll mind having you to myself for a bit," Wolf whispered, nuzzling the hollow of her throat.

Happy and content, Jessie wanted everyone to know the same incredible happiness. "You know, it's a shame that Jeremy will be so far away from Dove. I like your sister, and I think he's sweet on her."

Wolf groaned. "I for one am glad there're many miles between them. I don't think I could stand listening to all that fighting and arguing. Now, go to sleep. It's almost time to get up."

Jessie settled back and thought of James and Eirica. Jessie knew Eirica had a lot to sort out and come to terms with before accepting any man—including her fear that Birk could have survived. "Wolf?"

"What now, Jessica?"

"Do you think Birk really drowned?"

"Why are you asking?"

"Well, James and Eirica—"

Wolf lifted himself onto one elbow. "Absolutely not. No matchmaking. Let them sort it out on their own."

"I know. But James loves her."

Leaning down, Wolf brushed his lips over hers. "I can see that there will be no rest for either of us tonight. If you have enough energy to talk my ear off, how about trying this?"

Jessie's eyes grew wide at the suggestion Wolf whispered in her ear. "We can really do that?" she asked, her body tingling in anticipation.

Wolf grinned. "That and more. I love you, my Wild Rose."

Jessie pulled him down to her. "As I love you, husband. Now show me how."

Outside their tent, two animals lay side by side. Wahoska leaned over and licked Sadie behind the ears, rose onto his haunches and lifted his muzzle to the glowing moon above. He let out a long howl. When his master yelled out for him to be quiet, the wolf licked his mate once more, then curled up beside her and slept.

Author's Note

I hope you've enjoyed Wolf and Jessie's story. My *White* series continues with Wolf's brother, Striking Thunder as he finds new love with a captive woman named, Emma. For information on *White Flame*, check out my website:
http://members.aol.com/suanedw2u
or write me (an SASE would be greatly appreciated).

SHADOW WALKER
CONNIE MASON

Bestselling Author of *Flame*!

"Why did you do that?"

"Kiss you?" Cole shrugged. "Because you wanted me to, I suppose. Why else would a man kiss a woman?"

But Dawn knows lots of other reasons, especially if the woman is nothing but half-breed whose father has sold her to the first interested male. Defenseless and exquisitely lovely, Dawn is overjoyed when Cole Webster kills the ruthless outlaw who is her husband in name only. But now she has a very different sort of man to contend with. A man of unquestionable virility, a man who prizes justice and honors the Native American traditions that have been lost to her. Most intriguing of all, he is obviously a man who knows exactly how to bring a woman to soaring heights of pleasure. And yes, she does want his kiss...and maybe a whole lot more.

_4260-6   **$5.99 US/$6.99 CAN**

FALLEN ANGEL

CATHERINE HART

**Two-time Winner Of The *Romantic Times*
Reviewers' Choice Award**

**"Catherine Hart writes thrilling
adventure...beautiful and memorable romance!"
—*Romantic Times***

The nuns call her Esperanza because her sweet face and
ethereal beauty bring hope to all she knows. But no one at
the secluded desert convent guesses that behind her angelic
smile burns a hot flame of desire. Only one man can touch
that smoldering core and fan it to life with his blazing kisses.
But Jake Banner is a man of violence, not a man of God.
He is a feared gunfighter who takes lives instead of saving
souls. He is the stepbrother Esperanza has always adored,
the lover whose forbidden embrace will send her soaring to
the heavens, only to leave her a fallen angel.

_4016-6 $5.99 US/$6.99 CAN

Dorchester Publishing Co., Inc.
P.O. Box 6640
Wayne, PA 19087-8640

Please add $1.75 for shipping and handling for the first book and
$.50 for each book thereafter. NY, NYC, and PA residents,
please add appropriate sales tax. No cash, stamps, or C.O.D.s. All
orders shipped within 6 weeks via postal service book rate.
Canadian orders require $2.00 extra postage and must be paid in
U.S. dollars through a U.S. banking facility.

Name_____
Address_____
City_____ State_____ Zip_____
I have enclosed $_____ in payment for the checked book(s).
Payment <u>must</u> accompany all orders. ❑ Please send a free catalog.

ForeverGold

CATHERINE HART

**"Catherine Hart writes thrilling adventure...
beautiful and memorable romance!"**
—*Romantic Times*

From the moment Blake Montgomery holds up the westward-bound stagecoach carrying lovely Megan Coulston to her adoring fiance, she hates everything about the virile outlaw. How dare he drag her off to an isolated mountain cabin and hold her ransom? How dare he steal her innocence with his practiced caresses? How dare he kidnap her heart when all he can offer is forbidden moments of burning, trembling esctasy?

_3895-1 $5.99 US/$7.99 CAN

ATTENTION ROMANCE CUSTOMERS!

SPECIAL TOLL-FREE NUMBER
1-800-481-9191

**Call Monday through Friday
10 a.m. to 9 p.m.
Eastern Time
Get a free catalogue,
join the Romance Book Club,
and order books using your
Visa, MasterCard,
or Discover®**

Leisure
Books

Love
Spell

GO ONLINE WITH US AT DORCHESTERPUB.COM